Tamsin and The Grace

About the Author

As a history graduate, Harriet Temple has always felt drawn towards the Tudor period, and she is very interested in how women managed to cope and live through political events over which they had little or no control. She works in education and lives in West Sussex.

Harriet Temple

Tamsin and The Grace

Olympia Publishers
London

www.olympiapublishers.com
OLYMPIA PAPERBACK EDITION

A CIP catalogue record for this title is
available from the British Library.

ISBN: 978-1-80074-620-6

First Published in 2023

Olympia Publishers
Tallis House
2 Tallis Street
London
EC4Y 0AB

Printed in Great Britain

CHAPTER 1

'God's nails, girl! What are you doing, Tamsin Williams?' A squat shape emerged from the gloom of the backstairs in Penwarne Manor. Mistress Rowe raised the candle sconce higher to better examine the evidence before her.

I had fallen down the uneven back kitchen steps again. Every bone felt jangly, and my heart thudded. My basket lay upended, and a trail of cinnamon scented cakes showed the progress of my fall.

'Don't just sit there, you're late!' barked Mistress Rowe. She hauled me to my feet and giving me an impatient push, the housekeeper disappeared down the corridor.

And I was late. It probably hadn't been a good idea to try jumping the last four steps, but never mind. I still had all my arms and legs, and any bruises would have to wait. Picking up the last of the cakes and giving them a hasty wipe on my skirt, I ran along the corridor to the library, pausing outside to catch my breath.

As I tried to slide in quietly, I saw that the priest, our tutor, was distracted by my younger brother Daniel's Latin translation. Perhaps he would not notice my late arrival. I had reckoned without my elder brother Henry's nose for food – his sharp intake of breath alerted the tutor to my presence.

'Ah, Tamsin. How kind of you to furnish us with your company. Doubtless you have many important matters for your attention which take precedence over our lessons?' His gaunt face was angry, but I noticed his eyes gleam as he noted the presence of the basket, and his sharp nose sniffed the cinnamon scented air.

'My apologies, sir priest. I thought everybody would like one of my mother's cakes, but they took a little longer than usual to cook.' Hastily, I took up my place alongside my brothers.

'Sister, why is your face streaked with dirt?' asked Henry in a hoarse whisper. My younger brother, Daniel, stifled a laugh as the priest turned to glare at him.

'Silence,' he hissed. 'Daniel, let me hear your translation.'

I followed the text over his shoulder as he read aloud and saw that his Latin was accurate, as usual. This put the priest in a better mood and my lateness was forgotten.

When we paused for ale and the cakes, I managed to ensure that my brothers got the ones with the least dirt on them. The short-sighted priest did not seem to notice anything wrong, and I did not worry about Lord Boskeyn's only son, Edmund, eating a bit of dirt, as I had watched him accept a dare to eat mud in the previous year.

That morning, and a thousand mornings like them, passed by. I knew I was fortunate to be receiving an education – my brothers and I were very close in age and wherever they went, I was too. When it was proposed that my brothers be educated with our local lord's son, I had begged my father, Thomas, to let me join them. My mother, Elizabeth, was unsure, and the priest probably thought I would be bored quickly, but I was very proud of my learning.

I believe Lord Boskeyn and my father thought of my education as an interesting experiment. The experiment turned out successfully for me, but my brother, Henry, continued to grapple with Latin as his interests were more practical. He loved hunting and fishing and he was always first out for archery practice. Daniel enjoyed learning too, but the lord's son, Edmund Boskeyn, said he did not need to be very learned because he would have a secretary for anything needing reading and writing. Although Edmund was now nineteen and was meant to be studying law at Cambridge, he was frequently home. He was not popular with the local tavern keepers because he often seemed be involved in fights.

Henry and Edmund got on reasonably well but there had been a recent incident, witnessed by Daniel and me during archery practice in the grounds of Penwarne Manor. Suddenly, both Henry and Edmund were rolling in the mud and struggling to punch each other. They were evenly matched; Edmund was older, but Henry was as tall, and his love of the outdoor life had given him strong muscles.

'Stop this, you fools!' I'd yelled. They ignored me. Daniel was too young to intervene, so it was up to me. Next to a nearby cattle trough was an ancient leather bucket. I filled it to the brim. It was leaky, but if I ran there should be enough left. Running as fast as I could and skidding on the grass, I aimed it over their heads as they rolled around. With much spluttering and cursing, the fight came to a muddy finish.

Later, walking home, I asked Henry about the dispute.

'Edmund said I was too far forwards when I took aim.'

'Were you?' I asked.

'No. He's an arsehole, always thinks he's right,' he growled.

'Yes, well, you have a bloody nose, and you are covered in mud. You had better not let Mother see you. You can get the worst off if we stop by the well.'

Our house, Trenowden Manor, was half-way up a hill which overlooked the harbour of East and West Looe, twin towns in South-East Cornwall. There was a proper stone bridge between them and not some rickety old wooden contraption. I loved to walk from West Looe harbour over the bridge to East Looe, to watch the brown sails of fishing boats as they came home to drop their catches in the fish market.

My brothers thought I was peculiar because I also enjoyed going to mass. Every Sunday and on holy days, we trailed down to our church of St Nicholas, which jutted out over the harbour at end of a small street filled with houses and shop fronts. What they did not realise was that I enjoyed going there because I liked to watch the congregation, the dramatic arm waving of the priest and the light coming through the stained-glass windows.

Further along the cliffs, away from the harbour, was the beach at Hannafore, which had been our favourite place when we were children. When the high tide had been and gone, we would rush down to the rockpools to see if the sea had left behind any crabs or other shellfish. We would stagger home, proudly bearing our leather bucket full of squirming creatures for dinner. Our cook had to explain that the tiny versions we found would not feed a flea.

Experiments in keeping the tiny crabs as pets were not successful, despite Daniel's attempts to feed them seaweed. I still remember the terrible rotting smell that pervaded the upstairs rooms before the "pets" were poured onto the midden by exasperated servants.

Penwarne Manor had been built on top of the hill, and it was at least two hundred years old. Successive Boskeyns had added wings and outhouse and it was much larger than our home, Trenowden Manor, further down the hill. Doubtless, their sensitive, aristocratic noses needed more protection from the pervading smell of fish that hung around the harbour area.

I was very fortunate to have had a happy and secure

childhood, but all that had changed when I was sixteen years old. One summer evening, I came home from an errand to Penwarne Manor to find our house full of our female neighbours. I thought perhaps I had forgotten some pre-arranged social event, that I would have to rush upstairs and change my mud flecked dress. However, there was something strange: the women talked in whispers, and my smiles and greetings were not returned. I went to find my mother's friend.

'What has happened? Tell me, please, Mistress Pascoe.'

'Oh, Tamsin, your father's horse arrived home riderless. Your brother, Henry, went out with his friends to search for him and found your father insensible on a path. They managed to get him home, but he looked so bad that a priest was sent for, God rest him.'

'Is he dead?'

'You must speak to your lady mother, Tamsin.'

Hastening to the kitchen, I found my mother sitting by the fire. She held her rosary in her hands, her eyes were blank, and the waxy pallor of her face alarmed me.

Henry appeared, he looked distraught as he grabbed both my hands. 'Sister, you must be brave. Father has gone to God.'

'Is he really dead?' I said, my lips wobbling. Henry squeezed my hands and nodded. The world felt as if it had tipped sideways, and my knees threatened to give way. Surely this could not be happening.

'The priest is still with him, Tamsin.'

'Where is Daniel?'

'There he is, with Mistress Pascoe.' Daniel's eyes looked red and sore, but that good lady had put her arm around him, and he seemed calm.

'Henry, will you come with me to see Father? I do not think

Daniel should come up yet.'

Upstairs, Henry went straight in, but I hesitated on the threshold of the chamber, too frightened at first. When at last I entered the room, I found my father lying on the bed, his hands placed together. His face appeared calm. No injuries were apparent, although a rag had been tied around his head. I half expected him to spring up and tell me it was all an elaborate joke, but of course, no such thing occurred. The priest was on his knees by the bed, praying in a monotone. Henry and I joined him while we struggled to grasp this new reality.

The local coroner had been summoned by Henry, now man of the house at the tender age of seventeen. The subsequent inquest found that Father had died as the result of an accident, perhaps a sudden apoplexy which had caused him to tumble from his horse and cut his head. There was no evidence of foul play. Mother recovered herself enough to organise and preside over the funeral feast, and we were grateful for the number of neighbours who turned up with contributions of food and firewood.

Inevitably, life was grim for several months, but Mother started to regain her zest for life with the support of her friends and I tried hard to be helpful. Father's sudden death had left a big hole in our lives and it was difficult for us all to accept that he would never return. Once we had got through the first Christmas and the first birthday without him, it gradually became easier.

CHAPTER 2

The year 1532 rolled in and only Daniel continued to study at Penwarne Manor. Henry had taken over most of our father's daily duties with help from neighbours, and I now stayed at home to help Mother. Lord Boskeyn seemed very favourably disposed towards Daniel, and Mother expressed hopes that he would fund him to study at Cambridge. A career in the Church or the law could set him on a path to a prosperous future.

With her two sons on the road to independence, Mother turned her attention to me. I had always known that it was my duty to marry. However, with only a small dowry and without astonishing beauty, I suspected that I was unlikely to attract many suitors.

All the young men I knew seemed to regard me as a friend, an honorary boy, and it was true that I did not go out of my way to appear feminine. My hair was a good colour, being very fair, and there was plenty of it, but I kept it crammed under a coif for practicality's sake. My skirts were usually muddied because I resented the time needed to brush the hems daily.

One morning in the early autumn, an unexpected message from Lord Boskeyn summoned Mother and Henry to Penwarne Manor. I decided to help my mother's maid, Joan, to clean the windows, which had gathered deposits of salt from a recent wild storm at sea. I had just started shaking out some dusty old hangings when I heard Mother returning home.

'Tamsin, come immediately; I have such news!' shouted

Mother, struggling to remove her cloak. 'Lord Boskeyn has offered to pay for Daniel to attend Cambridge! His future is assured!'

I realised that I had not seen Mother this happy since she had been widowed. Her cheeks were pink, and she was practically dancing around.

'That is wonderful news, Mother. How very kind of Lord Boskeyn!' I said, as a burning smell erupted into the room.

'Forgive me, I must get back to the kitchen.'

Clouds of smoke billowed from the kitchen as I dashed in. I had thrown my apron down a little too close to the cooking fire when I had finished helping Joan, who now appeared to have vanished. The remaining servants were cleaning upstairs. Grabbing the burning apron, I unfastened the latch on the back door, kicked it open and rushed into the garden, hurling the apron into what passed as my vegetable patch. Fortunately, the remains of last night's heavy rain doused what now appeared to be a black rag.

Where was Joan? The answer became very clear as I rounded the corner of the garden to see Henry and Joan holding hands and staring into each other's eyes. Joan saw me first. She moved away from my brother, and there was a challenging look in her eyes as she turned to face me. Henry immediately dropped Joan's hand and moved towards me.

'Tamsin, what do you think of our improved prospects? Shall you like living in London?' As Henry had never demonstrated intellectual prowess, I assumed that he had muddled something.

'I really do not know what you are talking about, brother. Do come into the house. Mother was telling me about Daniel's future, but we were interrupted by a small fire in the kitchen.'

'Ah, Tamsin, there you are. I trust the fire is now safely extinguished,' said Mother, looking unexpectedly calm for somebody whose kitchen could have been destroyed. She patted the bench, indicating that I should sit beside her. Meanwhile, Henry drew up a stool.

'Daughter, Lord Boskeyn has good news for us...'

'Yes, I know, Mother,' I interrupted rather rudely.

'Pray, do me the courtesy of listening to what I have to say, Tamsin,' she said calmly. 'Lord Boskeyn has a cousin who resides in Greenwich, a Lady Sedley. She is the widow of Viscount Sedley, who died several years ago. Lady Sedley holds land and property in her own right. She is childless, but she has not yet remarried. She is seeking an educated lady in waiting to escort her on outings and make herself agreeable. Lord Boskeyn has recommended you for the position, Tamsin.'

Shocked, I enquired what "make herself agreeable" might mean.

'I would imagine she wants somebody to read to her and perhaps assist her with embroidery, music and all the pastimes that great ladies enjoy. She would also require you to escort her to the king's court when necessary. Just think, you could see King Henry and Queen Catherine!'

'Mother, I would need to travel up to London and live there! What do I know of fine society? I have never been up the country further than Plymouth. No, I am sorry, Mother, but I do not think this is suitable for me.'

Henry's face became stern. 'Tamsin, you know you must obey our lady mother and thank Lord Boskeyn for his kindness in thinking of you. You may even be lucky enough to meet a gentleman in London who will offer you marriage and security.' It was quite unnerving to be confronted by my brother – only one year older but attempting to puff his chest out and deepen his voice.

'Do not be pompous, Henry dear. I am happy here, I have plenty to do and perhaps one day a "gentleman" of Cornwall will offer me marriage!'

'Tamsin, you know that it is unlikely; there is only a little money set aside for your dowry and although you are pleasant looking, you do not have the advantage of great beauty to recommend you. Granted, you are virtuous, religious, and unusually well-educated, but there are not many local gentlemen of our class. I beg of you, consider your prospects before you make an over-hasty decision which you may come to regret.'

Then came the second bombshell. Henry cleared his throat and went on. 'I think that I should consider marriage soon, Mother. With Tamsin gone, my future wife could be company for you.'

I retreated to the kitchen to find Joan was pounding dough. Her face was redder than normal, and she seemed flustered. What was going on? Suddenly, the room seemed too small for me and I had to get out. Grabbing my cloak, I headed to the front door.

'Do not delay dinner for me, Mother. I will be back in time to call on Mistress Pascoe with you this afternoon.' After an uncharacteristic struggle with the latch, I got the door open and breathed a lungful of fresh air. I would walk to Hannafore and try to work out what I should do.

The harbour was mostly empty of boats. The tide was out and those left lay at awkward angles on the mud. I dodged around the few solitary old men standing around the quay. Wildly, I thought I could offer myself to one of them as a wife, anything to stay amongst everything familiar and loved and then imagined their responses. The likelihood of any of them thinking the over-educated and flighty daughter of dead Thomas Williams would make a good wife was remote, and they were hardly the "gentlemen" envisaged by my brother. Dejected, I returned home to find dinner over and Mother sewing in the parlour.

'Tamsin, now that you are sixteen, you must stop this wandering around by yourself. In future, take Joan with you. Young ladies need chaperones and we do not want people gossiping about you. Now, make yourself useful,' she said, holding out my latest attempt at embroidering a shirt. I chewed at an obstinate thread as Mother thrust scissors at me. 'Really, Tamsin, that cloth will be grey by the time you have finished the rose. Perhaps you should unpick it and start again?'

'Well, at least I can sew hems even if I cannot seem to embroider with these sausage fingers,' I said.

'Daughter, there is nothing wrong with your fingers. You are just too impatient, and you lack confidence in your skills.' She removed the grubby cloth from my fingers with a loud sigh. 'Well, at least you have your education to recommend you.'

'I can manage a garden and make meals from the most unlikely ingredients, too,' I said.

'That is most certainly true, and you could direct the growing of kitchen and medicinal herbs needed for a household. But you are unlikely to be required to cook if you marry appropriately. While you are not really a beauty, you are attractive. Your plentiful fair hair is an asset, and your teeth are good.'

Was I a horse? I thought. I felt that I did not want to discuss this subject any further.

'Did you hear the church bell, Mother? It is three o'clock. Are you going to change before we visit Mistress Pascoe?'

'No, this gown will do, but I think you should wash your hands because there is still soot in your nails from the kitchen

17

fire, Tamsin, dear.'

After I had washed my hands and disposed of the water, I realised that there were also black smudges on my kirtle. I went back to the kitchen jug to collect more water and scrubbed at my skirts. With any luck, it would dry on the walk up the hill.

By the time we had arrived at Mistress Pascoe's cottage, I was hot from the walk and not in the best of moods. Mother's friend prided herself on her ability to interpret the behaviour of others accurately and she was not shy about giving her opinion, wanted or not.

'Tamsin, my dear, I do hope you appreciate your good fortune. A lady in waiting to the Dowager Viscountess Sedley, what an honour for you and your family!' Mrs Pascoe was busying herself pouring us some of her home-brewed elderberry wine while fixing me with her beady eye.

'I have not yet decided,' I said.

'Your duty is to obey your mother and take the opportunity that God has offered.' Mrs Pascoe positioned herself opposite, just a little too close for comfort.

'Yes, Mistress Pascoe.'

'You should ask to see Lord Boskeyn and confirm your acceptance tomorrow. I saw him exercising his horse this morning, so I know he is in residence.'

'Very well, Mistress Pascoe. I will call in the morning.'

That settled, Mistress Pascoe subsided into her chair and sipped her wine. 'Elizabeth dear, do try these honey cakes; they are delicious, and I made them myself. You are still looking rather pale and peaky.' Mother and Mistress Pascoe busied themselves with dissecting all the latest gossip as I sat looking glumly out of the window.

'Does Henry have a lady in mind as a wife?' I asked Mother

as we walked home, full of cake. Fortunately, the return journey was mostly downhill.

'He may well do, Tamsin,' said Mother with a smile. 'When his marriage takes place, I shall remove myself to a smaller house. Trenowden Manor cannot have two mistresses! This could be another reason for you to accept the position in London.'

Later, in the chilly bedroom, as I removed my kirtle as fast as possible and jumped into the bed, I began to wonder. What if I did go to London? I must be brave and speak to Lord Boskeyn tomorrow. Surely there was no harm in finding out more.

The following morning dawned grey and chilly. When I peered out of my tiny window, I could see a sea mist creeping through the valley. The brown sails hung limp in the gloom as the boats prepared to leave the harbour. Not a day for a good catch; this could mean hunger for the fishermen's families. I prayed for the sun to burn away the mist and a breeze to blow it. Sighing, I turned from the window and picked up the water pitcher. A few minutes later, I was ready. With hands and face washed and wearing my best gown over my cleanest kirtle, I went downstairs to the kitchen.

'Good morning, Joan, is there any bread left over from yesterday?'

'I had to throw it out this morning, Mistress; the mice had been at it. I hope you do not mind me saying: the bread should always be kept high up, away from the vermin.'

'That is most strange, Joan, the bread is always kept on the top shelf. In truth, I remember placing it there yesterday evening.'

'Well, Mistress, either the mice have taken up climbing or perhaps, Mistress, you are mistaken.'

Listening to the pert tone in her voice, I began to feel tense.

I knew I had replaced the bread in its accustomed place. Perhaps Henry had cut a slice on his return from the tavern and forgotten to replace it on the shelf.

I enquired if there was ale or if the cat had fancied a drop and drained the cask. A gleam in Joan's eye showed that she had noticed my irritation.

'Mistress, there is plenty of ale and today's bread will be ready soon. Your mother says I am to accompany you to Penwarne Manor when you have breakfasted.' This was not good news, but I would have to make the best of it.

CHAPTER 3

After breakfast, we set off. Outside was the thick mist which seemed to muffle the usual sounds of our animals, but as we climbed the hill to Penwarne Manor, the mist became lighter. Joan had managed to keep up with me even though I set a fast pace, and soon we could see buildings ahead.

'Mistress Tamsin, I do not want to speak out of turn, but you appear hot and bothered and your headdress has slipped because you walk so fast. Perhaps you resent being accompanied and have tried to ensure that I refuse to walk with you in the future.' She was smiling at me and I could not help myself giggling.

'I fear you are correct, Joan!'

'Shall we pause while I adjust your headdress for you? After all, you will soon be a grand lady; you cannot appear a ragamuffin!' With my headdress now straight, I sailed on.

By the time we had reached Penwarne Manor, I had convinced myself that I was calm, dignified, sophisticated and wise for my years. Indeed, any aristocratic London family would be very lucky to make my acquaintance. I would be independent, I thought, and imagined myself sending money home.

'We would never manage without Tamsin,' said my mother in my vision. I pictured her with Henry and Daniel looking hungrily at a table groaning with bread and meat. The gratitude on their faces as they began to eat...

Before Joan could even knock at the ancient door, it swung open.

'What do you want?'

An ancient crone stood in the doorway. She wore a cap crookedly on her head, but her dress looked to be of good fabric, and around her neck was a necklace of pearls. She could not be a servant, and a guest was unlikely to answer the door. That left one possibility: this must be the reclusive Lady Elowen Boskeyn, a widow and the current lord's elderly mother. We curtsied hastily and I tried to sound confident.

'Good day, your ladyship. I am Tamsin Williams of Trenowden Manor and this is my maid, Joan Glasson. I wonder if I might see his lordship upon a matter of some importance?'

'Wait there, I will see if I can find a servant. God knows where they all are. Nobody tells me anything.' She moved back into the hall, leaving me standing on the doorstep feeling rather silly. 'Partridge!'

She had a surprisingly strong voice for such an elderly lady. There was the sound of hurried footsteps. A bulky man of indeterminate age confronted me. He looked me up and down.

'Please wait in the hall and I will see if his lordship is in,' he said pompously.

I entered Penwarne Manor, walking in what I believed to be a dignified and stately manner. As Partridge disappeared into a dark door at the back of the hall, I took the opportunity to have a good look around in the front of the house. My brothers and I had always used the back entrance when arriving for our tutoring. The hall was certainly large, but it had a slightly decayed air about it. At the back was a grand staircase, and dotting the walls were family portraits. Some of them would benefit from dusting, I thought as I surveyed the scene.

A cough from behind me alerted to me to the presence of Lord Boskeyn. I curtsied politely and noticed that he was looking rather harassed.

'Tamsin, my dear. Do come in and sit down. You too, Mistress Joan. I have all the information you will need about the matter. Indeed, I had a further message from my cousin, Lady Sedley, this morning. She is impatient for your answer.'

I could not maintain my former stately walking style because Lord Boskeyn set off at a fast pace. I scurried behind as we passed doors and yet more doors, with Joan scuttling behind me. Finally, he came to an abrupt stop outside another one and I only just avoided a collision with him. He stood back to let me pass and I found myself in a small parlour.

'Thank you for receiving me, your lordship. I was quite overwhelmed with gratitude when my lady mother gave me the news.'

'Of course, of course, but it is not so very surprising that we should think of you for this post. You are presentable and unusually well-educated for a lady. I hear good reports of your conduct and when my cousin enquired, I thought of you immediately.'

My first thought was to enquire about where these "reports of my good conduct" had come from, but this would be an inappropriate question from my new confident and sophisticated self.

Instead, I asked, 'What would be my duties, my lord?'

'My lady cousin needs somebody who can read to her, make conversation, see to her wants and accompany her on visits to her friends, some of whom are very high in the king's favour. The position does not require any heavy work and naturally you would be provided with your own servant. My cousin would prefer a young girl from Cornwall because of the family connections.' After this speech, Lord Boskeyn turned to me expectantly.

'May I ask where the lady lives, your lordship?'

'She has a large house with extensive grounds in Greenwich, not far from the Thames.'

Swallowing nervously, I asked if I would receive any monetary reward. This was important if I were to send any money home and gain the undying admiration of my family. It was probably an unladylike question, and I avoided Joan's gaze, but I could not miss the gasp from her.

Lord Boskeyn seemed lost for words. 'I do not believe so, but you would probably receive an allowance for clothing and such things and, of course, your board.'

Well, that ruined my vision of the future. Never mind. If I was very careful, I might be able to save something from a dress allowance.

'How would I make the journey to London, your lordship?'

'Our steward, Peveril Longshanks, will make the arrangements and inform you of the details.'

Suddenly, I felt the streak of recklessness that used to make me the first to jump a stream or climb over a wall. Before I could think, I found myself accepting Lord Boskeyn's offer. Through a haze of excitement, I heard him say that he would send a message to Lady Sedley to expect me forthwith.

Lord Boskeyn escorted us to the front door. Again, there were no servants to be seen. Just in time, I remembered my manners and curtsied.

'Your lordship, I offer you my grateful thanks for this opportunity. I shall do my best to provide excellent service.'

'Yes, yes, I am sure that we may count on you. Farewell, Tamsin. You will of course write to your mother and she will tell me how you are doing.'

With that, he shut the door in my face. I could hear hurried footsteps echoing in the hall as he moved away.

The mist did not seem to be lifting as we walked back It was fortunate that Joan and I were very familiar with the track.

As we went through the final field before the downward slope of the path, I heard hoof beats nearby. Who was out riding in this weather? The amiable face of Barnaby, one of Lord Boskeyn's horses, appeared to the side of me. He snorted and came up close, snuffling for any treats I might have. I guessed the identity of the rider and I was correct: Edmund Boskeyn leaned down to me.

'Good afternoon, Mistress Williams, and of course, Mistress Glasson. Have you perhaps been paying a charitable visit to my father's tenants, or are you hoping to catch a glimpse of our new steward?

'Why would I be wanting a glimpse of your new steward?'

Edmund grinned at me. 'He does not appear to have a wife. Perhaps you have seen my father and you are now deciding whether you will embark on your adventure in London or hunt down my father's innocent steward to secure your future here in Looe!'

'Oh, do be quiet. You talk a lot of nonsense, Edmund. Yes, I am resolved to go to London and hope that fortune smiles upon me.'

'The steward might not suit you, anyway. He is very serious, and he spits mightily when he talks. His mind does not appear quick either. But perhaps you could overlook stupidity and spitting, Tamsin? I expect you are very keen to marry,' said Edmund. Looking at his smiling eyes, I took a deep breath.

'I have no pressing need to marry, and I am looking forward to my new situation,' I said with dignity. 'You, on the other hand, will need to marry to get heirs to your father's estate. I wish you good fortune in your endeavours.'

'A man as handsome as me will not have any trouble in attracting a suitable bride. Consider the estate and my father's wealth.' He put his nose in the air and shook his glossy dark hair in an exaggerated manner. 'All the young ladies will be falling at my feet!'

Barnaby started to snort impatiently, having established that I did not have any treats for him.

'You are as conceited and ridiculous as ever!' I shouted at Edmund, all dignity forgotten. 'Your head is so big, it's a wonder you can get it off the pillow in the morning!'

With that, I turned and swept off, followed by Joan and hoping that I would not trip over the path. Fortunately, I did not. The sound of hoof beats faded into the mist.

'He is a clever lad and no mistake, Tamsin, but you must not let him goad you,' said Joan.

Further down the hill, all was silent. The lack of wind meant there were no familiar sounds, no sails flapping. No shouts and crashes as catches were unloaded. Standing by the door of Trenowden Manor, peering through the murk, I thought I could make out a ghostly figure. The figure became a man shrouded in a cloak. Clearing my throat, I stepped forward.

'Good afternoon, sir. I am Tamsin Williams of Trenowden. Do you require assistance?'

'Good afternoon, Mistress, it is fortunate that I encountered you. I am Peveril Longshanks, steward to Lord Boskeyn.' He bowed, as I curtsied and tried to stand back from the spittle flying out of his mouth. Edmund had spoken truly.

'I have funds for your journey, written instructions and a letter of introduction from my master to Lady Sedley. You will ride with a carter to Plymouth and then sail to Deptford. You will then find an inn called The Bear and send a messenger to Sedley House, and the family will send transport to collect you.'

'Thank you, sir,' I said, taking the small money bag and proffered paper. 'When am I expected to travel?'

'You should be at the crossroads by the sign of The Dragon at dawn on Monday. The journey will take about three days to Plymouth, provided there is no inclement weather. The sea journey should not be more than a few days.'

'Pray, please convey my grateful thanks to Lord Boskeyn for arranging my travel.'

Peveril bowed and turned to start his uphill journey back to the manor. I watched his long, spidery legs as he disappeared into the mist and mopped my face a little. It was difficult to separate the moisture of the mist from that of Peveril's spittle.

'Thanks be to God that you are home safely,' said Mother. 'Put your shoes by the fire – they look soaked through – and tell me what Lord Boskeyn said.'

As I removed my shoes, I realised that my feet were numb with cold and my hair full of moisture that could not all have been blamed on poor Peveril Longshanks. I limped towards the fire.

'I have decided to go to London and join Lady Sedley's household,' I said grandly. Mother shrieked with delight and embraced me.

'This is wonderful news, Tamsin. I knew you would see sense. God must be smiling on us, because today, Master Trewoody of Pelynt called on me to see if Henry might make a match with his daughter, Jenna.'

I tried to recall anything I knew about Jenna Trewoody. I knew the Trewoody family were prosperous merchants, but all I could remember about Jenna was that she was quiet with a delicate appearance.

'Master Trewoody has wide business interests, Tamsin. In time, he intends to trade with Newfoundland on the other side of the world! His daughter's dowry may well be substantial. If a match is agreed, Master Trewoody may eventually leave the business to Henry. As you will doubtless recall, he has no sons.'

'Would Henry like to be a merchant?' I enquired.

'It is true that Henry shows no aptitude for book learning, but he can reckon numbers well and I know Master Trewoody employs a secretary.'

'So, he might not need to read documents and suchlike?' I said. Mother nodded.

'With Daniel in the Church or practising law, and you now more likely to marry, events may work out better than I had thought. Perhaps I may spend my declining years with a brood of grandchildren!'

I knew that Mother was devoted to us, perhaps unusually so. Although she had three living children, there had been at least six other babies who either never took a breath, or only lived a matter of days or weeks. Grandchildren would be extra precious to her, and her excitement at the idea of her children marrying was understandable.

After a glass of rum with a dash of black treacle to help chase out the chill, I felt better, and going into the kitchen, I found Joan crashing pots and pewter plates around.

'Good evening, Joan. I wonder if I could prevail on you to place a warmed brick in my bed tonight?'

Joan looked at me blankly and her eyes appeared red and puffy. 'Yes, Tamsin, I will heat one up directly.'

Oh dear. Poor Joan, she has heard us talking about Henry's marriage, I thought.

Later that evening, Henry arrived home, stumbling slightly, with a smell of spirits about him. 'Greetings, Mother and my most esteemed sister,' he slurred. 'I have great news for you both. I am to visit Mr Trewoody tomorrow to ask for his daughter Jenna's hand in marriage. I have reason to believe that I will be accepted.' He staggered off to bed.

Mother had a satisfied smile on her face. I realised that negotiations must have been going on behind the scenes for some time. Evidently, Mother and Mr Trewoody had already paved the way for this event.

'This would be a very advantageous match for both Henry and Mistress Trewoody,' said Mother still smiling as she checked that the door was fastened securely and began to douse the candles. 'Henry will gain a suitable wife and Mr Trewoody gains the son he never had. Also, Mistress Trewoody will not have to live far from her family.'

'Does Mistress Trewoody really want to marry Henry?' I asked as Joan banked up the fire for the night.

'Well, one must assume so since she has apparently assented already,' said Mother, looking surprised. It came to me that Mother could not conceive of any circumstances in which a female would not immediately be overcome with gratitude at the prospect of marrying her elder son.

When I reached my bedchamber, I found Joan transferring the heated brick into the bed. She did not at first see me in the doorway. Loud sniffs came from her.

'Joan, whatever is the matter?'

'Nothing, Tamsin. I've put the brick in, like you said. I'd best be off now as I need to check that your boots and cloak are drying.' She hurried off downstairs.

I found I could not sleep. Instead I saw the thick sea mist, meeting Lord Boskeyn and Edmund, images of the steward announcing my travel arrangements, pictures of Henry announcing his marriage plans. Finally, I thought of Joan and her tear-stained face. I hoped that Henry had not taken liberties with her. Finally, I fell into an exhausted sleep.

The next morning, a quick glance out of the window showed that the mist had lifted overnight. The day was bright, and I felt full of energy. After a quick breakfast, I began to think about what I should take with me to London. Joan seemed more her normal self and I thought she would be pleased if I asked her opinion about what to pack.

'Mistress, I've got enough to do. These fish will not gut and salt themselves. I need to go over to the market in East Looe, and your brother walked mud everywhere when he came home last night. You should ask your mother.'

I found Mother sorting herbs for drying. She paused and rubbed her hands on her apron.

'Tamsin, you should take your two good dresses and your two best headdresses. Some caps, shifts and a dress for any rough work too. We do not know how much room there will be for luggage on your journey, so you had better take the smallest box. Remember, your new mistress will likely be providing you with other clothes. Joan will be accompanying you, as a young lady cannot travel so far unchaperoned. She can remain with you as your personal maid.'

'Mother, how will you manage without Joan?'

'Do not worry, Tamsin, Joan's younger sister, Bridget, will assist me. She is already twelve years old, neat and tidy enough, and her mother is anxious not to lose the income.'

I trailed upstairs, opened the clothes press and shook out my two best dresses, dropping sprigs of lavender to the floor.

Fortunately, the lavender had done its work and I could not see any moth holes. I had no idea if the dresses would be suitable in London, but they would have to do.

I took out my two gable headdresses. I was very proud of these, ordered from Plymouth three months ago and the very latest fashion. Wearing them would be uncomfortable as I was used to plain linen coifs, but the London ladies were bound to be wearing them, and I had heard that Queen Catherine favoured them.

Carefully, I folded my dresses and added the two gable hoods. There was scarcely any room for anything else, so I crammed my shifts at the side and added my small store of jewellery, my missal, and a silver crucifix. Finally, I added my rosary to the top so that I could reach it easily on my journey.

The rest of Saturday passed quickly in a flurry of last-minute tasks. Formal goodbyes to friends and neighbours could wait until after church tomorrow.

Sunday morning saw me sitting in our pew, suddenly aware that I might not see the church or the congregation for many years. With tears pricking at my eyes and my heart beating a little too fast, I listened to the familiar sounds, the call of seagulls and the distant sounds of the sea. Even the priest's usually dull sermon seemed weighted with heavy significance.

I plastered a bright smile to my face as I circulated amongst my neighbours and friends outside the church. They pressed forward with their farewells and I was alarmed that some of them were behaving as if we would never meet again. Did they expect me to meet my death in London? Or were they expecting to depart this life before I returned? Of course, none of them apart from Lord Boskeyn and Edmund had ever travelled to London. Many had not even ventured further than Liskeard or Polperro.

Walking back home, I realised that I was terrified. What on earth did I think I was doing? How would I survive without the sounds of the sea? The familiar faces? The long walks in the countryside? It was too late now; I was committed to my fate!

CHAPTER 4

Monday morning was dark and blowy. I had hardly slept, so afraid was I of missing the cart. Mother's face was tense as she lit the candles while Henry brought the horses out from the stables.

Joan appeared from the kitchen with a small parcel of food. 'I've done us pasties, honey cakes and ale,' she said, curtsying. I thanked her quietly and turned to Mother. I was afraid to say anything in case I burst into tears.

'Send us a message whenever you can, Tamsin dear, and make sure you attend mass regularly,' she said while holding me in a tight embrace.

Henry fastened Joan's bundle and my box to a small cart. He beckoned me to mount my horse. 'Hurry, sister, we must be at the crossroads by dawn.'

And then we were off. I turned to wave as we rounded the corner, and Trenowden Manor vanished from sight. What was I doing?

Henry shouted over the noise of the hoofbeats 'I hope you are not downhearted, Tamsin!' I held tight to my cap as the wind gusted. 'This is a great opportunity for you and for our family. Who knows what connections and acquaintances you may make!'

Fortunately, Henry could not see my wet eyes in the dark. 'Yes, of course,' I said bravely. 'I will do my best to do my duty and enhance the reputation of our family.'

Henry was not so easily deceived. 'Sister, don't be miserable. If it's really terrible, send a message and I will prevail upon Lord Boskeyn to arrange your return to Looe. However, you would still have to marry somebody. Perhaps Old Bartholomew, the fisherman, would suit you? He must be nearly one hundred. It is said that he has a secret horde of gold buried in a cave by Talland. He would not live long and then you would be a rich widow!'

I started to laugh and immediately felt better. The possibility of rescue brightened my mood. We reached the crossroads before the first glimmer of light in the east, and did not need to wait long before the carrier rumbled into sight. Henry leapt down and carried my box and Joan's bundle to the large cart. We made a brief farewell, my tears now dry, and I noticed that Joan appeared unaffected by Henry's departure. I was away on the road to my adventure!

The driver volunteered his name as Tom Morval, but he was mostly silent as we rattled through the dawn. Joan and I perched uncomfortably on a pile of tightly packed parcels whose owners had sent them up country with Tom. The carrier made slow progress over the rutted tracks.

Although we were given our own chamber when we stopped at each of the roadside inns, the prickly straw mattresses and the noise of downstairs merrymaking kept me awake. By the time we reached Plymouth, I ached all over and was sure I could sleep for a week. Joan and I were both looking forward to the sea journey.

Tom deposited our luggage and us at the Plymouth Customs and Excise office. Consulting my written instructions from Lord Boskeyn, I asked for directions to The Good Fortune. An officious looking clerk emerged from behind a pile of ledgers and gave us the directions. Fortunately, he also sent a male servant to carry my box. Arriving at the location specified by the clerk, I could see an enormous ship, much bigger than the Looe fishing boats. There were men swarming all over it, some up the rigging, others stowing a cargo of barrels and boxes. Nervously, I approached a man who seemed to be shouting instructions into the air and waving his arms.

'Excuse me, sir, could you direct me to the captain of this vessel?'

'Are you a passenger? You should make haste, we sail with the tide. See yon gentleman over there?' He pointed further down the quay, 'That be Captain Watkins.'

Walking as fast I could, with the man carrying my precious box scurrying behind, I made my way, trying hard not to trip over the coils of rope which festooned the quay. Joan followed clutching her bundle.

'Good morning, sir, I presume you are Captain Watkins? I am Tamsin Williams of West Looe and this is my maid, Joan Glasson. A passage to London has been booked for us. Could you tell me where we must go?'

'Good morning, Mistress. I am indeed Captain Watkins. Please proceed down the gangplank and go below decks. The Purser will show you to your quarters. You and your maid are the only paying passengers on this trip.'

Turning, I saw that the clerk's servant had already gone aboard and placed our luggage on the deck. He was now waiting expectantly. Congratulating myself on my experience of climbing in and out of boats in Looe, I set off confidently down the gangplank, remembering that I would need to pay the servant some small consideration for hauling my belongings into the ship. Distracted by feeling for my pocket, I slipped on the damp wood but managed to keep my footing until reaching the deck of the vessel, whereupon I staggered to maintain my balance.

A familiar voice came from above my head. 'Mistress Tamsin, how wonderful to encounter you! Pray, are you perhaps trying out some new dance steps to impress the Londoners?' he shouted, cheerfully. A small group of porters turned to stare at me. Surely, the irritating Edmund could not be here too? Looking up, I saw that he was indeed grinning down at me from the quay.

'You know perfectly well that I am not trying out dance steps, Edmund!' To cover my embarrassment, I turned to go below decks.

Meanwhile, Edmund had moved past us onto the boat, where he picked up our luggage. 'Allow me, ladies,' he said. Joan simpered and I glared at her. Nevertheless, I realised that it would have been difficult for us to get down the steep steps while carrying our stuff.

After depositing our stuff, Edmund bowed and stepped back up the gangplank, looking down at me. 'My apologies for the interruption, Mistress. I am here to send messages to London with your ship. May I wish you a pleasant and speedy voyage.' With another bow and a smile, he was gone. The Customs House clerk cleared his throat pointedly.

I extracted some groats from my pocket, restored the ties and went to go below. A bent little man scuttled out of what appeared to be a tiny cubby hole, rattling a set of keys. 'Excuse me Madam, I must secure my cash box and then I will conduct you below.' We watched him lock the door.

'Why do you carry a cash box? Surely people do not need money on a voyage such as this.'

'Madam, some of our sailors are foreigners and need to change coin into good English money. I will also need to organise the payments to the crew, who will leave the ship at London.'

'Of course,' I said. I had not thought of that.

We reached a small door deep in the ship. Edmund had left our luggage outside. The cabin was tiny with two cots, a jug and ewer, but I was pleased to see a small window.

'You must keep this window closed at all times, lest the sea enter,' said the Purser. 'There are some hooks for your clothes. You may eat with the captain, although you might prefer the food sent to your cabin. Now I must leave you as we are about to cast off. You may go up on deck when weather permits, but you must always obey the captain's instructions.'

After some minimal unpacking, I set off for the deck with Joan in my wake. She still showed no sign of distress from parting with Henry. Indeed, she had been surprisingly cheerful on the journey. Up on the deck, it was a hive of activity. Joan and I retreated to a corner from where we could see the ropes uncoiling, dropping into the sea, and being hauled up. The side of the quay was retreating.

Standing with Joan, I strained my eyes away from Plymouth to behind me, where I could just see the outline of the Cornish coast in the far distance. Tears blurred my vision, but the wind quickly dried them. Waves splashed the hull, and timbers creaked as the wind filled the sails of the ship. We were off to London!

The days passed slowly. Captain Watkins explained that the ship would travel close to the coastline to avoid any threat from the Barbary pirates who occasionally threatened these waters. By mutual consent, Joan and I spent as much time as we could on deck in the fresh air, only returning to the cramped cabin when necessary.

Fortunately, neither of us suffered ill effects from the motion of the sea, and we found that there was always something to look at, from a huge warship from the king's fleet on the horizon, to activity on the deck. The sight of sailors climbing the high rigging made me feel dizzy and I was always surprised when none fell off.

Joan appeared as excited as I was by the journey. I did not like to ask her what had happened with Henry and she did not volunteer any information. Instead, we discussed neutral topics and pooled our limited knowledge of the city we were fast approaching as we advanced up the great river Thames. Marshland and tiny villages passed by on either side.

'It's full of enormous buildings and a huge fortress where wild animals live,' said Joan. 'It has many markets with goods from faraway countries. The king lives in a palace with his wife, Spanish Catherine, and all the ladies of the court are covered with gold and precious jewels.'

'The queen is said to be a gracious lady. She is very well-loved, even though she has not presented the king with a son yet. Of course, she has a healthy daughter, the Princess Mary, but England cannot be ruled by a woman,' I said, bracing myself as a wave smacked the hull.

'No, of course not. It would be ridiculous,' Joan said straightening the hood of my cloak. 'In East Looe market, I heard that the king wants his marriage annulled. He wants to marry a younger wife who can give him sons. Surely, he cannot just get rid of his wife. Do you think we might see the king?'

'I suppose if he rides out in the streets, we might catch a glimpse, if we are permitted. Or perhaps I shall be asked to attend Lady Sedley on a visit to the court.'

After all our discussions about the future, it was a little shocking to find the future almost upon us as we neared our journey's end. Already, I could make out an increasing number of dwellings and church steeples in the distance. As we got closer to the port, I saw grand houses with gardens fronting the Thames. Many of them had decorative barges bobbing gently on the tide.

'Joan, look at those windows. Can you see the sun sparkling on them? They must all be made of glass!' We were silent. The windows must have been large if we could see them, and glass so expensive. These people must have been rich beyond our wildest dreams.

We were now entering a wide stretch of the river, and the number of crafts, barges and skiffs increased rapidly. Slowly, we were drawing nearer to the dock. There was a muffled thump and the ship juddered. The stone quay was now very close, and the deckhands jumped off, bearing massive coils of rope to secure the ship. We had arrived and our adventures were beginning.

CHAPTER 5

It felt very strange to be walking up the steady gangplank, and a very long time seemed to have passed since we had left Cornwall, even though it had only been a few days.

My first impression of London was the noise. The yells of the porters and the shouted instructions as consignments were unloaded from the hold, combined with the rattle of carts, felt quite overwhelming after the peace of our voyage. The ground seemed to move under my feet as we followed a porter with our luggage. A short walk took us to The Bear tavern as instructed by Lord Boskeyn where we were shown into a shabby parlour.

'I would like to send a message to the house of Lady Sedley, sir,' I said to the landlord as confidently as I could. To my relief, the landlord immediately called over a child of about ten years. 'Ned, take the lady's message and be back sharpish.'

'Wotcha goin' to give me?' enquired the boy, straightening a battered looking cap and glaring at Joan in an unfriendly manner. I watched her press a coin into his grimy hand.

'Here is a coin, and you shall have another when you come back with the answer.'

The boy, Ned, shot off bearing the written message I had composed onboard ship to tell Lady Sedley that we had arrived.

Joan clutched my arm as we sat in the parlour. Through the open door, we could hear shouted greetings, laughter, and voices speaking in different languages. It seemed to have been a very long time when Ned arrived back, out of breath.

'Lady says you're to wait in the courtyard and a cart will collect you and your maid at noon.'

As noon arrived, all the church bells began to ring from different areas. The noise was extraordinary. 'No danger of us mistaking the time, Mistress,' said Joan.

'No, indeed, I'm surprised all these people don't go around with stoppered ears. Perhaps they are all hard of hearing.'

We did not speak anymore because a cart had appeared in the courtyard and the driver was making straight for us. 'Mistress Williams and her maid?' he yelled over the cacophony. 'Wait here and I will ready the cart.' We watched as he pulled out a small step stool and gestured to us.

'I am Will, one of Lady Sedley's drivers. Is that all your luggage?' he said indicating the small bundle and my box. 'Will a carrier bring the remainder?'

'No, Will, this is all we have,' I said, trying to climb elegantly into the cart. Huffing and puffing, Joan followed me in, sitting down with her lips pursed as she surveyed the scene.

'Pray, make yourselves comfortable and we will be at Sedley House directly,' said Will.

'Is it perhaps market day? There seem to be many people abroad today,' I enquired as loudly as I could manage, as the cart rattled along.

'Nay, Mistress. It is always busy around here,' shouted Will.

The press of people and the pungent smells began to make me feel queasy. Although the streets and gutters, particularly of East Looe, were often filled with rubbish, the clean sea breezes helped to wash it away.

The London streets seemed very closed in and dark because houses on opposite sides of the road leaned towards each other until the upper storeys and roofs almost touched. The gutters ran with filth, but people seemed to ignore it, although I did notice some women using pattens to raise them out of the worst patches. The noise did not abate. If anything, it grew worse, as the drivers called greetings to each other as we made our way to Greenwich. The constant calls of street vendors shouting their wares added to the din.

We passed close to high walls around a white tower. 'Is that one of the king's palaces?' I asked Will.

'Aye, it is the Tower,' he answered. 'The royal family sometimes visit, and it is where we put our traitors!' he added with a chuckle.

'Is this another palace?' I enquired as we drew up outside what to me was an enormous mansion surrounded by a high wall.

'This is the main entrance to the residence of Lady Sedley,' yelled Will. 'The doorkeeper will open the gate in a moment.'

A large man shambled forwards and Will roared, 'Open the gate. Here is a young lady to stay with Lady Sedley. Take her box and find somebody to escort her to her ladyship.'

The gates opened to reveal a vast, gabled building of brick and timber set in well-stocked gardens with several smaller outhouses. We entered through a great door at the front and immediately, the noise from the streets was muffled.

A well-dressed woman appeared and introduced herself as Lady Margaret Presland, waiting woman to Lady Sedley. We followed her down several corridors and climbed an impressive, intricately carved staircase. At the end of a smaller corridor, Lady Margaret paused. 'Her ladyship's quarters are through here.'

The sound of footsteps heralded the arrival of another young lady dressed very finely. Lady Margaret smiled at us and then disappeared through a small door.

'Good day, Mistress Tamsin. I am Lady Ester Priddy. I will

show you where you will sleep and other necessities, then I will conduct you to Lady Sedley.'

I could not help but notice that she ignored Joan completely. Off we trailed down yet another corridor. This house was enormous. Did everybody have titles? How would I ever find my way around? I turned back to check that Joan was still following us. Her expression indicated that she was not at all happy. On turning back to follow Lady Ester, I saw that she had opened a door to reveal a large room with six beds, large wooden ornamental chests, and several tables.

'Your bed will be here by the window and you may put keep your clothes in this chest,' said Lady Ester. 'Your woman can unpack your possessions while I conduct you to her ladyship. She is most anxious to meet you.'

Joan looked startled. 'Where am I to sleep, my lady?'

Lady Ester looked surprised, as if a table had suddenly spoken. 'You will be found a bed in the servants' quarters, of course.'

'But I always sleep near Mistress Tamsin,' said Joan.

Lady Ester addressed me rather than Joan. 'This is London. There are armed guards patrolling the grounds and house. There will be no danger to your Mistress Tamsin,' she said condescendingly. 'We have our own servants if your mistress requires anything in the night.'

As she spoke, Lady Ester turned her back on Joan and it was fortunate that she could not see Joan's rude gesture.

'Come, Mistress Tamsin. I do hope that we shall be friends. Lady Sedley is in the company of her other ladies. I believe they are embroidering new altar cloths.'

As we approached, I could hear the soft sounds of a stringed instrument and a low hum of female chatter. Lady Ester stood aside as a page opened the door and stepped back, indicating that I should enter. Still feeling a little wobbly after the voyage, I walked carefully in, remembering to keep my head up and shoulders back. At the end of a room, in a chair somewhat grander than the others, sat the woman I identified as my new employer because of her apparent age and her extravagant jewellery.

'Ah, Tamsin, at last you have arrived!' My curtsy was a little unsteady and I stumbled as I straightened myself. 'God's blood, girl! Have you been drinking liquor so early in the day? You are positively staggering!'

'No, your ladyship, it is the effect of the voyage. I am told it takes time to become accustomed to dry land after a long sea voyage.'

'Did you lose your gowns at sea? That one is quite out of style. It appears to be decorated with something peculiar, and your headdress, well!' There was a titter from the heads bowed over their embroidery.

I gritted my teeth and managed to control my rising temper. 'Your ladyship, I bring you greetings and good wishes from your cousin Lord Boskeyn of West Looe.'

'Yes, yes,' she said, interrupting my speech. 'All was explained in my cousin's letter.'

She rose from her chair and stalked around me as I stood in the centre of the room. I could hear her tutting and sighing as she subjected my person to a close examination. I heard more low tittering from the ladies sitting behind me.

'Well, Tamsin, we shall have to do something about your clothes. You cannot accompany me out dressed in that manner! I will send the seamstresses to you and the other women will advise you on appropriate styles. Now, you may assist us with the altar cloth. Take a seat next to Lady Margaret over there.'

Weary, hungry and dejected by my reception, I perched on a low stool. The sun was now high in the sky; it must have been almost eleven o'clock. Surely dinner must be served soon.

Lady Margaret thrust a needle at me. 'You can begin here on the border if you like,' she said. Rather than expose my appalling embroidery skills, I offered to tidy the rather tangled box of sewing silks which lay at her feet.

Margaret gave me a friendly smile. 'Yes, of course, I loathe that task,' she said. 'I expect it is all rather strange for you here. You can use this opportunity to have a good look at us all and I can tell you more later,' she added in a whisper.

Feeling relieved at her friendly overtures, I began to sort out the confusion of silk threads. The general chatter in the room increased, the ladies turned away to focus on their work and I began to relax.

'Lady Sedley has an imperious and direct manner, but she is kind at heart,' whispered Margaret. 'I do not believe she wished to embarrass you, she just speaks her mind, and your clothes are a little out of fashion. Perhaps you are still in your travelling dress?'

I did not like to inform her that I had dressed in my best and newest clothes to create a good impression on arrival.

'When you have unpacked all your gowns, I will help you to pick out ones that will be more suitable, and it may be that ones that are not acceptable could be altered by Bridget, our favourite seamstress.'

I thought of my two other gowns and kirtles. I felt that Margaret would not find either "acceptable". Looking around, I saw that the other ladies all wore dresses in more luxurious fabrics. Precious stones glittered around their necks and all their hoods were in a different style to mine.

Thankfully, dinner was served soon. We all processed to a large hall, led by Lady Sedley. The trestle tables were all set out and I was placed next to Margaret. Lady Sedley sat at the top table with her guests and Lady Ester. The rest of the household filled the lower tables. There seemed to me to be an enormous amount of food. Course after course was brought in by the serving men, and I ate as much as I could.

Afterwards, in the chamber, all the other waiting women clustered around my open box. The expressions on their faces showed that my fears were confirmed. None of my clothes were "acceptable", apart from a pair of sleeves and my shifts.

Lady Ester summed it all up: 'Send for the seamstresses immediately!' she told a servant. 'Tell them to bring fabric lengths for all occasions.'

'But Lady Ester, I do not have sufficient funds to pay for all this,' I stuttered.

'You need not trouble yourself about that, Mistress Tamsin. Our clothes are necessary to maintain our positions and, as such, are attributed to household expenses.'

I still remember the sight of all the rich fabrics piled onto my bed as Lady Margaret and Lady Ester planned my new wardrobe.

'I think we need six kirtles, gowns, sleeve sets, stockings, some plain shifts and two cloaks, one for summer and one for winter. Mistress Tamsin will also need several headdresses, some plain caps and we must find her some more jewellery.'

Feeling rather full after dinner, I allowed the women to hold various fabrics against me and listened while they discussed my appearance as if I were not there. This was a peculiar experience as I had never paid much attention to my looks before.

'Her hair is her best feature. We need something which brings out the fair colour.'

'Yes, but she is so pale, and although her eyes are large, that shade of green is little more difficult.'

'Her teeth are good. We can solve her pallor with a little paint, and she would benefit from having her eyebrows plucked.'

'I do not want my eyebrows plucked. I like them as they are!' I was beginning to feel angry, and I could feel a headache building up.

'Fortunately, she speaks well, only a slight trace of a rural accent. We should go through court etiquette with her and ensure that she can move and dance gracefully. I noticed that she tends to stride along; she will need to take smaller steps. We will need to practise formal court curtseys with her too.'

'There is so much to do!' said Lady Ester to my embarrassment.

I had thought myself sufficiently sophisticated, but I was clearly wrong! There followed several days of standing still while fabrics were held against me and measurements taken. Experiments with face paint followed, with Margaret directing operations. 'Just a little to redden her cheeks, and perhaps her lips. Go carefully with the powder; it is making her sneeze, which will undo our efforts. We had better pierce her ears. Has anybody got a sharp needle?'

It was a strange experience, surveying myself in a full-length, glass mirror for the first time. A stranger clad in a silver kirtle, with a green gown and an unfamiliar curved French headdress stood there. Some rather uncomfortable shoes completed the ensemble, and around my neck was a string of pearls borrowed from Lady Margaret.

Repeatedly, I practised elaborate curtseys, dance steps and the art of moving gracefully across a room without stumbling, while carrying a heavy Latin grammar text on my head.

CHAPTER 6

My transformation from provincial Cornish girl to fashionable London lady was complete by late 1532. After many trips accompanying Lady Sedley to see friends locally, tonight I was going to be one of the two ladies-in-waiting accompanying Lady Sedley to the king's new palace at Hampton Court. I might see King Henry in all his glory and even catch a glimpse of 'The Lady,' as we called Anne Boleyn, who was not a favourite in Lady Sedley's household. Indeed, she was regarded as an evil and immoral hussy intending to usurp the place of our beloved Queen Catherine, but such things could only be said in private.

After extensive preparations, Lady Sedley was ready to leave and, to my relief, she had picked Margaret as her other lady-in-waiting. When her ladyship climbed into the coach, we followed her, settling into our seats opposite. Lady Sedley appeared to be wearing the entire contents of her jewellery casket and her face was painted thickly. The coach felt stuffy, so I leaned forward to adjust the window.

'Stop!' shouted Lady Sedley. 'We will catch an ague from the night vapours!'

Feeling rather silly, I subsided into my seat. What were these dangerous night vapours? The night air was not dangerous at home. It must have been something peculiar to London.

The carriage rumbled on down a track full of ruts, which jolted us as we passed groups of small dwellings. The cottage windows were mostly dark; presumably the inhabitants had gone to bed with the onset of night. Finally, the jolting ceased as we joined a smoother road on the approach to Hampton Court Palace.

The darkness began to lift as light streamed from large braziers and torches set into the outside wall. Guards stood aside to let Lady Sedley's carriage pass. The driver slowed the horses as we arrived at the entrance. All around us were many carriages and coaches: some extravagantly decorated, some very plain. Footmen and pages rushed around, lighting the way of the guests as they advanced to the entrance. I could hear the hubbub of low conversation and tinkling laughter as the gorgeously arrayed people passed by.

It took some time for us to extricate Lady Sedley from the coach with her stiff, jewelled gown, but finally, she was standing in the base-court. Fortunately, a page approached us without the need for me, as the most junior lady-in-waiting, to go and summon one.

'Greetings, ladies, may I light your way to the Great Hall?' he asked politely, setting off at a fast pace.

'Slow down, man!' yelled Lady Sedley. 'Where is your respect for my advanced years?'

'My apologies, madam, I quite mistook your ladyship for a younger lady,' he said with a secret wink at me. Lady Sedley tutted but she was not displeased.

A blaze of candlelight greeted us at the door of the Great Hall. It was difficult not to be dazzled by the combination of chandeliers and twinkling diamonds on the gorgeously dressed courtiers.

Lady Sedley swept ahead of us like a majestic ship. On and on she went, until she reached the far end of the Great Hall. Two guards blocked our way and enquired Lady Sedley's name.

Seconds later, they had retreated, and we entered a room whose walls were hung with beautiful tapestries.

Over the heads of the many courtiers, I could just see a dais with two beautifully decorated and padded chairs. A canopy depicting the royal arms of England was set on poles. This must have been where the king and queen sat to receive important visitors. Margaret was just pointing out the detail in the tapestry nearest to us when Lady Sedley ordered me to find refreshments for us.

The chamber was suddenly becoming more crowded, and the air smelt stuffy and unpleasant. The heavy mingling perfumes made for a noxious atmosphere. After pushing my way through the groups of courtiers, who all seemed to be shouting at the tops of their voices and laughing heartily, I found a page and asked him where refreshments could be found. He directed me to a low table, which I was pleased to see was topped with many wine flagons and drinking vessels. A team of servitors were presiding over the drinks, while pages carried them away.

Looking hastily at the assembled drinks, I hazarded a guess about the quantity of Rhenish wine based on the amount my brother, Henry, usually drank and requested three goblets. Carefully, I led the way back to our party, the page following behind with the heavy tray.

'God's blood, Tamsin! We will need to be carried if we drink all this! Whatever were you thinking?'

Just as I was passing a goblet to Lady Sedley, trumpets sounded, I jumped, and the red wine was deposited on my beautiful gown, and dripped to the floor.

'Do not react, Tamsin,' hissed Margaret in my ear, 'and nobody will see.' Smoothly, she handed another cup to Lady Sedley, who had turned around to look at the dais. Margaret stood in front of me, offering me a linen napkin to sponge the worst off. Gratefully, I took the cloth and mopped at my kirtle. The press of people was now so great that nobody would notice the stain.

I became aware that people were ceasing to talk, and from my vantage point, I could see people bowing and curtseying towards the dais. I had almost missed the entrance of the king!

Although I could not see much above the crowd, I saw a head wearing a large velvet hat with a feather studded with diamonds. The head belonged to a man in middle age with reddish hair and a broad, bearded face. The king must be very tall if I can see him over the heads of all these courtiers, I thought.

'Quick – curtsey!' Margaret hissed in my ear as, all around us, people sank down. Peering up, I tried to see what was going on, but the front rows were now standing which blocked my view. There was a fluttering movement and the head bobbed and disappeared; the king must have been sitting down on his ornate chair under the canopy.

Now what was happening? Everybody was standing again, and I could not see anything else. The general hubbub rose again, punctuated by loud bursts of male laughter from the dais area. Margaret and I did not dare try to push any further forward as there was no space.

'I can see the Duke of Norfolk speaking to the king,' said Margaret in a loud whisper.

'Is The Lady here?' I whispered, trying to stand on tiptoes discreetly.

'Hush,' whispered Margaret, 'it is safer not to make any remarks or questions that could be misinterpreted by any listeners.'

'No, of course. I will not,' I said cheerfully, emboldened by the wine, which seemed to be slipping down very easily.

'We'll speak later when we can talk more discreetly,' said Margaret.

Looking around, I could see several young gentlemen openly staring at us.

'Margaret, why are they looking at us?

'I believe it is because you are new to the court and they are wondering who you are.' We looked for Lady Sedley, but she had disappeared. Seconds later, we heard her loud, honking laugh ring out from somewhere near the dais.

'We cannot pass through this crowd,' said Margaret, 'so we had better wait where she left us. Doubtless, she will return soon.'

With nothing else to occupy our attention, we turned our backs on the staring gentlemen and examined the enormous and extravagant wall hangings.

'It is very impressive work,' I said, suppressing a hiccup. 'I do not think I could ever possess such skill with a needle.'

'Perhaps not,' said Margaret, 'but you can read better than any of the other ladies.'

There was a parting of the crowd in front of us which heralded the return of Lady Sedley, who appeared very pleased with herself.

'Ah, so here are my waiting women, skulking in the corner – and I see Tamsin has been partaking of the wine. Tell me, dear, are you partial to strong drink? I remember your unsteadiness on your arrival.'

Spluttering, I was about to deny this when I noticed that Lady Sedley was smiling at me.

'Do not worry yourself, I do but jest,' she announced with another loud explosion of mirth. 'Now, go and find our driver, I find I am very tired, and it grows late.'

It seemed very dark on our journey home, but the horses

seemed to be moving faster, perhaps sensing the return to their comfortable stables and a well-deserved rest. I watched as Lady Sedley's head lolled and she sank into sleep. Loud snores punctuated the air.

'Margaret, do tell me more about The Lady. We did not hear much news of royal events in Cornwall.'

'Anne Boleyn is a knight's daughter from Kent, but her uncle is the Duke of Norfolk and her father, Thomas Boleyn, is high in the king's favour. It is said that she has refused to become the king's mistress and will only settle for marriage. The king wants a son, and Queen Catherine has only managed to produce one living daughter, Princess Mary. The poor woman did produce a son, but he only lived a few weeks some years back, so the king fears the Tudor dynasty will be wiped out. Anne Boleyn is already acting as if she is queen, sitting in Catherine's place at feasts, and she has been given a suite of rooms next to the king's at Hampton Court.

'Of course, the king will not be able to annul his marriage as the Pope will surely not permit it, and nor will the queen's nephew, Emperor Charles. Queen Catherine must be restored. We must wait for these distressing events to pass,' said Margaret, settling back in her seat as the journey went on.

Several weeks later, after morning prayers, Margaret and I were walking in the garden. It was a cold but sunny autumn morning. We had Lady Sedley's permission to escape the great chamber and our sewing because we had reached a particularly complicated patch of the altar cloth, and neither Margaret nor I had the requisite fine skills needed.

We walked in the gardens at the back of the house. There was no wind so we could not detect any noxious odours from the Thames, and we could hear birds singing. The few barges out on the river sent little waves which twinkled in the sunlight as they passed by.

We were discussing the previous day's expedition to the court at Whitehall Palace. Margaret was in full flow.

'Did you like the look of Lord Burton, Tamsin? I thought he was rather handsome, and he has extensive lands in the Midlands. How about Master Biddup? He will inherit a large Wiltshire estate, eventually. Or did you prefer Lord Allerthorpe with his northern estate?'

'Margaret, I thought Lord Burton was rather high and mighty of manner. He clearly thinks that all women are desperate for his attentions. Mr Biddup was dull of mind and he smelled peculiar.'

'Ah, you like Lord Allerthorpe, Tamsin!'

'No, on the contrary. I hardly noticed him so I cannot think of anything to say about him, Margaret dear. I can say that I found Whitehall Palace one of the most confusing places I have ever been to. I could never marry anybody who had an apartment there. I should spend all my days wandering around lost! Why is it all such a muddle there?'

I noticed Margaret fiddling with her headdress. 'The king is making alterations because it used to belong to old Cardinal Wolsey. Tamsin, it has started to rain; perhaps we should seek shelter?'

I agreed, although I would have preferred to stay outside by the river, which was as close to the sea as I could get. I still missed Cornwall very much, and at times I felt as though I carried a stone in my chest when I thought about it, especially when I received messages from home.

Mother wrote every week, Daniel once a month in a beautiful secretary hand, and Henry had managed two scrawled missives since I had left three months ago. Sometimes, messages were delayed and the news was well out of date by the time I received it. However, the chances of me ever returning to Cornwall were quite remote. I could not see myself ever being able to build a future there. I should count my blessings and look forward to the future.

We retreated to the house, entered the chilly hall, and sat down on a bench. I kicked some mud off my shoes.

'Margaret, let us not hurry back to Lady Sedley. Instead, we could walk in the gallery; she will not be expecting us back yet.'

Margaret and I set off up the main stairs.

'Have you seen all the family portraits, Tamsin?'

'No, I always seem to be hurrying on some errand whenever I am in this area.' We were on the landing by then and Margaret sped off towards a wall which seemed to be covered in pictures.

'Look at this fierce old man in armour,' she said, pointing to one of the older looking portraits.

'He is so stout, as well; I'm surprised his horse can carry him,' I said, 'and look at the nose on this one. He must be a relative of Lady Ester.'

'That is not very kind of you, Tamsin, but yes, there is a resemblance. I believe most of the old families in this country are interrelated,' Margaret said, moving to a smaller picture further up the gallery.

'Ah, here is the nose again,' I said, pointing to a stern-looking, ancient woman dressed in black and smothered with diamonds. 'Another relation, I think.'

'Tamsin, you are disrespectful!' said Margaret with a mock stern face. 'Look, this one is new. I think I can still smell the artist's paint.' She was pointing to a portrait of a man in middle age with dark hair.

'He looks familiar.' I bent to make out the gold lettering. 'Yes, it is Lord Boskeyn of Penwarne. He sent me here to live with Lady Sedley. She is a cousin to him.' Resolutely, I ignored the pang caused by gazing on the figure who reminded me of home. 'Are any of your kin here, Margaret?'

'Yes, there is a painting of my grandmother on the far wall,' she said, leading me over. I was looking at a painting of a lady of indeterminate years, her hair scraped under a white coif. She appeared serene but I thought I could see humour in her eyes.

'Do you remember her, Margaret?'

'Yes, she lived with us, and in the afternoons, we would accompany her out on walks. She had so many stories and legends to tell us about where she came from in Sussex. She died of the sweat back several years ago. I miss her still.'

'That must have been terrible for you,' I said sympathetically. 'Did anybody else catch it?'

'Fortunately, none of my immediate family members, but three servants became ill and all died. The sweat kills so quickly. Grandmother seemed hale and hearty at dinner, but she was dead by early the next morning.'

Both of us had suffered a significant bereavement and we knew that the prospect of sudden death was real. It was therefore essential to never skip mass and to remember to say our prayers. We knew that danger lurked in the poisonous miasmas and bad smells of the city, and that many illnesses defeated the efforts of our best physicians.

Soberly, we descended the main staircase, it was time to return to Lady Sedley and the ladies before our absence was commented upon. We did not want to be refused permission to be absent from a task in the future.

I remember that day well because a chance event later that

day directed the course of my life in a direction I had not anticipated.

It was early evening, and all we ladies were in our chamber, picking out clothes for us to wear to attend a large court gathering at Greenwich Palace. Maids rushed hither and thither, bearing armfuls of kirtles, sleeves and headdresses. The air was thick with the scent of rosewater and lavender as our dresses were unpacked from our boxes and hung up or spread on beds to help us to choose.

Margaret was parading around in a tawny silk with crimson sleeves, which set off her dark hair well. As usual, I was still in my linen shift and struggling to decide. Thanks to Lady Sedley, I now had several gowns to choose from. My Cornish outfits, which I had thought so fine, had been given to the servants.

'Wear the blue silk with pink sleeves,' advised Margaret.

The gown which had received the wine stain all those weeks ago had been discarded as impossible to clean, but I still had the silver kirtle which had survived unscathed.

'I will wear the silver kirtle, the silver sleeves and the blue silk,' I announced. The maid laced me in and helped me to arrange and cover my hair under a black French hood set with tiny pearls. I tweaked some of my hair at the front because I fancied that the lightness of its colour could make me appear as if I could be bald. Margaret advanced on me with the cosmetics tray and added some colour to my cheeks and lips. She was fortunate to have naturally red cheeks and lips.

It was almost dark as we gathered in the courtyard to mount our horses.

'Will the king be at Greenwich Palace?' asked Lady Ester.

'I expect so,' said Lady Sedley. 'He is fond of Greenwich because he grew up nearby at Eltham Palace.'

I listened carefully and imagined a baby King Henry, but try as I might, I could only summon up a picture of a shadowy woman holding a miniature version of him, complete with beard and hat. Surely, this enormous and majestic king could never have been a baby.

CHAPTER 7

Fortunately, it was a beautiful evening, and the ride was short. With Lady Sedley in front, leading us like a flock of ducklings, we proceeded through the gates and entered the main courtyard of Greenwich Palace. As at Hampton Court, there were many people swarming around, noisily greeting each other.

In the Great Hall, musicians could be heard tuning their instruments and the main floor had been left clear for dancing.

'Now you will have the opportunity to practise the new steps you learnt in our chamber,' said Margaret, as a page handed cups of wine around to us. Lady Sedley had joined a group unknown to me and indicated that we were free to enjoy ourselves. I felt a sparkle of excitement as I surveyed the scene. The musicians began to play a lively tune and I itched to dance.

Lady Ester approached. 'Tamsin, perhaps you had better watch those of us more skilled in the moves before you attempt them.' Deflated, I moved back obediently, but almost immediately, a young man who looked familiar was standing in front of me.

'Mistress Tamsin, would you care to join the dancing?'

Curtseying demurely, I recognised him as Lord Allerthorpe, one of the young men introduced to us during my first outing to Whitehall Palace several days ago.

I placed two fingers on his arm as he led me on to the floor, which was already crowded. It was a dance which involved much skipping around and changing of partners. Fortunately, I remembered the steps even though I could not recall the name of the dance. As I whirled around, I became aware of some staring, and as soon as the music stopped, I left the floor with Lord Allerthorpe close at my heels. Wondering if my headdress was crooked or if I had made errors in the dance, I pleaded great thirst so that Lord Allerthorpe would absent himself.

As soon as he had disappeared on his errand, I looked for Margaret, but she was out on the floor with one of her admirers. Lady Ester stood there alone tapping her foot with an artificial smile.

'Lady Ester, can you please tell me if my headdress is crooked or if there is anything else amiss with my attire?' I whispered. 'I am sure I was following the dance correctly, but some people seemed to be staring at me and I wondered why.'

Lady Ester surveyed me. 'Your headdress is straight but a little of your hair has escaped which makes you look untidy.'

She stepped back as Lord Allerthorpe returned and a page carrying wine arrived. Relieved, I took a large gulp from the cup presented to me. 'My thanks, sir. It is a little hot in here.'

Lord Allerthorpe surveyed me calmly. 'Madam, perhaps we should take a short stroll in the courtyard? Some cool air might be refreshing. Do allow me to escort you.'

'I will accompany you, of course,' said Lady Ester, now standing close by. 'Tamsin cannot walk alone with a man and I too find that I would love to take some air.'

We three politely pushed our way through the crowd. Emerging into the cold night air, we began a stately perambulation around the palace courtyard. Thankfully, it was now less crowded, and the night air was cool and still.

Lord Allerthorpe was silent, but Lady Ester was clearly uncomfortable with the quiet. 'Are you staying in London for long, Lord Allerthorpe?'

'No, my lady,' he replied. 'I am just down from Yorkshire to see to my London affairs and then I plan to return home.'

'Does your Yorkshire estate keep you very occupied? Forgive me, I cannot remember its location,' said Lady Ester.

'Allerthorpe Castle is near York,' he replied. Silence fell again.

I was preoccupied with looking up at the stars in the night sky and was startled when Lady Ester contrived to stand on my foot. 'Tamsin, too, is far from home,' she said, looking at me meaningfully.

Lord Allerthorpe looked at me rather nervously. 'Yes, I believe you are from Cornwall? I recall Lady Sedley informing us that you live on the coast in a small town.'

'Yes, my lord,' I said, jolted to my senses by my rather painful toes. 'My family has a manor near Looe, a small place probably unfamiliar to you,' I said politely.

'Madam, I believe I have heard mention of it. I have an acquaintance who has an estate in that area. You may know of Edmund Boskeyn.'

'Indeed, yes, my lord. I had the privilege of sharing some of his education. Our parish priest was our tutor, and my brothers and I were included as company for him.'

'I cannot imagine that young man being very studious,' replied Lord Allerthorpe, beginning to look less nervous.

'No, he certainly was not. He would absent himself from lessons whenever possible. He seemed to believe that he would not require an extensive grasp of Latin or Greek in his future. Edmund was altogether rather arrogant.'

Lady Ester looked shocked at my frankness. 'I expect the gentleman will have servants to deal with these tasks when he comes into his inheritance,' she said quickly. 'Do tell us more about Yorkshire, Lord Allerthorpe. I have heard that it is a wild country.'

I looked at him with more interest. 'In what way is Yorkshire wild, sir?'

'It has miles of empty moorland and rocky coasts. The people consider themselves a separate race to those in the south and their allegiances are to the local northern lords.'

'I believe Cornwall to be "wild" too. As with the north, our people believe themselves to be different to the people of England and in many parts, English is not even understood. We also have our rocky coasts and even wild moorland.'

'Our people are generally very devout, and even small hamlets usually have a church,' added Lord Allerthorpe.

'Yes, we in Cornwall are most devoted to our Holy Mother Church,' I said.

'I am delighted to hear that we have so much in common,' said Lord Allerthorpe with a bow. 'But now we must get ourselves back to the hall before you are missed. Perhaps you would honour me with another dance tonight, Tamsin? And perhaps you would dance with me, too, Lady Ester?'

The rest of the evening passed quickly, as I found that I did not lack dancing partners, in addition to Lord Allerthorpe, who claimed four dances. All too soon, it was time to ride home. As I fell into my bed that night, I realised that I had enjoyed this evening more than any other since I'd arrived in London.

After morning prayers the following day, Lady Sedley summoned me. I found her in her dressing room with the seamstress, who was pinning the hem of her gown.

'Ah, Tamsin,' she said. 'Pray, leave us, Margery.' The seamstress nodded and curtsied. She could not very well have answered because her mouth was full of pins.

Lady Sedley sailed over to an ornate chair, patting a stool in front of her. 'Pray, sit, Tamsin. Would it interest you to know that Lord Allerthorpe has sent a message asking for my permission to call this afternoon, and he requests that you accompany him for a walk in the gardens?'

Startled, I blurted out, 'But why would he wish to call on me, your ladyship?'

'Do not be foolish, girl. You appear to have charmed him last night and it seems that he enjoys your company!' She went on, 'I promised my cousin that I would see that you were introduced to suitable young men. I must admit that I was thinking a little lower than the Earl of Allerthorpe. He owns a great deal of land in the north and his estate is prosperous. His family have connections to the former royal Yorkist families, and they lost much power and influence in their struggles with the Lancastrians in the last century. However, the present king has shown him favour and his lands were restored to him.'

'Madam, he is only offering to walk with me, he is not proposing marriage!'

'Tamsin, your tone is pert and unbecoming in a young lady! Surprisingly, you appear to be the first young lady to spark any interest in Allerthorpe since his arrival a month ago, despite introductions to the best families with marriageable daughters.'

It was clear that I was expected to make the most of this opportunity.

'Pray, please ensure that you are tidy and well-mannered this afternoon,' said Lady Sedley. 'You may take your servant, Joan, with you.'

After dinner, I called Joan to the bedchamber and we decided what I should wear. 'Practical would be best, as we are going to walk,' I said, reaching for the most serviceable dress of brown and grey.

'Nay, Tamsin, let me pick you something,' said Joan, her hand closing on one of my more ornate gowns. 'This one becomes you well; the pinks suit your fair colouring. Try it on.'

It did not seem worthwhile arguing with Joan and I also wanted the rare chance of talking to her while we were alone. 'Joan, tell me how you are doing now, are you settled in? Are the other servants kind to you?'

'Why yes, they are mostly pleasant to me, and when I am not helping you, I sometimes give a hand to the other maids whose mistresses are more demanding,' she said, scraping my hair back under a French hood.

'I am not demanding, then? That is not what you used to say when we lived at home,' I teased.

'Compared with some ladies I could name, you are a perfect angel,' Joan said, struggling with the laces of my pink kirtle. 'You decide what you want to wear without changing your mind and you do not require a lot of paint to disguise spots.'

We descended the main staircase, with Joan carrying my cloak in case of inclement weather. We were early; the church bells had not struck two o'clock. I arranged myself prettily with a piece of the hated embroidery in a side room with Joan perched on a stool close by.

We waited. As the bells struck the half hour, there was a commotion at the door. Shortly afterwards, a page came in and announced, 'The Earl of Allerthorpe presents his compliments, Mistress, and wishes to know if you will receive him.'

Smothering a giggle at his solemn tone, I confirmed in my grandest voice that I would be pleased to receive Lord Allerthorpe and asked the page to show him in forthwith. I ignored a snigger from Joan.

Lord Allerthorpe swept in. He seemed richly dressed but his clothing was marked with smears of mud. He bowed. 'Madam, a thousand apologies for my lateness. An incident on the road delayed me.'

I curtsied. 'Pray, do not distress yourself, your lordship. I was absorbed in my needlework and did not notice the lateness of the hour.' I waited until Joan had poured wine for Lord Allerthorpe and when he pronounced himself refreshed, we set out on our walk.

'What happened on the road, sir?'

'A cart had overturned, leaving a trail of cabbages in the mud. The street was blocked, the carter was dazed, and the horse distressed, and all the cabbages needed to be collected.'

'Was the carter injured?'

'Fortunately, he only had a few grazes and the horse got back on its feet. The worst bit was trying to collect the cabbages. A great crowd appeared from nowhere and I could not help noticing cabbages disappearing into shirts and aprons.'

'Did you tell the driver?'

'No, Mistress, I did not. Many of the people looked half-starved and a cabbage would have made a thin pottage more appetising.'

'Ah,' I said. 'You may call me Tamsin.'

'May I return the favour? My given name is Richard,' he said with a bow.

The walk passed very pleasantly and as there had been little rain recently, the footpaths, although muddy, were less of a quagmire than usual.

'Do you enjoy riding, Richard?'

'Yes, much more than you enjoy sewing, I believe. Despite your rapt attention to your work, your needle was not moving when I arrived!'

'That is most certainly true. I cannot manage complicated stitching, but I can do plain sewing. I do enjoy walking, but not so much here in the clogged city streets. My favourite walks are in meadows and across wild landscapes. Most of all, I love to walk by the sea. I can never get tired of watching it in the different seasons.'

'You must miss your home and Cornwall. Shall you go back?'

'I do miss my homeland, but I do not know if I shall ever have the chance to return. My family is in somewhat reduced circumstances since the death of my father, and we do not have the funds for unnecessary travel. My family are hoping that I will find a rich husband!'

There was a gasp from behind me. Too late, I clapped my hand over my mouth. Again, I had departed from polite conversation – I had implied to a young man that I must marry for money!

Horrified, I sought an acceptable follow up before he could respond. 'Richard, you must miss Yorkshire and your family too.'

'I do, Tamsin, and I must say that it is refreshing to hear a young woman so open about her situation. I will not think the worse of you. There must be a hundred young women at court engaged on the same mission!'

After that blunder, I was careful to stick to safe subjects of conversation.

Feeling somewhat sweaty and still embarrassed, I saw that we had finished our turn around the gardens. Joan slipped in front to summon the porter to open the door.

'Do come in and partake of some refreshment, Lord Allerthorpe,' I said formally. 'You must be fatigued after our expedition.'

'Not fatigued, but certainly a drink and a little more of your

66

company sounds delightful.' I saw Joan grinning as the door was opened and we went in.

Later, at supper, Lady Ester leaned over to me. 'Tamsin, I saw you return from your walk with Lord Allerthorpe. Did he mention a Lady Constance?'

'No, he did not, Lady Ester. Should he have done?'

'I heard talk that he and she are to marry. It may explain why Lord Allerthorpe has not shown any interest in London ladies. It would be so very suitable as their lands adjoin in Yorkshire. It is strange that he did not mention her.'

'Yes, I expect it would be a suitable marriage. But no, Lord Allerthorpe did not mention her to me.' I turned away from her and noticed that all Lady Sedley's ladies-in-waiting seemed to be staring at me. What had I said?

Joan explained later. 'It's because they think you must be hoping for a proposal from him yourself.'

'I had not thought of it like that. I like him because he is pleasant and knowledgeable, and he talks to me as if I am not an idiot – he is good company, nothing more.'

'I think some other young ladies, Lady Ester for example, might like him for themselves. I have heard that he is regarded as a great catch, and several ladies have expressed jealousy of Lady Constance up north.'

'How do you know all this, Joan?'

'You know me, Tamsin, I always enjoyed a gossip and us maids like nothing more than discussing our mistresses' private business!' It was true: back in Looe, Joan always seemed to know the latest news and she kept a sharp eye on all the "goings on" as she called them.

CHAPTER 8

The following week saw me out walking with Lord Allerthorpe most days, with Joan trailing behind holding whatever flower I had picked, along with a pocketful of interesting stones I'd found. While Richard talked about politics, the Church, and the recent marriage of the king to Anne Boleyn, of which I knew little, I found that I could educate him about nature, as our walks took us through the fields to the villages around Greenwich.

After church on Sunday, he appeared to escort me home as Lady Sedley had invited him to dinner. To my surprise, he had brought me a present: a beautiful pair of kidskin gloves.

'How very kind of you, Richard. Thank you, I shall wear them this afternoon and of course I shall treasure them. You do realise that if I were to drop one in the river, you would have to jump in and retrieve it immediately!'

'I should be honoured to do so, Tamsin!' said Richard with a bow.

After dinner, we followed a path down by the Thames approaching the Palace of Greenwich. Many people were out and about, enjoying a day off work. I stopped to dislodge some mud from my shoes when I noticed a barge approaching. The rich hangings and the royal crest marked it out.

'Who is that?' I said, shading my eyes. 'Is it the king and queen? I cannot see yet; there are guards blocking my view, but we should be able to see better in a minute.'

The barge was now in front of us, and we were joined by a

small group of women, who looked to be servants by their dress. I walked closer to the river, with Richard and Joan following behind.

'Tamsin, do not fall in or I shall have to dive for more than your gloves!' called Richard.

I had a much better view now. The king was not there, but in the barge was a small, slight woman with very dark hair, loaded with diamonds which flashed in the sunlight. The murmuring from the women in front of me increased in volume. They looked aggressive, and some were moving forwards. It was clear they had not come to applaud the queen.

Richard grabbed my arm. 'Stay back, there may be trouble.'

I strained to see and as I watched, the woman turned away, giving orders to the boat crew. Fascinated, I stared at her. Her black eyes were a little protuberant and although she was striking, she was not beautiful.

'So that is our new queen. She was fortunate that the women could not reach her. They looked hostile,' I said.

'There was an incident several years ago: an enormous crowd of women chased her off when she landed further up the Thames and tried to visit a nearby house. She was chased back onto her barge by a large crowd of angry women who shouted insults. This queen is not popular with the people, especially the women who blame her for the king annulling his marriage to Queen Catherine, whom they loved.'

Our walk home was more sober than usual. That incident had cast a pall over what had been a lovely day.

Later that evening, Lady Sedley sent for me. Surprised and wondering what I could have done, I hastened to her chamber.

'Tamsin, sit down and listen to what I have to say. Lord Allerthorpe requested a private meeting with me after dinner before he went for the walk with you, and he has asked for your hand in marriage. Fortunately, I had already noted his attraction to you and have taken the precaution of sending messages to your mother and my cousin in Looe to inform them of a possible match. I hardly think there will be any objections. There, what do you say to that?'

'Lady Sedley, are you sure you have interpreted him correctly? He did not speak of marriage while we were out this afternoon,' was my stunned response.

'My dear, Allerthorpe was very clear. He will not propose until consent is secured from your mother. He is prepared to overlook your humbler background and your small marriage portion. He is doing you a great honour.'

'But my lady, I thought he was as good as pledged to an heiress in Yorkshire.'

'I believe the families had hoped that the two young people would marry; it certainly would have been advantageous to both families. But it seems that Lord Allerthorpe has his own ideas. You will, of course, be married from here at St Alfege's Church and the wedding breakfast can be arranged here in the Great Hall. Your family home will not have the facilities required.'

'Lady Sedley, Lord Allerthorpe has not made any proposal to me. I have not had the chance to consider what is a very weighty matter indeed!'

'Nonsense!' snorted Lady Sedley. 'It is not a weighty matter. You have secured the admiration of a rich, unmarried man with excellent connections who is far above your station in life. Do you wish to live in hope for a better offer? You may end up unmarried and always beholden to others,' she said.

Lady Sedley was not finished. 'I do not think you realise the opportunities this would give you. Think of the benefits to your own family. Richard may assist them financially, and having a countess in the family will reflect very well on them. I consider this a triumph! He will declare himself to you shortly and, of course, you will accept him.'

Back in the sleeping chamber, which, mercifully, was empty, I confided the news to Joan. We had to speak quietly but her mouth dropped open and I was afraid she was about to shout, so I covered her mouth with my hand as a precaution.

'I do like Richard, but I am not sure that I would like to go and live in Yorkshire. It is even further away from Cornwall. I am also uncertain about getting married so soon. The idea of spending the rest of my life with one man and managing a large estate is a little worrying.' There was a muffled noise. Hastily, I took my hand away from Joan's mouth.

'Tamsin, Lord Allerthorpe is certain to have a full staff to do everything. I do not think you would have much to do – it will not be like our Trenowden Manor in Looe where everything is run on a shoestring. You could just wear pretty dresses and entertain!'

Seeing my downcast face, Joan added, 'Of course, there are bound to be exciting walks and new places to explore. It would not matter if you wore out shoes as you do now, either! Also, perhaps Richard will allow you to make regular visits to Cornwall. He has sufficient wealth to send you in an upholstered carriage, and you could stop at all the best inns on the journey, instead of making do with the flea ridden holes we used on our trip to Plymouth!'

'Would you come to Yorkshire with me, Joan? I know we have had our differences in the past, but I could not manage without you now.'

'Certainly, I will, if Lord Allerthorpe has no objection. I, too, might find myself a husband in the wilds of Yorkshire!'

'If I decide to marry Richard, it will be on condition that you accompany me, Joan.'

Later that night, I lay awake, listening to the soft snores of the other ladies. What would they say if they knew? Doubtless, they would advise me to accept the proposal.

Should I marry Lord Allerthorpe? If I did, I would have the security my mother had always talked of and I would be able to help my family. Richard and I were already friends and many marriages went ahead when the bride and groom hardly knew each other. The "love" and "passion" of which minstrels sang were not relevant to real-life marriages. In any case, Lady Sedley's messages would already be on their way to Cornwall, and I could not bear to disappoint my family. Now all I needed was for him to propose!

The following morning, Richard appeared as I was again sorting out Lady Sedley's embroidery silks and taking as long as I could over the task. The low hum of chatter ceased as a servant knocked. 'Enter,' shouted Lady Sedley.

'Lord Allerthorpe requests permission to walk in the gardens with Mistress Tamsin,' announced the servant. Richard appeared behind him.

'You may go, Tamsin. Richard, my dear, will you stay to dinner?'

'My thanks, Lady Sedley, I would be delighted to accept your kind invitation.'

Heart hammering, I nearly upturned the box of silks on to the floor. All the ladies turned to stare at me. Curtseying to Lady Sedley, I hurried out, feeling my cheeks grow hot.

'Good morning, Tamsin, you look somewhat flushed today. Have you been running or is it the excitement of embroidery that affects you so?'

'No, Richard, I am quite cool, I just need a little fresh air.' We went outside.

'Let us walk around the terrace.'

'That sounds like an excellent idea,' I said.

'I have something to ask you.'

Suddenly, he was down on one knee. There was a horrible crunching noise.

'Richard, you have just knelt on a snail. Pray, move back so that I can see if it can be saved. No, it is quite dead, but it has left its corpse on your breeches.'

'I am very sorry for the snail, but perhaps you would do me the honour of becoming my wife?'

'Stand up,' I said, 'and I will use my kerchief to remove the worst. Oh, and yes, I will marry you.'

'Tamsin, I shall do all I can to ensure that you never regret this decision.'

'You may start by always checking the ground for any small creature before you throw yourself down upon it, Richard.'

Richard leaned towards me and pecked at my cheek. 'Your mother appears pleased and Lord Boskeyn of Penwarne has indicated his approval. It is fortunate that Lady Sedley took it upon herself to forewarn them. I shall announce the glad tidings at dinner, and I will begin the arrangements for the ceremony. We shall be married as soon as possible.'

'It would not surprise me if Lady Sedley had already arranged for the bands to be called. She seemed most eager for this match,' I said rather acidly.

'She sees your beauty and virtues, and as do I, my darling.' Richard gazed at me with watery eyes. Amazed, I judged it wise to keep silent.

Predictably, there was a tumult of noise when Richard made his announcement. Men congratulated me and the sweeter of the ladies offered kisses and cooed at me. Lady Sedley sat with a triumphant gleam in her eye, but Lady Ester glared.

'Who does she think she is? She's nothing but a country

bumpkin from an obscure and poor family.' Her voice was low but designed so that I could hear. I itched to throw a plate of sweetmeats at her but managed to control myself.

Back in the sleeping chamber, Joan was waiting and hopping around as I expected.

'So, he proposed! Your mother must be so proud. You will be a countess and preside over an enormous estate. You do not look as happy and excited as I had expected, Tamsin.'

'I am happy, Joan, but you must understand that this is rather like a business arrangement, not a love match. You are fortunate in that you can marry for love whereas I cannot because I have obligations to my family, and I do not want to live as a dependant for the rest of my life. Lord Allerthorpe must marry because he needs an heir for his estate. However, he seems kind and we share interests. We shall manage quite well, I daresay.'

Joan was quiet for a few moments. 'This matter has moved very quickly. You may have received other offers had you waited.'

'No, Joan, we must be realistic. There cannot be many agreeable and rich men who would wish to marry an obscure Cornish woman from minor gentry without much dowry and no estate.'

'No, I suppose not.' She brightened up. 'Now we must think about what you will wear. Doubtless, her ladyship will have an opinion.'

'Yes, I expect she will, but *I* shall decide what gown to wear to my wedding!' I said happily.

CHAPTER 9

A beautiful May morning found Richard and I standing at the door to St Alfege's Church, exchanging our wedding vows. It was a great sadness to me that my mother did not feel able to stand the rigours of the journey from Cornwall. Daniel was by now deep in his studies at Cambridge University and could not travel either, as he had important examinations. However, I had the support of my brother, Henry, and his new wife, Jenna, who sailed up from Plymouth.

During the wedding feast, I finally had the chance to speak to Henry. I began to feel tearful at this link with home. He seemed to have grown and filled out further, and the beginnings of a beard sprouted from his chin.

'You have done very well for yourself, sister, much better than I expected. Mother and Lord Boskeyn are delighted.'

Irritation at his patronising tone prevented me from becoming tearful with homesickness. 'What do you mean "better than you expected"?'

'Well, you are not rich or of conventional beauty, but you do look fine in that get-up and your hair is actually very pretty,' he said, referring to my unbound hair, which cascaded from an Allerthorpe tiara.

'Your eyes are beautiful too, Countess,' said Jenna.

I looked around for the lady she was addressing and belatedly realised it was me.

'Why, thank you, Jenna. I am sorry that we shall not have

time to become better acquainted. I understand you must return to Cornwall very soon.'

'Yes, sister, we must catch the evening tide,' said Henry. 'There are urgent matters in Cornwall which require my presence.'

'I must ask Lady Sedley if she will allow me to pack some food for your journey.'

'Tamsin, you are the Countess of Allerthorpe now; Lady Sedley will not mind. Just ask the servants to organise it for you,' said Henry.

'Oh,' I said, feeling rather startled. 'Yes, I will.'

I did exactly that, and as Henry had predicted, some neatly wrapped food parcels and bottles of ale were delivered to Henry's servant as the couple climbed onto their horses. I stood waving as they disappeared around the bend, and this time I did cry.

The evening wore on and I drank perhaps more than was good for me, partly to blank out the homesickness and partly to mask my nerves about the wedding night. Fortunately, with my country upbringing, I already had an idea of what was expected of me. Joan, trying to be helpful, informed me that it could be painful, but otherwise reasonably pleasant and I should not be alarmed if I bled.

By the time the priest had finished sprinkling the bed with holy water and the last of the inebriated guests had been bundled out by Richard, I felt somewhat unsteady on my feet, so retreated to the enormous bed lent to us by Lady Sedley in honour of the occasion. There followed an awkward tussle as arms and legs collided and I lay back, examining Lady Sedley's extraordinary bed hangings. Depictions of fantastical animals were combined with unfamiliar flowers – the animals appeared to be moving. Most fascinating.

Richard appeared to have finished pumping at my inert form, for he climbed off me. 'My darling, you are so beautiful. I am honoured that you chose me for your husband.' He began to stroke my hair and kiss my face.

I bolted out of the bed, nearly fell, but managed to make it to a nearby ewer, where I found myself vomiting.

'Richard, I am so sorry,' I said as I regained control and started to feel better. 'I will ring for a servant to clear this.' A servant arrived so promptly that I even wondered if he had been listening at the door.

Silently, I climbed back into bed, feeling rather shaky, sore, and conscious of something sticky running down my legs.

'Women do not generally vomit when they are in receipt of my attentions,' said Richard. 'Am I so disgusting to you, wife? Or could it have been the quantity of strong drink you imbibed this evening?'

'The drink,' I mumbled, falling into a pit of sleep.

In the morning, Joan arrived, bringing a concoction of willow bark in a cup. 'This will ease your head, Mistress—I mean, your ladyship. You should rest this morning. Nobody is expecting you downstairs until later.'

'Where is Lord Allerthorpe, Joan?'

'He left early this morning, my lady. His servant said he had matters to attend to at Hampton Court. He went by the river and is not expected back until this evening.'

I lay back on the pillows, waiting for the willow drink to do its work. Joan appeared with food at dinner time, but I could only nibble some bread and sip the ale. With her help, I donned my best gown and descended the stairs.

'Good morning, Countess,' said the voice of Lady Sedley from the back of the room. 'I trust you slept well?'

Surprised, I wondered who had entered the room behind me and turned around to look. Then I realised, I had forgotten my new title again! There was an outburst of giggles, but some sympathetic faces too.

'Why, thank you, Lady Sedley. I slept very well indeed, and it was so kind of you to give up your bedchamber for us. Richard says we will move into Allerthorpe House soon. Would you like me to continue the piece I was working on last week, Lady Sedley?' I said, looking at the embroidery spread out around the room.

'That will not be necessary, Countess. Would you care to take a turn around the garden, or would you prefer to ride out somewhere? I can send one of the women with you.'

'That would be lovely, Lady Sedley, I would like to walk. May I take Margaret with me?'

'You may. Fresh air should restore you.'

Margaret and I made our way along the path to the terrace overlooking the gardens. We had just moved out of earshot of the gardeners when Margaret said, 'You look a little pale, Tamsin. I trust you are not worn out by bed sports!'

'Certainly not, but I may have imbibed a little too much last night.'

'Well, that will confirm Lady Sedley's earlier suspicions of you,' she said, giggling.

'Margaret, that is not very kind! It is precisely because I am unused to strong liquor that I feel like this today.'

'Of course, Tamsin. Oh, should I be addressing you as Countess? How is her ladyship's head and her other parts?' More giggles.

'Margaret, I can report that my head feels much better in the fresh air and my other parts are recovering too.'

'Indeed, I am glad to hear that you are improving. I suppose you are too grand now to give me any other information?' Yet more giggling.

'Well, I remember it was uncomfortable and rather boring, but mostly I remember Lady Sedley's bed hangings which appeared quite extraordinary – the animals seemed to move!'

'Tamsin, dear, that was the effect of the wine you had taken. I have seen Lady Sedley's bed curtains and I can assure you the animals are entirely stationary.'

'Did you enjoy yourself last night, Margaret? I seem to remember you dancing several times with Lord Presland.'

'Yes, I am hopeful that he will offer for me. He seems polite and kind and he is quite handsome. His estates are in Leicestershire and I believe his castle has been renovated recently. I think my parents would consider him worthy of me. We must all marry, and I am almost nineteen years old already!'

'I heard that Lord Burton and Lady Ester are to marry, so we shall not need to tolerate her condescension for much longer.' I said, cheerfully. 'Also, Margaret, as I am now a Countess, I will interrogate Lord Presland about his intentions to you when I next see him,' I said in my grandest tone, trying not to smile.

'Tamsin, promise me that you will not! You will frighten him off and I shall remain a sad old spinster.'

'Do not worry, you can come and live with me as a lady-in-waiting and I will make you do embroidery all day. Margaret, you will always have a home with me, and I am sure we will have no trouble with finding you a good husband if, of course, the idea of embroidery-filled days does not attract you!'

Laughing together, we went back inside. I felt better and occupied the rest of my day directing the packing up of my possessions which were to go to Allerthorpe House, a short ride away from Sedley House.

'Is the earl not back yet?' said Lady Sedley at supper.

'He has gone to Hampton Court. I was told that it was on a matter of some importance.'

'I expect the king wants something done. His Majesty never had any patience.'

'Have you met the king, Lady Sedley?'

'Bless you child, yes, on many occasions. I have known him since he was growing up at Eltham Palace. His mother, Queen Elizabeth, God rest her, invited me to play with him and his sisters. His older brother, Arthur, had his own establishment at Ludlow and Henry was just the Duke of York and expected to make his career in the Church. He was a handsome and clever child, always eager to show off his learning to anybody who would visit the palace.'

'It is such a pity that he cast off Queen Catherine.'

'Yes, it is, and we must learn to refer to her as the Princess Dowager in front of other people. It is sad about the poor Princess Mary. She has been separated from her mother and we are supposed to call her the Lady Mary now.'

'I do not think the new queen is very popular,' I said and briefly told Lady Sedley about how Richard and I had witnessed the hostile reception given to her by a group of poor women.

'Tamsin, you must be careful what you say,' said Lady Sedley. 'It is not for us to question the behaviour of the king, and his secretary, Cromwell, has spies everywhere, probably even in this household. You can be certain that he will have at least one spy in every noble house.'

With that sobering thought, I returned to my quarters to await the return of Lord Allerthorpe.

It was fully dark when I heard clattering on the stairs and

Richard entered. 'My love, I thought you would be asleep by now. How kind of you to wait for me.' He started nuzzling my shoulder, but I wriggled away and out of bed on the excuse of pouring him some wine. I wanted to find out what was going on.

'Richard, pray tell me what you were doing at Hampton Court.'

Richard looked surprised and drained his wine goblet. 'Wife, do not be concerned about matters of state, they are not for you. Instead, let us concentrate on making an heir for Allerthorpe.'

'Richard, I do not think I shall be able to conceive while I am worried about what the future holds. Do not forget that I am educated and may understand more than usual for a woman.'

'Very well, Tamsin. As you know, the king is now Head of the Church in England and Wales. I have been helping to implement the new law which stops the senior clergy from sending large amounts of money to the Pope. Also, I have been helping to organise the queen's coronation. She will be crowned on 1st of June at the Collegiate Church of St Peter in Westminster.'

'Is it true that she is already pregnant?' I asked, pouring Richard some wine from a flagon.

'Yes, I expect that is why the king married her in such haste in January.' Richard pulled off his travel-stained jerkin and made a lunge at me. 'To bed, Tamsin,' he said with a gleam in his eye.

I lay down trying to ignore the soreness between my legs from last night and distracted myself by wondering if I would be permitted to attend the coronation.

The following day, we were installed in the London house. I did not have to lift a finger as the servants did all the work. Smaller than Lady Sedley's establishment, it nevertheless benefitted from some beautiful gardens and it was not far from Greenwich Palace and the markets. Fortunately, Joan approved of it and I ensured that she was given her own room as befitting her improved status as the personal maid of a countess.

Once we were settled in, life proceeded smoothly, and I found plenty to occupy me. News that my brother, Henry, had a son arrived from Looe and I managed to make an embroidered shirt for him successfully, with some help from Joan.

To my delight, Richard and I were invited to Queen Anne's coronation. The streets were beautifully decorated, and fountains ran with wine, but the atmosphere was not joyful. The Londoners seemed subdued, and I heard jeers and rude comments. The queen was visibly pregnant, and I wondered how she endured the hostility of the people.

CHAPTER 10

Life at Allerthorpe House settled into an even rhythm. One year and then another went by. Richard was often away but I relished the independence that his absence gave me, and occupied myself with social events and charitable projects. The increasing availability of printed books gave me the opportunity to indulge my interest in reading, too.

One day in the early spring of 1536, Joan and I were wandering around the bookstalls of St Paul's Churchyard. Joan seemed happy to watch the people and chat to the two soldiers, Ranulf and Rolf, whose company Lord Allerthorpe deemed necessary on our outings.

We were standing by a stall, where a bookseller was trying to persuade me to buy a beautifully decorated Book of Hours, when Joan suddenly clutched my arm. 'Tamsin—I mean, your ladyship, there is a man staring at us.'

Turning around, I saw no such man, and forgot the incident as I bargained for the book. The light was failing fast when we began to retrace our steps home. Joan was chattering to Ranulf, described by her as the most handsome of the pair, when there was a scream from an alley on the right. I paused, intending to investigate, but was blocked by Rolf, the other retainer.

'Stay here, your ladyship. You too, Mistress Glasson. Doubtless, it is nothing,' he said grandly. They both clanked off down the alley.

Joan and I were left wondering what was going on, when

there was a sudden movement to my left. Looking down, I realised that my money purse had been cut clean away. All I saw was a young man running ahead of me, and seconds later, he had vanished into another alleyway.

Ranulf and Rolf came clattering back. 'Nothing there, my lady; all is quiet.'

'Numbskulls!' screeched Joan. 'While you were away, a sturdy vagabond cut my lady's purse strings and made off!'

'It is no matter,' I said, displaying a composure I did not feel. 'There was hardly any money left in the purse.'

Although I was disturbed by the incident, I also wondered how it would feel to be so desperate that a man would risk being hanged for stealing.

Richard was predictably furious about the theft and wanted to sack Ranulf and Rolf immediately, but I managed to persuade him not to. Without employment, they could end up in the same position as the thief who stole my purse. I would just have to ensure that I remained more vigilant and remember that I lived in the capital city, not a small market town.

'I have already decided that you would be more secure in my Yorkshire castle,' said Richard the following week. 'There is a small garrison of soldiers and the building is easily defended. London can be volatile city and the religious changes are causing some unrest. It is time you were introduced to my people. You will enjoy being mistress of a castle!'

'You may be right, husband, and I have news for you. I suspect I may be with child! Pray, do not grapple with me; I am still unsure!'

Richard released me from a bear hug and sat down suddenly. 'I cannot accompany you because there is much to do regarding matters of state, and perhaps you should not travel in your condition?'

'I would rather travel with you, Richard.'

'Yes, I am sorry that I will be delayed, but there is your safety and that of my heir to consider. I shall send twenty armed guards with your party and you shall travel in a litter, stopping frequently at comfortable inns and convents.'

I was almost sure that I was pregnant as my monthly flow had always been regular and there had been nothing for three months. I had not been quick to conceive, but again, Richard was often away, sometimes for weeks at a time. The thought of such a long journey in a swaying litter was not encouraging, but I comforted myself with the thought that no one would dare to stop me riding my horse once we were away from London. My hopes were dashed when Richard announced that his friend, Lord Waleby, was also returning north and would accompany us.

'It will be a comfort to me to know that Lord Waleby will be with you in case of any accidents or mishaps.'

'I do not need to be supervised on this journey, Richard. Joan and I managed to travel some two hundred and fifty miles from Looe to London, alone and with no incidents,' I said sharply.

'Nevertheless, Tamsin, I am your husband. You will agree to this. When you travelled before, you were but an obscure gentlewoman. Now, you are a great lady travelling through some remote and poor areas. There may be sturdy beggars lurking who will see your baggage train as easy pickings. I shall join you as soon as I am finished with the king's business.'

'Let us not argue. Perhaps Lord Waleby will indeed be of help to us. Meanwhile, I had better go and give instructions for the journey,' I said.

'There is no need for you to do so. I have already ordered the household to prepare for your journey. You should go and rest.'

As I was feeling rather tired, I acquiesced, but a part of me was irritated by Richard's assumption that I would agree to go north, and the fact that he had already taken charge of preparations.

Later that day, I was surprised to find that the baggage included a dismantled bed and other furniture. I went to find Joan.

'Surely I do not need to take a bed and all this equipment,' I said, waving my hand at all the boxes and parcels. 'Surely inns will have beds!'

'Yes, they will, my lady, but what did for us on our last journey will not do for a noble countess!' replied Joan as she wrested with an over-filled box.

'Can I help you? I cannot just sit around, and it is raining outside.'

'No, you may not help, and yes, you must go and sit down. Perhaps you could go and select books and suchlike for the journey. What a disaster it would be if your embroidery got forgotten!'

As servants were now running back and forth, loading the waggons, I took myself out of the way. We were to leave early in the morning, and I should check that all my medicinal potions and unguents were collected, as I did not know about the state of the herb garden at Allerthorpe Castle.

Richard was home by the late afternoon, and I rushed to greet him with more enthusiasm than usual.

'I am glad to see signs that you may miss me while we are apart!' he said, throwing off his gauntlets and handing the reins to a stable hand.

'Of course I will miss you, Richard. Will you be sad to see

me go?'

'Yes, my love, but I doubt I shall have much time to miss you, as Cromwell's errands and directives are increasing every day.'

'But you will be allowed to join me at Allerthorpe Castle soon,' I said, suddenly alarmed by the idea of being separated from my husband.

'I think we should not underestimate the impact of these religious changes and the king's marriage to Anne Boleyn. Some people are not happy with the events and the king does not like disapproval. He has convinced himself that his plans come straight from God, so he reacts violently to anyone who dissents. His mood is increasingly unpredictable, especially since Queen Anne has not yet presented him with a son.'

'He has his daughters, and perhaps she will produce a son in time.'

Richard threw himself into a chair and gestured that I should join him. 'Tell me, Tamsin, how do you think the poor survive in a bad harvest or when they are sick?'

'Well, they can go to the monasteries and convents for charity and treatment if they are sick.'

'The king is beginning to investigate some larger monasteries for abuses and deficits in religious practices, now. Commissioners are already identifying monasteries likely to be dissolved.'

'Surely the king will only close religious houses that are badly managed? I have heard that monks and nuns are being sent to other, more properly run, houses. So perhaps it will not make such a difference to the poor.'

'Tamsin, I would like to think that you are correct, but the religious houses also hold a large amount of land and gold.

Cromwell has already involved me in drawing up plans for inspections. Land and property will revert to the Crown and then be parcelled out to the king's friends. Although monks and nuns will receive pensions if they do not transfer to another house, there will be many servants cast out with nothing. They may well starve or turn to crime to survive.'

'If all this is true, Richard, it does not bode well.'

His face, normally so sunny, became serious. 'Tamsin, you must not speak of our discussion. The king does not like to hear of any dissenting opinions.'

'Of course, I shall not if you say so, and Lady Sedley has already warned me to be careful, but surely the people do not know what is happening. Do you think there will be trouble when they discover all this?'

'I believe that the matter is not widely known about yet, but yes, I believe there will be protests. I hear that some lords are already beginning to make it known that they would be pleased to buy additional lands from the king. Anyway, let us talk of something more pleasant. It is our last evening together for several weeks and you must not be downhearted, or it could affect my son!'

'What if it is a daughter, my lord? Will you decide to put an end to our marriage like the king did with Queen Catherine?' I said, aiming a stray napkin at his head.

'Yes, I would put you in a nunnery, where you would be forced to embroider altar cloths and vestments all day and every day,' Richard said with a grin.

We left early the next morning under instructions to meet Lord Waleby at St Albans. I peered out from the litter curtains and wriggled to try and get comfortable under the furs, for it was very cold.

'Joan, I really cannot stand to stay in this litter for the next ten days, or however long it takes us to get to Yorkshire. I shall riot if Lord Waleby does not agree to me riding a horse instead!'

'At least you are warm, my lady,' said Joan from her horse. 'You must try to remember your dignity; people will expect a countess to be transported in comfort.'

'This is not comfort!' I said, gritting my teeth as the litter swayed and bumped. 'I cannot adjust to the rhythm in the way I could on a horse, and I cannot see where I am going!'

Joan slipped from view and was replaced by the anxious face of Ranulf. 'Are you quite comfortable, your ladyship?'

'No, I am not. I shall be riding from St Albans.'

'Yes, my lady.' He disappeared and now Rolf was riding alongside the litter.

'We should be at the Angel Inn in about two hours, your ladyship.'

I nodded politely, as I was feeling rather nauseous.

At last, the Angel Inn loomed into view. It was a large, wooden building with several outhouses. At the front door were several men. One detached himself, bowed and moved towards me.

'Good day, your ladyship. I am Peter Sandon, the landlord of this establishment. Welcome to my humble inn. May I help you to descend, and perhaps you would like to take some refreshment and warm yourself by the fire while the horses are changed?'

Awkwardly, I climbed out of the contraption, cursing to myself. Nothing would make me get in that thing again.

'Please come this way and my wife, Maud, will bring you a posset to revive you. Your men may take their places at the table and food will be brought. I have set aside a room for you and your maid.'

We followed him to a small back room warmed by a brazier. When the posset arrived, I warmed my hands on the cinnamon-scented drink and drank it as quickly as I could. Master Sandon was correct; my throat and stomach immediately felt warmer. Joan and I were trying to identify the ingredients of the posset when the door burst open.

'Good day, my lady. Lord Waleby, at your service. I am here and ready to ensure that our journey proceeds without mishap.' He flourished an extravagant hat as he bowed.

'Good day, my lord. I am honoured to meet you and I am pleased to report that we have proceeded thus far without any difficulties.'

'I see you have a goodly band of men at arms. I have brought another six, including two of my best archers.'

'We shall have a small army, sir! I doubt any lawless miscreants will dare come anywhere near us.'

'Indeed, my lady. Shall I ask the innkeeper to bring food?' he said, pulling at his curly grey beard.

'Yes, please do, Lord Waleby,' I said, for I was suddenly feeling much better and even hungry.

After dinner, Joan helped me to dress in clothes more suitable for riding. However, I felt rather stupid when I realised that we did not have a spare horse for me to ride. I thought carefully. 'I have it! You will ride in the litter, Joan, and I shall travel on your horse. People will assume the countess travels in the litter, nobody will be any the wiser, and you will enjoy yourself!'

'What do I do if we pass through villages and towns?' asked Joan nervously.

'You can just wave your hand in a stately manner or perhaps

close the curtains so people will think the countess wishes not to be exposed to the common gaze. You may even scatter a few coins from my purse if the people appear very poor.'

Lord Waleby was presented with a fait accompli as Joan climbed into the litter and I mounted her horse, just as we were ready to leave.

'My lady, I must protest. You should not ride in your condition and your maid cannot possibly travel in the countess's litter!' His complexion became redder.

'My lord, please do not dispute with me. As you say, I am in a delicate condition and should not be crossed, and I feel that riding will be of benefit to my health. Joan is a little fatigued today; she will be much more use to me after a rest.' Before he could open his mouth, I hurried on, 'People will not notice. They will assume that Joan is the countess and honour will be maintained.'

Quickly turning my horse away, I gave my men the order to leave, which meant that the rest of the party was obliged to follow them. I found I was enjoying myself more, the wind was lessening, and I could now see the surrounding countryside. We passed several small settlements and could see smoke issuing from their fires, but we saw nobody outside the dwellings.

CHAPTER 11

That evening, we rested at a convent. The sisters made us welcome and sent the men off to a monastery a little further on. Joan and I were given a comfortable room and provided with supper. We were just finishing the meal when a young girl of no more than ten years knocked at the door.

'Please excuse me, your ladyship, I am Hilda. The abbess wonders if you would attend her in her quarters at your convenience.'

'Of course, child. We shall come directly. Perhaps you could show us the way?'

'Yes, my lady.'

'Hilda, you are very young to choose a religious life.'

'Oh, I did not choose it your ladyship. My parents promised me to the Church and delivered me here with a dowry when I was but two years old. I am a postulant and must take my final vows when I am older.'

'Are you happy here, Hilda?'

'Why yes, my lady. The sisters are kind and I have learned my letters, and I can write a little and cast accounts. I doubt I would have had as much education at home.'

We had reached the abbess's door. Hilda knocked, curtsied, and was gone. A voice called, 'Enter.' The abbess was a rotund woman who looked to be in her fifties.

We curtsied. 'My humble thanks for giving us shelter, Lady Abbess. I am the Countess of Allerthorpe, and this is my maid,

Joan.'

'Please make yourselves comfortable,' said the abbess. 'I understand that you have come from London and you journey to Allerthorpe Castle in Yorkshire?' She offered us wine as she spoke. 'We have heard rumours. We wondered if you would be able to provide us with more information about certain events?'

'Lady Abbess, I know very little, but I am sure I can trust to your discretion. I have heard that the king has ordered Thomas Cromwell to make a survey of the religious houses. Some say it is to root out abusive practices, but it is also thought that the king has his eye on the riches held by certain monastic houses. It is believed that some houses may be dissolved, their lands and possessions sold.'

'So it is not merely gossip. I have also heard that Queen Anne has only given birth to a daughter, followed by several miscarriages,' said the abbess, as she replaced her wine goblet on the table.

'That is indeed true. I heard that her latest disappointment occurred after the king fell from his horse during a joust, and that he is now very angry about his lack of an heir.'

'I fear for the state of the king's soul,' said the abbess. 'I hear that Queen Anne favours reform of the Church and the New Learning. There have been so many dramatic changes that I do not know what the future holds. We are an unimportant establishment and lack much in the way of material wealth.'

'Lady Abbess, if you do have any moveable valuables that could be removed discreetly, perhaps you should hide them now as a precaution. They say the king's commissioners are already visiting and surveying religious houses.'

'I will pray on this matter, your ladyship, and I thank you for your wise counsel. What times we live in!'

On the following morning, we rose before the sun was up. As the packhorses were reloaded, I passed Hilda in the corridor. The front of her habit was muddy, and she held a garden trowel.

'The abbess gave me permission to absent myself from Lauds,' she said with a curtsey.

'Do take care, Hilda, and if you should ever become homeless, apply to me and I will give you a position in my household.'

'Thank you, my lady, but I doubt that such a thing will ever happen.'

We assembled in front of the abbey in a sombre mood. Even talkative Joan was quiet, and Lord Waleby did not even raise his eyebrows as Joan climbed into the litter and I jumped onto my horse. Indeed, he continued morosely, only cheering up when he could mix with his men and drink ale at our stopping points.

The long journey continued, and we saw but few people in the scattered villages. However, as we travelled further north, when the Allerthorpe livery was sighted, some people paused to wave and call out greetings. This gave Joan the opportunity to wave from the litter. Looking around on one of those occasions, I saw that she was doing this very enthusiastically and hurling a substantial number of coins in their direction.

'Joan,' I hissed. 'Do not wave so violently. Remember, you are a rich lady who can barely condescend to acknowledge the greetings of such poor people, and pray, do not give away all my money before we reach the end of our journey!'

'But my lady, I am giving you a good reputation among the common people. They will remember that Lady Allerthorpe is a kind soul who did condescend to acknowledge them and scattered some largesse for their relief!'

There was no answer to that. The journey continued with

overnight stops at a variety of inns and religious houses. Every night, Joan prepared a posset for us, using as much of the recipe provided by Maud, the innkeeper's wife, as we could remember.

After at least three months with no monthly flow and certain other symptoms appearing, Joan and I had concluded that I was certainly pregnant. Fortunately, the tiredness and nausea stopped, and I felt fit and well despite the discomforts of the journey.

At last, we sighted the city of York ahead. Lord Waleby appeared revived and insisted that I should take my place in the litter for our grand entrance to the city. I could see Joan looking disappointed and so some devil in me made me refuse him.

'It will not matter where I am, my lord. Nobody knows me and nobody will notice anything different. Joan will wear one of my best cloaks and draw the curtains.'

'As you say, my lady, but I do not think Lord Allerthorpe will be best pleased when he hears of your conduct on this journey.'

'Do not presume to know my husband's mind, Lord Waleby. I will ensure that you will not be blamed. You could not have placed me in the litter by force, lest I injured myself and damaged the welfare of Lord Allerthorpe's son!'

As we made our way through the crowded streets of York, the press of people and traffic was such that we needed to pause at times. Joan was in her element, bowing and smiling at every opportunity. While some called out a greeting, not everybody looked happy to see us, and I became aware of muttered comments as I rode past.

'Who do they think they are? London lords from the king's court – give them a nice Yorkshire welcome!' A clump of mud struck my litter but missed Joan, fortunately. One of the soldiers drew his sword but the miscreant was long gone.

'Sweet Jesus! Joan, keep the curtains closed,' I shouted. 'There may be other missiles and I do not want trouble.' I rode back to my place in the procession, willing us to go faster.

Lord Waleby drew level with me. 'My lady, we must proceed with all haste to Allerthorpe castle. I fear the mood of the populace and would not want you exposed to any further insults. I am sorry to say that the king is not as popular as we would wish. People resent the changes in the Church and they do not like the king's new marriage.'

'Yes, Lord Waleby, we must not be the cause of any trouble. I have told Joan to keep herself hidden.'

Fortunately, York was nowhere as large as London, and we were soon out into the calm of fields and forests. We had only about twenty-five miles to travel before we reached Allerthorpe Castle. We might travel it in two days providing the weather held and the horses did not become lame. However, Lord Waleby advised taking three days to avoid over-tiring the horses.

The weather remained fine, and I was pleased that people seemed friendlier again. Children stood at the wayside waving and Joan enjoyed herself, waving and throwing the few coins left. Meanwhile, I made the most of what would probably my last opportunity to ride for some time.

At last, we were at journey's end. Allerthorpe Castle stood on a small hill, and I could see small figures scurrying around as our cavalcade approached. The drawbridge stood open as we clattered over the moat. We entered under the arch of a large gatehouse which led to a courtyard. Lord Waleby took control, addressing the small crowd that had gathered in a loud voice.

'Make way for the Countess of Allerthorpe. I am charged by the earl to ensure that his lady receives a hearty welcome!'

'Where's the earl, then? Why is he not here too?' shouted

voices from the back of the crowd.

Lord Waleby roared back, 'The earl has been detained on the king's business and will arrive in due course!'

To my amusement, I saw that various household officials were pushing past me and advancing purposely towards the litter curtains, which were shut firmly. A little girl appeared carrying flowers. What would Joan do? We had not thought of this.

I steered my horse to face the litter and said in my loudest voice. 'Joan, we are arrived! Do you feel up to alighting?' The crowd craned forward to see what was happening. I stood in my stirrups and shouted, 'Good people, thank you for your welcome. I graciously allowed another lady to ride in my litter as she had a malady which has now gone. Thanks be to God!'

People turned to stare at me, and a faint echo of, 'Thanks be to God,' echoed back.

Joan emerged from behind the curtains and accepted help down from Ranulf. She looked quite nervous and the crowd that had been pressing forwards stepped back suddenly. Joan quickly located me and gave a low curtsey in the muddy courtyard.

'Oh, how can I thank you, my lady? Your kindness in allowing me to use your litter has resulted in my complete recovery,' she declaimed at the top of her voice.

'I am happy indeed to see you now fully restored,' I bellowed back. The people looked at me askance. Belatedly, I realised that my hair was coming down from my headdress and my muddy travelling clothes did not make me look like a countess.

Lord Waleby appeared at my side. 'Lady Allerthorpe is exhausted from her journey and needs to rest. Kindly conduct the lady countess to her apartments forthwith!' he declaimed to the crowd. A middle-aged woman curtsied to me.

'Welcome to Allerthorpe Castle, my lady countess. I am the

housekeeper, Edith Fereby, and this is the steward, Tom Babthorp. Please follow us.'

An elderly priest stepped forward before I could do so. 'I am Father Anslem, your ladyship, and I am here to serve the spiritual needs of the household. Please send for me at your convenience,' he said bowing. He then retreated with Lord Waleby. I noticed that they had their heads close together. They were clearly conferring about something of great interest to them.

With Joan and the servants carrying my belongings, I followed the housekeeper and steward through a second gatehouse, which led to a smaller and cleaner looking courtyard.

'Your apartments are on the left, my lady, and they connect with those of the earl,' said Tom. 'Edith will fetch whatever you and your waiting women require and assist with your unpacking.'

Edith showed us into a small, square room containing cushioned chairs and a table. The walls were hung with tapestries and the windows looked out onto a garden. The floor had been strewn with clean herb-scented rushes, and a fire blazed in the large, stone fireplace displaying the arms of the Allerthorpe family.

'How did you enjoy being Lady Allerthorpe in her litter today?' I asked Joan, trying to flex my fingers, which had become chilled in my riding gauntlets.

'Very much, my lady, but I was right worried when they advanced to welcome me! More importantly, how are you feeling after the journey, my lady?'

'I am tired and little stiff, but I expect I will recover soon. I am not at all concerned about the baby. Ask Edith to bring us some wine and food to revive us and then you can go and supervise the unpacking of our goods.'

Hours later, my bedframe had been reassembled and made

up and my rooms were beginning to take on a homely air. Joan looked askance at the truckle bed provided for her.

'I expect you are now much too grand to sleep in that,' I said teasingly, 'but I will not need you to masquerade as me in my bed. I promised you a room to yourself so tell the servants to move your bed to the little room next door.'

I was up early the following morning, ready to explore my new domain. I was glad of my warm cloak when Joan and I reached the battlements of the castle as there was a cold wind. Peering through the arrow slits built into the stone walls, I could see many fields and strips of land dotted with small dwellings.

'The builders of this castle chose well; we can see for miles. The inhabitants would have had early warning of any attacks,' I observed. 'I believe the castle has been standing for at least three hundred years. Just think of the battles it must have seen, even in recent times. Richard told me how his father fought for the House of York. We are indeed fortunate that a settlement was reached.'

'You mean when the seventh Henry, a Lancastrian king, married Elizabeth of York, my lady?'

'Yes, Joan, and we must pray that the peaceful times continue.'

We descended to the chapel, where we found the Allerthorpe priest kneeling in front of the altar. After making our reverences, we waited quietly for him to finish his prayers. The priest appeared a young man, not more than twenty-five years old.

'My lady, I did not expect to see you so early,' he said, advancing down the aisle. He bowed and ushered us out of the chapel.

'I am sorry for intruding on your devotions, Master Priest. I could return another time if it is more convenient.'

'No, not at all, your ladyship,' he said, leading the way to a small chamber next to the chapel entrance. My eye was immediately drawn to a shelf of books. I itched to look at them, but I must remember my manners.

'May I pour you a cup of ale, my lady?' I accepted a cup and gestured to Joan that she could leave. 'Master Priest, you are very kind, thank you.'

'My lady, are you recovered from your journey?'

'Yes, Master Priest, I am recovered. Although long, the journey was interesting, although uncomfortable at times.'

'I believe you are accustomed to travel, my lady, as you are from Cornwall. Tell me, did you have your own chapel on your estate, or did you worship in your parish church?'

'We had only a very tiny chapel on our lands, so we attended the parish church for most services. We did not have a resident estate priest as the living was too small.' I pictured the walk down the stony path to the church, with its views of the sea, and felt a pang of homesickness.

The priest was staring at me. 'I beg your pardon, my lady, I did not mean to distress you. Tell me, were services regular and well-attended?'

'Yes, indeed. The tenants and local people always attended every service.' I did not mention how the older members of our congregation often slept through the sermons.

'Living in such a remote area as Cornwall, I would think that the people would be more vulnerable to heretical ideas and superstition, unless the priest were an educated and vigilant man. Tell me, was your priest vigilant against unorthodox practices?'

Determined to gain the upper hand in what was beginning to feel like a power struggle, I sat up straight, looked straight into his stony eyes and spoke in my coldest tone. 'I can assure you, Priest, that I saw no trace of heretical practices in the local population.'

His response was not unexpected. 'My lady, pardon me, but as a weak woman of limited education, you would not have the capacity to notice such things.'

Gripping the arms of the chair, I said tightly, 'You are wrong, Master Priest. I am educated. I was fortunate to be included in the tutoring provided to my brothers.' Swiftly, I went over to a bookshelf and selected a Latin text. 'Allow me to translate,' I said, selecting a page at random. The priest looked stunned, which was fortunate as I was concerned that my Latin might be rusty. Replacing the book, I picked up a Greek text and translated the frontispiece.

The priest interrupted me. 'My apologies, my lady, I see that you are in truth highly educated for a woman.'

'Tell me, are you not somewhat young for a priest? Perhaps your learning has come from books and from religious men who do not have experience of secular life. I understand that the king's daughter, Lady Mary, is highly educated, doubtless her sister Elizabeth will be too. Clearly, most women do not have the opportunity to study the classics, but it is certainly possible for some of them to do so.'

'Yes, I do not doubt that noblewomen may gain a smattering of the languages, but for most women it is impossible and would be dangerous to their health and conduct.'

Taking pity on this young priest who was not much older than me, I decided to switch to less contentious subjects. He brightened visibly when I began to ask questions about the estate's tenants, until it was time for breakfast.

CHAPTER 12

Sitting on a dais at a small table in the Hall after breakfast, I felt very important when the castle steward introduced me to the principal servants and the most important of the local tenants. I was unsure about what to say, but people seemed happy with my nods and smiles. It was made clear to me that an efficient system was already in place and that I would not be expected to interfere, although the steward warned me that the last harvest had been poor and that some tenants would be unable to pay all their rents this year.

After dinner in the Hall, I began to feel very tired, and retired to my chamber. I was startled out of a dream that I had given birth to a hissing cat with sharp claws, to find Joan looking agitated.

'Your ladyship, you have visitors. They have been put in the Hall and have requested to see you at your earliest convenience.'

'Do they look important, Joan? Do I need to get up?'

'Yes, my lady. They have announced themselves as Sir Nicholas and Lady Metcalfe. Sir Nicholas is the younger brother of Lord Allerthorpe. They seem impatient to see you. Edith has provided them with refreshments and their horses have been stabled.'

'Very well, Joan. Please help me dress as quickly as you can.' Joan wrestled my best French hood onto my head – I wanted to appear fashionable and sophisticated when meeting Richard's family, as I was concerned that they might be expecting an ignorant country bumpkin. Smoothing down my almost best gown, I entered the hall as elegantly as possible.

A short and portly man rose to his feet and gestured to a taller and thinner woman next to him. 'Lady Allerthorpe, Tamsin, at last! We have been most anxious to meet you.' He bowed as his wife and I curtsied to each other. 'This is my wife, Elinor Metcalfe.'

Taking a chair, I smiled encouragingly, 'I am delighted to meet you, Sir Nicholas and Lady Metcalfe. Have you ridden far?'

Lady Metcalfe looked me up and down. 'Only about five miles, but I would have thought Richard would have made you aware of where we live. We have a small manor to the south of this castle. You are, of course, welcome to visit at any time.' She patted her linen coif. 'There would be no need to wear court dress,' she said, eyeing my headdress.

'Yes, of course, Lady Metcalfe, I quite understand, and I must say that will be a relief.' I pulled off my headdress forgetting that in the hurry to get dressed, Joan had not secured my hair in a coif underneath. Down it fell over my shoulders and I heard a sharp intake of breath from Joan, stationed on a stool behind me.

I felt rather silly. 'Please forgive me, my condition requires me to rest in the afternoons and I did not have time to dress properly.' My career as dignified Lady of the Castle was not going very well. I attempted to tuck my hair back under the headdress with Joan's discreet help.

Lady Metcalfe's superior look changed in a flash as she absorbed what I had said. 'Your condition? Do you mean that you are expecting a child?'

'Yes, I expect a child in the late summer, I believe,' I said, watching Lady Metcalfe's face, which now appeared drained of colour.

'May we offer our heartiest congratulations!' said Sir

Nicholas. 'You must not hesitate to call on us if you need any help. You must be praying for a son.'

'Yes, indeed,' said Lady Metcalfe, looking as if she had eaten something nasty.

'Are you quite well, Lady Metcalfe? May I call you Elinor since we are now sisters?'

'Yes, thank you, Tamsin. I think it was the cheese I had with dinner. I am recovered now.' She clapped her hands and a serving man stepped forward holding a large flat square object wrapped in cloth.

'Sadly, we were unable to attend your wedding in London,' said Sir Nicholas portentously, 'but here is our wedding gift to you and to Richard.' He proffered the object to me and Joan darted forward to steady it. Together, we unwrapped the parcel. It was a portrait of themselves.

'It will help you to remember us in your prayers,' said Lady Metcalfe, 'and cheer you while you are separated from Richard. Family portraits do make a castle feel more like a home, is that not true, my dear Tamsin?'

'Oh yes, they do,' I said, gazing at the picture of the Metcalfes staring gloomily back at me. 'I shall treasure this portrait. Richard will be delighted to see it when he arrives.'

'Pray, when do you expect him?' enquired Sir Nicholas, helping himself to another cake and speaking so that crumbs fired out from his mouth.

'I am unsure, but I am certain that it will not be long. He is employed on the king's business.'

'Is he working for Cromwell, now our Vicar General?' said Lady Metcalfe.

'Yes, I believe he is required to help plan a survey of the religious houses. It is so terrible, there is talk that even great houses may close.' Too late, I put my hand over my mouth. Richard had said I should not talk about the subject, but surely it would not matter if it was to his family?

Looking at Richard's brother and his wife, I was surprised not to see the horror I expected on their faces.

'Well, Tamsin, it is all for the best,' said Sir Nicholas. 'I am sure the king and Cromwell know what they are doing, and it is true that many religious houses allow abuses and extract high tithes used for their own comfort.'

I looked carefully at Richard's brother and assumed what I hoped was a neutral expression. 'I expect you are right, my lord, but my husband is a little concerned.'

'Richard was initially reluctant to support the king in the break with Rome,' said Sir Nicholas, 'but of course he has sworn the oath of loyalty to the king, as you know, and his attitudes are now more realistic.'

'You will find the priest here very helpful,' said Lady Metcalfe, 'and if there is anything that is not clear to you, you must apply to me. As a woman, I understand how difficult these matters are for us to understand. I will explain it in terms that will make perfect sense to you.'

Gritting my teeth, I offered more wine and sent Edith to the kitchen for more cake. The conversation then turned to estate matters and the weather. Finally, as the church bells rang for four o'clock, they called for their horses and made their farewells. Politely, I escorted them to the door and stood waving enthusiastically as they disappeared into the valley. I asked Edith to clear away the remains of the refreshments and went to find Joan.

'Why did they look so shocked when I said I was with child? Why do they not seem concerned about the possible threat to our religious houses?'

'My lady, I am not educated, but I suspect that Sir Nicholas hopes to inherit the earldom should Lord Allerthorpe die. If you produce a son, he will lose the inheritance. Also, as a younger brother, Sir Nicholas's estate may be small. I expect they hope to buy land from the dissolved monasteries, so they may not be sorry if they close.'

'Joan, how could I not notice such obvious things? Of course, if I give birth to a boy, he will inherit, and you may be correct that the Metcalfes are eager to acquire more land. What shall we do with that depressing portrait? We must display it, or they will be offended!'

'Tamsin—I mean, my lady, perhaps you should lie down, and I will bring a lavender compress to soothe you. You are overwrought and it is not good for the child.'

The weather grew warmer, and I found that I loved to walk in the countryside near the castle. I felt settled, and most days passed happily. Lord and Lady Metcalfe's visits became less of a trial as they gradually became friendlier. I was missing the company of a close woman friend, although Joan did her best to compensate, and I felt a little lonely when a letter from Margaret brought news of her imminent marriage to Lord Presland. It did not make sense for me to make the journey back down to London in my condition, so I consoled myself by sending a set of decorative silver plates to her instead.

Regular letters came from Richard, but still he did not arrive. Finally, in mid-April 1536, there came the message I had been waiting for: he was expecting to be with us within the next fortnight.

One morning, Joan and I were sitting on a rug put down for us by Ranulf and Rolf, who always accompanied us armed – I felt, unnecessarily – with swords. It was a beautiful day: daffodils were all out and birds were chattering in the trees. It really felt that spring would be with us soon.

'Joan, can you feel the sun on your face? Just pull your hood down a little.' Her mittened hands struggled with the hood cord. 'There, can you feel it?'

'Yes, my lady, but look, what is that flashing in the valley?'

As I followed her gaze my heartbeat speeded up. 'It looks like soldiers. The sun is bouncing off their breastplates.' I walked a little away from the group. 'I cannot see the livery. I think we should pack up. If they are important visitors, I should be there to greet them.'

We set off down the hill, Ranulf carrying Joan's basket behind and Rolf leading the way. As we got nearer, I realised that the livery was that of the Earl of Allerthorpe – my husband was finally home! Setting off at a run, I hastened further down the hill, but found that I could not run as well as I used to because the baby seemed to be weighing me down. As I reached the courtyard, I realised my gown was muddy, and I was breathless. I slowed to a dignified walk as I could now see that my husband had brought visitors with him.

Richard jumped down from his horse and advanced towards me. 'My dear wife, I am very happy to be home again and to see you looking in such fine health, too!' He patted my bump and leaned down to kiss me. 'We will talk later. I am desperate for ale and a change of clothes.'

'Of course, husband,' I said, taking in his exhausted appearance.

'Before I go, I have a surprise for you, Tamsin. Look who has come from London to see you!' he said, pointing to mounted figures towards the back.

He waved and the riders came forwards. It was my old friend, Lady Margaret, and an unfamiliar man who were dismounting. I ran to embrace her. 'Oh Margaret, I am so pleased to see you. I have so much to show you, too!'

Margaret turned to the man. 'Countess, may I present Lord Presland, my husband.' He bowed and I curtsied.

'I am delighted to make your acquaintance, madam,' he said, kissing my hand. Lord Presland appeared surprisingly well-groomed for a man who had been on such a long journey.

'Margaret, I have been so looking forward to hearing more about your wedding. Richard could not attend because he was away on Crown business. He is always pre-occupied with his work and not much news reaches me here in the wilds of Yorkshire. Do come inside and while you take some refreshments, I will order the servants to make rooms ready for you.'

Inside the base courtyard, a busy scene greeted me. Horses were being led to the stables and soldiers were being unbuckled from their armour by younger squires. I sped to the kitchens to find Edith.

'Edith, we have unexpected visitors. Please ask the servants to make the two principal guestrooms ready for Lord and Lady Presland from London. I am sorry for the extra burden of work this will cause you, but Lord Allerthorpe did not inform me that he would bring guests. I suppose you already have accommodation for the extra servants and soldiers.'

'Yes, my lady, you need not worry. Lord Allerthorpe has a habit of forgetting to tell us when he is bringing people to stay, and so we always have plenty of linen available just in case. It will not take long to prepare all the accommodation. Meanwhile, my lady, I have taken the liberty of sending wine and sweetmeats to the small hall. By the time your guests have refreshed themselves, everything will be ready. I have also ordered the kitchen to produce a substantial dinner which should be ready by noon.'

'Edith, thank you, I am very fortunate to have one such as you to organise my household. Pray, make sure the steward assists you and if there are any difficulties, come to the small hall and give me a signal and I shall come directly.' I went to find my guests feeling suddenly euphoric. My husband was home, and my closest friend was here!

That evening, we all sat by the fire in the Great Hall while the musicians played softly from the gallery. When the servants withdrew, I turned to Richard.

'It is wonderful to see you home again safely, but you look tired. Would you like to retire early? With your leave, I should like to talk to Margaret and Lord Presland. They can tell me the rest of the news, so you do not have to tire yourself further.'

Richard got to his feet. 'Tamsin, you are very thoughtful. I shall retire to my own chamber tonight. Doubtless, you need plenty of space!' he said, looking meaningfully at my expanding waist.

'Yes,' I laughed. 'I feel as though I am the size of an elephant, and Joan tells me that I toss and turn at night. You should take your rest while you can!' I shouted as Richard left the room.

Presland stretched out his legs in front of the fire. 'Margaret has told me much of you,' he said. 'An unknown young lady from obscure Cornish gentry who managed the fearsome Lady Sedley, and then proceeded to net an earl as a husband without any apparent effort. You perhaps do not know of the stir you caused among several young gentlemen at court?'

'No, indeed, Lord Presland, I was unaware that I made any impact on anybody apart from Richard, and I think you are flattering me!' I turned to Margaret. 'Do tell me more about your wedding. Did you have many guests? Was the weather good?'

'Tamsin, we were fortunate in the weather. We had more guests than we expected, including the queen's brother and his friends!'

'George Boleyn, that was an honour for you. Perhaps he is an acquaintance of yours, Lord Presland?'

'I am one of a group of courtiers he likes to call on for archery practice and other sports.'

'And you gamble, visit taverns and sometimes get disgracefully drunk,' said his wife.

'That too,' said Presland, unabashed. 'It is difficult to refuse George Boleyn. He has such power, and he is close to the king.'

'How are the king and queen?' I asked politely. There was a short silence.

'It is a little difficult at court, currently,' said Margaret. 'The king and the queen appear to argue frequently. The only time I have seen them in harmony recently was in January, when Queen Catherine died, but shortly after that the queen lost another baby.'

'Hush, wife,' said Presland. 'You must refer to Lady Catherine as the Dowager Princess.' Margaret glared at him and continued.

'You will have heard of the king's jousting accident. The king tumbled from his horse and was insensible for two hours. Everybody thought he was dead, so the queen's uncle, the Duke of Norfolk, went to give her the sad news. Meanwhile, the king was revived, but soon after, the queen miscarried a son and it was on the very day of Queen Catherine's funeral!'

'The atmosphere at court is tense. The king seems more

short-tempered and suspicious. Cromwell is always with him and they often confer together away from the other members of the Privy Council,' said Presland.

'It is a relief to get away from London,' said Margaret.

'Did the Dowager Princess have an honourable funeral?' I asked.

'The Dowager Princess was buried quietly in Peterborough Cathedral, near to Kimbolton Castle, her last earthly home. Unfortunately, the king did not permit his daughter to visit her on her deathbed.'

'How very sad it all is. I shall pray for them both,' I said, 'and now the king still does not have the legitimate son needed to continue the Tudor dynasty.'

Our discussion seemed to cast a gloom over the evening, and shortly afterwards, Margaret and Presland announced they would retire to bed.

As I walked down the corridor to my apartments, all was silent, and it seemed unusually dark. My candle flickered in the draught and I felt a shiver go through me. It felt to me as if something evil was going to happen. I dismissed it as a symptom of my condition, but I was glad to reach the safety of my chamber, where a yawning Joan awaited me.

That night, I could not sleep. The baby seemed unusually active, and my mind was busy. Why was Richard so exhausted? What exactly had he been doing in London and elsewhere which kept him so very busy? I resolved to find out tomorrow.

CHAPTER 13

After morning prayers and discussing household matters with Edith, I set out to find Richard. He was in the stables, talking to the stable lad. I waited until he was walking back towards the house before I fell into step beside him.

'Richard, I trust you slept well? You look sprightlier this morning!'

'I feel much better, dear wife,' he said with a kiss on my cheek. 'You are certainly blooming, like a...'

'Like a what?' I said holding down my headdress in the breeze.

'A ship, my darling, a ship in full sail. I see that I am expecting a strong and active son.'

'I think you are implying that I am large. That is hardly surprising since I am only about two weeks away from going into confinement.'

'So soon? Time goes so fast, Tamsin. It does not seem long since our wedding.'

This gave me an opening to try and find out what Richard had been doing. 'Time seems to fly by when you are busy, Richard. Perhaps you have been busier than usual in London?'

'Yes,' he said, frowning. 'So many lists, plans and ledgers to examine. Cromwell expects us to work as hard as him. I'm not sure that he sleeps more than about four hours a night.'

'What is it that you work on? Are you permitted to tell a mere woman such as me?' I said teasingly.

'Do not be silly, Tamsin. I will tell you, but you must keep it to yourself and not tell Margaret, Presland, or Joan. Indeed, you must not repeat it to anybody.'

Mystified, I leaned closer to him to listen as we walked.

'It concerns the closing or dissolution of certain monasteries and convents. We now have a list of religious houses, and visits by the commissioners are underway. Tamsin, there are places under threat of closure in Yorkshire and all over the country, even in Cornwall.' We were almost back at the small courtyard by now, so he steered me around back to the gardens. 'It is a lovely morning and I think we should walk further to avoid anybody overhearing us, if you are not too uncomfortable, my darling.'

'I am not too delicate for a short walk and I must hear more,' I said, knowing that there was more he was going to say.

'It is all on a much larger scale than I had envisaged. I am worried about the consequences of closing so many of them. I think the impact will be worse because of the break from Rome, which ordinary people find hard to understand. The king is not so popular in the countryside as he used to be. There are rumours of further changes in religion, too. Some people believe that baptisms will be taxed!' Richard looked so downhearted that I paused to hug him.

'Husband, perhaps it will just be a very few religious houses that will be dissolved. There is nothing that you can do about this. We can only pray.'

'Of course, we cannot object openly about this; such speech would be treason. We must also hope that this year's harvest is better, because if it is bad, where will the poorest people go for relief if the religious houses are dissolved?'

'The nobles will have to do more to help the poor on their estates, and the towns will have to organise more help for those that are destitute,' I said.

'Not all noble families will consider it their responsibility,' said Richard, 'and the town parishes already provide alms for people in distress. But you are correct, something will have to be done if what I fear comes to pass.'

'Is there a chance that the king will change his mind about closing monasteries?' I asked.

'No, I doubt it. The king listens to Cromwell, who has great influence over him. Men see an opportunity to gain lands, so they do not argue against it. Of course, I believe there are some religious houses that are not well-run, but I cannot understand how so many can be suspected.'

'Is Thomas Cromwell an evil man?' I asked.

'No, not at all, he seems convinced that he is following the right course. He is aimable, generous and good company. He can do no wrong in the king's eyes and he keeps himself well-informed through a network of spies and informers. This allows him to tackle any problems before the king is even aware of them.'

'Do you think Cromwell has a spy here in the castle?'

'I think it is quite likely, which is why you must not repeat anything I have said or express any unorthodox opinions to anybody.'

Soberly, we returned from our walk and I went to find Margaret. I found her in the Great Hall with her husband. 'Tamsin, dear, you must have enjoyed your walk as you have been gone for so long.'

'Yes, I woke up feeling restless, and Richard and I decided to take some exercise before dinner.'

'Ah, you feel restless, perhaps it will not be long until the new little lord appears! When are you going into confinement?'

'Soon, according to my midwife. Never fear, she is already installed in the castle. I am better organised than I used to be!'

'The castle appears very well-run, the servants clean and willing. Was it difficult to manage them at first?'

'No, I was fortunate. Many of the servants appear to be from families that have served in the castle for generations. The steward is very efficient, and you have met Edith, who reigns supreme in the household. I do not have to do very much at all.'

Presland got to his feet, bowed, and announced his intention to visit the archery butts. 'I will leave you two ladies to discuss women's matters, as doubtless you are keen to do!' he said with a smile.

'Mind you are not late for dinner,' called his wife as he disappeared though the door. 'Now we are alone, Tamsin, I must ask you: what is it like to carry a child? You are so large, does it not hurt to walk?'

'I think it is because the child grows slowly, so one becomes accustomed to the extra weight. However, it is rather unpleasant when it seems to kick my ribs! Will you be able to stay long enough to keep me company in my confinement Margaret?'

'Yes, I believe we are to stay several weeks. Presland has business in the county and thinks to leave me here while he enjoys riding around the countryside, pretending to be a bachelor! Of course, you are hoping for a son to be an heir to Richard's title and estate.'

'It would be very convenient if it were a boy, but unlike the king, I do not think Richard would believe it a disaster if we had a daughter. Richard does have an heir – his younger brother, Sir Nicholas – and I suspect that he and his wife were a little distressed when Richard finally came home with a young wife likely to have children.'

'Why did Richard not marry before? He is quite old for a first marriage.'

'He was betrothed to a girl from Suffolk when they were both children and they were expected to marry as adults. Unfortunately, she died in an outbreak of the sweat when she was twelve. Before his father died, there was talk of Richard marrying a Lady Constance whose family live near here, but it all came to nothing. I do not think he was particularly keen to marry anybody. Richard has an unworldly and spiritual outlook on life.'

'Until he first spied you at Hampton Court and lost his heart!'

'Yes, apparently. Unfortunately, I cannot remember the first time I was introduced to Richard. However, I was impressed when he was late on his first proper visit because he had stopped to help a poor man whose load of cabbages had overturned on the street.'

'Tamsin, I am glad to hear that he is kind. Noble ladies cannot expect romantic love in a marriage. It is wonderful if we can get on with our husbands and establish a good day-to-day relationship.'

'Did you instantly fall in love with Presland?'

'Well, no, not really, but I felt fonder of him when he offered marriage and security!'

'Margaret, may I ask: do you have a good day-to-day relationship with Presland?'

'Well, yes, we get on tolerably well. As you can see, he is amiable, and he does not begrudge the money I spend on gowns. He is rather lazy and enjoys a quiet life. It would be better if he were a little more ambitious, but he has a large estate in Suffolk.'

'Does Presland have a position at court?'

'Yes, he is one of the king's Gentlemen of the Privy

Chamber, and he spends much time enjoying himself with the queen's friends. However, your husband appears very busy at court. I have seen him often in Cromwell's company, carrying ledgers and papers. Tell me: is Richard happy in Cromwell's service?'

I opened my mouth to tell Margaret about Richard's worries about the monasteries when I remembered that I must be discreet, even with my closest friends. 'I believe he is happy in Cromwell's service – he has a deep sense of duty and he likes to be useful.'

'He must spend so much time away from you. I wonder you do not resent it. Are you planning to return to London after the baby is born?'

'I have not minded being alone because of my pregnancy, which made me very tired at first. Also, I have occupied myself by meeting and visiting the tenants and their families. There have also been a few household tasks to perform. The stocks of cures were somewhat low, and it took time to plant, collect or prepare the necessary herbs. Of course, there was also the library to investigate and several books that required reading immediately! I am not sure when we return to London.'

'Of course, I have not forgotten your love of reading,' Margaret said as the bell sounded for dinner. 'Do you write as well?'

'Well, of course, I wrote to Richard when he was in London, but it takes so long for a letter to travel, although I suppose I could employ a fast messenger if there was some sort of emergency. I write down recipes including ones that my mother used to make. Fortunately, Joan can remember them. I am planning to make a book to be placed in the library.'

Joan appeared at that moment to inform us that dinner was

served in the Great Hall and that the earl and Lord Presland awaited us.

Two weeks passed happily. The earl and I were so occupied with entertaining our guests that we did not have the opportunity for many private conversations. I was now feeling huge and very uncomfortable, aware that I would soon be shut away in the dark while I waited for the baby to arrive. Margaret and Joan appeared excited, but I was now full of dread at the ordeal that awaited me, and I missed my mother. The priest counselled me to be of good cheer and told me to trust in God when I asked whether I should write instructions for my funeral.

Margaret sought out women servants from the castle who had produced healthy broods and brought them to visit me. Margery Keep, an ancient crone in her fifties who had borne fourteen children and raised nine successfully, took one look at me and announced that I would have no trouble because my hands and feet were large for a woman. This sounded so peculiar that I laughed and felt better.

One day in early May, after attending morning prayers, I said farewell to Richard, Presland, and my household before entering the room I had chosen for my confinement. My sister-in-law, Lady Metcalfe, Margaret, Joan, and the other women had been busy. All the windows were covered with hangings or blankets and a blazing fire was throwing out heat. I knew that this was to benefit me, but I was horrified at the reality of being forced to remain in this dark, hot room until the baby was born and for a month after.

'I must have at least one window that I can see out of and open if needed,' I announced to the assembled women.

'It is unhealthy,' said the midwife. 'Evil spirits or miasmas may gain entry and harm you and your baby, or the devil may enter the child before it is baptised.'

'Just one window might be permissible,' said Margaret, coming to my rescue.

'But it is tradition,' said the midwife, 'and I will be held responsible if any ill befalls my lady or the baby.'

'You shall not be held responsible. All these ladies here are witness to my request and to your advice. It is not your fault that I cannot comply fully,' I said.

We passed the time with sewing clothes for the baby, gossiping to each other and playing card games. It was strange to see no men at all, but I demanded that Richard come to the door each evening so that we could have a brief exchange of news. All food and drink was passed to a serving maid at the door of the chamber.

Fortunately, after less than two weeks of confinement in the middle of May, I began to feel niggly pains that came and went. The midwife advised that I should walk around the chamber, but I became hot and sweaty and refused to walk any further until my one uncovered window was opened. Outside, it was a beautiful warm day, and it was comforting to hear birdsong.

I was later told that I had an easy labour, but it did not seem that way to me. In a haze of pain, I clung to the arms of the birthing chair while my midwife and the ladies shouted encouragement. It felt as if I was giving birth to a very large turnip. I lost track of time, but it was very dark outside when I heard the midwife say: 'God be praised, my lady. You have a healthy daughter!' A furious roar filled the chamber.

'Give her to me,' I demanded as I was helped back into bed and the midwife was cleaning the baby. A small bundle with a red face was passed to me. The roar had stopped, and a pair of blue eyes stared up at me. Astonished, I checked her fingers and toes and lifted the head wrapping to see her hair: a short blonde fuzz.

All the ladies gathered around to coo at the infant. I could not help noticing that Lady Metcalfe looked particularly happy now that her husband was still heir to the Allerthorpe estate! Joan appeared ecstatic.

'Oh Tamsin—I mean, my lady, she is beautiful! Your mother will be so pleased.'

I lay back on the bed in a state of euphoria. I had survived childbed and I had a living daughter. Fervently, I prayed, giving thanks for my safe delivery and for the future health of my new daughter. As soon as the chamber had been cleaned of all the detritus of childbirth, Richard was permitted to enter. As he held his new daughter, he put a finger into her hand, her tiny fingers clutched it and I was touched to see tears forming in his eyes.

'Tamsin, you have made me a very happy man and I give thanks to the Lord that you have survived your ordeal.'

'I am sorry she is not a boy, but I expect I could repeat this experience in about ten years or so,' I said, smiling.

'Take no notice of my lady,' said Joan. 'She will forget the pain and be keen to provide you with your son and heir in a year or so.'

'What name shall we give her, husband?'

'I thought perhaps she could be named Alice after my dead mother.'

'Yes, that is a good name for her.'

Alice began to wriggle in my arms and seeing this, the wetnurse, Joanna came forward. 'May I take her little ladyship now, Countess?'

Feeling increasingly tired, I relinquished my child. Richard kissed my forehead and left the chamber, and I surrendered to sleep.

CHAPTER 14

Three weeks later, feeling much better, I was desperate to leave the lying-in chamber, so the priest agreed to conduct my churching a little earlier than usual. After the ceremony, I was officially free to go where I wished and do as I wished. After checking on Alice in her nursery apartments, I celebrated by going for a walk with Margaret and Joan, with Ranulf and Rolf walking behind us.

During my lying-in, I had noticed that the women kept to light topics and dissuaded me from asking for news from outside the castle. I was eager to find out what had happened while I was shut away. Remembering about what Richard had said about possible spies and intelligencers in the castle, I did not ask direct questions; instead, I asked for any news from the court.

Margaret and Joan both put on horrified but excited expressions. 'You will never believe what has happened while you were confined,' Margaret said. 'Queen Anne has been tried and beheaded for numerous offences, including witchcraft and incest, and the king is already set to marry again!' I gasped with amazement.

'Yes,' said Joan. 'It is true. We heard the news last week, but we did not disturb you with such news while you were in confinement. The king is to marry Queen Anne's former lady-in-waiting, one Mistress Jane Seymour from Wiltshire.'

'I do not recall her,' I said, 'but there were so many people at the court on the occasions that I attended.'

'She is pale, her hair is fair, and she is very quiet, nothing like the former queen. It is not surprising that you did not notice her,' said Margaret.

Although I had had no love for Queen Anne, having recently experienced giving birth, I found myself feeling a stab of pity for the woman who had endured childbirth and miscarriages, yet still was unable to provide the king with a son. I recalled the small, dark figure I had seen several years ago in her barge and the pregnant queen at her coronation. 'Well, let us hope Queen Jane soon provides the king with an heir for England,' I said.

'Also, Cromwell has already closed the smaller religious houses. Their buildings and land have been given to those who have supported the king,' said Margaret.

Aware that my husband's work involved contact with Cromwell's office and that there could be a spy in the castle, I stopped myself from reacting with horror and instead said, 'I wonder why this is happening.'

'Who knows?' said Margaret. 'As women, we cannot hope to understand all the detail of state policies.'

'No, indeed,' I said, swallowing hard and resolving to find out more information from Richard later.

'Your ladyship, may I speak? There is something else that has happened,' said Joan. I steeled myself for more bad news. 'Ranulf asked yesterday evening if I would marry him when circumstances permit. I would like to accept his offer if you have no objections.'

'Of course, you should accept him, Joan. I am so happy for you,' I said hugging her. 'We can have the wedding here in the chapel!' Suddenly, with horrible clarity, it occurred to me that she would leave my service. Fortunately, Joan had guessed my thoughts.

'I would not leave you, my lady, not unless I was blessed with children. Ranulf and I consider ourselves tied to the service of Lord and Lady Allerthorpe for as long as we are needed.'

I looked behind to where Ranulf and Rolf were trailing in the distance, engaged in a deep discussion which involved much gesturing and laughter. Joan had clearly recovered from her heartbreak over my brother, Henry, and it looked as if I would not lose her imminently. Some happy news in this uncertain world.

Later, in the privacy of our apartments, after telling Richard of Joan's news, I asked my husband what he knew of the dissolution of the monasteries and convents.

'Do not upset yourself, Tamsin. Lord Cromwell is only continuing the policies of Wolsey, who closed some small religious houses with the Pope's agreement about ten years ago. The revenues were used for the founding of colleges at Ipswich and Oxford. All the monks and nuns would have been transferred to other, larger houses. Haltemprice Priory in the east of our county is set to be dissolved in August, but it is a poor establishment which has been declining for many years. I do not regard it as a great loss.

'So Jervaulx Abbey will be safe?'

'I think it is unlikely that the larger religious houses will be affected by this policy. Now, tell me, how is Alice?'

'This evening she smiled at me when I went to visit the nursery. Joanna says she is feeding well and growing fast. We are fortunate.'

Richard kissed me. 'We are extremely fortunate, Tamsin, and I treasure the day that I first set eyes on you at Hampton Court, when I beheld that vision of a beautiful young lady with a red wine stain on her fashionable gown! Now, let us resume the business of producing an heir for our estate.'

Later that night, as I lay, unable to sleep, I realised that despite Richard's reassurances, I was still worried. There had been so many extraordinary events recently – the break from Rome, the execution of Anne Boleyn, and the Bible being made available in English. What had seemed impossible in the past might not be so in the future.

Lord and Lady Metcalfe called on us in early August. Richard and his brother disappeared into the steward's office to discuss business, and I was left to entertain Lady Metcalfe. As usual, she enquired after Alice's welfare and expressed a wish to see her. The nursemaid brought her to us, and the next half hour disappeared as we played with the baby. Lady Metcalfe appeared very fond of Alice and had brought her a gift of a little poppet in a silk dress. Alice could not hold her doll very well, but she spent a considerable time staring at it and Lady Metcalfe was enchanted.

'Next time, sweeting, Aunt Elinor will bring you a teething ring for your little toothies,' she announced to the baby.

'Sister, Alice does not have any teeth yet.'

'Ah, but time goes so fast. You will soon find little white teeth in those tiny gums, and something to chew on will be just the thing,' she said, waggling her head at Alice, who was now gazing at the diamonds on her headdress in fascination.

Richard and Sir Nicholas had been closeted together for some time, and they emerged with stony faces. 'Goodness, you gentlemen both look very serious,' I said.

'It is only estate business, Tamsin, nothing for you and Lady Metcalfe to concern yourselves over.'

I made a mental note to find out later what was wrong. It seemed to take longer than usual for the couple to climb onto their horses, and then Lady Metcalfe was delayed by blowing farewell kisses to Alice. All the way through supper, I watched Richard to see if he would give any hint of what was amiss. I began to wonder if I was imagining things, as everything seemed normal.

At last, it was time for bed, and we were alone. I decided to approach the topic carefully and began with, 'It must be pleasant to have your brother living so close to us.'

'Yes, it is good to have family close at hand,' said Richard.

'You usually enjoy each other's company, which is why I was surprised to see the pair of you looking so solemn when you joined me and Lady Metcalfe in the hall.'

'Tamsin, did I not tell you there is nothing to worry about?'

'You did, Richard, but as you say, you are proud to have an educated wife. Do not patronise me. I know something is very wrong.'

'Very well. There are many murmurs of discontent against the king and Cromwell regarding the religious changes, and signs that it will turn to unrest.'

'Is it the common people who are complaining? Certainly, our tenants have been asking me what is happening. They do not understand why their beliefs, the beliefs of their fathers and of generations before them, must change and they fear that taxes will be raised, which they will be unable to pay. The recent harvests have not been good, and they are afraid that bands of beggars will attack their homes.'

Richard nodded. 'You are correct, Tamsin, but there is something else worrying me. You must not repeat this to anybody, but I know that some local landowners and men of influence are also ready to revolt against the king's religious changes. It is very difficult for me because, as you know, I work for Lord Cromwell's office.'

'Do you think Cromwell is suspicious about your loyalty? I have seen you receive letters from his office. Is there anything in them that makes you think that?'

'No, there is nothing, but he does seem extraordinarily well-informed about our local affairs. I can do nothing except watch and wait while I am not called back to London. Somebody in this area seems to know our movements, so we must be doubly careful not to do anything that could be interpreted as disloyal to the Crown. You must make the most of this time as I do not know how long it will last. My brother and I have discussed the situation.'

'Your brother is more of the reformist persuasion, is he not? I doubt he has much sympathy with the country people.'

'While Nicholas favours reform and regards some previous Church practices as promoting superstitious nonsense, he is not without compassion. You may trust him absolutely, Tamsin. Elinor takes her lead from Nicholas. I know she can be irritating but, again, she would always do her best for a member of this family, regardless of any differences.'

'Richard, you tell me not to worry but I can tell that you are concerned, or you would not be telling me who I can trust. It sounds to me as if you really do expect a rebellion.'

'I very much hope not,' said Richard. 'Now come here and do your wifely duty!'

It was now September, and Margaret and Presland were still with us. I had grown so used to Margaret's company that I could not imagine being without it, but I knew the time would come when she and her husband would need to get back to their own estate.

We were harvesting herbs to replenish my store for the

approaching winter when I broached the subject. 'Margaret, have I not kept you away from your home? I do not want you to leave, but neither do I wish to selfishly keep you close.'

'Tamsin, I have had such a lovely summer staying with you and Richard. I do not want it to end, but you are of course correct. Our steward and other household officials are reliable and efficient, but we really should think about leaving soon. I will talk to Presland.'

'Where is Presland? I have not seen him since morning prayers.'

'I believe he is out visiting acquaintances in the area. He is probably drinking and gambling, as usual, and perhaps even trying his luck with the local women.'

'Do you not mind his behaviour, Margaret?'

'No, I just ignore it. He is always polite and considerate to me. I just would like to see him show a little more ambition rather than treating his life as one long pleasure-seeking mission!' Margaret smiled, but the smile did not reach her eyes. 'Richard seems quite ambitious. Am I correct?'

'Yes, I think he is, but he does not say much about what he does,' I said, mindful of Richard's warning about spies. Of course, Margaret could not be a spy, but if she were to repeat anything sensitive, it might cause difficulties for him. 'Margaret, it would probably be sensible to start your journey back to London before the autumn weather blows in and makes the roads muddy and impassable.'

'Yes, I know, but what about you? How long do you plan to stay in Yorkshire?'

'I am unsure. Richard will tell me when his current errands are completed, and I assume we will then need to return.'

At that moment, we could hear hoofbeats in the distance.

Margaret stood up and shaded her eyes from the sun. 'I think it is Presland,' she said, dropping a handful of parsley into the basket. 'I had better go and wash my hands of all this mud and then greet my dear husband! I will see you at dinner.'

Margaret walked away towards the castle, leaving me sorting through our harvest of herbs. There seemed to be enough for basic remedies, but I would need to walk out further afield to find the rarer plants. It was too late to set out now, so it would have to wait until tomorrow. I clambered stiffly to my feet and proceeded to the distilling room with my basket. As I hung up bundles of herbs to dry, I thought about the journey to London and realised that I did not want to return to our house. I was happy here, and the thought of enduring all the noise and smells of the capital was disheartening.

There was also the risk of infection in London; surely our castle in the country air was safer for Alice. Perhaps Richard would say that he had been ordered to remain here. The northern winter was bound to be harsh, but the castle had withstood all such weather for generations.

That evening, I ordered a fire in the hall as there seemed already to be a hint of autumnal chill in the air. The firelight played on the faces of Margaret and Presland, who seemed to be quieter than usual. Richard was dozing or, as he put it, resting his eyes after supper. Joan was handing out glasses of hippocras and plates of wafers, as Edith had retired for the night.

'We are so very grateful for your hospitality,' began Presland, 'but we believe we should be back on the road to London within a few days. It is nearly October already and, as Tamsin has noticed,' he said, waving towards the fire, 'autumn is coming on quickly.'

Richard gave a tiny snore and opened his eyes. 'As you wish,

Presland although it has been a pleasure to have you both here, as I am sure my wife will agree.'

I inclined my head while forcing myself not to plead with Margaret to stay longer. 'It has been a wonderful time,' I said, 'and I do not know how I should have managed if Margaret had not been here for my confinement.'

'You women love to gather in flocks, chattering to each other like birds in the trees,' said Presland, slurring his words slightly and reaching for more hippocras.

I looked at him with surprise. 'No more than men like to banter and argue with each other in taverns and suchlike.'

'Do not try to pit your wits against Tamsin!' laughed Richard. 'She will always have the last word.' Presland smiled lazily and downed the rest of his drink.

The following day dawned bright, and I decided to make an expedition to gather more herbs and suchlike for my stores. Margaret, Joan and I left after a quick breakfast of ale, bread and cheese. We had just reached a valley where wormwood was reputed to grow, when Joan shouted, 'There's somebody who looks like a messenger entering the castle in a hurry!'

I hoped it was not a summons from Cromwell for us to return to London and, shifting the basket on my arm, I decided to put everything from my mind except finding the plants I needed.

'We will find out if there is any news soon enough. Now, ladies, which of you can find the wormwood first and who will find a willow tree?'

About two hours later, once we were laden with various herbs, we returned to the castle in merry humour, fuelled by Joan's decision to bring a bottle of wine to sustain us on our outing.

Richard met us at the entrance. 'There are reports of disorder at Hexham Abbey. The king's commissioners are trying to enter, but the abbot has barricaded the monastery and is threatening to fire on them!' His face was serious as he continued, 'There are reports of local uprisings and disorder. The local landowners are trying to persuade the people to return to their homes.'

'Perhaps they will be successful and the people will settle down,' I said.

Presland had now joined Richard in the doorway. 'Richard, I think Margaret and I should leave tomorrow.'

'We shall be sorry to see you go, but it would be sensible. Although all seems peaceful here now, the situation may change rapidly.'

'Shall I ask Edith to send servants to help with your packing?' I called after them.

'No, thank you, our servants will be able to manage,' called back Margaret as she and Presland went to their rooms.

I looked at Richard. 'What shall we do?'

Richard answered, 'We must stay in the castle. I have not received orders from Cromwell, and as a landowner, I have a responsibility for the welfare of my tenants and the household staff.'

I felt a weight of dread on my stomach. Northumberland was not very far away. What if the trouble spread? My basket of herbs now appeared irrelevant, but I forced myself to act as if I was not all worried.

'Come, let us go to the kitchens, Joan, and sort the plants.' This occupied us for some time.

At dinner, we discussed the practicalities of Margaret and Presland's journey. They would return by the same route that had brought them into Yorkshire and they hoped to join a party of other travellers, as they had on the way up. A large group was always more secure in case of robbers on the road, and this was even more important in these troubled times.

Their goods were to be carried in panniers on the horses, as Presland felt that a carriage would be too cumbersome if they encountered any trouble.

The fact that there was still no word from Cromwell began to worry Richard. 'It is very hard to know what action I should take.'

'Husband, I think you should stay in the castle and concentrate on your usual duties,' I said. 'If Cromwell needs you, he will surely send word. It is not as if there is any trouble in our neighbourhood.'

CHAPTER 15

The following morning, we stood in the courtyard to say our farewells to Margaret and Presland. A cold wind was blowing, but it was now early October and so this was not surprising. Margaret was muffled up in a thick cloak and knitted cap. Finally, the horses were ready. The servants and men at arms took their places and it was time to say goodbye.

'I shall send messages whenever I can!' called Margaret. 'I hope to see you both back in London soon. We can celebrate Christmastide together!'

Wiping away tears, I stood until their party had disappeared into the distance. Straightaway, I decided to visit Alice, who always seemed cheerful and pleased to see me.

Richard saw my face as I went to go inside. 'Sweetheart, do not distress yourself. We have not heard about any new trouble and they are both experienced travellers. They are familiar with the route and they have an armed escort.'

'I know all this,' I sobbed, 'but I cannot seem to compose myself.'

Richard embraced me and patted my head awkwardly. 'I see you are on your way to visit Alice. She will cheer you up. Go now and I will send Joan to you later.'

After playing with Alice, I soon felt better. She put out her little fat hand, trying to grab my necklaces, and I could see little white marks on her gums where her lower teeth were coming through.

'She is a remarkably happy child,' said Joanna, the wetnurse, as Alice lay and kicked her legs. 'Easy to soothe, and she sleeps all night, which is not always the case with babies of her age. She is so active that I freed her from her swaddling bands a little earlier than is usual.'

I surveyed my fat little daughter and watched the sunlight catch her fine blonde hair. Her eyes had remained blue, and she showed promise of becoming a beautiful child. I considered myself lucky that she had survived so far. So many babies died before completing their first year and I feared for her health if we needed to return to London soon. Richard was already eager for another child – he did not hide the fact that he longed for a son, but there was no sign yet that his wish would be fulfilled.

The castle seemed empty without Margaret's lively presence, and I even found myself missing the sight of Presland sprawled on one of the castle chairs, wine in hand. I continued to busy myself with my remedies and cures, grinding dried herbs into little sachets of powder, ready for mixing when required, and checking on the bunches hung up to dry.

Next, I called Joan to help me sort my belongings into some sort of order, ready for the summons from London which I assumed would arrive soon. 'Joan, will you wait until we arrive back before marrying Ranulf, or shall we arrange the ceremony here?'

'We think that events are too uncertain now. It would be better to wait until we are back in London and I can invite members of the household down there. We would not run the risk of having to suddenly abandon our plans, and we could take our time to plan the wedding once we are back at home.'

I did not miss Joan's reference to 'home,' and thought it strange how much everything had changed since we'd left

Cornwall. I decided that now was the time to ask her about what had happened with my brother, Henry, even though I was nervous about what liberties he might have taken with her.

'Tamsin, you have no need to be worried. We kissed and cuddled, but I knew that to Henry, it was just a dalliance. I am still a maid. Yes, I thought my heart was broken when we left Looe, but it was nothing compared to what I feel for Ranulf!'

'Joan, I am so happy to hear you say this. I was worried that Henry may have behaved badly to you while you were under my family's protection.'

'Never fear, Tamsin, all is well. I should say that I am sorry for my bad moods before we left Cornwall, I was young and stupid, and I really thought that I was being deprived of my one true love! I now think of the London house as my home, even though I still hope to return to Looe one day.'

'In that, we are of one mind. I cannot think that I will never return to Cornwall again and I am determined that you and I shall go back on a visit to Looe one day.'

On the following day, a messenger arrived for Lord Allerthorpe. I waited in the hall while pretending to sew, hoping that he would see fit to share any information with me.

'Tamsin, I have a message from Presland. They met groups of angry people on the road near Lincoln, people who say they are determined to remove Cromwell and all the king's evil advisors. They were permitted to pass safely, but not until Presland had spoken to the leaders and agreed that their cause was just. Fortunately, he has a silver tongue, and he can be very convincing. I had been a little suspicious about some of Presland's activities while he was with us.'

'What do you mean, Richard?'

'Did you not notice how Presland was always out and about

134

in the area by himself?'

'Yes, but Margaret said that he was out drinking and gambling in taverns and suchlike. She also thought it possible that he had a woman somewhere.'

'I think that Presland wanted her and us to think that he was idling his time away, but I am convinced that he was gathering intelligence on the local area for Cromwell.'

'Do you think he was watching us, too?'

'Yes, I suspect that Cromwell is suspicious about my loyalty. I fear I have not convinced him of my passion for religious reform.'

'He cannot doubt your loyalty to the Crown. You took the oath to the king as Head of the Church, and you have done nothing to help these rebels. Presland cannot have reported anything suspicious because you have not done anything suspicious!'

'Oh Tamsin, you are a very loyal wife, but you do not know everything that has happened. It is true that I am worried that religious houses will be plundered for gain, regardless of whether there are abuses or not.'

'Richard, have you done anything that I should know about?' I asked. 'I have the welfare of Alice, Joan and all our household to consider.'

'It is best that you know nothing, wife, so that you cannot be implicated if I am called to account.'

'Richard, you are frightening me. I know you have a strong sense of right and wrong, but please have a care for our daughter, if not for me!'

He looked at me calmly. 'Of course, I care deeply about you and our daughter, but I will not give you any further details. That way, you are not involved, you know nothing, and nobody will suspect a baby of a few months of being a traitor!' With a quick kiss to my cheek, he walked away to the steward's room.

Suddenly, I felt as if the ground might give way beneath me. With a few words, my husband had tilted my world. I climbed the worn stone steps up to the castle battlements. I needed quiet and a chance to think before I could resume my role as the noble countess without betraying my apprehension. Holding my cloak close in the wind, I could see that everything looked normal. No armies were marching to arrest my husband. Indeed, all I could see was our own small band of men at arms practising archery, and the laundry maids struggling to peg out sheets in the blustery wind.

Returning to my chambers, I chose a book at random and settled in front of the fire. I found that I could not concentrate on the words and after reading the same page four times, I put the book down and decided to visit the kitchens and distillery rooms. I resumed chopping and grinding herbs and spices, and by the time I had finished, I had a comfortingly long row of labelled jars, ready for most hurts and ailments.

At supper, Richard seemed determined to discuss estate matters in greater detail than usual, but all I could think of was what might be happening outside.

Finally, after the servants had left the room, I blurted out, 'Is there any more news?' Richard seemed to be thinking before he spoke.

'Tamsin, I did not want to trouble you further, but I had a message from my brother that thousands more people have joined the uprising. They seem to be organising themselves now. They have been asked to disperse by local landowners like Lord John Hussey, but they have refused. They are approaching the Hambleton Hills, where it is thought they will set up camp.'

'Richard, that is only about a day's ride from us. Where are they going next? What do they intend to do?'

'I have heard they intend to march on London and force the king to get rid of Cromwell and others they describe as "evil advisors". They resent the investigation and closure of religious houses and I believe they are angry about changes in the way religious services are conducted.' Richard paused before saying more. 'We have also had a series of indifferent harvests, which are causing hardship. Conditions have been worsened by some landlords enclosing land to graze sheep. depriving their tenants of the opportunity to grow crops. I believe this situation is dangerous. However, the men keep saying that they have no desire to harm the king. They believe that he is unaware of the hardship caused to his people.'

'Have you heard from Cromwell yet?'

'No, I would have told you if I had.'

'What will you do now?'

'Tamsin, I fear that if I do not take some action, I will be accused of cowardice, and worse. I hope I can help with persuading the people to go home. I pray they will be reasonable, as they will surely be slaughtered before they get anywhere near the king.' Richard swallowed hard and looked at me gravely. 'I dread being asked to attack the rebels. Some of them may turn out to be our own people if this revolt keeps spreading. I will ride out and meet Nicholas at dawn with a small force of men at arms and leave the remainder to guard the castle. I intend to take Ranulf and Rolf, as I am certain of their loyalty.'

Suddenly, I felt cold. 'Richard, you will be riding into danger. What if the people turn on you?'

'I must take that risk, Tamsin. With my title and land holdings comes responsibilities. I have no choice other than to

137

act. I hope to be able to convince people that their objectives will not succeed and if that they persist, there is a high risk of much bloodshed.'

After a sleepless night, much of which I spent praying for the mob to disperse and for Richard's safety, I stood in the dark of early morning to bid him farewell.

'Be of good cheer, Tamsin; I will return safely. In the meantime, do not go outside the castle. If danger threatens, listen to the advice of the steward, and if the castle is threatened, go to Lady Metcalfe, who will give you and Alice shelter. Their manor is less conspicuous and unlikely to attract the attention of the people.'

He leaned down from his saddle and gave me a final kiss. Then he and the soldiers rode away. I listened to the diminishing sound of hoofbeats and made may way to the chapel. The chapel was empty. Only a few candles were lit, which gave the place a ghostly aspect. As I knelt and tried to focus on prayer, I wanted to howl in desperation. As a woman, I was powerless to influence events, and I knew that I must accept this. Fervently, I prayed for serenity and fortitude in the coming days. When I returned to my chamber an hour later, it was dawn, and I could see no sign of Joan.

After a few minutes, Joan appeared at the door. 'I have been down to the kitchen and prepared you a warming posset. Do you remember the one we had in the inn on the journey from London? Well, I have had another attempt at making it, so now you must drink some and then you must rest.'

The posset was indeed warming and relaxing, and I fell into a deep sleep. Upon awakening, I felt well-rested, but my stomach lurched as I recalled the recent events. I dragged myself out of bed, washed my face and hands and, with Joan's assistance, put on one of my favourite gowns. I had missed dinner, but I did not feel hungry.

Downstairs, I asked the steward to ensure that all the servants and estate tenants assembled in the hall, for I wished to address them. Joan was dubious. 'Do you wish to see even the kitchen boys and the gardeners?'

'Yes, everybody, Joan. Everybody on this estate is under my protection. They must know the facts, including that if they are tempted to join the uprising, they could be risking their lives.'

An hour or so later, I was waiting on the dais while the people filed in. I waited for the coughing and whispering to settle, and started to speak. My voice sounded strange and wavery to me, but as I spoke, I felt my confidence grow. I outlined all the news that I had received and warned them that they could be risking death if they were tempted to join the uprising. Finally, I thanked them for sparing me time away from their duties and signalled that the meeting was over. There was much muttering as they left, but I was pleased to hear some call out blessings on me.

CHAPTER 16

The remainder of the day passed with the usual routines. I went to visit Alice in the nursery and took the opportunity to ask the chief nursemaid to pack a small bag of Alice's belongings, in case we suddenly needed to leave the castle. I spoke as calmly as I was able and tried to sound as if this event would be very unlikely, but I could see a spark of fear in her eyes.

In truth, I was increasingly aware that I sympathised with the rebels. As a good Catholic, it had been hard for me to accept the religious changes, and I could not understand why some of the larger monasteries and convents now seemed to be facing dissolution. The religious houses seemed to me to be the bedrock of our society and I could not imagine a life without them. If Richard was correct and larger institutions were dissolved too, there would not be enough religious houses left to take on all the dispossessed monks and nuns, let alone their lay servants, so where would they find refuge?

As I knelt at the prie-dieu in my chamber that evening, I prayed that the people would disperse and go home; that the king would be alerted to the problems without any bloodshed; that he would take advice from more conservative advisors, shun Lord Cromwell, and consider the grievances of the people of the North. Then, Richard would come home, we could resume our sunny future and perhaps I would have another baby – a son to inherit the title and estate. I even pictured us with a brood of children, returning to Cornwall to visit my mother and brothers.

Tears pricked at my eyes as I imagined rushing into my mother's embrace and seeing her delight as she met my children. We could walk down to West Looe Quay, and my imagined son would be fascinated by the fishing boats coming home with the catch. We could walk in the fields to Hannafore and collect crabs and shells from the rockpools.

Abruptly, I was startled out of this happy reverie by the sound of shouting. The reflections of lighted torches bounced off the dark walls of my chamber. My first thought was that Richard had returned. Hastily, I put on a wrap and lit a candle. Joan was in the corridor her face pale with fear.

'Tamsin, there is a crowd of men outside.'

'I heard the noise. Where is the steward, or the captain of the guards?'

'They are both outside, too. I think they are trying to speak to the men.'

'Very well. I shall dress, go outside and find out what is happening.'

'The earl said that you were not to go outside, my lady.'

'The earl is not here, Joan. I will not hide in here and you must not prevent me leaving.'

'My lady, I merely thought I should remind you of your husband's directions.'

'I consider myself reminded. Now help me dress.'

Hastily, I put on a plain kirtle and warm over-gown, with my cloak over the top, as the night was bitterly cold. There was no time to fix my headdress, so I tied back my hair with a piece of ribbon. My hood would be up; nobody would see my hair.

'Stay here, Joan, there may be danger.'

'No, my lady, I shall not. I am accompanying you.'

'Very well, fetch your warmest cloak.'

Minutes later, we approached the front door. As I looked out, I was confronted by a large mob of men armed with pikes and sticks, and a few women. Many carried burning torches, and the effect was to light the whole of the inner courtyard, which looked strange against the black, starless sky. The steward stood seemingly paralysed and there was no sign of our guards.

'Madam,' hissed the steward. 'The soldiers have disappeared – they must have joined the mob. These people are saying they wish to replenish their stores and suchlike.'

I said, 'Well, we can hardly stop them now. You had better agree, but it must be an orderly process. I will speak to them.' Stepping forward, I clambered up on to a small mounting block. There was a rumbling from the crowd, and some stepped forward to see me better.

'Good people, I am the Countess of Allerthorpe. My husband is away from home, but I am willing to help you out of Christian charity, even though you have terrified my household with your arrival. You may take what you need from our stores, but I will only permit small groups in my castle. You will need to decide what you need and organise bands of no more than four men for each item you require. When you have organised yourselves, you may apply to my steward here, who will tell you where to go and when to proceed.'

The response was a series of shouts and jeers. I stepped off the mounting block and ran back to my chamber with Joan at my heels.

'Quick, Joan, get our bundles together. I will take my jewellery,' I said, stuffing a pouch under my skirts. I also added a small dagger. 'We will fetch Alice and her wetnurse and then we go down to the stables before the rebels reach them. We will then ride to a safe distance and watch to see what they do. If they disperse peacefully, we can return. If not, we will go to Lady Metcalfe at Scarby Manor.'

Risking a quick look out of the window, I saw that the men were lining up and things appeared orderly. However, we did not wait to see any more, and hurried to the nursery wing, where we found the wetnurse, Joanna, fully dressed, sitting by Alice's cradle.

'Joanna, there is not a moment to lose. We must leave now before they reach the stables. I do not know whether the rebels are a threat to us or not, but we are not staying to find out!'

With Alice fast asleep and wrapped up warmly, and us carrying our bundles, we crept out of the back kitchen door towards the stables. A dark shape came towards us. 'Ah, some beautiful ladies!' he slurred.

Quickly putting on a Cornish accent, I said, 'If you be looking for wine friend, go through that kitchen door and through the passage on the right.'

'Stay and drink with me, fair ladies!'

'No, we cannot stop. Our menfolk be expecting us to help them get food from yon castle larders. We must hurry!'

'Suit yourselves. I will find another lady, perhaps the beautiful countess. I saw her.' He staggered away to the kitchen door.

The horses were restless, probably disturbed by the unusual noises and lights. 'Give Alice to me, Joanna, I will tie her to my front. You and Joan take a horse each. We must be as quiet as we can. We do not know how long it will be before somebody else follows the path around the side of the castle!'

My fingers were clumsy with fright and cold, but I managed to get Alice tied securely to me without her waking. Speaking in whispers, we hastily put saddles and bridles on the horses, and when all were mounted, I steered my horse to the stable entrance. And then disaster – another shape appeared out of the dark.

'What have we here?' A pair of hands grasped my horse's bridle. Without hesitating, I brought my riding crop down across his hands. Squealing, the man fell backwards, as my horse reared in alarm.

'Go!' I yelled as other figures emerged from the darkness. Fortunately, our horses knew their home landscape well. Joan and Joanna moved ahead of me while I struggled to get control of my horse. Finally, I managed to calm him and set off at a gallop. We rode across the fields until we reached a clearing in the woods. Slowing the horses to a walk, we followed the track through the woods until we came out on higher ground. Now we could see the castle surrounded by tiny fires.

'It looks as if the rebels have set up camp,' I said. 'I do hope I have not dragged us all out unnecessarily, but I know what happens when men find large stores of ale and wine: they lose all judgement. There must have been at least one thousand men in that crowd. Reasonable men can lose their wits in a mob. To them, we appear only as hated landowners, and I fear that Richard's connection to Cromwell may be known, even though he was increasingly opposed to his policies.'

With a thrill of horror, I realised that I had in effect told Joan and Joanna that Richard could be a traitor to the Crown. I would just have to hope that they would share my feelings. Joan was loyal I knew, but what of Joanna? I cursed myself for my talkativeness, but it was too late now.

Joan stayed silent, but to my immense relief, Joanna said, 'Yes, it is a shame about what has happened. Cromwell must be an evil man, and I doubt the king knows exactly what is going on.'

After an hour of watching, we were tired and uncomfortable, and an icy drizzle began to fall. 'Ladies, we will go to Lady Metcalfe at Scarby Manor as Richard instructed. She will give us shelter for the night and then we can decide what to do in the morning.' I did not want to be reliant on charity from Lady Metcalfe, but we could not camp out all night with a baby of less than six months old and no bedding or equipment.

'Will Lady Metcalfe receive us in the middle of the night?' asked Joan nervously.

'Yes, of course she will. I am her sister-in-law and Richard had already made arrangements for us to be given shelter if there was trouble.' I sounded more confident than I felt as we turned our horses to the west, towards Scarby Manor. Thirty minutes later, we could see the house ahead, and as we approached, we could hear dogs barking frantically. A figure in white appeared at the door holding a lantern.

'By Our Lady, Tamsin!' shouted Lady Metcalfe. 'Quiet now, Carac—get down, Dick, these are friends!' The dogs slunk away.

'Whatever has happened? Lob!' she yelled. I looked round for another dog, but this looked to be a stable boy, rubbing his eyes and adjusting his hose.

'Stable these horses. Ladies, come inside quickly, you are soaking wet and cold. I will ask you what has led you here when we are by a fire,' she said loudly. 'Agnes, come down quickly and make up the fire!'

My limbs were trembling with fatigue and shock as I led the women into the house. Alice had woken up and seemed in the mood to play, but I knew she would require feeding again before she settled, and Joanna looked exhausted.

'Agnes, fetch hot wine and food. Our guests need reviving before we sort out where to put them for the night. Go and wake up Mary; she can make up the beds in the east wing,' yelled Lady Metcalfe. 'That girl never wakes up when she is needed.'

'She probably sleeps with a pillow over her head,' whispered Joan.

'Hush, she will hear you!'

'Not her, I reckon she has a problem with her hearing. She does not normally speak so loudly. Perhaps you could suggest a potion to relieve it tomorrow.'

Soon, the door was barricaded again, the fire was built up and we began to feel better as the hot wine warmed our veins. Alice, now fully awake, was staring at Lady Metcalfe in fascination, and when that lady advanced on her, Alice held out her arms.

'Oh, what a little poppet she is,' shouted Lady Metcalfe. I had thought Alice might be frightened of this loud personage in her flowing white nightgown, but no, she seemed amused by her. With Alice now established on her lap, Lady Metcalfe asked what had happened that we should arrive on her doorstep in the middle of the night.

I watched her face change as I described the recent events. 'Oh, my dear, of course you could not stay there and expose my niece to such danger. You have had no word from Richard, I suppose?'

'None, Lady Metcalfe.'

'In the morning, I will send out my most trusted men to try to find out what has happened at Allerthorpe Castle. Then, when we know more, we will try to get a message to Richard,' she said in a penetrating voice.

We went to bed having drunk several cups of good wine, and with a sense of security again, it was easier to sleep.

For a few seconds when I woke up, I could not think where

I was, but Joan immediately loomed over me.

'Tamsin, Lady Metcalfe's men have left for Allerthorpe Castle to see what it is happening, Alice is downstairs with Joanna and Lady Metcalfe, and I have brought you some breakfast. I brushed as much of the mud as I could from your gown, but it is still somewhat dirty from our ride.'

'Thank you, Joan, but do not worry about that. Just help me dress, please.'

Anxiety clutched at the pit of my stomach and I found it hard to swallow the oat cakes, but I was soon ready to go downstairs.

'Good morning, Tamsin,' shouted Lady Metcalfe. 'It is about seven o'clock and there is no news yet. I hope you slept well.'

'Thank you, Elinor, it is very kind of you to offer us hospitality, and I slept well enough.'

'I think you and your party should remain here until we have definite news,' said Lady Metcalfe, in what she imagined to be a very quiet tone but was more like the volume of a normal speaking voice. I agreed this was a sensible plan.

Fortunately, Lady Metcalfe did not produce a complicated tapestry or embroidery piece that needed finishing. Instead, I was set to hemming some sheets, which was well within my capabilities. After Lady Metcalfe had passed on news of local births and deaths, we sat in silence as we sewed, as there seemed nothing more to be said. Each of us was thinking of what might be happening outside.

Shortly after dinner – a hurried meal eaten in silence – we heard horses coming up the drive. Joan stood to go to the window.

'Joan, do not let yourself be seen,' I whispered.

Lady Metcalfe leaned forward. 'Do not be concerned; my servants have returned.' Seconds later, Lady Metcalfe's steward and her secretary were bowing before us.

'What news of Allerthorpe Castle? Come on, spit it out!' shouted Lady Metcalfe.

'The castle still stands, but there is some damage. Some of it is what would be expected after a large group of men have camped out, but they also appear to have ransacked many rooms. There is extensive fire damage in the main living quarters, also.'

'Did you see any of the wicked scoundrels?' yelled Lady Metcalfe whose face had assumed an alarming shade of red.

'No, all appear to have left. Some of the castle servants returned from the woods where they had been hiding when they saw us. According to them, the crowd held some sort of a feast last night, but at dawn, a messenger arrived. They then packed up and left in small groups, travelling in different directions. All except one young girl, who said she wanted to see you, Countess.

'What young girl? Did she give a name?'

'She said her name was Hilda and that she had met you several months ago when you stayed at her convent, now dissolved. She also said that your ladyship had said she should apply to you if she was in need.'

'What have you done with her?' I asked the steward.

'I told the servants to take her with them back to the castle.'

'Thank you. I will speak to her when I return. She seemed a capable girl, so she will join the servants for now and I will decide on her role later.'

'Yes, my lady.'

'As the rebels have gone, I think something has frightened them away. When they arrived, I got the impression that they were setting up a camp for at least a few days,' I said, trying to sound calm and controlled. 'Is there any news of my husband Lord Allerthorpe, or indeed, of Sir Nicholas?'

'My lady, we have not seen them or heard anything about

them.'

'We are grateful for your efforts. Now go to the kitchens and get some refreshments,' bellowed Lady Metcalfe.

Before Lady Metcalfe could pass any comments on this disaster, I felt that I needed to sit somewhere quiet and think about what I should do. I excused myself and let myself out of the back kitchen door. Walking in the fresh air had always helped me to think in the past. I just needed a plan.

I should contact the Allerthorpe steward and ensure that repairs were in hand. As the living quarters were now uninhabitable, it was clear that I could not return home. I could either stay here with Lady Metcalfe's household, or I had two other choices: I could set out to find Richard and the two soldiers, or I could make the long journey back to London.

I did not relish the thought of living with Lady Metcalfe for the foreseeable future, but neither could I take Alice and her wetnurse on long and uncertain journeys. Without any clear news, I did not know whether the uprisings had stopped or not. If there was still trouble, I could be risking danger.

Joan appeared behind me. 'I thought you might be here, my lady. You will be glad to know that I have persuaded Lady Metcalfe to try an oil cure in her ear to loosen the wax which I believe is causing her hearing loss.'

'That is good news, Joan. Did you find the ingredients in the kitchen?'

'Yes, my lady, and I explained to Lady Metcalfe that the volume of her voice is too high. She said that she had wondered why Sir Nicholas had taken to mumbling at her! We do not want her shouting about our plans when any old body might hear her.'

'Very wise, Joan.'

'I expect you are thinking about what we should do next, but

I beg you, do not take us off on a wild errand to find the earl, Sir Nicholas, Ranulf and Rolf when we do not know anything of their whereabouts.'

'That is true. We do not know where Lord Allerthorpe is, or even if he and his men are still with Sir Nicholas. He could be anywhere in Yorkshire, or Cromwell may have summoned him back to London. Either way, a messenger has been unable to get through to us in all this upheaval. I am considering asking Lady Metcalfe to continue to give shelter to Alice and Joanna. They should be safe with her.'

'Alice certainly seems to like Lady Metcalfe, and if Joanna is with them, the baby's needs will be met,' said Joan thoughtfully.

'You must be very worried about Ranulf too, Joan.'

'Yes, my lady, but I know he is a skilled fighter and I believe I would sense it if anything terrible happened to him.'

'You love him, Joan.'

'Yes, as you do Lord Allerthorpe, my lady.'

'It is not the same. Our marriage was a convenient arrangement. The earl wanted an educated young wife, and I wanted to marry an amiable and decent man who would not begrudge me sending money back to my family if needed. However, I must confess that I have become very fond of Richard and I would be devastated should something terrible happen.' The afternoon was vanishing into twilight and the wind was chill. We could not stand out here much longer.

'Joan, I have decided that we will return to London. Richard may already be on his way there. He was expecting a summons from Lord Cromwell when all this trouble began, and that might well explain why I have not heard from him. He could have taken a boat from Hull to London to save time.'

To my great relief, Lady Metcalfe appeared amenable to this plan. 'As you know, Tamsin, Sir Nicholas and I have not been blessed with children and I would be delighted to take care of little Alice for as long as is needed. They can have the two rooms in the attic. I will send Mary up to put it all to rights. Alice can sleep in the Metcalfe family cradle and I will employ a nursery maid to help Joanna. As for your plan to return to London, perhaps you should stay a little longer to ensure that order has been restored. Also, if Richard is still in the locality, a delayed message may still arrive.'

'Elinor, you have my grateful thanks for your kindness. I shall wait a while to see if Richard and Sir Nicholas arrive home and until the area seems calmer.'

CHAPTER 17

Another day passed, and I reflected that never had time seemed to move so slowly. Every sound outside sent us to the window, but there was still no news and no sign of Richard or Sir Nicholas.

In the middle of the following night, I heard the dogs barking and the bolts being drawn back from the door. Heart thudding, I climbed hastily over Joan, who was snoring beside me, and ran to the chamber door, grabbing my wrap as I went. Mary was standing by the door in her nightclothes, holding a candle and trying to open the door. Joan came stumbling downstairs and took her place beside me. We struggled with the remaining bolts and opened the door into the dark night air. It was Sir Nicholas with Ranulf and Rolf, but there was no sign of Richard behind them. They were filthy and unkempt looking.

'Tamsin, my dear, I am sorry to tell you that Richard is not with us.'

'Mary, would you light some more candles and then fetch some wine from the kitchen please?'

'Yes, my lady.'

Sir Nicholas threw himself into a chair and indicated that the guards should sit too. Mary returned quickly with a large jug and proceeded to pour large measures of wine. I waited until the men had drunk some wine before asking for their news.

'Richard has disappeared, Tamsin. We were together at the camp on Hambleton Hill. Never have I seen such a large crowd. There were many thousands of men, but it was largely peaceful and their behaviour was orderly, although groups broke away now and again. We were unsure about what to do as we felt that many of their grievances were justified. One of those groups that left the camp managed to capture a lawyer who was travelling south. His name is Robert Aske.'

'Another group forced their way into Allerthorpe Castle and ransacked it, which is why you find me here with my daughter and closest servants,' I said bitterly. 'But tell me of the circumstances in which Richard vanished.'

'Two days ago, we received news that Charles Brandon and Thomas Howard, the Duke of Norfolk, were marching with a huge army sent by the king to restore order. Many of the men became fearful and began to leave for their homes. They thought it likely that they would be massacred. All was confusion, but we four bedded down for the night, resolving to leave for home the following morning. However, when we awoke, Richard was missing. His bedroll had been removed and his horse was gone. Ranulf, pray tell Lady Allerthorpe what you saw in the night.'

'My lady, I awoke briefly, and I saw Richard standing up. I thought he was going to the latrines, so I thought no more of it and went back to sleep. We had drunk a large quantity of ale before bedding down, my lady.'

I turned to Sir Nicholas. 'Did Richard seem worried at all? Do you know if he received any messages?'

'Yes, a messenger arrived for him earlier in the evening while I was talking to somebody else. By the time I reached Richard, he must have read it and put the message away. I thought it would be from you and I meant to ask him about it later, but by the time we'd had supper and opened a cask of ale, I forgot all about it.'

'Did you notice anything about his mood later?'

'No, he seemed in his usual good temper, not worried about anything. We had already decided we would return home in the morning.'

'So there was nothing unusual at all about Richard's manner or behaviour last night, and he did not leave a message to say where he was going?'

'No, Tamsin, as I have said. His departure was a complete surprise to us all.'

'Thank you, Sir Nicholas. I am sorry to press you about the matter, but the recent events have made me more fearful than usual.'

'The invasion and ransacking of the castle must have been a terrible shock, and now my brother, your husband, appears to be missing. I think we must return to the castle to assess the damage and see what can be done to remedy it. We must hope that in the meantime, Richard returns or that we receive a message about his whereabouts.'

'I think you should all have some food, a wash and a change of clothes before we do anything else,' I said. 'Mary, go and rouse Lady Metcalfe, and Joan, you can tackle the kitchen staff, who are doubtless awake by now. It may be that Lady Metcalfe will know of some spare clothing that you can borrow.'

Two hours later, we were all dressed and breakfasted, and it was decided that Mary, Agnes and Joanna should remain in the manor with Alice, in case Richard should arrive while we were all away at the castle.

It was a beautiful autumn morning and I wished I could enjoy the ride, but inside I was full of dread about what we would find at the castle, and most of all, I could not escape the nagging worry about Richard. Was he lying injured somewhere? Had he been kidnapped? I did not believe that he would abandon us without a word.

Although she had been delighted to have her husband restored to her, Lady Metcalfe was uncharacteristically subdued and less talkative than usual as we rode, but I was pleased to see that Joan's potion seemed to have improved her hearing. The closer we got to the castle, the more the ground appeared churned up by feet and hooves. We passed the blackened remains of small campfires, empty ale barrels and discarded animal bones.

As the castle came into view, I sighed with relief to see that it looked normal from the outside. However, as we approached nearer, I could see that some of the precious glass windows had been smashed, and other windows seemed stained black by smoke. There were discarded wine bottles floating in the moat and the nearby grass had been turned to mud.

There was no sign of the gatekeeper or of any servants in the main courtyard, but the area was littered with yet more discarded bottles and casks. Tethering the horses at the gate, Sir Nicholas, Ranulf and Rolf led the way inside with their swords drawn. Torn tapestries and bedding lay on the floor of the great hall and I was disgusted to see human excrement in the corners.

The lingering smell of smoke in the small hall, soot stains and half-burnt, broken chairs and wall hangings showed where somebody had evidently tried to set a fire. There was extensive devastation in the kitchens; broken storage jars, and the contents of cupboards strewn across the floor. There was still no sign of any of the servants.

We moved up the stairs, Sir Nicholas, Ranulf and Rolf again leading the way. I could see more devastation through the half-open doors of the chambers as we went past. Finally, we found a small chamber with a closed door. The men at arms approached cautiously but Lady Metcalfe now seemed to have regained her confidence.

'Open the door immediately or we will break it down. The Countess of Allerthorpe seeks admittance!' she bellowed before I could say or do anything.

There was the sound of heavy furniture being moved across the floor. The door opened a crack and the worried faces of the gatekeeper and the steward peered out. I stepped forwards and when the gatekeeper saw me, he opened the door fully.

'My lady, you are safe! Thanks be to God. We were powerless against the multitude. They forced their way in and ignored our pleas for them to behave appropriately. We tried to distribute food in an orderly manner, but they became hostile and would not listen to reason. A group broached the winter stores and ransacked the wine cellar. We were afraid, and when some of the men began to paw at the women servants, we shut ourselves in up here.'

I entered the turret room to find about half my household staff sitting on the floor or propped against the wall. There were children among them, and they started to wail when they saw our party. At the far wall, I saw the former postulant nun, Hilda, looking exhausted and frightened.

'Hilda, I am so pleased to see you again. I know everything looks terrible now, but you will be safe with us. Where are the others?' I asked the steward.

'My lady, some left with the crowd and others appear to have run away. I heard the leaders in the courtyard shouting that they must go home now because the king was sending a great army to restore order and kill everyone involved in the uprisings. There was a great rush to leave, but we were not sure if all had left or if we might be attacked if we left the safety of this room.'

'You were right to hide yourselves, and I do not believe that anybody could have stopped this crowd unless they had an army at their backs. There is much destruction and disorder downstairs and I do not know if there is any food or drink left. My husband is unable to be here, but I know that he would agree that your wages will be doubled in the next quarter if you stay and help to clean up what we can. I will help you in the work.'

Lady Metcalfe looked at me in some surprise. 'This is the work of servants, Tamsin. The countess cannot work alongside them,' she said.

'My lady wife is correct, Tamsin,' said Sir Nicholas, who appeared considerably shaken by the scenes of devastation.

'Yes, of course, but these are not normal circumstances. The situation is extreme, but I do not ask you or any member of your household to work alongside me. You would both do me a great service by returning home and taking care of Alice.'

The steward bowed to me. 'Your ladyship, will the earl be joining us soon?'

'He is delayed by the events, but doubtless he will be with us as soon as possible. Let us start by seeing if any food or drink has been left behind and then we may at least be able to feed the children.'

'I will send sacks of grain, meat and some ale over to you on my return to the manor, along with brooms and suchlike,' said Lady Metcalfe. 'There should be enough for everybody as your servants are depleted in number, and of course, I will take good care of Alice and her wetnurse.'

The servants were visibly happier and started to get to their feet and organise their children. Together, we trooped downstairs behind Lady Metcalfe. I accompanied her and her party to the horses.

'Thank you very much, Elinor. I will not forget your

kindness to me and to my household.'

'You and Alice are family, my dear. The place will soon be set to rights and Richard will return home. It will be as if nothing had happened!' With that, Lord and Lady Metcalfe and their small party rode off back to the manor.

I will never forget that time – the hard physical work and the exhaustion. I had grown soft since I'd lived in Cornwall, but I thanked God that I had been brought up with some experience of practical housework. As I swept out foul floor rushes and scrubbed filth from tables, I wondered what Richard would say if he suddenly returned home.

I wore a sacking apron and a stained coif, and my hands were cracked and sore from being submerged in pails of hot water. The mood and energy of the servants doubled after the arrival of the promised food and drink from the manor, and an almost holiday atmosphere seemed to envelope the castle. Hilda became more confident and cheerful. She seemed to be recovering from her traumas and I judged it best not to enquire too closely into her experiences until she seemed settled.

Three days later, there was still no word of Richard's whereabouts, but Lord and Lady Metcalfe returned bearing more food for the household. Lady Metcalfe exclaimed over the improvement as she entered the hall. 'Tamsin, my dear, what a transformation! You must have all worked so hard. I can hardly believe it. Quite magnificent!'

Later, as we sat for a glass of wine, Lady Metcalfe tutted over the state of my hands and advised me to rub them with animal grease.

'Sir Nicholas and I have been thinking about how you can manage your household now. As all the stored grain and other foodstuffs have been plundered, you have no way of feeding your people over the coming winter. We see no alternative other than for you to leave a skeleton staff here over the winter. Fortunately, the mob did not have the time or opportunity to take all your livestock and we can supply enough grain to keep a small staff fed. They will, of course, need to forage for herbs and roots, but it should be possible to maintain a supply of pottage and bread. Then they can plant new crops to harvest next year.

'In the meantime, you should stay at Scarby with us, Tamsin, while we wait for news of Richard. When he arrives, he will of course make his own decisions, but it would be sensible for us to all be together until we are sure that order has been restored to the county.'

I thanked them for their kind offer and requested time to think the proposition over. Lady Metcalfe appeared surprised that I had not agreed immediately and asked that I send a messenger with my decision by nightfall.

Outside, trees were already dropping leaves, but the air was still and the sky blue. It was a perfect day for a walk, so I took the path around the castle to think about what to do next. It was easier to untangle my muddled thoughts without taking Joan.

My main concern was Richard's absence. I had begun to think that he must have been called urgently back to London by Lord Cromwell. Messages to me could easily have gone astray in the recent chaos. Therefore, I reasoned to myself, I must return to London, where doubtless he was already back in the Allerthorpe house.

Secondly, I was worried about how the castle household would survive the coming winter with our carefully laid down stores stolen. Some of the servants were from tenant families and would be taken in by them. There would be hardship – I could see no way around it – but I would leave money with the steward to buy supplies to feed those who were struggling.

I did not know what was happening in Yorkshire. Was there still disorder? I thought it would be sensible to travel inconspicuously so that I could blend in with other people on the road. I could feel my heart beating with excitement as I made my plans. Now all I had to do was to convince Joan that it was a good idea, especially as I wanted her to travel with me.

'Two women unprotected on the road in these uncertain times! No, your ladyship, it is a mad idea,' announced Joan when I put my plan to her on my return.

'We would travel as two serving maids taking up offers of work in London. I thought we would ride with a carrier in a group of other travellers.'

'Where would we find this carrier and the other travellers?'

'We could ride down to York, stay at one of the larger inns for the night, find other people travelling and leave in the morning. We would make for the port of Hull and find a merchant ship to carry us around the coast and down to London. If we cannot find a ship to take us, we will need to ride there.'

'My lady, you would only have to open your mouth and people would be suspicious. What if somebody from round here recognised you?'

'Joan, you have forgotten that I can easily adopt a Cornish accent as I did the night the castle was ransacked. Nobody will expect to see the Countess of Allerthorpe dressed as a servant. People often only see what they expect. Having been brought up with brothers, I also know how to defend myself if needed.'

Grudgingly, Joan appeared to accept the possibility that my plan might succeed.

'Joan, I must send a message to Lord and Lady Metcalfe by nightfall to say that I will remain here to wait for Richard.'

'But you are not planning to remain here, my lady!'

'No, I am not, but I thought I would send a message to them once we have left on our journey. Otherwise, they will certainly try to stop me.'

'What about Alice? Can you leave your daughter for so long? Will you not miss her?'

'Yes, most certainly I will, but she will be safe with Lady Metcalfe and Joanna. I think it is more important to find out what has happened to Richard.'

'You are fonder of your husband than you appear, my lady, even though you always tell me that your marriage was for practical reasons!'

'I cannot rest until I know what has happened to him.'

The messenger returned from Scarby Manor with an answer to my message to say that Lord and Lady Metcalfe understood the countess's desire to wait for news of her husband in the castle and concluded with advice to return to them if there was no news after seven days.

That night, Joan and I picked out clothes for our journey, after I had been to the steward's office to arrange a system of relief for those servants and tenants who found themselves in need for the months to come. The steward agreed readily to my proposals, but I did not tell him then that I planned to leave for London.

Sorting out clothes and items for the journey, I felt much happier again. At last, I was doing something instead of waiting helplessly for news. On Joan's advice, I picked out my warmest and most practical clothes, and she removed decorative embroidery and ribbons to make my dresses plainer and more serviceable looking. We packed ourselves two small bundles and I sewed coins and jewellery into my shifts and pockets. I did not forget my dagger.

CHAPTER 18

We decided to leave before dawn. Fortunately, the gatekeeper was visiting his family and his replacement was young and inexperienced. Joan had intercepted a kitchen maid and managed to slip a dose of valerian into a jug of wine. This she presented to the bemused young gatekeeper, explaining it as a perk of the job. The stable boy also received an unexpected jug of the strongest ale, again doctored with valerian.

I wrote a message to the steward to announce my plans and asking him to avoid telling Lord and Lady Metcalfe of my absence for as long as possible. My prayers that night were longer than usual. I was excited and impatient to leave, but also nervous. What was happening in the outside world, away from our little corner of England?

By three in the morning, we were away, riding towards York. I could hardly believe that we had got away without notice. It was very dark and difficult to see the track, and a freezing wind moaned through the trees, numbing my hands as I struggled to keep a tight grip on the reins. I was glad of the dagger hidden under my cloak, which gave us some security. The road was unsurprisingly empty in the night, but I was hoping that we would run into a group of respectable travellers in daylight to keep us company on the remainder of the journey.

At about eight, we stopped at a roadside inn to break our fasts and were fortunate enough to find a merchant who introduced himself as Master Fish. Even better, he was leading a group to the port of Hull. All we needed now was for him to accept us in his travelling group.

Joan did the talking and introduced herself as Cecily and me as her friend, Lizzie, explaining that we were travelling to Hull where we hoped to find a sea passage to London. She added that we were to be employed in the household of an imaginary Lord Denton, who had sent money for our journey. With a sigh of relief, I saw that Master Fish believed the story and even told us that he knew the owner of a ship due to take a cargo of woollen cloth to Tilbury dock, and that the ship had space for a few passengers.

Buoyed by our breakfast and the prospect of a solution to the most difficult part of our journey, we set off again, this time with Master Fish and his group, which included a cleric on his way to another living and two widows, who were going to see relations in Hull.

Joan, now transformed into Cecily, inquired if there was any news. Master Fish looked surprised at the question.

'You must have heard of all the trouble we've had down in Lincolnshire: folks who wanted to take to the road to see the king, to tell him that things were being mismanaged? There was a great mob headed for London, but many of them fled back to their homes when they heard that the Duke of Suffolk was on his way north.

'But the talk now is that Yorkshire people are assembling again, and this time, they are organised and led by a one-eyed lawyer named Robert Aske.'

Aware that everybody was listening intently, he continued in an excited manner.

'Aske has compiled a list of the grievances to send to the king and he is even being helped by some of the local lords. I do not know where they all are, but I heard they are marching south. We have not seen them so we are hoping that we will reach York, and then Hull, before they do. Robert Aske has given this crowd of people a name: The Pilgrimage of Grace. Apparently, they have all sworn an oath to behave well and they are marching like a disciplined army.'

'Why is it a "Pilgrimage of Grace"?' asked one of the widows in our party.

'They call it a "pilgrimage" because they believe they are making a holy journey to see the king, who is Head of the Church, and the word "grace" expresses the love and peace of God. They aim to persuade the king to reinstate closed religious houses and reverse the religious changes.'

'What is the king doing about this?' asked Joan. 'Is he sending another army up the country?'

'I do not know, but all seems quiet, does it not?' replied Master Fish.

I prayed that we would reach York, and then Hull, ahead of any rebels or armies. We would have no hope of finding anywhere to stay if the area was swarming with thousands of people.

Our ride to York was difficult and slow, as rain had turned the tracks to mud and the horses struggled to find their footing at times. Master Fish's news was worrying, and I wondered aloud to Joan that I might have made a terrible mistake; we would end up sleeping in a ditch if Aske and his men had already reached York.

Joan's sensible response was that she thought the rebels would be more likely to pitch camps outside the city, as they would not have the money to buy accommodation.

By the time we reached the outskirts of York, every bone in my body seemed to be aching and I was finding it hard to maintain my role as Lizzie. Keeping my mouth shut as much as possible had seemed the safest option, so Joan had told the other members of the party that I was very shy.

It was already twilight and as we rode, I became aware of lights in the distance, interwoven with dark patches. As we got closer, the lights proved to be small fires and torches, the dark patches were makeshift shelters and finally, I saw masses of dark moving shapes. It looked as if Aske's pilgrimage had already arrived at York.

In York, as I had feared, accommodation was short, and we were repeatedly turned away. But we were fortunate, as Master Fish finally took us to an inn where he thought he knew the proprietor from his youth. The façade was neglected, but the owner recognised Master Fish. Ten minutes later, we were sitting in front of a long table where an unappetising pottage was being served. I ended up passing most of my food to a lurcher sniffing around in the filthy rushes. At least the ale was drinkable, and there was plenty of it.

Later, Joan and I were able to identify the privy by sniffing the air and following the direction of the smell. We found that we were laughing hysterically on the way back into the inn, due to the strain of the journey and the effects of the strong ale. Now it was time to find out where we were to sleep.

My heart sank when I saw the room that Joan and I were to share with other women. There were stained straw mattresses with dirty looking blankets laid out on the floor and the window was only covered with a cracked shutter. It was freezing cold, but at least we had protection from the rain now pouring down outside. Joan and I did not bother with undressing, and I sank into an exhausted sleep.

The next morning, I found I could hardly move; every muscle seemed to be sore. But I forced myself up, off the mattress and down the stairs with Joan, whose face was the colour of cheese.

'Perhaps we had better have a lot more of that ale to set us up for the journey to Hull?' I asked.

'No,' she hissed. 'Do you want to spend time squatting in the bushes by the side of the road?'

I accepted the wisdom of her words and contented myself with a small mug of ale together with some rock-hard bread. Joan went to pay the innkeeper for our stay, and soon we were reunited with our horses and back on the road through the drizzle towards Hull.

In daylight, the Pilgrimage camp looked vast but there seemed to be no disorder. All were moving purposefully around on what looked like domestic tasks as they readied themselves for the day.

A small party of richly dressed gentlemen rode in front of us, turning off in the direction of the camp. They were too far off for me to see if any of the gentlemen might answer to the description of Robert Aske.

'If we make haste, we will reach Hull ahead of this crowd,' said Master Fish. 'I believe the distance is about thirty miles and if we are lucky, we might reach one of the surrounding villages tonight.'

We stopped for dinner at a small inn where the landlord was eager to talk about the pilgrims. After we enquired about what he knew, he told us that he had heard that the rebels were heading to Pontefract Castle, where royal troops were stationed, and that thousands of local people were joining them every day.

'Surely Pontefract Castle will not surrender to them?' asked Master Fish.

'They say that Thomas Danby, the lord of the castle, may be sympathetic to the cause of the rebels,' said the innkeeper. 'Also, I do not believe that the castle is in very good condition, so perhaps they will surrender to them. Many people think that the cause of the rebels is just,' added the innkeeper.

'But surely they will be committing treason against the king!' I said before I could stop myself. The innkeeper gave me a puzzled look, as well he might, because I had forgotten to speak in Lizzie's voice. Other members of our party turned to look at me and I wanted to hide under the table.

'Treason or not, it's nothing to do with us, Lizzie,' said Joan hastily while elbowing me.

'No, indeed, Cecily,' said Master Fish. Fortunately, bread and fish was brought to the table and nobody said anything as we ate hungrily.

Joan's face betrayed nothing about my slip, but I dreaded her comments when we were alone. Fortunately, there was no opportunity for her to berate me for my carelessness before we encountered a problem.

It became obvious that we would not reach Hull before nightfall, because the track was blocked by a mass of people travelling up from the south. We had to slow our horses down to pick our way between the walking men, horses and the baggage train following behind. In the end, our party waited on the grass beside the track as it became too difficult for us to pass through them.

I watched the procession as it marched by. It appeared orderly and calm, as the pilgrims in York had seemed. My horse pawed the ground and snorted as if it wanted to join them. I wondered what it would be like to be one of the pilgrims. There were women and children among them, some riding in the baggage carts. Perhaps they were there to cook for the men, or possibly there were whole families marching together.

That night, we stopped for shelter at a convent which had not yet been closed. The lay sisters showed Joan and I to a small bedchamber with clean floor rushes, which seemed like paradise compared with our former accommodation on the road. It contained two small beds with clean coverlets, and a jug of water and a basin for washing. It was a relief to change our clothes and remove the lice, but I also had to listen to Joan's scolding about forgetting that I was supposed to be Lizzie, a poor serving maid.

'My lady, you must control yourself or our deception will be discovered and you will be returned to your castle, where you will have to sit and wait dutifully for news of Lord Allerthorpe. If you want to get to London without any interference, you must remember your role.'

As we were getting ready to leave the following morning, I could hear a commotion at the front door. The door to our chamber was open and I saw a nun rush by, looking flustered. A few minutes later, the stately figure of the abbess passed our door on her way to greet whoever had arrived. Hastily, Joan and I collected the last of our things and set off downstairs. In the hall were three men whose clothing marked them out as officials of some sort. As I drew nearer, I heard scraps of conversation.

'Lady Abbess, please consider your position and come to terms. In the meantime, we will finish our survey of the abbey and you and the sisters will not hinder our progress.'

So these were some of the king's commissioners, come to list the convent's possessions. It certainly sounded as if the convent's fate had already been decided. I realised that I had clenched my fists, but I managed to keep my mouth closed. A serving maid would not offer an opinion to Cromwell's commissioners – not unless I wanted to be thrown into some prison.

Master Fish and the others were already mounted outside. Thanking the stable boy, I took my horse's reins, mounted, and quickly took my place in the group. Even Master Fish had nothing to say as we left the abbey's precincts. The hectoring tone of the commissioners and the evident distress of the abbess seemed to have shocked us into silence.

As we stopped for dinner outside Hull, Master Fish told us that the convent was already designated to be dissolved, and that last night, the abbess had said that she was powerless to prevent it.

'It is possible that we were the last traveller guests that the house will ever see,' said Master Fish. He looked at us all furtively, and I wondered whether he was afraid that if he commented adversely on the end of the convent, one of us might inform on him to the authorities.

It was a subdued group that finally entered the town of Hull. Some left the group to join family and friends locally, while Master Fish, Joan and I headed for the dock area on foot, having left our horses at an inn on the road into Hull.

'We are looking for The Hope, a three masted carrack,' said Master Fish. 'The captain is a stout fellow by the name of Jerimiah Fox. He takes paying passengers alongside his cargoes. Once we have found him and booked our passages, we will know our sailing time.'

The sound of the seagulls was bittersweet to me. It reminded me of my home in West Looe, and for a minute, I experienced a pang of homesickness so sharp that it almost made me gasp. It seemed like a lifetime ago since I'd lived in Cornwall. Joan seized my arm. 'Now is not the time to dream, Tamsin. We need to keep our wits about us. Make sure you have your purse and jewellery safely hidden.'

The docks were swarming with people, merchants, sailors and noisy women with garish clothes and painted faces. It was quite mesmerising for me. A triumphant yell from Master Fish alerted us. Picking our way around boxes of freshly landed fish and bales of wrapped goods, we walked hopefully down the quay.

'Over here, Cecily and Lizzie! Here is The Hope! Now, where is Captain Fox? Wait here. Do not move while I go and look for him.' He bustled off full of self-importance.

'If Captain Fox will take us, the worst bit of our journey is over,' I said. 'We can hire new horses at wherever he decides to land, or if we are near enough to London, I will send a message to Allerthorpe House for us to be collected.'

'My lady, we still have to endure the sea voyage. What if we get shipwrecked or kidnapped by pirates?'

'That is unlikely, Joan. I suppose there is a risk of autumn gales, but we managed to survive on the voyage from Cornwall. As for pirates, this time we will be sailing from the north east, so I should think Barbary pirates are scarce. Look, here is Master Fish returning.'

Master Fish was accompanied by a heavily built man who looked as if his nose had been broken in the past. Although the man was large, there was a peculiar grace to his movements as he sidestepped the crates and boxes on the quay.

'Good afternoon, ladies. Master Fish told me that you both require passage to London. You may travel with us. There are two cabins for passengers with all meals included. We shall leave at five precisely and if you are not here, we shall go without you. I aim to put in at Deptford, God willing, but the length of the journey will be in the hands of our Lord.' After directing us to a crew member to pay for our passage, Captain Fox boarded the ship and disappeared below. Joan and I went to buy provisions for the journey.

True to Captain Fox's word, the ship left as the church bells struck five. Joan and I settled ourselves in our tiny cabin and with a lurch and a grinding noise, the anchor was raised, and we were off.

CHAPTER 19

I did not find this journey as exciting as the one from Cornwall, probably because I was continually aware of the fact that Richard was missing. I did not allow myself to think about what I should do if he was not in London because I was convinced that he must be there.

I was excited to be going back to London and Allerthorpe House, and imagined myself there with Richard again. We would return to Allerthorpe Castle after Christmastide, where Joan would be reunited with Ranulf and we could collect Alice from Lord and Lady Metcalfe. The steward would run the estate in our absence. I hoped that the harvest of 1537 would be good. As the ship plunged on through the waves, I thought how wonderful it would be to live in London again, near the centre of power. At least I would not be isolated from news, and I could call on Lady Sedley and see Margaret, who would be able to tell me about any interesting scandals and events I might have missed.

Joan persuaded me to practice my needlework to pass the time in our cabin. The crew did not seem to like us to be up on deck. I wondered if any of them secretly thought it bad luck to have women on their ship.

'Ouch!' I said surveying a tiny blood spot on a tiny dress that I was attempting to embroider for Alice.

'Give it here, my lady,' said Joan irritably. I wondered if she was missing Ranulf.

'It will not be long until you are reunited with your beloved again,' I said, patting her arm in commiseration.

'No, and nor you with your husband and daughter.'

'I try not to think of her too much. Mother always said that she tried not to get too attached to her children until we reached the age of five.'

'Yes, 'tis very sad how many die so young,' said Joan.

'I wonder if Queen Jane Seymour is with child yet.'

'We shall find out all when we reach London,' replied Joan.

It was misty and still when we sailed up the Thames, and Captain Fox ordered the sails trimmed so that we could catch the tide. All we could see was the odd black mast looming up at intervals in the wide estuary. The banks were too far away for us to see them. As we came closer in, we saw signs of poor wattle and daub cottages and decayed jetties. Gradually, the signs of human habitation increased, and we saw smoking chimneys on more prosperous looking houses.

'Mistress Cecily, tell your friend we cannot disembark until the customs agent has boarded and checked my cargo,' shouted Captain Fox, noticing us trying to keep out of the way. 'You would be better off below while we wait for him.'

Obediently, we descended the steep ladder to our cabin and occupied ourselves with tying up our bundles securely and checking that my money was easily accessible. We heard the noise of oars and the thud of footsteps overhead.

'It must be the customs man. Not long now, I hope,' I said.

It seemed like hours until Captain Fox put his head down the hatch and yelled, 'All passengers prepare to disembark!' but really, it was only about half an hour. We proceeded unsteadily up the gangplank into the chill of a Deptford morning. There were some small dwellings, but dwarfing them was a large building site with at least one completed enormous shed-like construction, surmounted by a large smoking chimney.

'What is that?' I called to a sailor leaning over the rail.

'No idea, mistress, but it looks like it is set up for metal work,' he said, pointed to two men in protective leather aprons pushing a barrow into the building.

As we walked up the muddy track, I was thankful to see that one of the smaller buildings was an inn of sorts. 'Perhaps we can hire horses here, or at least pay somebody to take a message to Allerthorpe House.' We entered the inn, which was dark and dusty looking. It seemed to be deserted until I banged on the wall hatch.

'Good morning, I am the Countess of Allerthorpe, newly arrived on The Hope, and I need transport for myself and my servant.'

A man appeared. 'And I am King Harry himself!' he responded. 'Peter,' he shouted over his shoulder, 'we have two women here, probably escaped from Bedlam or something. One says she is a grand countess!'

Of course, I had forgotten that we were dressed as poor serving maids and that our clothes, which had started off clean, were now dirty and crumpled. A man who I took to be "Peter" arrived and before he could say anything, I reached for some coins.

The ground felt unsteady under my feet, but I stood as tall as I could and said, 'How dare you address me thus. I am the Countess of Allerthorpe. This is my maid, Joan, and we are in urgent need of transport to London.'

The gold and my haughty tone seemed to make them uncertain. Their expressions changed and they looked at each other.

'My apologies, your ladyship. Your clothing confused me.

Some wine to restore you after your journey?'

'No, thank you. Do you have horses available to hire or is there anybody who can take a message quickly to London?'

'We have two excellent horses which can be hired.' He looked greedily at the coins in my hand.

'Very well. Bring round the horses so that I may inspect them,' I said grandly.

'Peter, go and fetch Bluebell and Snowdrop from the stables.' Peter, who had been standing by open mouthed, hurriedly left the room.

'Would you ladies like to sit, and are you sure you will not take any refreshment?' Having observed the dirty tabletops, I declined, although I sensed Joan would have accepted some ale. We could stop somewhere cleaner on the ride to London, I thought.

Peter returned, leading two horses which looked to be in reasonable condition. We went outside for a closer look. The saddles looked ancient and greasy, but the horses seemed amiable. 'Yes, these will suit us,' I said. In truth, I would have accepted a donkey, so desperate was I to reach Richard and Allerthorpe House.

I handed a half angel to the proprietor, who said, 'Tell your servants to return them to the Boar Inn near Fleet Street by tomorrow midday and I will arrange for their collection.'

We left Deptford, calling at a roadside inn for dinner. When I requested a private room in my normal voice, my clothing and general dishevelment caused some curiosity, but I was past caring by now.

Soon, the noise and stink of London began to assail our nostrils. The road became busier, and it was frustrating to be caught in slow moving traffic. After the peace of the sea journey, the noise and general hubbub felt overwhelming. My shoulders were aching with tension, and I was desperate for the sight of Allerthorpe House.

It was early evening when we finally arrived. We led our horses to the front door, which was answered by an unfamiliar women servant. 'Go away, we don't want no beggars here,' she said rudely, trying to shut the door in my face.

'Open the door immediately, you insolent woman, and send someone to stable our horses,' I shouted at her. 'I am the Countess of Allerthorpe returned from Yorkshire.' The woman looked shocked and bobbed a curtsey hastily.

'Please forgive me, I am new to this house and did not recognise your ladyship. I will send for a stable boy immediately!' Pushing past her, I strode into the house, followed by an exhausted Joan.

'Your ladyship, I am so pleased to see you returned,' said the porter, who looked as if he had been sleeping. 'We had no word that you were expected and will need to open up your rooms forthwith. Shall I tell the servants to send refreshments while we do this?'

'Where is the earl?' I asked desperately.

'Why, we thought him in Yorkshire with your ladyship. Is he also returning? We have had no word of this either.'

The effect of this news was to make my knees feel like water and I sank onto the nearest stool. Joan stood by me looking stunned. 'Are you quite certain that his lordship is not here?'

'Well, yes, my lady. Even if he were staying elsewhere in the city, he would have sent messages to inform us, surely?'

'Do not be concerned,' I said. 'I expect a message has gone astray. I shall contact his friends tomorrow. Please bring a jug of wine and ask the cook to send supper here.'

'Very well, my lady, I shall see to it immediately.'

'Joan, I know you are tired, but would you ask the kitchen to heat water, as I think I need to take a bath after our travels. When you have done that, return to me and share the wine and supper I have ordered.'

'I am not sure that is appropriate now, your ladyship.'

'Do you mean that as we are no longer Cecily and Lizzie, we may not sit and eat together? Well, I do not care a fig for what the servants may say. You have shared my hardships, so for tonight, we will not be mistress and servant. You may even use my bathwater after me if you are so minded.'

'Oh no, your ladyship, that will not be necessary. I prefer to wash as I have always done with a basin and ewer.'

My chamber was cold that night, despite the fire which had been hastily lit. However, I was so exhausted that I did not care at all.

After a long and refreshing sleep, I awoke to hear the early morning noise of London, but I did not get up immediately. Instead, I planned the day ahead of me. Somebody must know where Richard was, and I would go to Lord Cromwell and even the king himself if I could get no news of him.

After breakfast in my chamber, which was brought to me by another unfamiliar maid, I summoned Joan. I was pleased to see that she looked more like her normal self. She said that she had slept well and had a chamber to herself because of the reduction in household staff while we were away.

'Joan, after sending a message to Lord and Lady Metcalfe to tell them that we have arrived safely, my plan is to call on Lady Sedley to enquire for news of Lord Allerthorpe. I must hope that she can give me some clues, and she can also tell us what has been happening in the country. If she does not know of the whereabouts of my husband, I will make a list of his friends and acquaintances and call on them. If this does not provide us with information, I will request an audience with Lord Cromwell, as he may hold the key to this mystery.'

'Yes, my lady, that all sounds very sensible.'

'Joan, we must try to appear calm about this situation. I do not want people to pity me and think that my husband has run away because he could not bear to live with me!'

'How could anybody think that, Tamsin? I mean, my lady. Everyone knows how devoted he is to you.'

Later, as I stood at the entrance to Lady Sedley's house, I could not help but recall my arrival some four years ago as a naïve girl from Cornwall, daughter of a country squire. Now I was a countess, so I must act like one.

The doorkeeper's face lit up when he saw me, for which I was profoundly grateful. 'My lady countess, it is good to see you again. Would you like me to enquire if Lady Sedley is available to receive you?'

'Yes, thank you, Potts. Please tell her that I do not wish to inconvenience her as I am calling unannounced, but that I would be grateful for a few moments of her time.' Potts hurried off.

Seconds later, he was back and beaming at me. 'Her ladyship says she will be delighted to see you now,' he said, leading the way into a large chamber.

Lady Sedley was rising to her feet from a chair by the fire as I entered. 'Tamsin, how lovely to see you again, and looking so well too. I see you still have Joan with you too.'

I curtsied to Lady Sedley. 'It is good of you to see me without notice Lady Sedley.'

'Sit down, do. I will send for refreshments and you will tell me all about your baby daughter. Where is Richard? Will he arrive later?'

My heart sinking, I sat down. 'This is difficult to explain, Lady Sedley. In truth, I do not know how to explain it, but the fact is that Richard seems to have completely disappeared.'

'What on earth do you mean, child? Did he not accompany you on your journey from Yorkshire?'

'No, Lady Sedley. He was last seen when he left the castle in early October with his younger brother, Sir Nicholas, and two of our men at arms: Ranulf, who is Joan's betrothed, and Ralf. He had heard that there was a large band of rebels camped not far from us, and he felt that it was his duty to go and investigate what was happening.'

'Yes, we have all heard of the northern rebellions and the Pilgrimage of Grace. So, what happened next?'

'Sir Nicholas and the two soldiers returned to the castle a few days later to say that Richard had vanished in the night. A witness thought he saw him walking around and presumed that he had gone to the latrines, but when Sir Nicholas and the soldiers awoke, Richard was not there, and there has been no message from him or even any word of where he might be,' I said, feeling tears run down my face. Furious at my weakness, I mopped my face on my sleeve.

Lady Sedley remained silent for a minute. 'I have had no word from Richard either, since the message you sent to announce the birth of your daughter. I thought it was because he was enjoying married life and busy on his estate. I must confess I had started to feel irritated by the silence, and now here you are!'

'I must apologise for my weakness, Lady Sedley. It is just that I was convinced that Richard must have been called back to London, perhaps on some secret mission for Lord Cromwell.

There has been some chaos in Yorkshire, and I decided that a message to me must have been lost. At least now I am here I should be able to find out something.'

'Nonsense, my dear, you do not need to apologise. It is no wonder you are upset. It is a very strange business, and I shall be pleased to help you to discover the truth about your husband's whereabouts. I was a great friend of his parents and I have always been fond of both Richard and Nicholas. I was so pleased when Richard picked you as his wife. Some might have said that he was marrying beneath his station, but I could see that you would suit him perfectly.'

'Yes, Lady Sedley, I did not expect to end up a countess and it has taken me some time to become accustomed to my role, but although I may be flattering myself, I think I have met people's expectations.'

'I believe you have. Richard's London steward had nothing but praise for you when I spoke to him after you had left for Yorkshire.' Lady Sedley had more to say. 'Tamsin, it seems you have been cut off from news recently. Did you know that Robert Aske travelled to the court and spoke to the king?'

'I can scarcely believe that. Mr Aske was the leader of the rebels when last I heard.'

'It is true. The king has made much of him and has given him to understand that the demands of the pilgrims will be considered. The king has also issued a general pardon to all those involved in the Pilgrimage of Grace, provided that they lay down their arms and go home.'

'Why would the king do that? I heard talk of a great army coming north to put down the rebellion, and I assumed that there had been mayhem while Joan and I were travelling by sea to London.'

'It is thought that the rebels were so great in number that the king's army feared they could not tackle them. Also, the king was worried that some of the local northern lords would join the rebels,' said Lady Sedley.

'Well, at least I know that Richard would not have done that, Lady Sedley. He was always loyal to the Crown, even though he had his doubts about some of the recent polices.'

'No of course, he would not do such a thing,' said Lady Sedley.

CHAPTER 20

For the remainder of the morning, we compiled a list of people who were known to have associated with Richard in the past, and I began to write messages to each person. It was decided that I would ask the senior male staff members of my household to check various taverns that Richard and his friends had been known to frequent. It was agreed that if nothing more was known after seven days, I would seek an audience with Lord Cromwell.

I returned home to Allerthorpe House after dinner with a list of people to contact. My list included Margaret and Presland, who had returned to London ahead of me, but I found it hard to bring myself to write to them because of Richard's suspicions that Presland was one of Cromwell's informants. I missed Margaret, but it would be hard to speak to her without her husband knowing.

Finally, I wrote a short message to Margaret alone announcing my return to London and inviting her to call on me. I hoped it would result in her coming without her husband.

Talking to Joan as she helped me undress that night, I asked her if she would like to include a message to Ranulf in the stack of letters I was writing.

'I am not sure how much Ranulf can read,' said Joan, 'but I suppose he could get someone to read it to him. I will make sure that my words are all such as can be read out in public. By our lady, Tamsin, it takes much longer to undress you when you wear your London clothes!'

'Unfortunately, a countess cannot run around in a simple kirtle and kerchief over her hair in London. It will not be too long before we return to Yorkshire and then you can see Ranulf, and I can wear more comfortable clothing again. I just need to find out where Richard is.'

Six days later, there had been no reported sightings of Richard. Nobody had admitted to having had any contact with him since the summer. After a consultation with Lady Sedley, it was agreed that I would now send a request for an audience with Lord Cromwell himself.

I had only just despatched the message when Margaret was announced. I was delighted to see that she had come without her husband.

'Tamsin, I am so happy to see you safe,' she said, embracing me. 'It seems ages since we were together in Yorkshire. I have heard that you are seeking Richard. How terrible that he seems to have vanished without trace. We have heard nothing from him. How are you? How is Alice, and how did you travel from Yorkshire with all that unrest going on? I heard that Allerthorpe Castle was ransacked.'

'I am very well, although of course I am very worried. I have left Alice with her aunt in Yorkshire as it was too dangerous to take a baby on such a journey, and Lady Metcalfe tells me that she is thriving. Joan and I travelled together dressed as serving maids so that we would not attract attention. We saw some of the thousands of people march by in what they call the Pilgrimage of Grace. They seemed orderly and sober, and we did not have any problems with them.'

'But Tamsin, did they not invade your castle?'

'I believe the mob that invaded the castle had broken away from the main assembly. They did not murder anybody, they just wanted food, drink, and shelter, but they did a lot of damage and stole our winter stores.'

'Could your guards not see them off?'

'There were too many in the mob and they arrived without warning. I hoped they would just ask for some food and be on their way, but I was mistaken. They left us with scarcely any food stores, and I was obliged to ask some of the household to return to their families. Of course, the harvest was bad too and I fear that many may starve if the monasteries and convents are dissolved. Who will provide them with food and medical care when the religious houses are gone?'

'Presland tells me that there are plans to use funds obtained from the dissolution of the monasteries to increase the number of schools and make a better system to relieve the poor. However, I do not know if anything has been done about these plans yet.'

'Does your husband work for Lord Cromwell, Margaret?'

Margaret blushed as she spoke. 'Yes, he does sometimes work for him, as I believe Richard does.'

'You did not mention this to me in Yorkshire. Instead, you implied that Presland lived off family money, did not work and spent his time drinking, gambling and whoring.'

'Tamsin, I did not know of it when we were in the north,' she said heatedly. 'I only discovered it on our return to London, when one of the servants let it slip that he had been told to wait outside Cromwell's house for Presland last week.'

'Perhaps Presland has worked for Cromwell for some time, Margaret. Of course, he would not share information with you because, in common with so many men, he will have a low opinion of women's intellect!'

'What do you suspect might have happened to Richard?'

'I am beginning to think that something sinister has

occurred. Richard always kept me informed, even if he was delayed. This is all so out of character for him. I can only think that he is being held somewhere against his will, or perhaps he has had an accident.'

'Richard is an earl, an important man. He cannot just disappear!' said Margaret forcefully.

'No, I think not, and that is why I am seeking an audience with Lord Cromwell tomorrow. I believe that he knows much more than is generally known about what is happening in England.'

'Tamsin, you must be careful. I hear that Cromwell is a very powerful and proud man with much influence over the king.'

'Do not worry, I will be respectful and wide-eyed. I will even act like a ninny who has a great love of embroidery if required. It is almost eleven, Margaret, do stay to dinner. It is a fish day, but my cook can make delicious sauces.'

'Thank you, I will. If the sauce is as good as you say, I shall ask for the recipe, because our cook only seems to produce very plain cheese or parsley sauces.'

After dinner, we spent the afternoon discussing mutual friends and acquaintances and then moved on to the royal family. 'Is the queen pregnant yet?' I asked.

'I have not heard that she is and there are rumours that the king is becoming impatient,' said Margaret.

'Poor lady. She must produce a boy. It must be a terrible strain for her.'

'On the occasions I have seen her at court, the queen looks paler and quieter than ever,' said Margaret. 'Did Richard mind that you produced a daughter first?'

'No, I do not think so. He appears besotted with her, and we have time to have more children.'

'Of course,' said Margaret. 'Now I must think about leaving; the shadows are growing longer, and I do not enjoy riding around London in the dark.' I summoned Margaret's maid and her guards, and her horse was brought from the stables. 'Now remember about what I said about your behaviour when you are granted an audience with Cromwell. Do not let your tongue run away with you. He is the son of a blacksmith but very clever, so treat him with respect!'

'Yes, Margaret, do not worry. I will behave perfectly!' I said as she rode off into the chilly February twilight.

I looked around the street. Lights were appearing at windows and all seemed as quiet as London ever was. However, there was a strong stink blowing from the direction of the Thames, so I hastily went back inside before it could contaminate the whole house.

That night, I dispatched a messenger to Cromwell's house at Austin Friars, politely requesting an audience with him at his earliest convenience. The following morning, I received a polite message stating that Lord Cromwell would be pleased to receive the Countess of Allerthorpe at two o'clock that day.

I dressed carefully, aiming for stately but sober. Joan was straight-faced as she helped me with one of my most expensive gowns which was black and silver.

'Do be careful, Tamsin. They say Cromwell is a crafty old fox and his ambition knows no bounds.'

'I do wish everybody would stop warning me about him. You are all making me nervous and that really will not do. I am perfectly calm, and my enquiry about my missing husband is hardly a matter of state.'

Nevertheless, having announced that I was not nervous, I was aware of sweat on my back as I rode into Central London with my escort.

'Make way for the Countess of Allerthorpe!' shouted one of the guards ahead of me. It was strange to see people stand back to allow me to pass. Beggars darted forwards with hands outstretched, risking being trampled by the horses. Fortunately, I had brought some coins with me and was able to throw them to people. It was shocking to see so much poverty, and it was with some relief that I arrived at Cromwell's house.

I was faced with a large red-bricked house of three storeys. There was a small crowd of what appeared to be beggars standing to one side of the house, and guards posted all around. Further along, I could see other buildings, one of which was the house of the Austin Friars order.

'What are all these people doing?' I asked the nearest of my guards.

'Lord Cromwell's staff distribute alms to them regularly, my lady. Perhaps it is almost time for a dole.'

Cromwell's house guards stepped back and bowed as I neared the entrance. A stable boy came running for our horses. I climbed down as elegantly as possible from my horse and we were led through a high and sumptuous doorway into the house.

I was expecting a house full of shadows and deathly silence to fit the picture of Cromwell I had formed in my mind. I was surprised to see the house was full of men, busy on errands and moving purposefully. Two clerks staggered by holding enormous ledgers and I sensed that this was where many important matters were decided. We were shown into a parlour and wine was brought by a young female servant.

A man appeared, bowing. 'My lady, Lord Cromwell sends his apologies. He is delayed by his work, but he will be with you directly.'

Joan and I were just examining an expensive looking wall hanging when a door opened in the opposite wall. A large, middle-aged man was coming towards us. His features were heavy and weathered by the sun.

'Lady Allerthorpe, it is a pleasure to meet you. A thousand apologies for my lateness but there was an issue that required my immediate attention.'

I stood up and curtsied, and as did Joan.

'Pray follow me. Your servant,' he said, 'may wait here in the parlour. My secretary will be in attendance.'

I followed Lord Cromwell into what appeared to be a very large and untidy office. There were ledgers, piles of documents and crates everywhere. 'Please sit down, my lady,' he said, pointing to a chair which was, mercifully, free of objects. I sat down carefully, remembering to keep my chin high and my gaze fearless.

'I confess, I was intrigued by your message. In truth, I was so eager to see you that I have delayed setting out for Hampton Court to see the king. Pray tell me, why you have come, Lady Allerthorpe?'

'My lord husband, the Earl of Allerthorpe, seems to have vanished off the face of the earth. Extensive enquiries have not revealed his whereabouts. I wondered if you would be kind enough to help me to locate him. His disappearance is out of character and I can think of no reason why he would have abandoned his family, friends and property without a word to anybody.' To my horror, I could feel the treacherous tears at the back of my eyes. I fought to control them while I waited for Cromwell's answer.

'My lady, you surprise me with your enquiry. Do you really have no idea where he might be? I can see from your face that you do not. You will need to prepare yourself for bad tidings.' He looked at his secretary. 'Fetch a glass of brandy for the countess.'

'For pity's sake, sir, please tell me what you know.'

'You will know about the Pilgrimage of Grace, madam.'

'Why, yes. I understand the king in his great mercy has pardoned the rebels who have now disbanded, and that Robert Aske, their leader, was even entertained at court by the king at Christmas. I did hear that there were some negotiations with the rebels, but I do not know the outcome.'

'The outcome, madam, is this. There is news that new rebellions are taking place in the North. The king has lost all patience with the rebels and even now, the Duke of Norfolk is preparing to lead a great army into the North to impose martial law and eliminate any further resistance to the king. All the leaders will be caught and will face justice. Madam, I have received reports that your husband the Earl of Allerthorpe is in the North.'

'You mean that you know he is alive, Lord Cromwell. This is most happy news! I expect he will be helping local landowners to regain control of the area for the king. Of course, he will have been on the move, and perhaps his messages to me have gone astray.' I suddenly felt like jumping up and dancing around the room, but I felt a jolt when I realised that Cromwell was looking at me with an odd expression, almost as if he felt sorry for me.

'Madam, it grieves me to tell you that the Earl of Allerthorpe is a traitor to the Crown. He was sent by me to discover information about the rebels, but instead, he has supported them in their treason, and he is now named on documents in which the demands of those deluded idiots are stated.'

'There must be some mistake. Richard would never turn traitor. He must have been kidnapped by evil people and forced to join them.'

'That was my first thought, madam. I confess that I was surprised by his reported actions, but when I sent another agent to check, his report confirmed that the earl was with the rebels of his own free will. Indeed, he has been very busy on their behalf. I can see that this has come as a shock to you, my lady. You look ill. Drink your brandy. Shall I fetch your servant in case you faint?'

All I could feel was cold shock mixed with increasing anger. I stood up straight and spoke as haughtily as possible. 'I thank you for your news and the explanation for my husband's absence. I cannot believe my husband capable of the actions and folly you describe, but in the want of any other explanation, I can see that I must. Why are you so certain that my husband is a traitor?'

'I have an agent who has been watching him for some time. Your husband did not keep his disapproval of certain changes a secret.'

'Is Lord Presland your informant?'

'You will understand that I cannot divulge that information,' said Cromwell. 'Sit down, my lady – Tamsin, is it not?' I sat down. 'You do not look at all well. Fortunately for you, it was decided that you had no part in your husband's plotting, otherwise you would be in the Tower. From your reactions, I believe that to be correct.'

'If I had known, my lord, I would hardly have come here to seek your help! I cannot answer for my husband's opinions or conduct, but I am certain that he would never seek to betray the Crown.'

'My lady, make no mistake: your husband will be hunted down, tried and no doubt executed as a traitor. If you should hear from him, it would be sensible to plead with him to give himself up, as then His Majesty may be inclined to mercy. As he is a convicted traitor, all lands and property belonging to the Earl of Allerthorpe will be forfeit to the Crown. You should make arrangements for your future living.'

I do not remember how I left that building or the journey home. I just remember Joan's anxious face, and then lying in my bed, shivering, unable to stop my teeth chattering. I was told that I lay in my bed with a fever for five days. The fever gave me dreams in which I was chasing after Richard, but my feet were sinking in mud and I could not catch up with him.

CHAPTER 21

On the sixth day, I felt more like myself and struggled to get out of bed. The morning light was streaming into my chamber and I could hear the servants downstairs. I was sitting on the bed when Joan burst in.

'Tamsin, my lady, you are better! You should get back into bed. Or if you will not, you may sit in a chair and I will bring you some breakfast.'

'Yes, please do, Joan. It is important that I regain my strength quickly, and you must tell me everything that has happened since I fell ill.'

She brought a basin of water to me. The cool water felt good on my face and hands but when I tried to stand, I found that my legs were wobbly. Joan pushed a chair next to the bed and carefully I transferred myself into it. I sat quietly, trying to remain calm, as pictures of the scene with Cromwell came back to me. Joan returned with some ale, cakes, and an evil smelling potion in a small cup.

'Drink this. It will strengthen you, my lady.'

I looked at it dubiously. 'It smells disgusting, Joan. What on earth is it?'

'It is a restorative mixture made up by the apothecary for you. Drink it straight down and I will pass you some ale to take the taste away. Then you must try eating something.'

The mixture did not taste as bad as I had feared, and I felt a warm glow in my stomach. The potion probably contained some form of spirits.

'Now, Joan, you must tell me what has happened while I have been ill.'

'Well, you were carried in, almost insensible, and I discovered that you had a high fever. At first, the servants were terrified because they thought you had the sweat or even the plague, but you did not die quickly or develop any swellings and there was no rash.

'The apothecary said that you had been exposed to a miasma from riding in London's streets and that this had unbalanced your humours. He bled you and told us to keep you warm to burn the contagion out of you. We all prayed for you and God heard our prayers!'

'Has there been any word of Richard?'

'No, my lady.'

'Joan, are you aware that Richard has been identified as a traitor, and that if he is convicted, his estates will be forfeited to the Crown? Cromwell enlightened me about this.'

'Yes, my lady, it is now commonly spoken of everywhere.'

'And do people believe that my husband is a traitor?'

'My lady, I am sorry to inform you that people say that there are witnesses who have given sworn evidence that they heard your husband repeatedly condemning the dissolution of the religious houses and speaking against the king. They also say that rather than supress the rebels in the North, Lord Allerthorpe joined them.'

A cold finger of fear crept into me as I remembered the sunny days of our courtship, and Richard asking me what I thought would happen to poor and sick people if the monasteries were closed. Of course, it made sense. He was a man of conviction and he did not let the opinions of others sway him. He had ignored the fact that I was only from a minor gentry family when he married me, when as an earl, he could have sought the hand of higher placed eligible heiresses. I realised that it was unlikely to be a misunderstanding. I was indeed married to a traitor!

'My lady, take heart. From what I have heard, there is much sympathy for the northern rebels, but the problem is that people are too frightened to speak out because they fear arrest and worse.'

'I expect there are also lords who hope to gain monastic lands and buildings from the closures. They will not speak out,' I said bitterly. 'Perhaps they plan to make fortunes by building cheap tenements in holy buildings for rent, or they may plan to covert monastic buildings into large homes. Perhaps the lands will be enclosed for sheep so that lords may make fortunes from woollen cloth. Richard was right to be concerned about the welfare of the poor and sick!'

'Hush, my lady, please control your tongue. What if you are overheard by some busybody who seeks a reward for information?'

'You have no need to worry, Joan. From now on, I will be in perfect control of myself, and I intend to behave as if everything is normal. After all, Richard has not yet been arrested that we know of, and there has certainly been no trial or conviction.'

'You may have to deal with nasty comments, my lady, and it is possible that some ladies of the court may shun you.'

'I am aware of that possibility, but I will ignore anything like that.'

Later, as I sat by the window looking out at the grounds, I became aware that I was feeling increasingly angry about Richard's behaviour. Why could he not have faked illness when sent an urgent message to leave the camp and help restore order in the North? Other nobles had done this or said that their armies were too small. Then he would not have had the chance to rebel. Why did Richard have to stand true to his principles and risk his life for the sake of his beliefs?

It was several days before I was strong enough to go out into society again, but I had enlisted Margaret's support, and we picked a reception for the Spanish Ambassador at Whitehall for my first appearance back at court.

'You look as if you lost weight when you were ill, Tamsin,' said Margaret. 'Your face is thinner, which makes your beautiful eyes stand out more, and somehow this sickness has made you look taller!'

'Why, thank you, Margaret. The problem is that I have also lost weight from my bosoms. I will have to endure a very tight corset to force up what little I have!'

After the maids had helped us to dress, we raided my cosmetics box. 'Tamsin, most of these paints are still new – we should open them up and make ourselves look like visions of beauty!' said Margaret.

She brought out the pots and bottles and lined them up on the table. 'Now, I think red paint for our lips and some of this black stuff for our eyes. What about rouge?' By the time we had finished and had a little wine, we were convinced that we would outrival any of the court beauties. Indeed, a quick glance in the mirror showed me that Margaret was very skilled with face paints. I resolved to ask her to teach me how to apply them.

I summoned the carriage to take us to the palace of Whitehall because it was raining, which threatened our carefully applied face paint. I ignored the little voice in my head which said I was being extravagant and concentrated on enjoying myself. By the time we reached Whitehall, we were very merry, but underneath

I felt brittle and tense.

The great sprawling palace was busy on our arrival. 'Thank you, Jefferyes, we will alight here, and please ensure that you return at midnight,' I said to the coachman.

'The Countess of Allerthorpe and Lady Presland,' shouted the usher. To my horror, there was a lull in the conversation as people turned around to stare at us.

I plunged towards a lady of my acquaintance. 'Greetings, Lady Dorothy. It is very busy tonight, is it not?' The lady mumbled something in my direction and moved away to a nearby group, who all turned their backs on me.

We were saved by Lady Sedley, resplendent in yellow satin. 'Tamsin, my dear, how wonderful to see you quite recovered from your illness and looking so well – and you too, dear Margaret.' I was grateful to see that people seemed to lose interest in us and general conversation resumed.

Curious looks were cast in my direction as we moved through the crowded hall, but I remembered to hold myself erect and appear confident. Once we had found ourselves space to stand and had secured drinks, Lady Sedley began to interrogate me in a low voice. She asked what Lord Cromwell had said and if I heard any more news of Richard. It did not take long to acquaint her with the facts of the matter, and I found myself drinking my wine rather too quickly as I explained what I knew to her.

'Well, my dear, the most important aspect is that you do not seem to be under suspicion of treason yourself. I must say that I always knew that Richard was rather idealistic, but I did not expect him to act so recklessly.'

'No, indeed, Lady Sedley. It was a shock to me, and I must confess that I am angry about the risks he has exposed us to. If he is guilty, Richard is certain to be executed, thereby depriving Alice of a father. She and I will almost certainly be destitute, as the property and titles will revert to the Crown if he is declared a traitor.'

'Yes, that is so. We must hope that it does not come to that, my dear.'

'Lady Sedley, would you think me very rude if we did not talk about this subject further? I realise that I am powerless to take any action to alleviate the situation and I have a desire to enjoy myself here, for what may be the very last time.'

'No, of course, you and Margaret must enjoy yourselves. I see Presland is not with you, Margaret.'

Margaret looked embarrassed. 'No, I believe my husband may have been sent to watch Lord Allerthorpe on our visit to Allerthorpe castle last autumn and report back to Cromwell about his actions. I did not encourage him to accompany me tonight in case he distressed Tamsin.'

We were now following the flow of the guests, moving through an archway to a larger room where musicians were already playing lively tunes. I hoped that some young man who did not know my identity might ask me to dance. Fortunately, I did not have to wait long. A nervous looking youth with a face full of pimples sidled up to our table. He bowed to me and requested the honour of the next dance. With a brilliant smile, I accepted, put my hand on his arm and allowed him to lead me on the dance floor.

There was a fanfare of trumpets heralding the entry of the king with Queen Jane and we curtsied, waiting politely until they had settled on the dais and the king had indicated that the festivities could continue. The alcohol I had consumed loosened my inhibitions and I realised I was enjoying myself. Other men offered themselves for the next two dances and I became aware that people were staring at me, but I found that I did not care.

'Who are you, beautiful, mysterious lady?' said my third partner, an over-dressed, dark-haired man.

'I am surprised that you do not know. I am the wife of a missing traitor earl!' I said loudly and cheerfully. I was unable to restrain myself from laughing as he melted away into the crowd, a look of shock on his face. There was a hand on my elbow as Margaret appeared beside me.

'Come. Tamsin, I am fearfully hot. Let us go outside and get some fresh air,' she said as she propelled me out through a side door into the gardens. The rain had stopped, but the air was chilly.

Our footsteps crunched on the gravel as we walked, and I could see a frost was forming. 'I decided that it would be sensible to encourage you to leave the room,' said Margaret. 'Many people were watching you, and several young men enquired about your identity from Lady Sedley. They appeared disappointed to discover that you were already married, and then when they found out the identity of your husband, they almost ran away!'

'I am sorry, Margaret, but I felt such a wild desire to dance and enjoy myself. I just could not resist it. Perhaps the devil is in me.'

'Nonsense, it is just that you have been living under a great strain for the last few months.'

'Perhaps we had better go back in. Besides, I have not had a chance to see the king properly. It is difficult to take a discreet look when one is dancing.'

'Pray, let me adjust your hood, Tamsin; your hair is escaping again.'

'Why do my headdresses always slip? How do you keep

yours so sleek and smooth, Margaret?'

'I use a net to catch up all my hair first, sometimes a cap too, and secure it with pins. Your Joan probably did not pick up such hairdressing tips before you became the countess. Let us hurry back – I am starting to freeze!'

Music and light and the rumble of people enjoying themselves came through from the main door as it was opened for us. We made our way from the reception hall towards the main hall, but were then stopped by a row of people blocking the door with their backs to us.

'What is happening?' I asked a palace guard.

'The king is dancing with the queen, so the people give him space,' he answered.

Peeping around a large matron, we could see the king and queen dancing the pavane with a group of young people. They moved in a slow and stately manner. The king moved rather stiffly, and I noticed that he seemed to be fatter than when I had last seen him. Suddenly, I felt a wave of anger that this man, who had turned religion on its head to marry Anne Boleyn and now threatened to destroy religious houses that had stood for centuries, could also order the death of my husband according to his whim. Yes, there might be a trial, but the verdict was likely to be a foregone conclusion.

At a signal from the king, other couples joined them in the dance. We looked for Lady Sedley and saw that she was surrounded by a large and noisy group of courtiers, some of whom were known to Margaret. Suddenly, feeling rather tired, I found a windowed alcove and sat down, telling Margaret to go and join her friends and that I would meet up with her later. Now left by myself, I surreptitiously wiped the mist from the window and wondered if I would be able to make out the Plough's shape in the stars. I was interrupted by a man I recognised as my third, somewhat overdressed dance partner from earlier.

'Beautiful, mysterious lady, there you are again, but I know who you are now. You are the Countess of Allerthorpe, whose husband is a fugitive and a probable traitor.'

'Sir, I am afraid you have me at a disadvantage since I do not know who you are,' I replied rather acidly, as I did not appreciate being disturbed from my reverie.

'Allow me to introduce myself. I am Thomas Seymour, brother to our queen.'

Crossly, I got up and curtsied. 'I am honoured to meet you, my lord.'

'You do not look as if you are honoured, my lady. I am intrigued, because most wives in your position would be seeking to speak to anybody with influence in this court to try to seek a pardon for their menfolk.'

'My lord, I am well versed in the ways of our times and I do not believe that anything I can do or say will make any difference. I await the king's justice with equanimity,' I said, swallowing down my true feelings.

'Your husband's situation looks very unpromising. I understand that his commission was to try to persuade the rebels to disband, but instead he appears to have joined them. In effect, he has betrayed both the king and Cromwell. However, you could still try appealing to the king for mercy for Lord Allerthorpe. The king is always polite and amenable to an attractive noblewoman in distress.'

'I shall consider what you say, my lord. However, as my lord does not appear to have been arrested yet, I shall not act prematurely.'

'My lady, you should know that the Duke of Norfolk and a

very large army are already on the way to the North to apprehend all the rebels. In the meantime, may I fetch you another glass of wine? Or perhaps you would prefer to dance again.'

'I think I would prefer to dance, my lord.' Seymour offered me his arm and we processed to the dancing. I could not help but notice that this time, other dancers moved back respectfully to give us space.'

This time, I found that I could not lose myself in the music and dance. Instead, I was conscious that many pairs of eyes watched us, and at one point, I saw one pair of small glittery eyes in a puffy round face looking straight at me. Shocked, I realised that the king was staring at me!

Of course, Queen Jane's brother was well-known at court whereas I was unfamiliar, and I had the added attraction of being wife to a presumed traitor. It was not surprising that I should be the centre of attention, but it was not a pleasant feeling. When the dance ended, I excused myself and returned to my alcove, where I found Margaret waiting.

'Tamsin, everybody was watching you!' she said excitedly. You were dancing with one of the most popular men at court. The king himself looked at you and then made some remark to the queen, but I could not hear what was said.'

'I would not wish to know,' I said. 'Thomas Seymour appears well pleased with himself, does he not? But I think his clothes somewhat ridiculous – that enormous codpiece and, I'll swear, his doublet was so well-padded that he looked as if he might topple over!'

'Hush, Tamsin, someone might hear you. Let us go and find Lady Sedley and then perhaps we should think about leaving; it is getting late.'

Lady Sedley was still surrounded by courtiers and there was

much laughing and shouting around her. We stood politely, waiting for a gap in the conversation.

'Ah, the countess is back,' she announced with amusement in her voice. To my horror, it seemed that the whole group turned to stare at me. Putting on my haughtiest expression, I curtsied to her and announced confidently that Margaret and I were leaving and that we wished her an enjoyable evening.

'Lady Allerthorpe has only just recovered from a severe illness,' announced Lady Sedley. 'She must be fatigued, as I believe this is the first social occasion she has attended since then.'

I heard some mutterings at the back of the group, and I was sure I caught the words "traitor" and "Cromwell". But I ignored them, smiled at Lady Sedley and the whole group, curtsied again, and left with Margaret.

'I think everybody must know who you are now!' said Margaret as the carriage jolted over the uneven road.

'That is a pity. I do not seek notoriety, but I do not see why I should behave as if my husband has already been tried and condemned. Thomas Seymour advised me to approach the king himself and plead for my husband, but I said I would not consider it until a verdict has been given. Otherwise, it would look as if I already knew that my husband was guilty.'

'That is wise,' said Margaret. 'You look exhausted. You must promise me that you will rest tomorrow.' Soon, the carriage had reached Margaret's house, and I waited until she had been admitted before ordering the driver to proceed.

On my arrival home, I noticed a man who seemed to be lurking outside the house. It was too dark for me to see his features. I watched as he stepped back into the shadows as my carriage drew up. I asked the doorkeeper if any of our guards had been posted outside the house, but the man said no. Joan appeared in the hall, trying to stifle a yawn as she untied the strings of my cloak. It was such a relief to be home and away from all those eyes and the sense of tension.

Lying in my comfortable feather bed after hasty prayers, I reminded myself that I must not become soft and over-reliant on luxurious living. It was likely that Richard would eventually be detained and arrested, the state's remorseless judicial machinery would turn, and I could become a homeless and penniless widow.

Although I was tired, I could not sleep. Instead, I found that anger and despair was keeping me awake. There must be something I could do to save Richard. If I were a man, I could jump on a horse and just keep riding until I reached York, and then I could ask around and find out where pockets of rebels might be. My imagination was carrying me away, I realised, as I pictured us secretly fetching our daughter and fleeing the country. Finally, as I heard a cock crow and birds starting to twitter in the trees, I fell into a heavy and troubled sleep.

CHAPTER 22

The following morning, I asked Joan to bring me a lavender poultice as my head was aching. I had already planned to speak to all the household together about what would happen if Richard were taken and condemned, but I had repeatedly delayed, telling myself that nothing was certain yet. That morning, I was sure that disaster would inevitably overtake us.

'Joan, would you take a message to the steward and chamberlain requesting that all staff assemble in the hall at two o'clock. I wish to speak to them all about the future.'

'Yes, my lady.'

When the church bells rang the hour, I was ready in the hall. All the servants entered, right down to the lowliest kitchen maid.

'As you will all know, your master, the Earl of Allerthorpe, is currently somewhere in the North, where there has been rebellion. It is thought that he has disobeyed instructions from the king and Lord Cromwell to work to disband the rebels and has instead joined the rebels. We do not know where he is, and he did not accompany Sir Robert Aske down to London at Christmas. It is thought that he is helping to foster further rebellion. Now, I know as you do that Lord Allerthorpe is a man of high principles. He is also charitable, religious and has always been loyal to the Crown. I cannot believe that he has betrayed the king, but nevertheless, this is what is believed. The Duke of Norfolk is now on his way up the country to mete out justice and restore order.' I paused to clear my throat.

'You must all understand that if Lord Allerthorpe is condemned as a traitor all his lands, possessions and titles will be forfeit to the Crown. This means that all the earl's houses will be shut, and staff turned out. Now, it may be that whoever is awarded the lands and buildings will need servants, but I cannot guarantee that they will retain any of you. You should therefore start to plan for your futures. I hope that some of you may have families that can take you in and I shall ask around my friends for any vacant positions. You cannot know how very deeply I feel for you and I wish with all my heart that this situation had never occurred.'

A voice called out. 'There will be great hardship, my lady. Some of the London religious houses that use to provide relief to the poor are already being closed.'

'Yes,' shouted another voice. 'The reason I came down to London is because landowners are throwing poor tenant farmers off land that has been farmed by their families for generations, and all because greedy men seek to enclose fields for sheep to graze. They can make a lot of money by doing that! Meanwhile, men who are not fortunate to obtain employment end up begging in the streets and worse.'

A woman called out: 'It is all right for the ex-monks and nuns; they have pensions. But the monastery servants just get thrown out with nothing and they have to beg or starve too.'

I knew that everything they said was true, but I still feared that I was being watched for any evidence that would strengthen the case against Richard. I could not have my people openly criticising the king's policies.

'Good people, I agree that there is much hardship, but I feel sure that the king is aware of that and will shortly take some measures to improve the lot of those living in poverty. I have heard that some of the funds from the dissolution will be used to establish schools and hospitals.'

I thought it best to close the meeting before anything else controversial was said. I was just leaving the room after thanking them for attending, when somebody called out: 'My lady, what will you do if the earl is executed?'

'I will return to my family in Cornwall and live quietly,' I said, swallowing hard. I hurried out, determined to make a list of all my acquaintances and connections so that I would be ready to recommend any staff who could not secure alternative employment, or who did not have families to take them in.

Although the afternoon dragged on, my headache disappeared and by dusk, I had two lists ready. With the help of the steward, I'd compiled two lists: one of all my household and one of all my acquaintances in London, with suggestions about suitability in the margins. I knew I should do the same for Allerthorpe Castle, but I would need the help of the other steward for that. As for the other manors that Richard owned, I could do not do much as I had not had the chance to visit them with him during our short marriage.

That evening, I sat by the fire with Joan and pondered about what my next action should be. Joan seemed to be in favour of a journey to Allerthorpe Castle, as she was sorely missing Ranulf and no reply to her message had come from him. However, if I were to leave London suddenly, it might look as if I had gone to join Richard, which could result in more trouble.

'Joan, I think you are right. We should return to Allerthorpe Castle, but this time I will do so openly. In fact, I will demand an audience with Cromwell and tell him that I plan to return to the castle because I am concerned about the welfare of my staff, given our perilous situation.'

'Do you think he will permit you to do this, my lady?' asked Joan.

'Oh yes, he may,' I said. 'If Richard has not yet been captured, Cromwell will think that Richard will hear of my arrival and be unable to resist the temptation to meet me. Then Cromwell will send troops to flush him out. I believe that if Richard has already been apprehended, he will not allow me to leave as he will already be preparing a case against him. He will want all the main players here in London and he may wish to use members of this household as witnesses.'

'So, although nobody seems to know if Richard has been captured or not, you will know from Cromwell's response. That is clever, my lady!'

'Well, what is the use of a good education if I do not use my brain?' was my response. Looking out of the window at the darkening sky, I thought: Dusk comes early in the winter; it is not too late to send a message to Cromwell. I went to my writing desk and wrote a polite note requesting an audience on the morrow. 'Please take this downstairs and get it dispatched, Joan.'

The bells were tolling for seven o'clock when the messenger returned with Cromwell's answer. He would be pleased to receive me at nine in the morning.

The following morning dawned bright and sunny, although the streets were treacherous with frozen mud and rubbish. It was extremely cold, and I was glad of my thick cloak. I left plenty of time for the journey because I knew that the horses would not be able to travel quickly.

We reached Austin Friars about five minutes before the appointed hour. I threw some coins to the beggars outside and proceeded to the front door, where two stable boys hurried up to take our horses.

This time, we were both shown straight into Cromwell's study, which seemed to be piled with even more paper now. A servant brought us hot wine and asked if I would like my cloak taken. I agreed because there was a large fire roaring in the grate, and I did not want to feel hot and bothered in front of this man.

'My lady countess, it is good to see you again. How are you?'

'I am very well, thank you, my lord. How are you?' I said as politely as possible, hoping that Cromwell's ears were not so sharp that he could hear my thumping heartbeat.

'As you see, I am as ever working hard for the good of the Crown,' answered Cromwell. 'Now let us dispense with the polite formalities. Why do you wish to see me?'

'My lord, I am considering travelling up to Allerthorpe Castle. There are household matters I must attend to and I wish to see my daughter, who is currently staying with Lord and Lady Metcalfe. In view of the difficult situation my husband appears to be in, I thought I should inform you of my whereabouts.'

Cromwell paused and shuffled a pile of papers in front of him as I sat, waiting and maintaining the innocent expression of a matron only interested in domestic matters.

'Are you aware that the Duke of Norfolk's army marches north? There are likely to be some skirmishes as he reimposes the king's rule over this county. You may be caught up in some disorder.'

'I do not think so, my lord, as I plan only to go to Allerthorpe Castle. My steward has sent messages to me to inform me that all is quiet.'

'I am aware of that, madam.'

He is having all our messages read, I thought to myself.

'I intend to leave tomorrow, my lord, and I will take only a small retinue: my maid, Joan, and some guards for protection against robbery or mischief on the road.'

'If you keep to the main highways, you should be safe, my lady. Providing you are aware of the possible dangers from rebel groups, I see no reason why you should not undertake this journey.'

Cromwell indicated that the interview was over and even went as far as to wish me Godspeed on my journey. Keeping my expression neutral and confident, I curtsied politely and left the room.

By the time we had reclaimed our horses and were clear of Cromwell's house, I was fairly bursting with excitement.

'Joan, they cannot have captured Richard yet!'

'True, my lady, but what if Richard hears of your arrival and tries to see you? You have already thought that a trap might be laid, but how are you going to stop this happening?'

'I am not sure, Joan, but I will think of something on our journey.'

We spent the rest of the day assembling everything we would need. The process seemed easier this time as we were now experienced travellers. As before, coins and jewellery were sewn into my garments and we added old sheets to the horse panniers to protect us from dirty inn mattresses. I included a fur wrap against the cold and my dagger.

After sending messages to Margaret and Lady Sedley to tell them of my journey, I felt much happier when I went to bed that night, both because I was no longer passively waiting for events to unfold and because I would soon be reunited with Alice again.

By dawn, we were on the road out of London to the North. The weather continued cold but there was no sign of snow, for which I was devoutly thankful. We had decided against taking a carriage because of the risk that it would get stuck in mud in the winter weather.

For the first few nights, we stopped at prosperous looking inns with good stables so that the horses could rest properly. We did not want to have to hire horses, and so we took great care of them. There were a few families of people who had clearly fallen on hard times marching along the road but other than brief acknowledgements, we had no communication with them. The weather remained cold but clear, and we met few people out and about. In the towns and villages, doors remained firmly closed and any children running to look at us were hauled back inside by their parents.

On the fifth night, we stopped at a roadside inn, where the landlord seemed reluctant to welcome us in at first, until he had seen the members of our party. As he led us into a poorly furnished chamber, I asked him why he had seemed so suspicious when we arrived.

'My lady, I did not mean to offer any insult to you and your servants, but we have had Norfolk's army march through on this road. The soldiers billeted with us were rough and not inclined to pay for their food and drink. One of my female staff was assaulted by one of those drunken oafs and we were very glad to see them ride off after one night. Now we are reluctant to open the doors to strangers.'

'Did they say why they were marching north?'

'Yes, my lady, they mean to search out and kill any remaining rebels and they say that the Duke of Norfolk will impose martial law on the North. Anybody who speaks against the king or the religious changes, or who argues against any other laws, will be arrested and hanged. Your party is only a day or so behind them, my lady. You should be very careful that you do not encounter them.'

I thanked him for his information and advice and went to check that the horses had been stabled comfortably. We might need them to ride quickly if we met any trouble.

After a tolerable meal of meat and vegetable pottage, we retired to our chamber, spreading our old sheets on the prickly, straw mattresses.

'My lady, are you not worried that we will meet this rabble army on the road?' asked Joan.

'We cannot hide here, Joan; we must press on. Presumably, these men have a chain of command. If we should run into them, I will announce my identity. Richard has not yet been declared a traitor so they will not dare to molest us, especially if I threaten to report them to Cromwell. I shall describe him as a close friend,' I said with a wicked grin.

'Very well, my lady, but I shall make sure we both have our daggers within easy reach,' said Joan grimly.

After a very early breakfast of rather sour ale and oatcakes, we saddled the horses and set off again. Again, we were fortunate with the weather, but I did not like the look of the heavy cloud blowing from the east. There was no sign of Norfolk's army, but the track seemed very churned up and muddy.

By late afternoon, we had arrived at Lincoln, where we installed ourselves at an inn near the centre of the town. After booking our rooms and stabling our horses, Joan and I decided to walk around and perhaps buy some ribbons and trimmings for our dresses. We had not had the chance to wander around any of the other places we had passed through. We had not walked far when we came to a row of shops built on a bridge.

'How strange,' said Joan 'I did not realise there were other bridges with shops on them like London Bridge.'

'Nor did I. Let us go inside and see if they have anything we need.'

After an enjoyable time comparing ribbons and trims, we left with a small packet of purchases. 'The blue satin ribbon will look lovely on Alice,' I said, my heart skipping with excitement at the thought of seeing her again.

As we returned to the inn, Joan said, 'Tamsin, do not look round but there is a man that I think I saw at the inn we stayed at yesterday. He has stepped out of sight into a shop doorway now.'

'It would not be unusual for travellers to follow the same road and he may be buying gifts for his family. Perhaps he will appear again, and we will see he is just another person going to York!'

We had an enjoyable evening sorting our purchases, helped by the feeling that our journey's end was now in sight. Joan was still preoccupied by the man she had seen walking behind us. 'I cannot help thinking about it, my lady. He had a furtive look about him and I have not seen him in this inn.'

'Joan, you are overly nervous. There are many inns in this town and why should anybody want to follow us?'

'It may be that Cromwell expects you to arrange a meeting with Lord Allerthorpe before you reach the castle, and he has sent someone to follow us on the journey in case his lordship should appear suddenly!'

'If Cromwell has, the young man will be disappointed. I intend to find another way to try to send a warning to Lord Allerthorpe when we are settled in the castle, if I can find out where he might be.' I blew out the candle. 'Now go to sleep and try to stop worrying!'

CHAPTER 23

The following morning, we woke to a light covering of snow, but the sky was clear, so I hoped there would be no more of it today. The road to York again showed tracks from many horses, and we passed areas with the blackened remains of many campfires and holes in the ground where posts had been inserted.

'My lady, it is certain that a large army has passed along here very recently,' said one of our armed escort. He shaded his eyes and looked out over the fields 'Some of those fires are still smouldering. We should be on the alert for stragglers and hangers-on from the baggage train who may wish to cause trouble.'

However, all seemed quiet, and I admired the way that snow transformed the bare and scrubby countryside into a glittering landscape. As we rode, the way became increasingly hilly and we passed occasional tiny settlements which appeared deserted. I noticed our two soldiers looking around alertly. 'Is there anything wrong?' I asked.

'My lady, it is odd that we have not seen any people near the villages we have passed. Also, we have not seen any other travellers on the road recently.'

'Perhaps it is too cold for them?' I ventured.

'No, my lady, people up here are tough and used to all weathers. A little bit of snow would not put them off.'

We were passing through a small valley when disaster

struck. A band of armed men suddenly appeared in front of us. They must have been waiting to ambush us. I signalled to our party to halt immediately.

'Kindly move out of our way, good sirs!' I yelled as confidently as I could. 'I am the Countess of Allerthorpe returning to my castle. I have permission from Lord Cromwell to travel.'

One of the men rode forward and leaned over me, I noticed that he had a fearsome scar running down the side of his face, which puckered his eye. 'We are commanded by the Duke of Norfolk, who orders you to accompany us.'

'You will have to show me some warrant or letter of authority before I accompany you anywhere, you ill-mannered churl!' I yelled back.

The scarred man stepped back, and seconds later I realised that he had thrown a small axe at one of my soldiers who now fell from his horse to the ground. Blood seemed to be everywhere.

'That is my warrant, lady!' shouted the man with the scar. Joan sat frozen with horror.

'Best to see what they want, my lady,' said the other soldier. 'There is nothing I can do against this lot.'

'May God save us,' muttered Joan.

'It seems you leave me with no choice,' I shouted. 'But first I will see what I can do for this man.'

I climbed off my horse to see what I could do for the soldier, but it did not take long for me to realise that he was beyond help. I noticed that his sword was still in his scabbard. Some of the ruffians stepped forward and tied the man's body to his horse.

'You will remain here while my men re-group around you,' said the scarred man. 'Anybody attempting to ride away will be cut down immediately.'

I felt as though I was in a nightmare, but the wetness of the man's blood on my travelling cloak was real enough. We rode on for perhaps another half an hour until we arrived at an enormous camp of soldiers. As far as I could see, the landscape was filled with small fires and makeshift shelters. We were led further into the camp until we arrived in front of a grander looking tent in the colours of the Duke of Norfolk.

The scarred man ordered us to stop and indicated that I should dismount and enter. Joan went to follow me, but the scarred man shook his head at her. 'Your mistress will not need her woman.'

I drew myself up to my full height and stalked into the tent. I had not met the Duke of Norfolk before, but I had glimpsed him at court in the past. I saw a grizzled and grey bearded man wearing a high-quality breastplate and gold chains. He was loudly cursing some minion as I went up to him.

'Good afternoon, your lordship. There seems to have been a terrible mistake,' I said through gritted teeth. 'I have been rudely apprehended by a band of ruffians who say they work for you. One of my men at arms has been murdered most foully. I am the Countess of Allerthorpe, and I look to you to remedy this situation immediately. I seek justice and a Christian burial for my servant, and of course, the release of myself and my party.'

'Ah. the Countess of Allerthorpe! You are unlikely to retain that title for long as we are set to capture your treacherous husband, you stupid woman. Do you seek to aid him? Is that why you are travelling up here?'

Trying to control my temper, I responded meekly. 'Oh no, sir, I have no idea where my husband is, and I do not care either. My business is with the tenants of Allerthorpe Castle. There are outstanding debts that need to be paid and land disputes that must be settled.'

'Surely your steward can deal with this.'

'Oh yes, of course, the steward can prepare the paperwork, but my signature is needed on various documents as my husband is a fugitive. Thank goodness I learned to write my name! My steward will tell me where to sign. As you can see, sir, I simply must resume my journey. Lord Cromwell was informed of my errand and gave me consent for it before I left London.'

I was surprised to see a dark expression pass over the Duke's face at the mention of Cromwell's name. Had they fallen out? Would this prejudice the Duke against me? I could see that he was thinking so I pressed on hastily.

'Would not the king want a smooth handover of the estate? When all is settled, I mean to make my way back to my family's home in Cornwall.' I rounded off my speech with a respectful curtsy.

'There is some merit in what you say, my lady. It is to your credit that you have accepted the fact of your husband's disgrace with such equanimity. I will allow you to proceed with your journey, but you will now be escorted by a small band of my troops. We would not want you to be distressed by any stray bands of rebels.'

'Very well, sir,' I said meekly. 'Can I be assured that you will give my servant a Christian burial and investigate the circumstances in which he was most foully slain?'

At this point, the scarred man whispered in the Duke's ear. The Duke laughed and patted his back while inwardly, I burned with fury.

'Madam, your servant was resisting arrest by my representative and threatening violence by drawing his sword.

There is no illegality involved, but rest assured, he will be buried according to the rites of our Holy Mother Church. You may prepare to resume your journey. May I offer you some refreshments before you go?'

'No thank you, sir, I do not require anything.' I walked back to the entrance and a soldier stepped forward to lift the tent flap for me. Outside, I found my party waiting anxiously. 'It is all right, we can continue. But first, we must wait for an escort provided by the Duke of Norfolk.'

I whispered to Joan, 'It is best that we do not discuss anything other than everyday matters from now on and do not express any opinions about anything! But rest assured I will avenge our guard.'

'Very well, my lady, but will our man be buried with the proper rites?'

'Yes, Norfolk says so.' I mounted my horse and waited impatiently for Norfolk's "escort".

Finally, the escort arrived, and I was pleased to see that they looked like new recruits, not battle-hardened veterans. I hoped they would be easy to manipulate. How fortunate that the Duke of Norfolk seemed to have such a low opinion of women!

After a short and uneventful journey, we sighted the city of York. We pressed on because I was desperate to reach the castle by nightfall. There would be plenty of time for rest when we arrived. We arrived when it was almost completely dark. I led the party in so that I could reassure the gatekeeper. His warm welcome caused tears to form in my eyes and I was pleased to see that my rooms were prepared.

At last, after greeting all the household staff, arranging accommodation for Norfolk's soldiers, ensuring that everything was in order and visiting the chapel, I was able to retire to my rooms and call Joan to attend me.

'Well, Joan, I hope your reunion with Ranulf was satisfactory!' Her smile was my answer. 'Would you ask a servant to bring wine and food to us? You look as if you need something to revive you too, Joan, and then you can spend the rest of the evening with your beloved!'

'Thank you, my lady, but I keep thinking of our poor guard felled by that monster's axe.'

'I have been to the chapel to pray for his soul. He died only because he was doing his duty by trying to protect us. Do not worry, Joan, I hope to take revenge for his death. Fortunately, the Duke of Norfolk thinks I am practically illiterate, and he will not be overly suspicious that I might write or read messages. However, I feel sure that we will be closely watched because I think they suspect that Richard might attempt to contact me now that I am back up here.'

'What will you do now, my lady?'

'I will behave as if nothing is wrong. We will follow a normal routine and be polite and considerate to those boys Norfolk has sent. Now drink up your wine, Joan, and off you go. I will not call you early tomorrow.'

I found it very hard to sleep that night. It still felt strange to be here without my husband, and images of blood and the scene in Norfolk's tent repeated themselves in my mind.

I slept late the next morning but managed to get myself washed and almost dressed without Joan's help. I put on a plain kirtle and gown, but as usual, I could not fix my headdress securely. Finally, I decided to forget the boxy headdress which was now in fashion again due to Queen Jane's influence and just twisted my hair into a long plait. I was just about to venture downstairs when Joan appeared.

'Tamsin, my lady, you are a married lady. You know you cannot appear with all your hair showing!'

'No, I realise that I should not, but it seemed so silly that I could not even dress myself without your help when I managed perfectly well in Cornwall.'

'That was all a long time ago, my lady, and much has changed. I will send for your breakfast, and then the steward has asked to see you.'

'When I have dealt with the most pressing estate matters, I should like to ride over to Lord and Lady Metcalfe's manor. I can hardly wait to see Alice again!'

'Very well, my lady. Shall I send a messenger to see if they can receive you this afternoon?'

'Yes, but please try to do it in front of one of those soldiers and make it a verbal message.'

'You want them to think that you can hardly write your letters?'

'Yes, Joan. I fear we shall have to be very careful.'

The morning was spent with the steward, signing documents under the watchful eye of a soldier. I congratulated myself because I knew I was a fast reader and under the guise of carefully writing my name I hastily scanned as much as I could. To add realism, I asked him to read out some sections of the text. If the steward wondered about my behaviour, he was too polite to comment.

When the messenger returned with a verbal message to say that I was welcome to visit the manor at my convenience, I was relieved that Sir Nicholas had not sent a written note which of course I would be "unable to read".

We rode to Scarby Manor in the early afternoon accompanied by two soldiers, and I was delighted to see Alice standing between her aunt and uncle. I leapt from my saddle and ran to her, but instinct slowed me down. What if she did not know who I was or, worse, was frightened of me?

As I approached carefully, Alice surveyed me from head to foot. To give her the chance to observe me further, I concentrated on greeting Lord and Lady Metcalfe who invited us in. Mindful that I must keep the soldiers sweet, I asked for ale to be sent out for them.

Sir Nicholas retired to his study, as he said, 'To give you two ladies a chance to discuss your womanly news.' Thankfully, he said this in the hearing of the soldiers who were now distracted by a game of cards.

I managed to push the door almost closed, noticing that the soldiers were ignoring me. Elinor Metcalfe quietly asked why I had brought the men with me. Hastily, I whispered a quick recap of the main events of the last two days.

'So that bullying fool, Norfolk, is responsible for them?'

'Yes, Elinor, but they are much better mannered than some of his men, scarcely old enough to shave, and I must keep them in good humour. Norfolk thinks that I can barely write my name, that I am stupid and so I do not constitute any threat. I intend to maintain this fiction for as long as possible.'

'Ah, so that is why a verbal message arrived from you. Sir Nicholas said we should reply in kind because you must have your reasons for not writing as usual.'

'Thanks be to God that he did, or the soldiers might wonder why a woman known to be illiterate would receive a written message from close relatives!'

I turned to Alice and dug into my bag. 'Look, sweeting, I've brought some pretty ribbons for your hair.' She toddled up to me and it was all I could do to stop myself grabbing and embracing her.

'Alice, this is your lady mother who has come a very long way to see you,' said Elinor.

Alice turned her face up to me and regarded me solemnly with Richard's blue eyes. 'Mama,' she said.

I got down on the floor to her level and tied one of the ribbons in her hair. 'There now, you look beautiful!' It was true. Alice's features were regular, her hair light gold and her smile very sweet. For a second, I wanted to burst into tears because Richard was not there to see her too.

Elinor must have picked up my thoughts because she turned and whispered to me. 'Richard has seen her! He was here about one month ago, but he could only stay a short time. He picked up a few provisions and clothes and was gone again. Do not worry, nobody knows he was here except one of the servants, who will never speak about it.'

'Did he say anything or give you clue about where he was going?'

'He said nothing about it. He said that if we did not know then we would be safe.'

'He said much the same to me when I saw him last.' I swallowed hard and turned to Alice to distract myself.

She was now attempting to put a ribbon in her doll's hair. 'Let me help you, darling. Bring the poppet over to me.' She went to fetch it and, returning with it, sat herself down in my lap, holding out the doll to me.

'Elinor, I cannot thank you and Sir Nicholas enough for your good care of Richard's daughter. It is clear she is happy and well looked after. May I ask you to take care of her a little longer? The current situation is dangerous, and I do not know yet what the future holds.'

'We should be delighted, Tamsin. I was a little afraid when I heard you had returned to the castle that you would arrive and demand your child back.'

'Much as I miss Alice, I believe that children need stability, routine and a feeling of safety. She is happy here and I think that when she is older, she will understand why I cannot have her with me now.'

'Of course, it is normal for the daughters of noble houses to be sent away to other aristocratic houses to learn the skills they will need to run a great house. However, if Richard is declared a traitor, we know that all his titles and lands will revert to the Crown, so Alice will not be expected to do this,' said Lady Metcalfe.

'I intend to teach Alice as much as I know, and I hope that she will one day attract a husband who will want her for herself and not for lands, titles, or riches,' I said.

'Do you plan to return to Cornwall if the worst happens, Tamsin?'

'I think I will have no alternative.'

'You could come and make your home with us. When I married, I brought lands and property with me which are not connected to the Allerthorpe inheritance. The king cannot confiscate those. Also, Sir Nicholas has not been involved in any of the rebellions. Perhaps he will be allowed to keep his own title so Alice will still be from a good family which would make her a more attractive prospect in the marriage market!'

'That is a very kind offer, Elinor. I will think about it,' I said.

We talked for the rest of the afternoon until, at last, one of the soldiers poked his head through the door and asked a servant to see if I was ready to leave, as twilight was fast approaching. I could tell that Lady Metcalfe was about to tell him to mind his manners, but I hushed her and demurely answered that of course we would leave soon.

It was hard to drag myself away from Alice but at least I did not have to act a role for the soldiers. What was more natural than a mother being distraught at leaving her only child?

On the ride back to the castle, to my amazement, one of the soldiers said gruffly, 'Your ladyship, do not distress yourself. I am sure that the Duke of Norfolk would expect a mother to make several visits to such a young child. We will be happy to accompany you on another such expedition.'

Hastily, I turned my big tear-stained eyes on him and said innocently, 'Oh, do you think so? What a kind man the Duke must be!'

CHAPTER 24

A week went by and the weather worsened. Snow covered the ground, and it was difficult for us to keep warm in the draughty castle. Freezing winds from the east hammered at the walls and snow was driven in through the arrow slits. Still, I heard nothing from Richard and still I did not know where he was. My wild plans to somehow contact him failed because of Norfolk's guards. No matter where I went, one of them would appear silently, and any messages that arrived for me were read by their captain. The only place in which I could be sure of privacy was my bedchamber.

One afternoon, I managed to arrange for Hilda to enter my bedchamber with clean linen because I wanted to find out how she was settling in to castle life. I told her to sit down and was relieved to discover that she seemed happy.

'What happened when your convent was dissolved, Hilda?'

'The abbess and the professed nuns took pensions as there was no room for them anywhere else. I was very worried about the oldest ones. Some had not lived outside since the last century and they were feeble and confused. They headed for St Albans, but I fear some may have perished by now.' There were tears in her eyes as she continued.

'I went on to London as a servant to a group who had not taken final vows. When we reached London, nobody wanted me, and I nearly starved to death until I was rescued by a kind priest who employed me as a servant. I then travelled to Lincoln with his household, but the priest died of a fever there, so I went on the road to the North, surviving by begging until I joined the train of a knight as a laundry assistant. I remembered the name Allerthorpe and left the knight's train to find you, but then I got caught up in a large mob who were intending to rob your castle. The rest you know, your ladyship.'

'Oh Hilda, I am so sorry to hear of your suffering. You must stay with me no matter what happens. I will always find you work somehow.'

Later, I was sitting reading and Joan was sewing, both as close to the fire as we could get safely, when we heard a noise downstairs. We looked at each other.

'I should go and see what is happening.'

'Surely you will be called if you are needed, my lady?'

I did not want to rise from my warm chair but felt that I should investigate. I could now hear men shouting at each other. Pulling my fur wrap closer, I hurried towards the source of the disturbance.

I could see several of Norfolk's guards holding up lengths of dress fabric while one was holding onto a thin young man. When the young man saw me, he called out: 'My lady, I was just delivering your goods when these ruffians demanded to search my cart. Look, they have unwrapped all your fabrics and they are already muddy from that fellow's boots!' he said, pointing angrily.

I was stunned, I had not ordered any materials and I did not recall seeing them before. Could somebody have sent me a gift? But who? Suddenly it flashed into my head: could it be Richard? Was there a message for me hidden somewhere in the folds of cloth? If so, I thought, watching the soldiers shaking out the materials, it will be discovered before I have read it.

'Pray, please stop disordering the fabrics. They will be quite ruined,' I said, pretending to look horrified, and indeed the floor was already covered in melted snow and mud. 'I have been impatient for these to arrive.'

'Have you indeed, my lady?' said the captain of the guards. With a sinking feeling in my stomach, I saw that he held a small packet in his hands. 'What is this?'

'It must be the needles,' I said demurely. 'Please do not drop them on the floor.'

There was a tearing noise. 'This is not a packet of needles, my lady. I ask you again, what is this?'

'I have no idea and I cannot see what you are holding.'

'It appears to be a message from your husband, the disgraced Earl of Allerthorpe.'

'From my husband, are you sure? Give it to me and I will take it to the steward. He will help me read it and it may contain instructions about estate matters anyway.'

'Madam, do not play the innocent with me. I will read your message to you now.' The message the captain read out was short. ''Thorsby Copse, midnight, Friday.' Put this fellow in the dungeon, I will question him further.'

'But I know nothing. I have no idea how that message got into the packages.' Protesting loudly and casting desperate looks at me, the cart driver was dragged away.

'Really, Captain, is this entirely necessary? The dungeons are in a terrible condition and have not been used for the last fifty years as far as I know. As for that message, it must be a stupid joke, intended for someone else. I do not make assignations to meet people in the grounds late at night!'

'My lady, I can assure you, it is entirely necessary. This message may, as you say, be a prank, or it could be an attempt to contact you by your fugitive, traitor husband. In the meantime, you will be confined to your chambers while I seek advice from the Duke of Norfolk.'

'How dare you refer to my husband as a traitor? He has not been convicted of anything.'

'When we catch him, I believe he will be. There is already much evidence against him.'

'Oh, do you mean evidence that has been tortured out of poor souls?'

'Madam, watch your tongue or you may find yourself in your own dungeon.'

Shaking with fury, I was escorted to my chambers. Joan met me, wide-eyed, at the door. As I entered, I heard two of the guards settle themselves down outside my door. Using a mixture of gestures, I managed to indicate that we should be careful what we said as the guards would be listening.

'There has been a terrible misunderstanding, Joan! A mischievous person has sent a foolish message to me wrapped up with my order from the draper's workshop in York. It is quite ridiculous, but the captain of the guards thinks that it is a secret message from my husband asking me to meet him in Thorsby Copse on Friday at midnight!' Fortunately, Joan seemed to have understood the circumstances.

She spoke clearly. 'Well, fancy that, my lady! How could the earl have known that you placed that order? Indeed, I remember it well. Somebody is teasing you.'

'I am exceedingly displeased. The men dropped the fabrics on the floor, which is splattered with snow and mud!'

'We must hope that the cloth is still usable, my lady, or how shall we make your dresses?'

'I think I shall need to lie down and rest after this. I shall have to hope that the captain soon realises his mistake, as it is most inconvenient to be confined to my chambers.' I said as loudly as possible.

'Very well, my lady. I shall help you onto your bed and leave you in peace,' said Joan.

We quietly left the room and withdrew to the privy, which opened off the main chamber.

'Joan, I do not know what to do. They will be waiting for him on Friday night,' I whispered.

'If you do not appear, he will know something is wrong. There is a good view of Thorsby Copse from Larch Hill. Surely he would not arrive without checking that you were there and alone first,' she whispered back.

'Of course, why did I not think of that? I feel calmer now. Thank you, Joan. But wait, I forgot, the captain of the guards has taken the cart driver to the dungeon for questioning.'

'My lady, I think it likely that the packet was slipped in before the cart was loaded. The merchant will not drive his own stock around the country. He will have employed one of the many local men and he will know nothing. The message would have been slipped into the cart while his back was turned.'

'Yes, that is likely. We must hope that the driver really knows nothing and cannot incriminate Richard. I also hope they do not question him roughly. We must continue to pretend that I ordered the fabric myself.'

We padded silently back, and I lay down on the bed to wait for events to unfold.

Joan asked loudly, 'My lady, may I bring you some wine?'

'Yes, please, Joan. I would like it heated today.'

Joan tried to open the door, but it was locked. 'Kindly open this door, my lady needs some wine!' she shouted.

The door was opened by one of the younger guards. Joan gave an audible sniff as she exited. 'Does your mother know that your duties include locking up defenceless women who have done nothing wrong?' she demanded. The reply was muffled as the door closed, and there was silence.

Supper was brought to the door later and passed to Joan. With nothing further to do, we amused ourselves by cutting a paper pattern for a dress to be made from the unsolicited fabric.

The winter darkness fell early, and we loudly decided to get ready for bed. That was a terrible night which I remember well. I prayed fervently for God to protect Richard and all of us. Towards dawn, I drifted into an uneasy doze, to be woken by a loud hammering at the door.

I heard Joan speaking quietly at the door. 'My lady is still asleep. I will not have her woken up yet unless there is a fire!' Out of my half-closed eye, I saw the door close again and heard heavy footsteps retreating.

I could see beams of early sunlight reflecting off the polished surfaces of my jewellery box. The weather was better today but I did not feel heartened. Instead, I was full of dread. What was going to happen now?

As I breakfasted, Joan said that the captain of the guards had been demanding to see me. 'He says he has received a message from the Duke of Norfolk concerning you, my lady,' she said loudly. 'I told him that you would not see him until nine o'clock.'

'Thank you, Joan. Of course, I must say my prayers first, but I will be pleased to see him after.'

'It is getting harder to play the placid, ignorant woman,' I whispered, gesturing that Joan should follow me to the privy. 'But I must let him think that all I care about is having my cloth back. I shall act as if I think that message is purely a prank by some bored apprentice or suchlike.'

'Now, my lady, what shall you wear today?' Joan said after we had crept back into the main chamber.

'Such a difficult decision, I do hope the captain will let me have my parcels today. I am so short of dresses!' I said loudly.

When I was ready, Joan knocked on the door and we were escorted downstairs to meet the captain. 'The Duke himself has given orders that you will go to Thorsby Copse on Friday at midnight accompanied by us.'

'Will that not be a waste of time?' I answered demurely. 'This is sure to be a hoax played by some silly apprentice.'

'You will follow the Duke's instructions, or your waiting woman will find herself in the dungeon.'

'This is a little excessive, Captain, but since the Duke requests it, I suppose I had better comply. Have you now released the cart driver?'

'That is not your business, but yes, he has been released as he had nothing useful to tell us.'

'I am glad to hear it. Now, if you have finished searching my materials, I would be grateful if you could send them to my chamber. I am eager to start sewing. Will you now remove the guards from my door as it is most inconvenient to be locked up.'

'Yes madam, but you will remain on the castle premises until Friday night. If you wish to take exercise in the grounds, you will be accompanied by the guards, and you may not visit your daughter.'

'I shall obey the Duke's commands, of course,' I said with a straight face.

'The fabrics will be sent up to you shortly. Now please excuse me as I have many pressing matters to attend to.'

I sailed off sedately followed by Joan. 'Pompous arsehole,'

I muttered to her.

'Yes, indeed, your ladyship.'

'I am going for a walk around the castle so that I can check that everything is functioning as it should. Come with me, Joan.'

I noticed that the mud and melted snow had been cleared from the hall floor and fresh rush matting put down. In the kitchens, everything appeared normal, and the servants seemed cheerful, but when I met the steward, he wore a harassed expression.

'I am glad to see your ladyship looking well after the unpleasant scenes yesterday. I realise this is a difficult time for you, but do you know how long the Duke's guards are staying? The feeding of them and their horses is putting a strain on resources, especially after the rebels took over the castle last year and depleted much of our stores.'

'I am sorry, but I cannot say exactly. It depends on the Duke of Norfolk's wishes and on what happens in the county. If there is more trouble, perhaps they will be called back to join Norfolk's army. I suggest you apply to the captain and explain the situation. Perhaps he will see fit to pay the estate for their keep?'

The steward looked around anxiously before he leaned down and whispered to me. 'I have heard that a lord called Francis Bigod is trying to provoke another uprising in the north because he feels that Robert Aske and his friends have betrayed the cause by agreeing terms with the king. There could be more trouble very soon.'

'Very well, Master Steward, thank you for informing me. If you should obtain more news about what is happening in our area, would you please pass it to me immediately?'

'Of course, my lady, you can depend on me.'

'Thank you, Master Steward.' I was pleased to see that he

looked more cheerful now. I headed for the stables and the brewery building, but as soon as I approached an outer door, two guards appeared by my side. 'Do not worry yourselves, I am merely going out to the stables to check on the welfare of my horses, but you are welcome to accompany me, of course,' I said calmly.

All appeared normal in the stables. I made a quick visit to my horse to give her a rather shrivelled carrot and then I went to look at the army horses. They were larger than usual and did not have a lot of space in their stalls. I felt rather sorry for them, being trapped here, but the weather was still ferociously cold. At least they were warm and dry.

When we returned to my chamber, I saw that the fabrics had been delivered. Joan went to examine them, and I watched as she shook out the folds.

'These are beautiful, my lady. Whoever...' I held my finger to my lips to hush her as I was unsure if there was anybody outside my door.

'Yes, they are very fine and just as I remembered them,' I said loudly for the benefit of any listeners. 'We will start work after dinner. I think the yellow silk would be best for the kirtle.'

The materials were certainly lovely and close to what I would have chosen myself. It had to be Richard who had organised this; nobody apart from Joan and perhaps Margaret knew my taste so well. I remembered how somewhat unusually for a man, he would always pass comments on new gowns and even suggest colours he thought would suit me. It was wonderful to have something that Richard has chosen for me even though it had really been a method of concealing a secret message.

CHAPTER 25

Inevitably, Friday morning arrived, and the captain of the guards asked to see me alone.

'You will be leaving the castle about half an hour before midnight, accompanied by me and all the guards. You will enter the clearing by yourself while we hide in the undergrowth. Your maid will also accompany us. She will remain with the soldiers. If the earl approaches and you attempt to warn him, my men have orders to slit her throat immediately.'

I was horrified. 'This is very melodramatic, sir. Firstly, the earl will not appear because the message is a piece of mischief making, and secondly, why would I attempt to warn a traitor to the Crown? I would then be committing treason myself! Surely you cannot think me a traitor, Captain?'

'No, my lady, but you must understand that your husband is a dangerous man who consorts with those who rebel against the king.'

'I cannot believe that, sir, but I will do as you ask.'

Shocked and angry, I went up to walk on the castle battlements. I must calm down before I saw Joan. As I climbed the narrow steps towards the battlements, I was not surprised to see one of the guards appear behind me. The view from the top was bleak but I hardly felt the cold wind because of my anger.

'Do not worry, I will not fly away,' I said to the shivering soldier.

After a time, my breathing steadied, and I felt more

controlled. I would say nothing to Joan and if by any chance Richard did appear, I would say or do nothing that might endanger her. I reasoned that I owed loyalty to Joan, who I had known since childhood and who was here through no fault of her own, whereas Richard appeared to have chosen to join the rebels and put himself and us in danger without my agreement. Once I had acknowledged this, I felt ready to return into the castle. I would be strong and determined, and I had not forgotten our murdered guard. I would find a way to exact revenge on the man with the scarred face.

Back in the castle, I realised that I was extremely cold and hastened to the fire in my chamber, where I found Joan absorbed in her sewing. 'My lady, you look frozen. Where have you been? What did the captain want?'

'Joan, I will answer your questions in order!' I said loudly for the benefit of any listeners. 'Yes, I am cold because I went for some air on the battlements, and the captain wanted to tell me the arrangements for tonight. I am to accompany him and the guards to Thorsby Copse tonight. You will be in attendance too in case I need anything. Of course, it will all be very boring, and we shall come home again freezing cold and nothing will have happened, but nevertheless we must do as the Duke of Norfolk requires.'

'I will make sure your warmest cloak is ready for you to wear, my lady,' said Joan.

'Thank you. Now let us resume our sewing, I do so love stitching, and I am anxious to wear my new dress!' Joan smothered a giggle.

As we sat there, with Joan stitching away and me tacking seams for her to sew, the day passed, supper was served, and eventually I realised that that it was now time to dress for our expedition. Joan had to help me more than usual because I felt sick with fear.

The horses were already saddled when we arrived downstairs shrouded in cloaks, and both of us carried our daggers within our skirts, although I could not see how they would be useful. The moon was full. Of course, that was why Richard had picked tonight. We would not need lanterns that could give us away. I prayed that he would not come, or if he did, that he would see that I was not alone.

Soon we arrived at the designated clearing. We secured our horses and I walked alone to the centre of the clearing, asking Joan to remain behind with the guards. Fortunately, she accepted this and did not insist on accompanying me further. I could hear the soft noises of night creatures, scuffling in the undergrowth. I waited quietly as instructed. Was there anything I could do to warn him? Nothing came to mind. I was stuck here as helpless bait and if I made a wrong move, Joan would die horribly.

There was a rustling in the undergrowth, and I froze, but it was only a bird disturbed from its roosting. How much longer would I have to stand here?

There was another noise, a cracking of a twig on the ground and the shape of a man was outlined in through the trees. Mindful of the decision I had made earlier, I managed to control myself and not shout a warning.

The captain had risen to his feet. 'Richard, Earl of Allerthorpe, you are under arrest for treason and plotting against the king's Majesty,' he shouted.

Suddenly, there was chaos, as all the guards rushed forwards and disappeared into the woodland. Joan and I were left standing there alone. We embraced each other and waited. Once the crashing noise of heavily armed men had retreated, there was just silence. All the woodland creatures must have been hiding in terror.

About half an hour later, the captain and the guards arrived back. He looked furious. 'The traitor got away for now, but I have every hope that others of the Duke of Norfolk's men will apprehend him soon. You ladies mount your horses we will return to the castle as there is nothing more to be done here tonight.'

As we climbed back on the horses, I realised that I had a pounding headache. Had that been Richard himself in the woods? Or someone else, perhaps a poacher? Whoever it was had moved very quickly. Perhaps he had a fast horse waiting nearby. I could feel tears in my eyes, and it took all my control not to cry openly. The guards seemed disappointed to be cheated of their prey and nobody spoke on the return journey.

When we arrived back at the castle, the captain spoke to me. 'You did not try to warn your husband, my lady.'

'No, because I could not see how it could have been him. I believe you frightened off a poacher, sir.'

'If he was a poacher, he took care to bring a fast horse with him. Most poachers travel on their two feet to avoid detection, my lady.' With that, the captain turned and clanked off to join his men.

I was relieved to reach the safety of my chamber at last. Joan fetched my store of oil of lavender to massage my forehead and I started to feel better. We whispered together in the privy.

'Do you think that was the earl himself?'

'I do not know, Joan. It might have been, but I am glad that whoever it was escaped safely. These men are vicious.' She had no idea how close to death she had been.

'Oh, they are not so bad, my lady. They are only doing their jobs and they are always polite to me.'

'I am very tired, and I am going to bed now, but my head is

better,' I said. 'I do so want to see Alice again.'

The next morning, we left after morning prayers to visit my daughter. Fortunately, the captain had agreed, provided we were accompanied by two guards. It was a beautiful morning, and it was wonderful to be able to ride out again, even though we were still being watched. However, last night's events were still imprinted on my mind and I found it hard to indulge in my usual chatter with Joan.

We stayed to dinner at Scarby Manor and Sir Nicholas Metcalfe arranged for the guards to be fed in the kitchen, which gave us the chance to speak more freely about last night's events, although we kept our voices low.

'Did you see anything that made you think the person you saw could have been Richard?' asked Sir Nicholas.

'No, the woodland and undergrowth was so dense, and the person was wearing dark clothes and some sort of head covering – I cannot be certain that it was him.'

'I think there are those who may be meeting in secret and plotting more rebellions. Perhaps you encountered somebody else up to no good, but it is difficult to get any reliable news,' said Sir Nicholas. 'Many poorer people are struggling to survive. We have not raised our rents, but others are not so forbearing. You might have seen a poacher trying to catch a rabbit for the pot. There is a lot of hunger locally.'

'What do people say? Will there be more uprisings?' I asked.

'Tamsin, you must not repeat what I say as it could be interpreted as treason. People are becoming increasingly unhappy about the king's religious changes. Many still believe that the Pope is the only real head of the Church. People say that just because he has made himself Head of the Church it does not mean that what the king decrees is the will of God.'

Sir Nicholas sighed. 'Worse is that people now seem to be blaming the king himself rather than evil advisors, since Robert Aske's negotiations seem to have come to nothing. There are increasingly rumours that the contents of dissolved religious houses are being used to enrich greedy men. Also, it is looking likely that many more abbeys will be closed, including some of our most important ones. I cannot see how the situation can be resolved, especially with so many people who used to make a living on the land finding themselves living in poverty. The whole of the North is like a tinder box, ready to ignite, and I do not think it will take much to spark yet more rebellion.'

Elinor Metcalfe coughed loudly, and one of the guards appeared in the doorway. They must have finished their dinners.

We fell to talking about Alice, her new tooth and all her latest achievements. I sat full of pride as I heard how she could build towers from bricks and how happy she was.

'Indeed, she hardly ever cries. She is such as sunny child, and strong too. She will wake from her nap soon,' said Elinor. 'It is most considerate of her to sleep for an hour so that we could talk without interruption! The nurse will bring her down when she awakes.'

'Elinor, are you still happy to take care of her? I feel she is secure here and I do not know what the future holds. My position is precarious.'

'Certainly, we will be happy for her to live with us for as long as you see fit. You need have no anxieties about Alice – we love having our niece living with us!'

Alice was brought down bleary-eyed by her nurse, but she soon seemed to finish waking up, and watching her playing helped to revive my spirits.

Leaving her later was very hard, as was waving farewell to

Lord and Lady Metcalfe. But on the way home, Joan and I occupied ourselves by talking about Alice, who was truly the most marvellous and forward child in the whole wide world!

On our arrival back at Allerthorpe Castle, the captain asked to see me. 'The Duke of Norfolk has sent an order that you must go to York.'

'But why? I am not disloyal, and I have had no part in my husband's activities!'

'It is not for me to say, my lady. I have my orders, which must be carried out. You will make ready to travel to York tomorrow at first light.'

'Am I to be allowed a waiting woman or must I go alone?'

'The order specifies you only. It does not mention anyone else.'

'Does it say for how long I must stay in York?'

'No, madam.'

With a heavy heart, I went up the stairs to tell Joan of my news. Predictably, she was horrified. 'My lady, you cannot go alone. All those rough men, and who will look after your clothes?'

'I think my clothes may be the least of my concerns, Joan. I am most worried about being accused of treason or of being forced in some horrible scheme to entrap Richard.'

'How long will you be away, Tamsin—I mean, my lady?'

'I do not know. Please help me to choose practical clothes and supplies that I should take. There is no point in making a fuss about this. It will not change anything, Joan.'

I was ready to ride for York at dawn. The captain looked startled and not long out of bed when I appeared, for it was still very early. 'I see no point in delaying, sir. Are my guards ready to leave?'

'They will be with you soon. I shall order your horse to be brought from the stables and ensure that the panniers are attached.'

Soon, it was time for me to leave. I embraced a weeping Joan. 'There is no need for tears, I will be back soon enough. But if anything should happen to me, can I be assured that you will take care of Alice's welfare?'

'Yes, my lady, I swear it. Alice shall be safe. I will take her myself if anything should happen and find the means to get us both to your mother's house in Cornwall.'

'Thank you, Joan. I knew I could depend on you.' With that, I rode off into the dawn, accompanied by four guards.

CHAPTER 26

We stopped for dinner at a wayside inn, where I was treated with great respect when the guards announced my identity. I wondered what the landlord would think if he knew that I was really a lady under suspicion, being forcibly escorted to the Duke of Norfolk. When he asked me the purpose of my journey, I said merely that I was visiting the Duke.

We arrived in York mid-afternoon. The streets seemed quiet and there were many soldiers in Norfolk's livery in the streets. The city had a neglected air about it. There was much rubbish lying in the stinking alleys and the market seemed scruffier than I remembered from my first visit on the way to Allerthorpe Castle. We proceeded up to the castle, which had a dilapidated look about it, and the guards presented the message from the Duke to the sentries at the entrance.

The inner walls of the castle looked damp and there were cracks in the brickwork. I was taken to a small chamber on the second floor and told to wait. The chamber was furnished with two chairs and a table which was covered with documents and rolls of paper, some of which looked ancient.

I sat down on one of the chairs and looked out of the crudely cut window. I could see the great stone wall of the keep. The sky was grey and heavy, a complete contrast to yesterday's weather. I heard heavy footsteps, and seconds later, the door was flung open. In walked the Duke of Norfolk and two secretaries carrying paper and ink.

'Ah, the Countess of Allerthorpe. Welcome to York Castle, I hope you have been enjoying the view. May I offer you some wine?'

'Yes, please, some wine would be welcome. The journey was most tiring,' I said as pathetically as possible.

'I have a few questions to ask you. First, have you seen your husband or heard anything from him since the night that he managed to evade my guards?'

'No, my lord, I have not seen him or had any message from him. I have no idea where he is, and I do not know if he is even alive,' I said.

'My informant tells me that you thought the man who was almost apprehended several days ago was probably a poacher, is that correct?'

'Yes, my lord. Why would my husband return secretly to his own castle?'

'I ask the questions here, madam!' shouted the Duke. 'I do not trust your protestations of innocence in the matter of your lord's whereabouts.'

'I really know nothing about his exploits, or I would find and berate him for his foolish behaviour, which threatens my future and that of his daughter, not to mention his household and tenants!'

'You use a convincing tone, madam, but I am not yet persuaded. You will remain in York in close confinement until such time as I see fit.'

'Excuse me, my lord, what crime is the lady accused of?' asked one of the secretaries, who had been scribbling busily.

'The Countess of Allerthorpe is suspected of plotting against the Crown, Master Rigby. I believe her behaviour has been treasonous.' It was quite horrifying to hear this said and I was immediately angry and frightened, but I realised that perhaps it would be better to say nothing more than another denial.

'I am not a traitor and I have not plotted against the State, and nor would I wish to.' I spoke slowly so that the secretary would transcribe my words accurately. The Duke opened the door and roared down the stairs for guards to escort me to a secure chamber.

Down some slippery steps we went, and I began to worry that I would be confined in some dark dungeon. Fortunately, the guards paused at the first floor and led me down a long and dank corridor. A door with a large padlock hanging from it was opened and I was pushed in.

'Wait, may I have some ale, and some water to wash in please, sir,' I asked the biggest of the guards.

'Yes, my lady, I will order it to be sent up. You are to be confined as befits a noble lady. A fire will be set for you shortly and your goods brought,' said the guard politely. The door crashed shut behind me and I heard bolts slide into place.

It was freezing in the chamber. A small window opening was covered with cracked horn and behind the inadequate covering were thick bars. I hoped the weather would not deteriorate. The door rattled again, and a girl entered carrying a jug and a cup. She was followed by a young man with my panniers around his neck, carrying a basket of kindling and another jug which presumably contained water. I sat down on one of the chairs and surveyed my new home. A narrow bed, a table, two chairs and a chest. On the top of the chest was a cracked stoneware bowl for washing. The floor was covered in rushes which thankfully appeared clean.

When the fire was made and the ale poured, I was left alone. A chamber pot had been placed in the corner and I was grateful that I would not need to squat on the rushes. Time seemed to pass very slowly, made worse by the fact that I had nothing to do other than read my little Book of Hours and pick out some of the cleaner and shorter rushes and weave them into little mats. However, nobody had searched me, though doubtless my luggage would have been, and I still had my dagger hidden in my skirts. Some hours later, there was a rattle at the door, which opened to admit one of the guards.

'Your ladyship, the Duke of Norfolk bids me say that you will be accompanying him on his journey north to Carlisle. You should be ready to leave at six o'clock tomorrow morning.'

'Why is the Duke going to Carlisle?'

'I believe it is all part of his campaign to restore order in the North, my lady.' The guard left the room and shortly afterwards, the girl who had brought my ale reappeared with a bowl of pottage and a hunk of bread for my supper. I seized the opportunity to talk to her.

'What is your name, girl, and how old are you?'

'I am Mags, my lady, and I am twelve years old,' she said, looking at me with surprise. Perhaps she was not used to prisoners asking her name.

'Mags, I get little news and I do not know what is happening in the outside world. Are there uprisings in York or anywhere else?'

'My lady, I am not supposed to talk to the prisoners, but yes, there has been some trouble in the area. But the Duke and his soldiers have caught and executed many of the rebels and it is quiet now. They say he will leave for Carlisle tomorrow and do the same thing there.' Her expression was glum as she gave me this news.

'Thank you, Mags. I do not wish to get you in to any trouble so I will not ask anything else.'

Mags was silent for a few seconds and then she burst out, 'It is awful, my lady, so much killing, and people are so frightened. I do not understand it because I heard that the king had pardoned all the rebels at Christmas.'

'Yes, indeed, Mags, it is all very difficult to understand. We must hope that the trouble passes swiftly, and all is calm again soon.'

'Yes, my lady.' She curtsied and looked at me nervously. 'Please do not tell anybody that I spoke to you. I have a mother at home who depends on my wages.'

'Mags, I will say nothing of what you said. You have my word.'

After a fitful sleep, I got myself up at five o'clock, it was easy to mark time from the bells of the Minster Church. I had some difficulty with tying up the laces on my gowns because my fingers were stiff with cold, but I was thankful that I had packed my simplest and warmest clothes. After a quick breakfast of ale and bread brought by Mags, I was ready.

At six, I was escorted down the stairs to the courtyard, where my horse stood snorting in the freezing air. Looking at the blue sky, I was hopeful that it would warm up later. My panniers were attached to the horse, and I was told to wait for the Duke of Norfolk's party. My heart sank as I beheld a long column of fully armed soldiers; it looked as if the Duke was expecting a struggle.

Finally, we were off, and I had the chance to look around. I saw few people on the streets other than those opening their shop fronts. People seemed to be deliberately ignoring us. Any looks directed at us were unfriendly or fearful. Soon we had left York and were now in the desolate looking countryside. Such settlements that I saw had ancient dwellings, no more than long wooden huts where people lived together with their animals. I wished ardently that the weather would warm up. Surely things would be better in the spring.

The grim journey continued. When we stopped for dinner, the Duke sent for me. 'I wish you to ride next to me in the front,' he said. 'I want people to see that I have the Countess of Allerthorpe as a prisoner.'

'I doubt anybody would be interested. I am not a prominent person in these parts.'

The Duke did not answer but merely laughed without humour. I curtsied and moved away to fetch my ration of pottage from the cook's cauldron.

As we set off again, I rode up to the front of the procession, where the Duke waved me to a place on his right. The men near him looked at me in an unfriendly manner and grudgingly moved to accommodate my horse. The ride seemed to go on for ever. My legs and back were aching, and still we went on. When darkness came, the way was lit by riders holding torches. At last, the Duke called a halt. We were in a small town, but I had no idea of its name.

'We will pitch camp here at Northallerton!' he shouted. I sat on my horse, unsure what to do, watching as the men rapidly erected numerous tents. Some disappeared into the nearby woods and reappeared with armfuls of branches and logs. Cauldrons were hung over fires which had just started to smoke.

A soldier appeared and told me to follow him. With great difficulty because of my stiff and aching limbs, I dismounted, and he led the horse. I found myself stumbling over small hillocks as I followed. Eventually, we arrived at a tent indistinguishable from the others save for a fluttering pennant bearing the Duke of Norfolk's arms where, to my surprise, I found Mags, the castle servant. The soldier ducked under the tent flap and threw my panniers on the ground.

'I will fetch us some food and drink,' said Mags, and she vanished out of the tent. I was left alone so I took the opportunity to look out and see what was happening. The fires of the soldiers seemed to be burning brightly now and I could smell roasting meat. The men all seemed very cheerful and there was much loud laughter as they passed jugs of ale around. I was not happy to see that the Duke of Norfolk's tent, a larger version of mine, was pitched next to me.

Mags reappeared in our tent carrying two bowls followed by a soldier carrying a jug. She had obviously charmed him into carrying it for her. I felt in my purse for a small coin which I handed to the man. 'No, madam, I reckon you need it more than me, being a prisoner and all that,' he said.

The bowls contained pottage again, but at least there were a few pieces of meat floating in it. I asked Mags why she had joined us.

'The Duke said that he needed a woman to attend a female prisoner of high rank,' she said, 'and the cook picked me. The Duke said that there would be extra money for me if I came, so I agreed.'

'I am sorry if you have been inconvenienced, Mags, but it is good to see a friendly face here.' We ate our food in companiable silence; the tent walls were thin, and I did not want to get Mags into trouble.

We were just finishing our ale when the jingle of spurs alerted me to the fact that somebody was approaching the tent. The Duke of Norfolk's head poked through the tent flap. 'Ah, all settled, I see. You keep a close on the lady, Mags, and if there is any trouble you need only to call the sentry out here.'

'Very well, sir,' said Mags quietly.

As no pot was provided, Mags and I needed to find somewhere to relieve ourselves. The guard followed us as we walked to the back of the camp.

'The soldiers will have dug latrines are over there,' said Mags, 'but they will not be suitable for ladies. We could take it in turns to go in the bushes.'

'What about that guard? I am not going in there with him watching!'

'I will ask the guard to face the other way and wait with him, but please, madam, do not make a mad bid for freedom. It will not succeed and will probably result in you being kept more closely and in worse conditions.'

'Do not worry, I have no intention of running off into this wild, dark place, Mags,' I said as I headed for the biggest bushes.

As we made our way back, I was amazed by the guard's ability to locate our tent in the dark. But, as Mags said, it was not very difficult to pick out the Duke of Norfolk's grand tent!

CHAPTER 27

After an uncomfortable night, punctuated by sounds of merry making followed by much shouting and singing, we were again up at dawn and ready to ride on. The Duke of Norfolk's face looked puffy in the morning light and I guessed that he had been drinking until late. When he saw me looking at him, he scowled and shouted at me. 'Today you shall see what the might of the Crown can achieve!' This was followed by another humourless laugh.

The weather seemed a little milder, but there was a slight mizzle in the air. 'Hope this stops soon, my lady, or we will be soaked through by the time we make camp tonight,' said Mags. I looked at her thin cloak. It did not look as if it would keep out the rain for long. 'When we stop for dinner, I will fetch out my spare cloak for you. The fabric is stronger and will keep out the wet.'

'Thank you, my lady, you are very kind.'

We rode on past more poor looking villages, until the Duke called a halt on a patch of woodland and I busied myself extracting my spare cloak from the panniers. It was a little long for Mags, but would do well enough while she was on horseback, and she seemed grateful.

Checking that nobody was in earshot, I said to Mags, 'It is a pity that many religious houses no longer exist as we could have sought hospitality in them.'

Mags looked scared. 'Yes, my lady, but best not to talk about that.'

After dinner, we passed yet another poor settlement, but this time a hideous sight met my eyes. There were many gibbets placed by the roadside, from which hung the bloated and decaying bodies of men and women. They looked like ordinary country people. Some were elderly and some scarce more than children.

I turned my face away and met the gaze of the Duke. 'This is what awaits all those who rebel against the Crown,' he said in a triumphant tone. 'Of course, the nobles who rebelled are beheaded, but the result is the same. Look carefully, my lady, and consider your options. Perhaps the king would be inclined to grant you mercy if you informed on your husband.' I was immediately furious, but it did not appear seemly to shout back at him in the presence of all those poor souls.

'As I have said before, I have no knowledge of the whereabouts of my husband, and I am entirely innocent of your preposterous assumptions.' I heard Mags gasp as the Duke rode towards me.

'Madam, you will mind your tongue!' he said as he grabbed the hair that had escaped my hood. He pulled back hard, and my scalp felt as though it was on fire. He pushed his face close to mine. 'You think you are so clever, but I am wise to your devious ways!' He released my head and rode off. I was conscious of many eyes staring at me. The Duke of Norfolk was known for his rough manners so perhaps they were not surprised.

We rode on in silence and when people had stopped watching me, I attempted to adjust my headdress, as my hair was now spilling out down my back. I did not know how far it was to Carlisle, but I suspected that there would be several more days of this hard riding. I prayed for fortitude and for help in maintaining control of myself.

After what seemed like an endless ride, we stopped at another piece of woodland and, as before, the camp was set up surprisingly quickly. The soldiers were certainly efficient. When we gained entrance to our tent, I watched until I saw the Duke walk away to confer with his troops.

Mags spoke first. 'Please be more careful, your ladyship. That is the man who helped to condemn his own niece, Anne Boleyn, to death. He is a bully without heart and what is worse, I overheard two soldiers discussing him. Apparently, he fears that the king may not trust him and so he is determined to kill every rebel to prove how loyal he is.'

'You should not listen to gossip, Mags, people always exaggerate.' However, I recalled that last year, Richard had said that Norfolk and Lord Cromwell hated each other. Norfolk despised Cromwell as the son of a blacksmith and thought that the king gave him too much power. Perhaps Cromwell had tried to undermine Norfolk to the king, and I knew that just as hunted animals at bay can be dangerous, a desperate man might be too.

That night, there seemed to be less of a holiday atmosphere and comparative peace fell on the camp. Perhaps even the battle-hardened soldiers had found the sight of so many ordinary looking citizens hanging dead beside the road rather unpalatable. After a meal of yet more pottage and a necessary trip to a clump of trees, we retired for the night. I felt that I was filthy from travelling, but I was so tired that I lay down on my allotted patch of ground without washing and fell asleep.

At about midnight, I woke up thinking I'd heard a disturbance, but all I could hear were the loud snores of the Duke of Norfolk from the neighbouring tent. I was just settling myself to go back to sleep when a hand suddenly covered my mouth. I was terrified. Was I going to be secretly murdered and explained away as an unfortunate death caused by an attempt to escape? It was very dark in the tent, but I could make out the shape of Mags snoring gently. I was trying to twist around to see my attacker when a familiar voice whispered in my ear.

'Tamsin, do not make a sound, or we may all die. I have come to rescue you!' But it was not the one voice I now longed to hear. It was not Richard. 'I will take my hand away if you promise not to make any sound,' said the man. 'Move your hand if you will be silent.' I waved my hand feebly.

'We are leaving now. I have a horse for you.' I grabbed my cloak as he pulled me up and out of the tent. I did not stop to think. Instinct took over; I wanted to be out of this camp, and I might have gone with the devil himself.

Outside, I nearly fell over a prone guard. The man dragged me along with a tight grip on my arm as we moved quietly through the dark. I could see very little as he led me away from the main camp into the adjacent woods. I knew only that he was taller than me. As we walked, he held branches back and pulled me up when I stumbled over tree roots. Then we came to a clearing, where another man waited with three horses. Standing close to an ancient oak tree for shelter, the mysterious man lit a torch.

I stepped back in shock my mysterious rescuer was none other than Edmund Boskeyn from Penwarne in Cornwall. 'I see you are as delighted as ever to encounter me, Tamsin!' He gave an exaggerated bow. 'Or should I say, your ladyship?' I regarded him steadily. This was no time for silly banter.

'If you are, as you say, "rescuing me" should we not leave this place immediately?' I was aware that my absence could be discovered at any moment.

'Why, yes, my lady. Before we flee, may I introduce my

friend, Stephen?' Feeling absurd, I curtsied politely to Master Stephen, who immediately led a horse over to me. 'Here we are, he is a calm animal and dependable. Allow me to assist you to mount.'

'Thank you,' I said politely, even though I did not need any assistance.

'I will lead as I know the area. Your ladyship next and Edmund last.'

We rode on through the night and I found I was drooping in the saddle as the first signs of daylight appeared. What had happened when my flight was discovered? Was Norfolk even now pounding Mags to a pulp to find out what had happened? Was the guard that I had stepped over now lying dead? I concentrated on keeping upright, while all the time listening for sounds of pursuit.

At last, we halted at a small village. Through the trees, I could see glimpses of the sea. We stopped at a medium-sized stone house. Feeling as though I was in a fog, I was half helped and half hauled off my horse by Edmund. Stephen took the horses around to the back of the house and Edmund knocked quietly on the door. It was opened by a young woman who appeared anxious.

'I was so worried, I thought you had been caught. I see you have succeeded in getting the lady. Come inside, please, we do not want to attract any attention.'

Inside was a comfortably but plainly furnished hall with a staircase leading up to a small gallery. I noticed that candles had been lit and a fire burned steadily.

'I will take this lady upstairs. You two may remove the mud from your boots. Please follow me, my lady.' I followed her up the wooden steps, taking care to hold the banister as my legs felt shaky. The woman led the way into a small bedchamber. 'I am Mary, and this is my house. I know who you are and what has happened, so you do not need to explain anything to me. I will bring up some water for you to wash, and some food and drink. We are about the same size, so I will bring you some a clean shift and some clothes from my chest. You can take your wet stuff off and I will see what can be done about it.'

'I cannot thank you enough, Mary. I am desperate to get out of these muddy garments and I have been unable to wash since I was imprisoned in York. May I ask where we are? I thought I caught sight of the sea.'

'You did indeed. This is Petyt, a small fishing village. You have no need to worry, you are safe here. I doubt the Duke of Norfolk even knows this place exists.'

True to her word, Mary returned with hot water and refreshments. I managed to get out of my wet clothes, wash myself, put on the clean shift and kirtle and drink some ale, but I could not tackle any food. My stomach felt as if it was clenched up tight. After making a neat pile of my muddy clothes, and remembering to remove my dagger from the pocket I had sewn into my skirts and hide it under the pillow, I lay down on the bed and slept.

Several hours later, I opened my eyes, wondering where I was. As I remembered, I sat bolt upright, but all was quiet downstairs, so I slumped down again. After a doze, I shook myself awake, washed my face and hands in what appeared to be a fresh bowl of water, and went to look out of the window.

There was the sea, and I could even hear the calls of seagulls in the distance. Perhaps I would be permitted to walk near it later. Turning back from the window, I found a shelf containing three books. Two seemed to be densely printed religious texts that I had never heard of, but the third was The Obedience of the Christian Man by William Tyndale, which must have been imported illegally. It seemed that the people who lived in this house were interested in the "New Learning". I had heard of Master Tyndale's work but had never seen a copy of one of his books. My husband would never have allowed one of these books in our house. Such a thing would be complete anathema to a man with conservative religious values, who had allied himself to the Pilgrimage of Grace.

I dressed in the sober clothes that Mary had provided. I was unsure about what to do with my dagger, but I hid it on top of the door frame and hoped it would not be noticed. As I went down the stairs, I heard distant church bells striking for ten. I must have slept for about five hours, but I felt much better for it.

'Good morning, Tamsin,' said Edmund from where he was sprawled in an armchair. 'Mary has gone to the market to get some provisions and Stephen is feeding the horses. I trust you slept well.'

'Yes, very well, thank you. Now are you going to tell me what is going on? How did you find me? And why?'

'Tamsin, your tone is almost threatening. Most women would have flung themselves at my feet to express their extreme gratitude for being rescued from that nasty old villain, the Duke of Norfolk!' he said with a mocking smile.

'Of course, I am grateful, and yes, you have my thanks, but I do not wish to go anywhere near your feet. Instead, perhaps you could answer my questions. Why are you up here in the North?'

'Please do not ask any more questions, Tamsin, or I will forget the ones you have already asked. You are too impatient, but then you always were,' he said with a grin. I swallowed my rude reply and forced myself to wait patiently.

'Your acquaintance, the Duke of Norfolk, is engaged on a mission to eliminate all further opposition to the king's reforms. Did you know that the Pilgrimage of Grace almost succeeded? No? Well, the fact is that the king did not have enough troops and loyal local lords to suppress it, so he had to play for time.' Edmund's face was serious. 'All that inviting Robert Aske to London for Christmas and considering the requests made by the leaders of the Pilgrimage was just a ploy. In the meantime, the king was readying troops to repress all dissent with extreme savagery. Doubtless you saw the many corpses hanging besides the roads?'

I nodded quietly.

'Norfolk has not yet completed his mission. He is still rounding up any lords and leaders who either joined in the rebellion or at least did not actively stop it. Along the way, he is stopping to make further examples of what happens to poor people who dare to oppose the Crown. Some of the lords will be executed, but I imagine that those who grovel and pay large fines may be allowed to live if they are useful to the Crown in some manner.' Edmund paused to laugh in a cynical manner.

'Edmund, did you kill the guard outside my tent?'

'No, I only knocked him out. You will be glad to hear that I only kill when I have no alternative.'

'How did you know where I was?'

'I found you, Tamsin, because I work for Lord Cromwell, your old sparring partner. Cromwell and the Duke of Norfolk dislike each other.'

'Why?'

'The Duke feels that he as a premier duke and others of his rank should be the ones to advise the king, not commoners like Cromwell. Norfolk believes that Cromwell has too much influence on the king and that he is promoting religious reform that goes too far. Cromwell is in favour of the "New Learning", for example, allowing everybody to read the Bible for themselves. He wants to see greater reform of the Church. Norfolk is suspicious about this.'

Edmund stopped to flick his dark curls away from his eyes. 'As you have doubtless realised, Cromwell runs a vast network of informers and spies throughout the country. There is not much that happens that he does not know about. He knew about the incident at Allerthorpe Castle when the Duke had tried to use you as bait to flush out your husband, but he got away.'

'Was that really Richard? The man I said was probably a local poacher?'

'Yes. Norfolk cannot bear anybody to outwit him so he decided to take you up North and exhibit you openly, hoping that Richard would try again to see you.'

'So that was why he ordered me to ride next to him on the journey and arranged for my tent to be close to his.'

'He hoped that Richard would do something foolish to see his wife and break his cover. He is known to be very attached to you, Tamsin, and now likely to be a desperate man because he knows he is being hunted.'

I dreaded asking my next question. 'Edmund, is there really definite proof that Richard was involved with the rebellion?'

'I know you will not want to hear this. As you know, Richard and his younger brother went to investigate reports of uprisings in their local area. Then, it is certain that he left his camp in the middle of the night. We now know that he travelled to the rebel camp and was received by Robert Aske. He was then seen marching with the Pilgrimage by several different informants. He did not go to London with Aske at Christmas to meet the king but instead became friendly with another rebel, Francis Bigod. Unfortunately, Richard then got tangled up with another rebellion in Cumberland when Bigod accused Aske of betraying the principles behind the Pilgrimage of Grace.'

I started to feel rather sick, but Edmund continued speaking.

'The Duke of Norfolk, helped by Robert Aske, led an army against the Bigod revolt and it was completely crushed. Norfolk took Richard prisoner, but he managed to escape, which explains why he is so keen to re-capture him. The Duke does not want Cromwell to be able to tell the king that he is too lenient with the rebel nobleman.'

'So, if my husband is not dead yet, he soon will be because if he is caught, he will be tried as a traitor and there is plenty of evidence that he is a traitor. That is a fact, is it not?' I said, trying to sound composed. Oddly enough, I found I was still angry that Richard had joined a revolt with no warning to me and that helped me to control myself.

'Yes, and if he is found by the Duke of Norfolk or his associates, Richard will be at greater risk because the Duke has taken his escape as a personal insult – he fears it makes him look incompetent to the king. He may take the chance to exact a personal revenge.'

'You mean that if he is not condemned by a court, he might have him murdered?'

'It is possible, Tamsin. It is best that you know all the facts.'

'I still do not understand why he did not tell me anything before he left for the last time.'

'What would you have done?'

'I would have talked him out of it. He had no regard to the safety of his daughter, his family, his household and me.'

'Richard is an idealist and an optimist. He probably thought that the rebellion would be successful because he felt the cause was just. Perhaps he expected some temporary upheaval, the implementation of the demands of the rebels, and then a better life with Cromwell and his cronies eliminated.'

'Yes, I see.' Despite my iron control, I had a desperate desire to burst into tears. If I were not already a widow, I would very likely soon be one. 'I would like to go for a walk by the sea. I have missed it recently.'

'I will accompany you in case we meet any of the locals. I will introduce you as my unmarried sister who is seeking refuge from the upheaval in York. You will say as little as possible.'

CHAPTER 28

We set out with me wearing my cloak, dried and brushed by Mary. The air was chilly, but the sun was shining. We walked in companionable silence and as we reached the edge of the cliffs, I started to feel less tearful. Waves were crashing on the beach and I could hear the sucking noise as each wave landed and retreated down the slope of the sand and shingle.

Fortunately, there was no one in the immediate vicinity that I might need to be introduced to. Further out to sea, I could see little day boats busy in their work. 'Is there a fish market here?' I asked.

'Not here, but there is one on the other side of the headland,' said Edmund.

'The scenery is impressive,' I said politely.

'But not as attractive as your beloved West Looe?' said Edmund teasingly.

'No, but it is lovely,' I said.

'Do you still miss Looe, Tamsin?'

'Yes, even though I have travelled further than I ever thought I would and seen much that I have liked. I am still proud to be Cornish.'

'The Cornish are regarded as a savage and rather backward race by many people. Do not forget that we rebelled against the present king's father in 1497.'

'Yes, I used to hear stories about that from aunts and uncles, but nobody from my family was involved.'

'I am actually surprised that you did not join the northern rebellion yourself, Tamsin. I can just picture you clad in armour, riding down to London waving a sword. I am sure you have a bloodthirsty streak!'

'You talk nonsense, Edmund,' I said while remembering the dagger I had hidden on the top of the door frame. 'I was too busy being a good wife and mother.'

'How is Alice?'

'And how do you know her name? Yes, of course, Cromwell's informers. Presland was one, was he not?'

'Yes, he is rather a good one. No one suspects lazy and over-indulged men like him to be spies. Your friend, Margaret, is very worried about your wellbeing. She is back in London, still trying to stop her husband from spending too much money at the gaming tables.'

We were down on the little beach by now. I could not help myself running towards the sea. Edmund was occupied with trying to find suitable stones for skimming in the sea. The wind filled my cloak like a sail and my cap slid sideways so that my hair started to unravel. I did not care because suddenly I felt happier than I had done for weeks. As I stared out to the horizon, I did not notice a bigger wave until it broke over my ankles and filled my boots with icy seawater. I looked down at my soaked boots and burst out laughing, then I hastily ran backwards as another wave approached. All the tension seemed to be falling away from me.

'Walking back in my sodden boots,' I said to Edmund. 'There is nothing more I can do, is there? I have put my daughter in a safe place, and I have escaped from the Duke so he cannot use me to trap my husband.'

'Excuse me, my lady, I was the one who arranged your

escape from the Duke. Do I not get an acknowledgement in your summary, or even possibly some thanks?'

'Very well, Edmund,' I said, poking him in the arm. 'I am most grateful to you and I suppose that I would not have managed to escape without your help, but you are still as annoying as ever. Now, I must get back so that I can remove these boots. I am sure there is seawater sloshing around in them.'

I looked up him. He was laughing again, and we were at the gate of the house. 'Lean on me, take your boots off and you can pour it out before you go in,' he said.

'I cannot lean on you; your shoulder is too high,' I said, stretching up to him.

'Would you like me to kneel, my lady? You can then rest your fair hand on my undeserving shoulder!'

'Yes,' I said crossly. Of course, he knelt as if in church and folded his hands, gazing up at me as if I were a church icon. At this point, the woman I knew as Mary appeared from around the corner carrying a basket. 'May I ask what has happened?'

'I am helping this lady to remove her boots after a small accident with the sea,' said Edmund smoothly.

'Bring them in and put them by the fire,' she said as I heaved the second boot off, whereupon Edmund leapt forward to carry in Mary's heavy shopping basket, causing me to lose my balance and sway dangerously before I managed to right myself.

'Thank you, Edmund,' said Mary, following him to the kitchen.

After offering help in the kitchen, which was politely refused, I wandered upstairs to fetch one of the books I had seen earlier. I was particularly curious about the one by Master Tyndale. Bringing it carefully downstairs, I settled into a chair to read and found myself totally absorbed.

Over dinner, I brought up the subject of what was known as "The New Learning". 'I hope you do not mind, but I have been reading the copy of Master Tyndale's work that I found in the chamber you have so kindly provided me with. It is very interesting, and I can see how the book must have influenced our king. It supports his position as Head of the Church and says that all people must do to live a holy life is to obey God and the king. There is no place for the Pope.'

'I believe that Master Tyndale's interpretation of Christianity is the true one,' said Mary.

'We do not need all the flummery and mummering of the priests,' said Edmund. 'We can have a simple and direct connection with God. You may not know, Tamsin, but Master Tyndale was betrayed and burned at the stake in Flanders last year.'

'That is terrible. Many evil things seem to be happening in the name of religion,' I said. 'May I continue to read the book tonight?'

'Of course, you may,' said Mary, 'and I hope you will find it illuminating.'

Later, when Mary had retried, Edmund and I were sitting by the fire. 'Edmund, you and Mary are both advocates of the New Learning, are you not?'

'Yes, we are, and I hope that in time you will be too,' said Edmund I noticed that, unusually, there was no trace of levity in his tone. His brown eyes were serious. 'But you must be careful not to discuss these ideas openly yet.'

'Mary is well educated,' I said. 'Is she a relation of yours?'

'Like you, she benefited from parents who believed that a good education was necessary for a girl and, like you, she shared a tutor with her brothers. But unlike you, there was no handsome young man being taught alongside her!'

'Now you are being silly again. I liked it when you spoke seriously, and you have not answered my question. Who is Mary and why do you and she live together?'

'Mary is a distant cousin of mine. Cromwell pays her an allowance to maintain her house as a shelter for those who work for his interests. There are several other staff employed. People usually just stay a short time.'

'What do the village residents think of a young woman living without a husband here?'

'Mary is from an old Yorkshire gentry family. She is thought to be a little eccentric, but she is also known for her charitable works in the village. She runs a little school for local children, girls as well as boys, in the back rooms of this house.

'We cannot stay here for much longer, Tamsin, and so we must make plans for what to do next.' Edmund yawned and lay back on the chair. 'I am rather tired. It must be all that exertion last night and the effects of the sea air.'

'Nonsense, you are just lazy. Do you remember when you paid me for doing your schoolwork? I believe it was a Latin translation and my reward was not money, it was a visit to the stables to see one of the cats who had a litter of kittens. I still remember those little fluffy creatures. What happened to them? I cannot remember.'

'The steward said he would drown them, but he never did. I believe we kept three as mousers and the other three were given to neighbouring farms. Now, we really must think about what we are going to do next. We should leave here by tomorrow before anyone takes too much notice of us.'

'Edmund, is there anything else I can do to find out what has happened to Richard?'

'No, I cannot think of anything. I believe we must get back to London and throw ourselves on Cromwell's mercy. He should be able to protect you from the Duke of Norfolk,' he said. 'We will leave tomorrow as husband and wife and get a passage on a boat down to London. I have contacts who can arrange a swift passage. If we ride down, we could be seen and captured. Once we are on a boat, it will be much safer. It is also a faster means of transport.'

'Very well, but why must we be a married couple?' I asked.

'Because any alerts will be warning about a lady travelling alone. It is very unlikely that the Duke knows that I am here.'

'But what about Joan? I cannot leave her. She will be worried, and I still have unfinished business in Yorkshire. I mean to find a way to avenge the murder of one of my guards, a local lad whose mother will be devastated and probably left destitute by his death.' I told the story of the incident and of how the Duke of Norfolk had dismissed it as a justifiable killing.

'Tamsin, sometimes we cannot do everything we wish to. Joan will survive, she will not be regarded as important, and you can send for her when you are safe in London. You will be able to do something to ensure that the guard's mother is does not become destitute, but if you are plotting to kill the murderer yourself, you are unlikely to succeed. Even if you hired someone to do it, the Duke would not rest until he had hunted down all those responsible. The scarred man of whom you speak is an old friend of Norfolk. You would end up on a scaffold somewhere. I will not permit you to behave in such a reckless manner.'

'Well, I will find another way to do him harm.'

'I can see that the passing years have hardened you, Tamsin. You would never have spoken in such a way in the past.'

'No, that is true. It is my experience of men's behaviour that has made me more ruthless, I believe.'

Edmund gave me a crooked smile. 'I can see that I must be very careful not to annoy you,' he said, stretching out his long body. 'Now, I must send a message to a friend to arrange for us to leave tomorrow.'

Early the next morning, after gratefully thanking Mary for her hospitality, we set out for a small harbour usually only used by fishing boats if temporary shelter was needed in a storm. I was dressed in clothes provided by Mary. Covering my hair was a severe white coif. I also wore a plain kirtle and a woollen overdress, but I insisted on taking my own warm cloak.

'I am Master Trout, a fish merchant, and you are Mistress Agnes Trout, my devoted wife,' said Edmund, flourishing some documents, an evil grin on his handsome face.

'Very amusing, Edmund!' I said crossly. 'What about the horses? Who will take them back to Mary?'

'We will leave them at the usual place, and they will be collected by Mary's servants later.'

After an uneventful ride, we left the horses tied to a field post and set out on foot. I noticed that Edmund kept a tight grip on my hand as we walked. 'You need not fear that I will run away. There is no need to wrench my hand off!' I said snappily. Eventually, we arrived at a tiny river, inlet with a small natural harbour. There was room for only one or two boats. We sat down on the grassy cliff to watch for the ship. As it appeared around the bend, we scrambled down to the harbour.

It was too big for the harbour, but after some careful manoeuvres, the crew was able to position it so that a small boat could be rowed out to collect us. Fortunately, the sea was calm. Eventually, we were brought on board after a worrying climb up a rope ladder. A young man bent down and grasped my wrists to haul me up and I landed on the deck in a heap.

'Your missus ain't used to this, is she, Master?' said the young man cheerfully to Edmund.

'She normally waits at home while I travel for the business,' said Edmund. 'But I think she wants to keep an eye on me, make sure I do not get up to any mischief with the ladies!' he added with a conspiratorial wink to the young man. Laughing merrily, the young man showed us to a cabin with two truckle beds.

'Stop your nonsense, Edmund!' I hissed. 'We could be on this boat for a week, and I do not want to be laughed at!'

He bowed very low and said, 'My most humble apologies, your ladyship!' He was still smiling in an infuriating manner. I could not think of any suitable retort and so stalked out. Perhaps a walk on the deck would calm me. I was going to have to live with this man in a very small space, so I would have to find a way to stop myself getting irritated.

Out on deck, I saw we were already out in the open sea, although the coastline could still be seen in the distance. Somewhere on that landmass was Richard, and I could sail past him and never know. A tear rolled down my cheek, but the freshening wind dried it quickly. Back down the ladder I went. There were two cabins: the captain's, and the one Edmund and I were to share. He was stretched out fast asleep. At least he did not appear to snore. While he slept, I unpacked a spare kirtle given to me by Mary, hanging it on a hook, and checked that my dagger, retrieved from its hiding place, was in position under my skirts. I then found myself nodding over my Book of Hours, so I slept too.

About two hours later, I awoke to Edmund carrying a jug of ale and two pies. 'It was hellish descending the ladder. I thought I would have to balance the pies on my head,' he said.

'I am not certain that I wish to eat a pie that has been on your somewhat dirty looking hair,' I said, looking at his dark mop of curls which looked wilder than ever.

'You do not need to worry, Tamsin, I solved the problem by carrying the pies in the bag with my teeth,' he said cheerfully. The fresh air and rest had made us hungry, so we quickly devoured the food and drank all the ale.

'I will go and fetch you some more,' said Edmund. 'I did not realise that you were such a heavy drinker, lady wife.'

'You drank more than half yourself,' I shouted as he disappeared up the ladder. Minutes later, he was back with another foaming jug. When the jug was empty, it became obvious that we must go to bed. Edmund flung himself onto the bed that I had chosen and looked at me challengingly. Immediately, I flung a rather dirty looking cushion at his head.

'Get off, you are sleeping in the other one!' I yelled.

'Now, now wife, where is your obedience to your lord husband?'

'You are not...' My angry shout was cut off by a hairy hand.

'Do you want the entire ship to know that we are not married?' he said quietly. 'And you can put that sharp dagger somewhere safe unless you are planning to fight me for the bed,' he added.

'How do you know I have a weapon?' I asked, horrified.

'Unless you have grown a strange abscess on your leg like our noble king, I believe you are carrying a dagger, Tamsin. Give it to me and I will look after it for you. You may have it back when we disembark, as long as your behaviour is beyond reproach,' he added with a smile.

'No,' I said. 'My life has shown me that danger lurks everywhere, and I will not be unprotected.'

'It is the custom to hand over weapons when receiving hospitality, lady wife.'

'This is not your ship so you cannot offer hospitality, Edmund!'

'You are misinformed. It is most certainly my ship and one of two that I own. How do you think we obtained a passage so easily?' Edmund answered mildly. 'You can be quite sure that you are safe. The crew know my identity, but they do not know yours.'

'So I do not have to pretend to be Agnes Trout at all.'

'No. Such a pity, it would have been amusing to introduce you as Mistress Trout!' he said, grinning again.

'Do you laugh your way through everything? It is exhausting,' I said as I lay down on the bed I had not chosen.

'I find that it helps to smooth the path to me getting what I want,' he said with a gleam in his eyes. 'May I wish you goodnight, Mrs Trout? I do hope that you do not snore. Here is your goodnight kiss, my dear.'

He lunged towards me and to my astonishment, I felt excited.

'Stop it, Edmund, I am a married woman!'

He moved back in an exaggerated manner. 'I beg your pardon, your ladyship. I was unable to restrain my passion. Pray, forgive me!'

As I drifted to sleep, I could not help but smile to myself in the darkness. Yes, Edmund was very irritating, but it was difficult to feel miserable in his company.

CHAPTER 29

The next few days passed smoothly, helped by the good weather. Edmund and I arranged a routine that we would each leave the cabin when the other needed to be private.

The stiff breeze filled the sails and carried as ever onwards. I was happy to sit and watch the sea and the changing view of the coastline for hours. It felt as if I were suspended outside time and I almost wished the journey would go on for ever. Both the Duke of Norfolk and Lord Cromwell seemed very far away, and I did not want to face the reality of arriving in London.

All too soon, we were back in the Thames and passing the hamlets I recognised from my travels with Joan. The customs official came onboard and checked the cargo of packets and letters at Deptford and we were free to leave. I saw Edmund in conversation with the captain of the vessel as the crew brought out the gangplank. Men in ragged clothing waited on the quay, hoping to earn a little money from unloading the cargo.

'Well, wife, do you have all your belongings?' Edmund said, looking meaningfully at the area of my leg where the dagger he had returned this morning was stowed. 'Let us depart this muddle,' he said as he waved his arm in the air.

Seconds later, a groom I recognised from Lady Sedley's household arrived, leading two horses.

'We are going to the Sedley house, where the good lady has already agreed to receive you. I believe she is eagerly awaiting your company. Doubtless she has alerted your friend, Lady

Margaret, to your arrival so I daresay you will find yourself happy enough.'

'I wish to go to Allerthorpe House and see that everything is in order first,' I said firmly as we rode along.

'No, Tamsin. Not now. The house will have been searched for evidence of treachery and the servants have probably fled. Perhaps go tomorrow when you have recovered from the journey, and do not go alone. I will see Lord Cromwell later and see what the situation is.'

I felt tired and dispirited. 'Perhaps I should leave it until tomorrow, then.'

Soon, we were within sight of Lady Sedley's house. 'Where will you stay, Edmund?' I asked. Suddenly, I felt that I did not want him to leave me.

'I have several places that I can stay. Do not worry about my wellbeing, Tamsin. Here is small purse of coins which you may have need of until we know your financial situation. Do not be embarrassed, I am just being practical.'

We had arrived. The stable boy ran forward to take my horse's reins. Edmund halted his horse and bowed extravagantly, sweeping off his hat. 'Farewell, Mistress Trout, I will see you again soon!' He wobbled theatrically in the saddle as if he would fall, grinned again, and then rode off quickly.

I was ushered straight into Lady Sedley's presence, where I curtsied to her. 'Tamsin, dear, I am delighted to see you again. You must be exhausted. Where is your luggage?'

'I did not have the opportunity to bring much, Lady Sedley. Indeed, most of the clothes I am wearing are not mine but were kindly lent to me.'

'Yes, I have heard an account of what happened to you. There is still no news of Richard, I suppose?'

'No, but I fear it is very likely that he is dead. I hope to see Lord Cromwell soon, as he may have news.'

Lady Sedley clapped her hands and a lady-in-waiting – very young, as I was when I had first arrived here so long ago – walked quickly over to her. 'Isabel, take the countess to the rooms that have been prepared for her and send to the kitchens for hot water, food and wine.'

Isabel indicated that I should follow her. 'I am Isabel Torville. This way, my lady, I hear you have had a gruelling journey.' She led the way into a well-appointed and comfortable chamber. 'I will send a servant to you who will help you with anything you need. There is a communal clothing chest for us ladies-in-waiting and I am sure there will be something to fit you.'

'I used to be a lady in waiting here,' I said, 'and I remember that chest of clothes. We used to look through it whenever we were going to an important event. It was a happy time. Is this still a happy house?'

'Oh yes, my lady,' Isabel said, rummaging in the chest. She held an orange brocaded dress against me. 'This is pretty but perhaps not for your fair colouring. This one is better,' she said, holding up a dark blue one with a grey trim. 'We are fortunate. Lady Sedley is so kind, and we have the opportunity to go out with her to all sorts of places. Sometimes we go to court!'

I remembered myself, giddy with excitement, going to Hampton Court before I had met Lord Allerthorpe. It seemed a very long time ago.

'We sometimes see important and famous people and, of course, we hear things,' she said with a conspiratorial look. 'Oh, have you heard, my lady? There is a rumour that Queen Jane is pregnant!'

'What delightful news. The king will be very happy if that is true,' I said.

'Yes, indeed,' said Isabel as three maids entered with large jugs of hot water. 'I have taken the liberty of ordering the bath for you, your ladyship.' Two men entered carrying a wooden bathtub, which they placed in front of the fire.

'Well, that will be a welcome luxury,' I said.

'Lady Sedley always says regular bathing is good for one,' said Isabel, 'and it is true that her ladyship is in excellent health for her advanced age – she is almost fifty years old!'

Linen towels were laid in the bath to pad it and the jugs of hot water upended. Isabel scattered some dried herbs into the water. 'It is lavender, my lady, and chamomile to calm your mind.' The maids put screens around the bath to protect against dangerous draughts and withdrew. I saw Isabel's eyes widen as she saw me remove my dagger from its hiding place.

'It was for protection on the roads,' I said. 'I am sure I will not need it now!' I handed my filthy shift to Isabel and stepped in. It was blissful to lie back in the hot water and feel my muscles relax.

I stayed in the bath until the water went cold. The business of drying my hair with towels and in front of the fire took an age but I used some of the time to write an urgent message to Joan, telling her I was safe and arranging her passage to London along with Ranulf and Rolf.

When I entered the hall for dinner, there was an awkward silence as I entered, and many faces turned to look at me. Lady Sedley stood up and showed me to a seat next to her.

'Some of you may remember Tamsin, who lived here before she married the Earl of Allerthorpe. She is a friend who has fallen on uncertain times through no fault of her own. I bid you all to treat her with Christian kindness.'

I sat down gratefully and was pleased to see that people were resuming their conversations. After nibbling at some venison pie and braised rabbits, I found that I was not hungry. I decided to slip away unobtrusively and see if I could arrange a horse so that I could go to Allerthorpe House. I was burning to go there, no matter what Edmund had said.

With a polite apology to Lady Sedley, who was so taken up with her conversation that she barely acknowledged me, I went to find a warm cloak. Fortunately, my muddy boots had already been cleaned and my own cloak brushed. I borrowed a placid grey mare and set off with one of the pages, who seemed happy for an excuse to go outside. The streets were just as noisy and crammed with people as I remembered, but I had forgotten that a short journey in Central London took longer because of the need to manoeuvre around the many people on foot. Even so, it seemed extraordinarily crowded to me.

'Page, is there some event or celebration today? There are so many people.'

'Yes, my lady, there are rebels to be hanged at Smithfield this afternoon. Folks are going to get a good position.'

'I see,' I said wearily. 'Do you know a quicker way to Allerthorpe House that would get us out of this crowd?'

'Yes, my lady, please follow me.' The page led me through a series of dark and stinking alleys, where the tall houses were shabby and the gutters full of rubbish. I was very pleased when we emerged into the leafy street where Allerthorpe House was.

We rode up to the front door and I gasped with horror. Planks had been nailed across the door and on all the downstairs windows. Then I saw a guard in the Duke of Norfolk's livery pacing up and down armed with a sword and an evil looking pike.

Hastily, I motioned to the page to move back; I did not want to be seen.

'I see my house appears inaccessible today,' I said calmly to the page, leading him to a clump of trees. 'We had better return to Sedley House.'

'Yes, my lady. Which route would you prefer on the way back?'

'The quick way, please. Would you wait while I adjust my saddle? I fear it is loose.' There was nothing wrong with the saddle, but I wanted a chance to examine the house again because I was plotting to gain entry later. Yes, all the upstairs windows at the front were not barred which meant it was likely that the back ones were not barred either. The guard was now on his way back to the front.

I froze in horror because the guard's face was fully in view now. It was none other than the man who had thrown an axe at my guard on the way to York – the man with the scarred face! It was imperative that we leave now before he recognised me. I leapt back up on my horse, dug my heels in and called the surprised page in front to lead me. Once my back was turned to that man, I felt safer, and as I rode back, I felt the comforting weight of my dagger under my skirts. I had not forgotten my promise to avenge my guard.

Candles were being lit on our return, and a servant carried a sconce before me as I went upstairs to take off my outdoor clothes. I found Isabel in the passageway as I walked to the room that had been allotted to me.

She looked at me curiously. 'Good afternoon, my lady, or should I say evening, as it is already getting rather dark. Have you been on an errand? I saw you slip away at dinner.'

'Yes, I have. Please excuse me, Isabel, I must remove these

boots.'

'Shall I send a servant to you?' I shook my head. Isabel smiled politely and her skirts rustled as she passed by. 'I will leave you then, but do come down when you are restored. Lady Sedley has arranged for musicians to entertain us this evening.'

When I got back inside my chamber, I sank down on the bed, feeling miserable. My own home barred to me. I must see Cromwell without delay. Although I felt that I did not like him, I also realised that I trusted him more than any of the other "great men" I had encountered. I went to fetch writing things from the small table and noticed that some gloves that I had laid down on the left side of the table had now mysteriously moved to the right side. My first thought was that a maid had been in to tidy, but this seemed unlikely as the room had only been got ready for me a few hours ago. Everything else, including a shawl that I had left on the bed in a crumpled heap, seemed undisturbed.

I thought carefully: had I placed the gloves on the right side? No. Due to my tendency to lose things such as gloves, I had long ago agreed with Joan that I would put gloves on the left of a table or chest and hair pins or ribbons on the right. It was then easier to see if I had lost anything.

Somebody has been snooping in here, I thought. But why would anyone do that? I had nothing at all beyond my clothes, of which most were borrowed, and my dagger. It was good that I had taken the dagger with me as Lady Sedley, while understanding the past need for it, would certainly require me to hand it over for safekeeping now. It was all a puzzle. If somebody had indeed been searching my rooms, they would have been very disappointed. I decided not to voice my suspicions but to watch and wait. I quickly wrote a polite message to Cromwell requesting an interview at his convenience and passed it to a page in the hall as I made my way to supper.

At supper, musicians were indeed performing. 'Did you know that they often play at court when the king's own musicians are not available?' said Isabel, who had taken the place next to me at the table.

'No. Their music is very fine,' I whispered back, trying hard to focus on the beautiful melodies.

'Listen, they are playing "Greensleeves". It is said to be a piece composed by the king himself,' said Isabel, who seemed to be ogling a handsome lute player. 'Look at him, is he not divine?'

'Yes, he has beautiful brown eyes,' I said. With a jolt, I realised that the man's eyes reminded me of Edmund.

I had another sip of wine and tried again to listen to the music, but all I could think of was Allerthorpe House, boarded up and guarded by the man I had sworn to be revenged on. What was happening? Whatever it was, I had to get inside that house somehow. By the time supper had finished and the musicians had bowed and collected their fee, my mind was made up. I would go out tonight and get into that house. I remembered that the back of the house had a low extension built on. If I could get up on the roof, I could gain entrance from a first-floor window. I had plenty of experience of climbing trees and the occasional cliff in Cornwall. Surely I would remember what to do. The only difficulty would be climbing in a dress. I would have to somehow borrow some men's clothes, preferably those of a working man, as jewelled doublets and puffy jackets would not be helpful.

Isabel interrupted my reveries. 'Tamsin, there is a very handsome man downstairs asking leave to speak to you!'

'Are you sure it was me he wanted to see?' I said.

'Yes, quite sure. I heard him ask after the Countess of Allerthorpe. The porter was saying that it was too late for you to receive him.'

'I had better go and see what is happening. It is probably a mistake because I do not know any handsome men who would call on me in London.'

Isabel trotted behind me, chattering excitedly, 'I will come with you as a chaperone!'

I arrived at the head of the staircase. 'Oh, it is only Edmund, an old family friend. My thanks, Isabel, but I will not need a chaperone.'

'Oh, but you are a married lady – you can introduce me to him!'

'Very well, Isabel.'

Edmund bowed as we reached the bottom of the stairs. 'Good evening, ladies,' he said.

'Good evening, sir. Edmund Boskeyn, may I present my friend, Mistress Isabel Torville?' Isabel curtsied low, probably to display her large bosoms better, I thought uncharitably.

'I am very happy to make your acquaintance, Mistress Isabel, but I fear I have a business matter to discuss with Lady Allerthorpe. Would you excuse us please? I hope to see you again in the future.'

'Yes, of course,' said Isabel, whose face I saw was now excessively rosy in colour. We waited until she had left, and I led the way into a small room that Lady Sedley used in the mornings.

'Why have you come, Edmund? Do you have news for me?'

'No, I am sorry I do not, but I can see from your face that you are anxious to tell me something.'

I checked the passage and closed the door. I had to explain everything quickly before Lady Sedley got to hear that Edmund was in the house, as she would doubtless summon him to her presence immediately.

'I went to Allerthorpe House today and found it boarded up and the door padlocked, but that is not all. I recognised the guard outside. He is one of the Duke of Norfolk's men, the one who threw an axe at my guard and murdered him for no reason other than to intimidate us.'

'Tamsin, I knew the house was boarded up. That is why I prevented you from going straight there on our arrival yesterday. I did not know that guard was there, but I think I know his identity if his scar is like this.' He drew a curving line down his own face that mirrored the one on the murderer's face.

'Yes, the scar is exactly like that, and he wore the Duke of Norfolk's livery.'

'His name is William Hayes and I fear he is a brute of the first order. He is a favourite of the Duke.'

'Edmund, I made a promise to avenge my murdered guard and I am trying to see a way to do it.'

'I hope you are not going to order me to kill him for you. I am not sure my fighting skills will be sufficient.'

'No, of course not. I intend to deal with him myself and I have already thought of a plan…'

'Please tell me you are not going to creep out of this house at dead of night in some disguise, make your way to Allerthorpe House, break in, probably through an unbarred upper window by way of the low roof at the back of the house, and then challenge Hayes to a duel and run him through the heart? I see, I am correct!'

'Yes and no. I had not intended the duel. I have not thought on my strategy yet.'

'No, Tamsin. It is a crazy plan. There may be more than one guard. Hayes may have finished his shift. You will be arrested and thrown into the Fleet Prison as a common housebreaker. And that is before we get to you climbing the house. I know your climbing skills are good for a girl, but they are not that good. No, you cannot, and you must not even think of it. There are other ways to get your revenge which do not involve you putting yourself in certain danger and bringing disgrace on your husband's name and that of your own family.'

'Kindly illuminate me. Doubtless you have a much better plan!' I shouted, forgetting that we should be quiet.

'I do have a better one. You will see Lord Cromwell and report the murder of your guard.'

'But the Duke of Norfolk will protect him, and no action will be taken,' I said despairingly.

'I think not. Cromwell is not a monster and he has some compassion towards ordinary working men. It may be because his own background is humble. He may welcome the chance to undermine the Duke of Norfolk, who as you know despises Cromwell for his low origins. I think he would use the case to embarrass Norfolk if he did not agree that charges should be pressed against William Hayes. Then justice would take its course and you would have the satisfaction of knowing that you took the action that made it possible.'

At this point, a servant knocked on the door. I went to the door and flung it open.

'My lady, Lady Sedley has heard of your guest's presence and she desires that he is brought to her as soon as possible.'

'Of course,' said Edmund smoothly. 'Pray tell your mistress I shall be with her directly.' The servant looked at me curiously as I stood by the fireplace with folded arms.

Edmund waited until the servant left the room. 'Tell Lord Cromwell and try to act like a helpless woman who only seeks justice. No talk of considering knifing him yourself, Tamsin.'

'Of course, I will not. I am not silly, Edmund. I have already written to Lord Cromwell to ask him to see me.' With another bow, he left the room and sped up the stairs to Lady Sedley's rooms.

CHAPTER 30

I was left with nothing to do except return to my chamber. I could not help but think that when spoken aloud, my plan had sounded reckless. Perhaps Edmund was right. I should ask Cromwell to help me get justice for my guard.

As I went towards my door, Isabel burst out of her chamber. 'Your ladyship, do come and sit with me. I have a jug of wine and some sweetmeats.' She opened the door invitingly and as I did not wish to offend her, I agreed.

'Who is Edmund Boskeyn and why have I not met him before?' said Isabel.

'He is the son of Lord Thomas Boskeyn from Penwarne in Cornwall. Our families were great friends, and my brothers and I shared a tutor with him for several years. He was really calling on Lady Sedley but requested to speak to me as a courtesy.'

'Is he married or betrothed?'

'He is not married, but I am unsure if he is betrothed.' I realised that I had never asked Edmund about that.

'Do you not think he is devastatingly good looking?'

'No, not really. Please do not tell him, he will become unbearably conceited, Isabel.'

'No, that would be forward of me. Does he have a house in London?'

'I believe he stays with friends when he needs to be here.'

'I should like to meet him again, your ladyship. Would you help me to do this?'

'Certainly, I will if I can, but I do not know how long Edmund plans to stay in London.'

'I have a sizeable dowry and I should like to marry soon. After all, that is why we women come here, and you managed to marry an earl! But of course…' She paused in an embarrassed manner.

'Yes, you were going to say, 'he is now accused of treason,' Isabel. Do not be afraid to say it. I can see that everybody thinks he is guilty, even though he has not been tried and convicted. But I must emphasise this: I did not "manage to marry" the earl, he pursued me. It was quite a surprise to find myself suddenly the Countess of Allerthorpe!'

'I do apologise, your ladyship. My mouth runs away with me sometimes,' Isabel said, laughing loudly. Her laugh sounded forced to me. I did not believe she was sorry at all and my instincts told me not to trust her friendly overtures either. After one cup of wine, I pleaded tiredness and went to my chamber. This time, it appeared undisturbed. I found I was exhausted when I lay down and within minutes, I was almost asleep. I was dimly aware of a commotion at the front door and Lady Sedley shouting "farewell" and then I was asleep.

The next morning, I was up as soon as the maid had been to light my fire and bring breakfast. I was eager to get downstairs and see if there had been a message for me from Cromwell. As I descended the stairs, the porter stepped forward. 'Message for you, my lady, from Lord Cromwell's office.' Thanking him, I broke the seal and read the contents. With relief, I read that I was to present myself at ten o'clock in his office at Austin Friars.

At ten minutes before the hour, I was admitted through the gates along with two guards and one of Lady Sedley's servants.

One of Cromwell's many clerks politely asked me to wait as

his master was just finishing another matter. I was in an agony of impatience as I waited, and finally Cromwell's head appeared through the door. 'Henry, bring a flask of brandy and two glasses.'

'Yes, my lord,' Henry, the clerk, said with a bow and sped off. Looking back, I see now that I should have noticed that it was strange to offer brandy to morning visitors, but all I did was to wonder why Cromwell needed brandy so early in the day.

'So many Henrys around the place these days, it is very confusing,' said Cromwell.

'Yes, even I have a brother named for the king,' I said, arranging myself in the chair that Cromwell indicated. He tapped a book on the desk in front of him. Again, looking back, I see that he was perhaps a little apprehensive about the interview he was to have with me, but then, I noticed nothing.

The brandy arrived and Cromwell asked for two glasses to be poured without asking me if I wanted any. The glasses were very beautiful, decorated with intricate patterns, and I looked at them carefully as I had not handled much fine glassware before.

'Yes, the glasses are lovely, are they not? They come all the way from Venice,' he remarked conversationally.

'My lord, I expect you know of my movements.' I noticed that he had the grace to smile politely. 'I asked to see you because I have heard nothing from my husband for a long time and I wondered if you had any news of him?'

'My lady, you must prepare yourself for an unpleasant shock.' He gestured towards the brandy. I took the glass obediently but did not drink because I wanted to hear exactly what Cromwell had to say.

'I am grieved to have to inform you that your husband Richard, former Earl of Allerthorpe, has been tried and convicted of high treason and the appropriate sentence has already been carried out.'

I sat stunned and an icy chill swept over me.

'For God's sake, woman, have a swallow of brandy.' I did so mechanically.

'When was he convicted and when and how did he die?' I asked, dreading the answer.

'He was convicted in March, my lady, at the Duke of Norfolk's Great Assize. Other nobles sentenced to death included Robert Aske, Lord Darcy, Robert Constable and Bigod. Some sentences were carried out in the North. Robert Aske was sentenced to be hanged in chains from York Castle. Your husband was beheaded.'

I gasped, but Cromwell had not finished speaking.

'The head of the former Earl of Allerthorpe is displayed in York as is normal for traitors. He was fortunate not to be hung, drawn and quartered. I received confirmation of the executions today. I must also inform you that all your husband's estates, possessions and his title revert to the Crown for the king to award as he sees fit.'

Suddenly, Cromwell's voice sounded very far away, and I felt sick.

'You may remember that I warned you of this eventuality. I hope you have been sensible and taken measures to provide for your own future. You will be reassured to know that you are not suspected of any wrongdoing. Of course, the Duke of Norfolk was furious to lose you, his bait to trap the Earl, but that is another matter.'

'I did not ever really believe it would come to this,' I said, standing up and staggering slightly. No, I thought, that is not true. I have always known in my heart that this would happen.

'Sit down, lady, I do not want one of those Venetian glasses smashed.'

'No, of course you do not,' I said with a deep breath, straightening my shoulders. The room had become darker, now a hailstorm bounced off the mullioned windows. I must control myself, I thought.

'My lord, I also have a favour to ask of you. No, it is nothing to do with the earl. It is a story of another tragedy which affects a poor family.'

I told him the story of my murdered guard and the identity of the scarred man.

'I have heard that you can be compassionate to those who have little,' I said, swallowing hard. 'This man left a poor widowed mother with no means of support. Obviously, I can do nothing in monetary terms for her now, but I have a burning desire to have justice for my guard. Norfolk's man said the guard drew his sword and resisted him, but he did not, my lord. I saw it all. That man threw his axe for no reason other than to terrify us and ensure my cooperation. It was wrong, sir, very wrong and he thinks that he will escape justice because his patron is the Duke. Please help me, my lord. I ask nothing more and I will leave shortly. You will not see me again.'

Vaguely, I heard Cromwell say that his powers were limited when it came to the Duke of Norfolk's own men, but he would see if anything could be done. Then I realised that I must leave quickly before I broke down. I stood up, replaced the glass carefully on Cromwell's desk, curtsied quickly and heaved the great door open, not waiting for the clerk to open it. I marched out with my head held high, summoned a stable boy for my horse, sprang on without the usual assistance given to a lady and rode away. The way was clearer because the hail shower had caused people to go inside and take shelter.

As I made my way back to Lady Sedley's house, ignoring the dampness seeping through my clothes, I prayed quietly for Richard's soul. As I arrived back, the sun came out and I felt a curious lightness. The worst had happened, and I need not worry about Richard anymore. He was now beyond all hurt.

My first action on returning to Lady Sedley's house was to write a sympathetic message to Richard's brother and his wife. I assumed that they would already have heard about the execution. I considered writing another message to Joan but thought it was likely that she would have already left for London. I then wrote a message to my mother in Looe to inform her of my terrible news and that I planned to return to Cornwall.

I took the messages down to the porter, urging him to send them urgently together with the coins to pay whatever was needed. Looking at the remainder of the coins given to me by Edmund, I realised that I was going to have to ask to borrow some money from Lady Sedley to be able to return to Cornwall.

As I was returning to my chamber, Lady Sedley appeared in the hall. 'Tamsin, my dear, are you unwell again? You are very pale.'

To my horror, I burst into tears. 'Richard has been executed as a traitor, Lady Sedley. Do not worry, I will leave your house as soon as I can, but could I prevail upon you to lend me some money to pay for my journey back to Cornwall?' I sobbed.

Lady Sedley looked shocked. 'What terrible news! I can hardly believe it. Are you sure it is true?'

'Yes, your ladyship. Lord Cromwell himself told me this morning. His poor head is displayed in York.' Servants appeared looking horrified at the scene I was making but I did not care.

'Tamsin, come and sit with me now,' ordered Lady Sedley.

'Go and fetch some hot wine, quickly,' she ordered Isabel, who appeared agog at the disturbance. We went to a small room off the main hall and Lady Sedley pushed me into a chair by the fire. 'Your clothes are wet. Come closer to the fire or you will take a chill.'

Isabel entered with the wine. Wordlessly, I took a cup. 'Now, drink that up and then we will talk,' said Lady Sedley. The wine was spiced, and I felt warmth spread through my chilled body.

'Before you make any plans, you will rest,' she said.

'I must go to the chapel and pray for him,' I said, standing up again.

'No, not now. Wait until you are more composed. Sit down, Tamsin! Richard will be safe with God by now.'

'Lady Sedley, I forgot to ask where the rest of his body is buried!'

'Do not think about that now. I will find out for you later.'

'Lady Sedley, you have been very kind to me, and I shall be eternally grateful, but we both know that you cannot have the widow of a traitor living in your establishment.'

'Why ever not? You have not been found guilty of any offence, have you? Allow me to decide who lives in my house! You will stay for as long as you like.'

'Nevertheless, I feel I must leave London.'

'Do you feel that Richard committed heinous crimes, Tamsin?'

'No, I think that he was a man of principle who held a strong conviction that the Pilgrimage of Grace had right on its side.'

'Does it occur to you that many people may share your belief? Some may indeed feel that rebels were badly treated by the king, but they will not dare voice such an opinion. The Duke of Norfolk is not popular with the people and indeed many nobles secretly regard him as a brute. Unfortunately, the king needs men like him to maintain order and he is now in a position of great power. In short, I believe that many people will be sympathetic to you,' said Lady Sedley.

My tears had stopped as I listened to her. 'There is wisdom in what you say, Lady Sedley. I have taken the liberty of sending for my servant Joan and two of my guards but unfortunately, I have realised that as my husband's estates and possessions are forfeit to the Crown, I have no money to pay them and certainly not enough to fund our journey to Cornwall. Would you be kind enough to lend me some money until such time as I can repay you, Lady Sedley?'

'Of course I will, child, but please do not make any hasty decisions. Await the arrival of your servants and then see how things are.'

I retired to my chamber and found, to my surprise, that I was already beginning to feel better. I was increasingly realising that since Richard had disappeared, I had somehow always known that events would not turn out well. It was fortunate that our marriage had been based more on friendship than true love or it could have been so much worse. I knelt by my window, praying to God to look after Richard in heaven. As I got up, I was flooded with a strange sense of calm. After that, I lay down on my bed fully dressed and thought about my future.

I had not committed any offence and yet I was being severely punished. I had no money of my own and no way of obtaining any for some time. The widows of other executed traitor noblemen would be likely to come from powerful and prosperous families who would take them in. Doubtless they had doweries that might not be included in the Crown's confiscation of property.

I knew that I would never starve if I went back to Cornwall, but money was tight in my family. Would I have to go and live with Henry and his wife and perform the role of a nursemaid to his children? Or could I live with my mother? With my education, I could set up a small school for local children, but I would need premises which would cost money to rent. Would old Lord Boskeyn help me? He might. It all seemed unfair, but as a woman, I knew that I had no power to change anything. I must accept my fate and continue to live by the rules of men as decided by God.

I thought of King Henry, sitting on his jewelled throne, taking lands and titles from families with no consideration for those who were guiltless but nevertheless suffered. I had my daughter to think of. How would she marry with no dowry? I had no means of knowing if Sir Nicholas's title had been removed. He should have been the new earl, but the title and the lands would probably go to one of the avaricious nobles who craved yet another title. Doubtless Cromwell would whisper the name of a likely candidate in the king's ear.

Lord Cromwell! I felt a wave of anger. Why had he not summoned Richard back to London before he fell under the spell of the rebels and given him a safer mission? He had clearly misjudged Richard by sending him to infiltrate the rebels without realising that he shared some of their values. And Richard, how could he have been so stupid?

Feeling irate, I composed a long letter to Cromwell outlining his error in sending Richard to negotiate with the northern rebels. Finally, I reminded him of my request that he do something about the man who had wickedly murdered my guard. I had no intention of sending it, of course, but writing it made me feel better. I slid it under a book and lay down again.

Supper was brought on a tray as I did not feel as if I could face the rest of Lady Sedley's household, but I could not eat anything because I felt as if I had my stomach had disappeared from my body. I longed to see Joan.

The next morning, dressed in the only black dress I possessed, I forced myself out into the garden and walked down to where it sloped down to the Thames. The sky was grey and the river a muddy brown. I watched the barges and cogs move past me. People were getting on with their lives. I must too.

I went back inside to see if Lady Sedley was in. A servant directed me to the orangery where Lady Sedley was directing the movements of various potted plants.

'Please excuse me, Tamsin, I am just sorting out the dreadful muddle in here!' she said in earshot of a gardener whose face was impassive. 'Go to my chambers, sit down and I will be with you directly.'

About ten minutes later, she sailed in, her complexion redder than usual. 'Bring some of the better ale,' she said to Isabel, who appeared to be engaged in tidying up. Isabel left the room and Lady Sedley enquired how I was today.

'Thank you, your ladyship. I am somewhat recovered, and I have made plans which I would like to discuss with you. If you allow, I will wait here for Joan to arrive and then make my return to Cornwall.'

'Yes, as I said, you may do as you please, but why deprive London of your presence? Eventually, you will need to remarry, and you will have a much better choice of candidates here than you will in Cornwall!'

'I have no plans to marry again, Lady Sedley, and I should imagine there will not be a queue of suitors for a traitor's widow with no dowry.'

'Nonsense! How will you survive? What about your daughter's welfare? There are always men looking for wives. Perhaps an older man, a widower who has been left with young children?' I looked at Lady Sedley. Now was not the right time

291

to tell her about my plan to start a school and worse, ask her to invest money in it. No. I would just have to be seen to go along with her plans for the moment.

'Perhaps I may consider marrying again in the future, your ladyship,' I said quietly.

CHAPTER 31

When I trailed back upstairs before dinner, I felt quite low and dejected. My plans, which had seemed so exciting and indeed sensible previously, now sounded rather silly and impractical. I really needed Joan to be here with her opinions. I hoped they were making good progress on their journey south.

When I entered my room, I could tell that somebody had been in there while I had been downstairs with Lady Sedley. It was probably a servant as my bed coverlets had been straightened and my table tidied. As I was leaving the room again, something occurred to me. I hoped the servant had not seen my letter to Cromwell, but of course the servant would not have been able to read it so it would be all right.

I looked quickly back at my desk. The edge of the letter was not showing from underneath the book where I had left it. Of course, it would have been straightened with my books. I must take that letter now and put in the hall fire now. To my horror, the letter had vanished! A swift search of the room showed no sign of it. Somebody had removed it, but why? I castigated myself for my folly, remembering how I had suspected somebody had been in my room recently when my gloves seemed to have moved all by themselves.

Feeling a little shaky, I went downstairs to locate a servant. 'Avis, has anybody been in to clean my chamber today?'

'I do not know, madam, I will go and find out.' I waited nervously. Lady Sedley and Isabel swept by with the other ladies on their way to dinner.

'Tamsin, why are you lurking here?' asked Lady Sedley. The ladies tittered sycophantically. 'Do hurry up, dinner will be served shortly!'

'Yes, your ladyship. I was just checking something with the servants.' Lady Sedley and her entourage disappeared through the doorway.

Avis returned looking out of breath. 'Madam, nobody has cleaned your room today. I am so sorry, I will send a girl up without delay.'

'No, Avis, please do not worry. It is just that I mislaid something and wondered if a servant had accidentally put it elsewhere.' Oh dear, now all the servants would know that I had lost something. I would have to think up some story about finding the object quickly or more questions would be asked.

'Oh Avis, I am so sorry, I have just recalled. I left it – the book – downstairs. How silly of me! I am sorry to have bothered you.'

'Not at all, madam, you have had a lot on your mind, I am sure.' She curtsied and sped off. I hoped that would prevent any talk in the servants' quarters. Now I must try to find out what had happened to my letter. How stupid I had been not to burn it immediately! I took my place at the table and was thankful that I was just in time.

'Ah, there you are, Tamsin. Is everything all right? said Lady Sedley.

'Yes, thank you. I thought the servants may have mistakenly removed something from my room, but I was wrong,' I said adjusting the napkin on my shoulder.

'You do not mean the letter that was lying upon your table?' said Isabel. 'I saw it signed and ready to be sealed and I took it downstairs to save you the effort.'

'Isabel, I did not realise that it was part of your duties to tidy my chambers,' I said neutrally.

'As Lady Sedley's waiting woman, I naturally tidy her chamber and since you are a guest and you have been much troubled, I decided to tidy yours as a favour to you, Tamsin!'

'Thank you, Isabel, you are very kind,' I said as calmly as possible.

'It was no trouble, I assure you,' said Isabel.

'Do you happen to know if a messenger has taken it?'

'Why yes, I saw it was addressed to Lord Cromwell, so I gave it to the page and told him to see that it was dispatched swiftly,' she said. I was not mistaken, there was a gleam in her eye that told me she had read the contents.

'Thank you, Isabel, most thoughtful,' I said smoothly. Now I was certain to be in deep trouble. My letter had been frank to the point of rudeness and certainly not the sort of letter that should be written to somebody who was the most powerful man in England next to the king! I picked at food, all the time listening for the heavy tread of marching feet. I would probably be arrested and flung into the Tower for this!

The afternoon passed slowly. As a woman in mourning, I decided that I would not be expected to be seen outside but it was difficult, being unsure of the correct behaviour for a traitor's widow. I thought that another walk in the garden would be acceptable, so I managed to pass an hour watching the Thames traffic. The weather seemed to be warming up gradually and it was more pleasant outside than I expected. At supper, I tried to behave normally but it was still difficult to eat, and whenever I looked at Isabel, her eyes seemed to slide quickly away from me.

An evening of sewing beckoned, but Lady Sedley called me

outside and kindly told me that my presence would not be required. She suggested that I go to her private library and choose a book instead to read in my chamber. Gratefully, I did as she asked and to my astonishment, I found a copy of the book by Master Tyndale that I had been reading in my northern hideaway. Was Lady Sedley interested in the more modern ideas too? I was surprised as I had assumed that she would still be discreetly sympathetic to the traditional forms of religion. I retired with the book and soon found that the hours passed more quickly.

After a rather restless night, I was up early. It was a beautiful morning and I felt more fatalistic about Cromwell's reaction to my letter. It was even possible that being so busy, he had handed it to one of his secretaries to deal with without even reading it. I went downstairs to check if there were any messages for me. There were none, so I found a sleepy-eyed servant to bring me some ale and food.

After a quick breakfast, I headed to the garden. It was indeed a glorious morning: birds darted around collecting bits for their nests and I could feel the warmth of the early sun. If Lady Sedley had seen me, she would have ordered me to wear a hat to preserve my complexion, but luckily, she was probably still fast asleep. I found what looked like an old mooring post for a boat which was just the right size for me to sit and survey the view.

I heard the church bells chiming for nine o'clock. The time had passed quickly with the busy Thames to watch. I made my way back into the house slowly. Perhaps Lady Sedley would send me out on a small errand or give me something to do which would make time past faster and Joan arrive sooner. I hoped that she was enjoying her journey in the company of her sweetheart, Ranulf.

As I entered the house, Isabel met me with an avid face. 'Tamsin, there is a message for you from Lord Cromwell's office.

I noticed the seal, but I could not find you anywhere in the house. Here it is!' Immediately, I was filled with horror. Was I going to be despatched to the Tower forthwith? No, the letter merely requested me to attend a meeting this afternoon.

'I expect there are formalities to go through for the transfer of Richard's estate to the Court of Augmentations,' I said calmly.

'Do his lands go there, then? I thought that was where the lands and possessions of dissolved religious houses went,' said Isabel. Was it my imagination or did she look disappointed? Perhaps she too was expecting my immediate arrest for offending Cromwell!

'I would imagine that the lands forfeited to the Crown for other reasons might go there too,' I said.

The rest of the morning was taken up with going through the contents of Lady Sedley's clothes chests.

'I feel I must prepare for warmer weather when I will need lighter garments,' she said. 'Isabel, check very carefully for moth holes.' We piled the kirtles and overdresses on to the bed.

'It seems that moths have not dared to approach these dresses, your ladyship,' I said cheerfully. 'No doubt the lavender helped to deter them!'

At dinner, again I found that I could not eat very much, but this time Lady Sedley's sharp eyes noticed the way I was pushing the food round my plate.

'Tamsin, you are shrinking before my eyes. Have a care or you may fade away to nothing!' Everybody turned their heads to look at me. Hastily, I said, 'It is just that I have temporarily lost my appetite.'

'Tonight, we will have venison pie for supper and a dish of larks, food that all sensible people enjoy. I shall expect to see you eating more heartily by then.' Rather hysterically, I wondered if

I would even have a head with a mouth to put food in then by then!

At last, the meal was over, and I went to prepare for my appointment with Cromwell. I decided to not to change but to wear my black dress, which seemed to have dried itself since my morning excursion, along with a sober looking gable hood.

Ten minutes before the hour of two saw me dismounting my horse and passing the reins to a groom outside Cromwell's house. I felt strangely calm. I had expressed my true feelings in the letter and yes, I did think that Cromwell had not handled Richard's mission well.

As before, I was shown to a chair outside the office to await my summons and as before, the scene was very busy. I wondered how many messenger boys and clerks Cromwell employed; I was sure I had seen at least twenty different ones in just a few minutes.

The door creaked and my stomach lurched. The familiar face of Cromwell's secretary peered out. 'Lord Cromwell will receive you now, madam.'

'Thank you,' I said and followed him into the office where Cromwell sat at his desk, his expression unreadable. In his hand was my letter.

'Madam, I see that you have a grievance against me, but before we discuss the matter, may I offer you some wine?'

'Yes, thank you,' I said, hoping that I would not be presented with the delicate Venetian glasses again. I saw that I was to receive a pewter goblet instead.

'I thought it wise not to send for the precious glassware again,' observed Cromwell, 'since you are liable to react quite passionately, and its safety could not be guaranteed.'

'No, my lord,' I said politely, bracing myself for the angry outburst that must surely follow.

'In your letter, you say that I showed poor judgement in sending a man like Richard Allerthorpe to spy upon the rebels. A man, you say, who always saw both sides of an argument and who was therefore vulnerable to changing his mind, but who always acted according to his principles. You accuse me of making an error!'

'My lord,' I interrupted, 'I must tell you, the letter was written for my own benefit, to relieve my distress. It should never have been sent and indeed the person who removed and sent it did not have my authorisation.'

'Are you saying that you did not mean what you have said?'

'No, my lord. I must admit that I said what was in my heart,' I quailed. Surely now he would fall into a rage.

'And then, madam, you go on to say that your husband was a man who put his principles above, shall we say, more earthly considerations and who did not give any thought to the effects of his actions on others such as his family, household and tenants. You are angry about this.'

'Yes, my lord, I am.'

'You know that I could have you sent to the Tower on some trumped-up charge of, say, aiding your husband in his treason for your insulting comments?'

'Yes, I am aware of this, my lord, but I think that you are a fair man overall, who would not stoop to such actions.'

'I might, if the Crown's security depended on it, madam. But fortunately for you, I believe there is a grain of truth in what you say. Perhaps Richard was the wrong man for this mission, and it is very unfortunate that all turned out as it did.'

'Richard was a good, kind and honourable man, your lordship, but perhaps not as wise as he could have been.'

'No, indeed. Do drink up your wine. You will not be going

to the Tower today, madam.'

'I am happy to hear it, my lord.'

'As for the matter of your slain guard. He is a favourite of the Duke's and has been with him for many years. I cannot take any further action at this time. I believe I warned you of the difficulty.'

'Yes, my lord, you did. May I ask if you happen to know where my husband is buried?'

'The remains of his body, apart from his head, will have been buried in the parish graveyard nearest to the location of his execution. I do not have immediate access to the records, which are currently with the Duke of Norfolk's clerks and secretaries, but doubtless I shall see them eventually.'

He paused to take some wine.

'Now, on another subject, I am aware that you have in effect been made destitute by your husband's actions. The Crown must always take the titles, lands, and possessions of treacherous nobles. However, there may be a way for you to make financial provision for yourself and your daughter. You could appeal directly to the king himself.'

'Surely I would be barred from the court before I could even approach the king.'

'You would normally, but I could arrange that you are invited to a court function. Are you brave enough to make an appeal to the king? You could throw yourself on your knees in front of him as a friendless widow, left alone with a helpless child. The king is always susceptible to a pretty woman and I have reason to think that he is likely to be in a good mood because the queen is expecting a child. He may be inclined to make you a grant of money or even a small dwelling.'

'I am willing to attempt it, my lord, if you advise that I

should.'

Cromwell got up from his chair and walked around me. 'You should ensure that your hair shows beneath a smaller black hood, and that dress you are wearing now will be suitable. You are too thin, but that adds to your appeal. Perhaps you could get a woman to help you paint your face very discreetly. You do not want to appear as a wailing corpse-like wraith.'

'No, my lord. I shall do as you say.'

'You are an unusual young woman, Tamsin, and I wish you good fortune in your endeavours. I will send word of when you should present yourself at the court.'

'Yes, my lord. Thank you for your help.' I curtsied, and the door was opened for me by a page, who was so prompt that he must have been listening at the door. I collected my horse and rode back to Sedley House in what can only be described as a state of shock.

Isabel appeared shortly after the doorkeeper had let me in. 'Good afternoon, Isabel,' I said. 'I see that you are surprised to see me back in one piece after seeing Lord Cromwell. Perhaps you thought that he would smite off my head himself in fury after he read the rude comments in the message which you oh-so-innocently sent off to him. I believe that you knew that I did not intend that message to be despatched and you had no business to be poking around in my private papers!' I stalked up the stairs with Isabel hurrying behind.

'My lady, you must have taken a fever. You are making no sense. I merely sought to help you with a chore.'

'Perhaps you accidentally did me a good turn,' I said, entering my chamber. 'Cromwell was sympathetic to me and he is arranging for me to make a personal appeal to the king concerning my circumstances.'

'I am certainly most glad to hear that,' said Isabel, who was not looking glad at all. She looked out of the window. 'There are some strangers arriving. I had better go in case I am needed.'

'Yes, you should,' I said, shutting my door firmly and collapsing on my bed. What was wrong with that woman? She was clearly hostile to me, but I could not think why she should be. I could hear some sort of altercation at the door, and I thought I caught my name being said. Now, what could it be?

As I arrived at the head of the stairs, I heard the familiar tones of Joan. 'We have recently arrived in London and we are here to see Lady Allerthorpe.'

I heard the porter speak. 'Wait there and do not move. Ah, Mistress Isabel, these people wish to speak to Lady Allerthorpe.'

I was just in time to hear Isabel say, 'If you seek alms you should go to the kitchen door.' I ran down the stairs, hardly daring to believe what I could see. There in front of me were Joan, Ranulf and Rolf, looking very bedraggled and tired.

'Joan! I am so happy to see you. And both of you too!' I said, looking at my guards. 'Porter, please take these two men to the kitchens for food and drink. They are my guests. Joan, bring your bundle and come upstairs with me. I will send for refreshments. You look exhausted.'

I relieved Joan of her burdens and made her sit down in a chair by the fire.

'Did you get a passage by boat? How long have you been travelling? How did you know where I was?'

'Tamsin, please do not ask so many questions at the same time. It makes it difficult to answer them, as I have been saying to you since you were twelve years old!' A jug of wine was delivered by Isabel, who was clearly agog to hear any information about the identity of the travellers.

'Lady Isabel, this is my personal maid Joan, who has been with me for many years. The two men are guards employed by my husband. They have just arrived from Yorkshire. Please explain to Lady Sedley that I must look after my guests and that I will not be at dinner today. Thank you, Isabel.'

After Isabel had left the room, I poured wine for Joan. 'Drink this, it will help to restore you.'

Joan took a few sips and then looked around the room. 'Very nice,' she said. 'Who is that cheeky mare?'

I tried not to laugh. 'The woman is Lady Isabel Torville, a waiting woman to Lady Sedley who has kindly given me refuge at this difficult time.'

'Why are you not at Allerthorpe House, Tamsin? We went there expecting to find you, but the house was all boarded up so we thought we would call at Sedley House to see if they knew where you were.'

'Joan, some dreadful things have happened. I did not send a message because I knew that you would have already left Allerthorpe. In short, Richard has been executed as a traitor. The foolish man was sent by Cromwell to investigate the northern rebels, but instead he decided to join them. He was convicted at the Duke of Norfolk's Great Assize in March and later beheaded.'

'Oh, Tamsin, may God have mercy upon him.'

I paused because a lump in my throat threatened to stop me relating my story. 'Joan, if a lord is declared a traitor, all his lands, possessions and titles are forfeit to the king. That means that I am destitute, depending on the charity of others. I have no money for your wages.'

'Do not worry, mistress, something will turn up.'

'The worst thing was that I had no idea about what was happening until I arrived back in London. It was Lord Cromwell himself who enlightened me.' Joan embraced me and it was hard not to weep on her shoulder. 'Fortunately, Lady Sedley has been very kind. She will allow you and the men to stay while we prepare to return to Cornwall. I have written to Mother to inform her of the sad turn of events and asking that she will take us in on our return. I have not heard back from her yet.'

'Oh, Tamsin, my dear. I do not know what to say to you. Richard was such a good man. I cannot think of him as a traitor.'

'Joan, if he joined the rebels as is said, then he was a traitor. He must have known the risks and he chose to ignore them! What news of Alice? Is she still happy with Lord and Lady Metcalfe?'

'When I last saw Alice about three weeks ago, she was healthy and merry. Lady Metcalfe brought her over to the castle to give her space to practice her walking. Such a sweet little thing. Of course, we had probably left on the ride to Hull before all these terrible things happened.'

'I am sure that they will know all by now, but I have sent a message to them to ensure that they do. It is so isolated up there and I have heard nothing from them. They must be very upset. I will write again when things are clearer. Is Lady Metcalfe's hearing still restored?'

'It seems normal. It was just wax in her ear and the oil cleared it completely.'

'That is a relief for everybody, I would think. I cannot tell you how pleased I am to see the three of you again! I will ask for food to be brought up here.' I left my room to find a servant and requested some bread and cheese to be brought up.

While Joan was still eating, and I judged that dinner must be over I went to see if I could speak to Lady Sedley. I was intercepted by Isabel, who informed me that her ladyship was resting and was not to be disturbed until three o'clock.

'Humph!' said Joan when I returned with the news. 'That woman does not like you. I expect she is jealous!'

'Why would she be jealous of a destitute widow, Joan?'

'Tamsin, you are about the same age, but you come from a place that London folk think is wild and backward. Your family is not grand and yet you secured an earl for a husband with no apparent effort. Maybe there were some young ladies whose noses were put out of joint. Also, you are better looking than her and she probably thinks that she will need to fight you now to get a husband!'

'Isabel seems to have a taken a fancy to Edmund Boskeyn. However, she will not need to compete with me for any husband. I have no intention of remarrying. I have told everybody!'

'Yes, but you did not set out to marry Richard, did you? Then look what happened!'

'That was different, Joan. I always knew I would need to marry somebody and when Richard presented himself, I thought we would get along well, and I could help my family too. Indeed, he was a lovely and kind man and was most generous to my family.'

CHAPTER 32

The next three hours went by quickly. When I heard the bells ring for three o'clock, I left Joan snoozing in her chair and set off to see Lady Sedley.

'Ah Tamsin, I have heard about your visitors and I was wondering when you would come and see me.'

'Isabel said you were resting, your ladyship, and that you were not to be disturbed until now.'

'I see. Isabel is very conscientious about her duties. Well, what have you to tell me?'

I told Lady Sedley about the arrival of Joan and the two guards and asked if she was sure that we could stay until such time as we could leave for Cornwall. To my relief, she confirmed her assent, and I was fulsome in my gratitude.

'Never mind that. You know that I am not short of funds and accommodation. The two guards may sleep with the menservants and Joan could have the little room opposite yours. They will have board with my servants, of course.'

'One day, I hope to be able to return your hospitality, my lady.'

'Yes, I am sure you will. Now, what of Cromwell? What did he say to you?'

'He did not say much other than to give me the news.'

'You must have been devastated,' she said, leaning towards me.

'Yes. Cromwell also told me that he could not do anything

about the soldier William Hayes, who murdered our guard, because Hayes is a long standing and favoured employee of the Duke of Norfolk who would block any enquiries.'

'Norfolk would not want anything revealed that might make him look bad in front of the king. Yes, you will have to watch and wait, Tamsin, if you still want to pursue this.'

'I made a promise to see that guard avenged and that is what I will do, your ladyship.'

'Tamsin, there is something else I need to tell you. I am sorry to say that it is more sad news, this time from Cornwall.'

'Oh no, please not my family...'

'No, it is not your family, but it is someone close to them. My cousin, Lord Thomas Boskeyn of Penwarne, died of a fever about ten days ago.'

'I am so sorry, your ladyship. God rest him. He was such a kind man, always reliable and fair to everybody. I cannot imagine Penwarne Manor without him.' A wave of misery swept over me. Two deaths. Was there to be a third?

'The funeral will have already taken place,' said Lady Sedley. 'I wondered why Edmund had not been to see me recently. He must have ridden for Cornwall as soon as he got the news.'

'I will write to his daughters. Please excuse me, your ladyship, I must return to Joan.'

'Very well, Tamsin, I will see you at supper.'

I went upstairs passing Isabel in the passage. 'Tamsin, I was wondering, is Edmund expected to call again soon?'

'I have no idea,' I said curtly, 'and his father has just died.'

'Oh, how sad,' said Isabel. As before, her facial expression did not match her words. 'Still, I suppose he will inherit his father's title and property now. You did say that he only had sisters?'

'Yes, Isabel, he does not have any brothers and yes, I will introduce you if he should call again,' I said, trying to keep the exasperation out of my voice.

Up in my chamber, Joan said, 'It is hard to see the way through all these sorrows. We must pray that happier times are coming.'

'Joan, there is something I have not told you or Lady Sedley yet. As you know, I am left without property or funds now that Richard has been executed as a traitor. Cromwell thinks that I should try a personal appeal to the king to see if he will grant me a pension or suchlike. After all, I am entirely innocent as Richard did not involve me in his unwise behaviour.'

'You mean to talk to the king himself!'

'Yes, Cromwell has said that he will notify me when the circumstances are favourable. He has also given me advice about how to conduct myself if I am granted an interview!'

'You mean, Cromwell will notify you when the king is in a good mood and more likely to grant a request?' said Joan. 'Well, that is extraordinary! You must tell Lady Sedley, Tamsin.'

'It is risky, but I have nothing to lose, really, so I am resolved to try, and yes, I will warn Lady Sedley. I shall need you to accompany me. I will find you something respectable to wear, but we should dress soberly.'

A week later, I received the promised message from Cromwell ordering me to present myself at Whitehall Palace at eight that evening and to gain admittance by showing his message to the guards.

Lady Sedley again gave me leave to rummage in the chests of clothes kept in the quarters of her ladies-in-waiting. Remembering Cromwell's advice about my dress, I had it brushed clean and selected a plain, small black hood which showed off the colour of my fair hair. I added a plain string of pearls borrowed from Lady Sedley. A plain dress in grey and a discreet gable hood were found for Joan. Also, following Cromwell's advice, I used the paints in the cosmetic box to emphasise my large eyes and added some reddening paste to my lips.

I was proposing to take a wherry down the Thames to Whitehall stairs, but Lady Sedley would not hear of it and insisted that we take her small carriage. 'You do not want to enter the court with mud or worse splashed on your skirts,' she said.

I found that the prospect of being able to take some action was making me much happier and I found my appetite returning at dinner that day. 'I am glad you are being sensible,' said Lady Sedley. 'After all, it would be ridiculous if you fainted at the king's feet for lack of food. You would not even be able to make your appeal!'

Later, as we were seated in the carriage, I said to Joan, 'This is an adventure, and we must do our best to enjoy ourselves. If nothing comes of it or the king will not see me, it is almost certainly the last ever visit to the court so let us make it a good memory!'

'I never thought I would see the king, so I am intending to enjoy myself. Do you think Queen Jane will be there?' asked Joan.

'I do not know, but I have heard that she is a kind lady. Edmund said that the queen seems to have traditional religious views so she may have had some sympathy for those connected with the Pilgrimage of Grace.' I looked out of the small window as the carriage lurched and swayed. I saw groups of apprentices, some staggering out of taverns singing lustily, and tired workers making their way home. Some brightly illuminated shopfronts had not yet closed for the night and there were still plenty of customers abroad.

Large houses replaced the shop fronts as we came nearer to the palace and the singing apprentices and shoppers disappeared. People who looked like palace officials were moving quickly and purposefully and on the approach to the palace, we saw many gorgeously dressed nobles on their way into the palace yard. Several carriages passed us, but the blinds were drawn; doubtless they contained courtiers or important people who regarded themselves as too grand to be subjected to the common gaze.

The sprawling buildings of the king's Palace of Whitehall were now in front of us as the coachman slowed the horses. Minutes later, we found ourselves dropped off in front of the vast entrance hall and I brought out Cromwell's letter. A page took us down long corridors to a large room with an enormous decorative fireplace, where drinks and refreshments were laid out. Around us stood little groups of expensively dressed people and I noticed some curious glances cast our way.

'Who are those women? They look as if they are dressed for a funeral,' said one tittering, over-dressed dowager pointing rudely at us, her face chalk white with some thick potion. I was maliciously pleased to see that cracks were already forming in her complexion. I heard some whispering and laughter and was aware of others staring.

'Come, Joan, let us fortify ourselves,' I said, turning my back on them and pulling her towards a table. I selected glasses of ruby red wine for us and then scandalised her by drinking mine quickly and going back for a second.

'Tamsin, be careful; you do not want to be tottering in front of the king!' she hissed.

'And nor do I want my teeth chattering with fear so that I cannot make myself understood. A little wine is steadying.'

Joan did not reply but her pursed mouth signalled disapproval. A blast of trumpets indicated that the king had arrived, and there was a rush for the door as courtiers competed for good positions in the Great Hall beyond. As apparent nonentities, we could not claim any precedence, so we waited at the back of the queue as it slowly filtered in.

When we finally arrived, I could see the king and the queen seated on a dais in chairs of state under a canopy. I could make out the royal arms of England and Wales, but I could not see if the king's claim to France was depicted too. Courtiers swarmed near the dais and I could hear much loud laughter. I noticed that there were musicians tuning up in the gallery; evidently, there was to be dancing later. A movement near the dais caught my eye and I saw that Cromwell had arrived. He was talking quietly to the king and I saw the queen lean her head over to hear what was being said.

I waited impatiently. The atmosphere became warmer, and the press of bodies brought with it the sweaty, sour smell of unwashed clothes. Some of the dresses worn by the ladies and the men's doublets seemed to be encrusted with jewels and I could not see how such garments could ever be washed clean. A young page appeared at my side. 'Madam, Lord Cromwell desires that you should make ready to approach the King's Majesty now.'

'Thank you. Come along, Joan,' I said, assuming what I hoped was a sweet and innocent expression. Cromwell signalled to us to wait near him. I was again conscious of people staring and wondering what Cromwell wanted with this dowdily dressed young woman.

The king seemed larger than when I had last seen him, his eyes sinking further into his round face. Beside him, the queen looked tiny and although she was equally gorgeously dressed, she was not beautiful. The king's voice sounded surprisingly high pitched for a man with such a barrel shaped chest. Every finger on his hands seemed to be adorned with a large, flashing ring. I waited, quaking with fear.

At a signal from Cromwell, I walked in front of the thrones as elegantly as possible and threw myself on my knees in front of the king and queen.

'Mistress, what do you wish to say to us?' said the king.

'Your Majesties, pray forgive me for interrupting your evening, but I am in sore distress and I beg for help for my young daughter and myself.'

'Ah, the widow of the traitor, Earl Allerthorpe, is it not?' said the king.

'Yes, Your Majesty, I am the innocent and destitute widow of that man.' I peeped up at him and fluttered my darkened eyelashes. I remained on my knees while Cromwell muttered something in the king's ear.

'Pray rise, madam.' I clambered to my feet. 'You have nothing to fear. We understand that you are left destitute by the consequences of your husband's ill-advised behaviour. You were in ignorance of your husband's treachery?'

'Yes, Your Majesty. I understand and accept that my husband's titles, property and estates are forfeit for you to dispose of as you see fit.' I curtsied very low and looked him in the face and was gratified to see a trace of admiration in his eyes.

'Lord Cromwell advises us that you have a young daughter and that your own family lack the means to keep you. I am minded to grant you a small pension.'

'Your Majesty, I can hardly believe it. Thank you, you are indeed a great and merciful Christian monarch and I shall be grateful to you until my dying day!'

The king almost seemed to be purring. 'Let everyone mark my generosity and Christian kindness to this unfortunate and blameless noblewoman. We hope that you may grace our court again one day, Mistress.'

I chanced a quick glance at the queen and was relieved to see she was smiling kindly at me. Cromwell signalled to me to withdraw, so I backed carefully away from the presence of Their Majesties and sought to conceal myself in the crowd.

Now everybody was openly staring at me, but nobody appeared hostile, for which I was grateful. Joan appeared back by my side. 'Oh, Tamsin,' was all she could say.

'Yes, indeed,' I said. I felt quite faint with relief. I would not be destitute and with luck, Alice could still make a respectable marriage.

A man cleared his throat close behind me. As I turned around, I saw it was one of the queen's brothers, Thomas Seymour, trying his luck again.

'May I congratulate you, madam, on your successful appeal, although I must say that success would not have been assured had you been old and ugly.' He bowed to me. 'The king clearly liked the look of you, as do I, Mistress Tamsin. You should be careful; the queen's happy news means that the king may be seeking a mistress for the next few months.'

'The king must be so happy to have the prospect of a son,' I replied, ignoring the comment about the king's bedtime habits.

'Yes,' said Seymour, 'we are very hopeful that we will have a prince.'

'I will pray for it, my lord.' I moved back from him because he seemed to be doused in a cloying perfume which made me want to sneeze. 'Please excuse me, my lord, I must leave now.'

'Will you not stay for one dance, Tamsin,' he said in an over-familiar tone.

'You do me great honour, my lord, but as I am recently widowed, it would not be fitting for me to dance,' I said firmly. I looked around for Joan to remove me from this situation. 'Ah, there is my waiting woman. Joan, kindly arrange for our departure. I am very tired.'

'Of course, madam,' said Joan with a glare directed at Thomas Seymour. However, he merely looked amused.

'I hope to see you again soon, fair lady,' he said, bowing low.

'Yes, my lord,' I answered, praying that he would not. There was something repellent about this brother of Queen Jane, despite his good looks.

CHAPTER 33

At last, we were trundling home in the carriage. The streets seemed quieter now and there were fewer candles in windows. The shops were all shut and there was hardly anyone around, except for night watchmen with their flaming torches. It was chilly in the carriage but fortunately, I was still a little affected by the wine I had taken so I sat in a warm haze.

Joan seemed to be lost for words apart from, 'What would your mother say? A daughter of hers demanding help from the king himself!'

'I did not demand it, Joan, I just played the role that Cromwell advised. Really, I have him to thank for this and you should be happy that I had the courage to do it. It may mean that I shall be able to continue to employ you, your future husband and Rolf! Had you thought of the alternative?' I asked crossly.

'I had thought that we would all throw ourselves on the mercy of your mother.'

'But you know that we are not rich, Joan. I was thinking of opening a small school in Looe to earn some extra money.'

'A former countess cannot become a schoolteacher!' said Joan in a shocked tone.

'Well, what would have been the alternative, Joan? Should I have found an unpaid position as a waiting woman with only my board in an obscure family with no means of employing all of you? Or should I have sold my body on the streets?'

I knew I was being unfair, but I also knew how precarious

315

my position had been and I guessed that Joan's solution would have been for me to marry any man who offered as quickly as possible.

'I am sorry, Joan, I did not mean to be so sharp with you. Thank God we are nearly back, my bladder is bursting.'

'You could have gone to the palace privies. Perhaps the holes in the board are studded with jewels!' said Joan.

'I was afraid I would get lost and blunder into some forbidden room!'

At last, the carriage halted, and I dashed out, not waiting for a groom to help me down. The porter bowed and looked at me curiously as I shot past. We had supper in my chamber by the fire, gossiping about the king and the people we had seen.

'Tamsin, you should avoid that Lord Seymour. He has a lecherous look about him, and I must say that I did not like the way in which the king looked at you either.'

'Do not worry about them, Joan. It is very unlikely that I will ever have cause to see them again. I wonder what will happen next. I assume that I wait for Lord Cromwell to summon me to discuss the details of whatever award the king makes me.'

That night, I went to sleep feeling happier than I had felt for a long time. Just before I slept, I thought of Edmund. Was he very upset about his father's death? What would he say when he heard that I had appealed to the king?

The next morning, a message from Cromwell was brought to me. I was asked to present myself at three in the afternoon. Joan was keen to accompany me in case I needed protection from that "devil". In vain, I tried to persuade her that Cromwell was not a monster.

As the church bells struck three, we were shown to the waiting area outside the Cromwell's office. This was almost turning into a routine, I thought to myself. Ranulf and Rolf handed over their weapons to the porter and were told to wait outside the room. A few minutes later, the secretary appeared and ushered us to the office door.

We paused and curtsied politely. 'You may remember Joan Glasson, my maid, from our previous meetings?' I said to Cromwell 'I do not have secrets from her. May she stay?'

'Yes, Mistress Glasson may remain,' said Cromwell. 'Please sit down. You have been awarded a pension from the Crown. The details are here.' He indicated a document. 'Perhaps you would like your legal advisor to look through it before you sign?'

'No, thank you, my lord. I will read it myself.'

Joan looked proud. 'Our Tamsin is a very learned lady, my lord!'

'I have no doubt that she is,' said Cromwell with a slight smile.

I read through it carefully. All looked in order and so I signed where indicated by the clerk, who also passed me what felt like a heavy purse of coins.

'Madam, it is advance payment of the first quarter of your allowance,' said the clerk.

I observed that Cromwell had returned to his desk and was reading a stack of letters with a frown.

I signalled to Joan that we were to leave. 'Thank you for your help, Lord Cromwell, I am most grateful.' I curtsied and the clerk bustled forwards to show us out.

As we followed the clerk back to the front door, I noticed that Joan was looking very closely at every wall hanging, ornament or candle sconce. 'I want to be able to describe all this to Ranulf,' she whispered to me.

Back at Lady Sedley's house, I went to find Isabel. 'Do you

think Lady Sedley will receive me now?'

Isabel give me a puzzled look. 'What has been happening, Tamsin? You disappeared on a mysterious errand this afternoon and someone said that you had been seen speaking to the king himself last night!'

'Isabel, if Lady Sedley will agree to see me now, perhaps she will allow you to stay and then you will hear the full story.' The speed at which she went to find Lady Sedley was noticeably fast and she was back equally quickly, slightly out of breath. 'Lady Sedley will be pleased to receive you now,' she said.

We climbed the stairs to Lady Sedley's rooms. 'Your ladyship, it is good of you to receive us at such short notice,' I said. 'I have a story to tell, and I wondered if you would permit Isabel to remain.'

'Aha, very clever,' said Lady Sedley. 'If Isabel hears your story, you will save yourself the bother of repeating it because she will ensure that the whole household has a full account before nightfall!' Isabel was blushing and I felt a little sorry for her.

'I will start at the end of my story, Lady Sedley, so that you know the bits that relate to yourself first. I have been granted a pension by the king which will give me independence if I live carefully. Therefore, you will not have to bear the cost of giving hospitality to me and my servants for much longer. Last night, as you know, I went to Whitehall Palace as advised by Lord Cromwell.'

'He is not a bad man,' interrupted Joan, 'even though he has an evil reputation in some places.'

'No, but I imagine he would be a dangerous enemy,' I said.

'Go on with your story, girl!' said Lady Sedley.

'Well, at a signal from Cromwell, I threw myself down on my knees at the king's feet and said that I was the innocent but destitute widow of a traitor who was begging him for help. I was terrified, but he was most gracious. He told me to rise and after a brief whispered conversation with Cromwell, he told me that he was minded to help by awarding me a pension.'

Isabel's mouth fell open. 'Oh, Tamsin, you are indeed fortunate,' she said.

'Hmm, I think that the king was influenced by your good looks and doubtless you gave an impression of a sweet, innocent and defenceless woman!' said Lady Sedley.

'I may have done that, but it does not matter. The only thing that is important is the result, which makes a big difference to our future.'

'Yes, certainly,' said Lady Sedley. 'Did you see the queen? How did she look?'

'Yes, she was there. She looked smaller than ever, or perhaps it is the king's increasing size which makes her look tinier. I did have a discreet look at her stomach area, but I could not see any visible signs of pregnancy. She certainly appeared happy, and she gave me a very kind smile.'

'It is probably too early for her to show very much,' said Isabel.

'Have you decided what you will do next, Tamsin?' asked Lady Sedley.

'I am considering renting a small house for a few months until the weather is reliably warm, and then returning to Cornwall.'

'I will call for the steward to see if he has heard of any available houses,' said Lady Sedley. She paused. 'I do have a small house on Cheapside which might be suitable for your purposes, but I will need to ask Master Steward about its current state.'

That afternoon, Joan and I rode out to try and find suitable areas, accompanied by our two guards. The task was quite hard as there were so many churches in London and I really did not want to live next door to loud church bells clanging constantly. We tried asking shopkeepers if they knew of anywhere, but they all said the same thing. They did not know of any houses to rent and we would need contacts among the landowners or the city guilds to find out more. Feeling rather dejected, we returned to Lady Sedley's house. When the porter opened the door, he said that Lady Sedley had left a message for me to see her on my return.

We took off our cloaks and I went to find her. Lady Sedley was in her parlour with Isabel, who was working on a rather complicated looking piece of embroidery.

'Tamsin, could you sew the hem of this cushion cover?' said Lady Sedley, passing it over to me.

'Yes, your ladyship, I could certainly do that without making a muddle.'

'Sit yourself down. I have spoken to my steward and I wish to show you something.' She leaned forward and picked up some documents. 'These papers relate to a house close to Cheap Street, which is the one I mentioned to you earlier. The steward said that the last tenants left several months ago and there is no reason why you should not have it for a short time. It is quite small, but the rent is reasonable, and it should be sufficient for your needs.'

'Thank you, Lady Sedley. I must confess that I was starting to wonder how I would ever find somewhere suitable. I was told that I needed contacts with landowners or city guilds to stand a chance of finding a respectable vacant house to let.'

'Well of course, I am a landowner, and I am indeed one of your contacts!' said Lady Sedley triumphantly. 'It has a large downstairs area with a fireplace, larder and storeroom and four bedrooms upstairs. I believe there is a small area of land with a stable for two or three horses at the back. If the stable will not hold all your horses, you may leave some here until you leave for Cornwall.'

'May I go and look at it tomorrow?'

'Of course you may, and I even have the keys ready for you.' Lady Sedley produced two heavy iron keys. 'The steward will give you directions tonight.'

'It sounds suitable,' I said. 'May we take cleaning equipment with us? After all, we could give it a quick clean even in the unlikely event that it is not suitable, as you will need to find new tenants for it at some point. As you have been so kind, it is the least I can do.'

A relaxed evening followed. I decided that we would all go together early in the morning, myself, Joan, Ranulf and Rolf. It was difficult to sleep that night because half of me wanted to rush out in the dark and see the house now, but Joan sensibly pointed out that it would be much better to view it by daylight.

We were all up at dawn for a hasty breakfast. The cook had very kindly packed us a picnic of bread and cold meats to fortify us if needed. We had scrubbing brushes, rags, mops and two leather buckets.

We followed the steward's directions eagerly. Arriving outside the house, I saw a wooden-framed building of two storeys with a garden and a small stable at the back. The windows were of glass, which was a relief. I tried the key in the large oak front door and was pleased that the door was not warped with damp. Inside was a large room with panelled walls and a modern fireplace set in the wall. Further on was a kitchen, pantry, and a small store. The privy was a separate building in its own little hut. The garden looked as if it had been cultivated quite recently – there were some overgrown vegetables and a small herb plot. Upstairs was one large bedroom and three smaller ones, and I was pleased to see that the largest bedroom included one large bedstead.

'This will do for us, and there is room for Alice if I need to bring her here!' I said happily to everybody. It was decided that Joan and I would tackle the cleaning.

Although there was a fine layer of dust everywhere, it did not look particularly dirty, and it did not take long to sweep it. After fetching water for cleaning from the public conduit, Ranulf and Rolf decided to check the area for me. Joan and I understood that this meant that they would look for a tavern.

'It will be easier to clean this place up without those men under our feet,' said Joan, brandishing a broom at a bedroom ceiling to release cobwebs.

The fireplace was difficult to clean. Soot seemed to fly up from everywhere and I was glad I had worn my oldest dress. After much sweeping, Joan and I decided that it was fit to use. We then turned our attention to the windows and the larder. Fortunately, there were not too many mouse droppings to clear up in the larder.

Ranulf and Rolf appeared back looking slightly unsteady and reported that the area seemed quiet and respectable. 'There were only goodwives doing their shopping, the odd merchant and a few apprentices on the street,' said Ranulf.

'Doubtless you found a tavern or two to refresh you on your expedition,' said Joan. 'I think we had better eat our dinner now, so you two sozzle-wits have something to mop up the ale.'

In the afternoon, the men pronounced the stables to be of good standard. 'There is room for two horses,' said Rolf, 'a small area for grazing, and the building seems watertight. There is also an area next to the horses where a stable boy could sleep.'

When we heard the bells of St Peter's church mark five o'clock, we decided it was time to think about leaving. I was exhausted and looking forward to washing off the muck. As we left, I had a sudden prickling feeling in the back of my neck. I turned around and caught a glimpse of a tall man who immediately disappeared around the corner of the street.

I told myself not to be silly. Nobody would need to follow me now. Cromwell had no need to send spies and he would have my new address in the morning.

It was a strange feeling to be locking up my own house. I had never needed to lock Allerthorpe House or Allerthorpe Castle; the servants did that, and we did not lock our house in Looe.

Joan and I talked about wall hangings, floor rushes and the possibility of obtaining a feather bed for the bedstead. We were just discussing truckle beds for the small bedrooms and a table and stools for the main room when we arrived back at Lady Sedley's house. There was a horse I did not recognise tied to a post by the house. The porter opened the door and we almost fell in. Passing the main hall, I heard voices behind a closed door. One was Lady Sedley, another was Isabel, the other was a familiar man's voice.

The door was opened by a servant. 'Ah, madam, Lady Sedley requests that you join her.'

I entered the room to find Edmund sitting in a chair with Lady Isabel perched on a stool next to him. His face looked drawn and paler than usual.

'Your ladyship, I must apologise for my appearance. We have just returned seeing the house. It is just right, Lady Sedley, and I would be delighted to rent it from you. We did do a little cleaning too.'

'It looks as if it involved removing a considerable amount of soot,' said Lady Sedley. 'There are also cobwebs hanging off your hood.'

Isabel giggled. I noticed she appeared pink and flustered. 'Yes, Lady Sedley. I was going to wash myself before appearing in front of you.'

'Well, never mind, we have an unexpected visitor, as you see. I am sure he will excuse your dishevelment.' Edmund stood up and bowed, and I curtsied.

'Go and give orders to your servants and then come straight back here,' said Lady Sedley. 'I can hear them clattering around outside.' I went outside and told them to replace all borrowed items and then go to their quarters and have a rest.

When I returned, Lady Sedley had poured me a large cup of wine. 'This will revive you, Tamsin, dear.'

Taking the cup, I turned to Edmund. 'I was so sorry to hear of your father's death, God rest him. He was such a good and kind man, and he will be sorely missed.'

Edmund's face looked unusually serious. 'I thank you. He was a good age, and he had a fortunate life.'

'Did the funeral go well?'

'Yes. I had not realised how popular he was until that day. Your mother, your brother, Henry, and young Daniel all attended, along with over sixty friends and relations. We could not fit them in the church.'

'He must truly have been a good man,' put in Isabel, leaning towards Edmund as if she might pat him as you would a pet dog.

'I was so sorry that I could not be there. I did not know until Lady Sedley received the letter. I had so much to thank him for.'

'I only just got there shortly before he died by riding like the devil himself,' said Edmund. 'You also have suffered a rather more catastrophic bereavement, I know.'

'Yes, and I imagine the whole of London and probably much of the North knows the details. I would prefer not to talk about it.'

'Of course. Did you know that you also have a streak of soot on your face?'

I ignored that. 'As Lady Sedley will doubtless have told you, she has been kind enough to offer me a tenancy on one of her houses. It has lain empty for some months and required some cleaning.'

'Tamsin,' interrupted Isabel, 'I will tell the servants to bring up washing water to your room. Doubtless you will need plenty of time to change before supper.'

'Yes, I do. Thank you, Isabel.' I knew that she wanted Edmund to herself, but I was surprised that she would be so open about it. 'I will go up now,' I said with a curtsey for Lady Sedley. As I left the room, I could hear Isabel telling the servants to bring up the bath and heat the water to fill it. Ah, so I was to have a proper wash and be away for longer to give her a chance to pursue Edmund!

I was only just in time for supper because it took a long time to carry up the jugs of hot water to fill the bath, but it was wonderful to be able to remove the soot and all the engrained dirt that I had picked up.

I was amused to see that Isabel had seated herself next to Edmund. She had engaged him in a conversation, which she punctuated with little trills of laughter and coy smiles.

'Oh, your lordship, I do so adore a country walk, and do you know, I have never really seen the sea!' I could not make out

Edmund's replies, although I listened as I hard as I could. Lady Sedley's voice was drowning him out as she explained to me which tradesmen I should favour with my patronage.

Later that night, as I got ready for bed, Joan was full of outrage on my behalf. 'He scarcely said a word to you, he was so busy fawning over that Lady Isabel. Were you not upset?'

'No, why would I be?' I was lying because I was a little put out that Edmund had barely spoken to me. Perhaps I had got too used to being the centre of his attention on the journey from the North? Perhaps it was just because we had passed much of our childhoods together?

'Isabel really should have given him some peace. After all, he has been bereaved recently,' I said.

'That woman, Isabel, has Edmund in her sights, Tamsin. She wants to be the new Lady Boskeyn because of his inheritance. A large manor house and estate to go with it. I expect many other young ladies will chase after him too, now there is a vacancy for a new Lady Boskeyn!' said Joan.

'Well, what is that to me?' I said. Joan pursed her lips and we said no more on the topic.

CHAPTER 34

The next few days passed in a blur of visiting furniture stalls and markets. We also sorted through pieces that Lady Sedley could spare from her household. Some things had to be made; it was not sensible to buy previously owned feather beds as they could harbour lice or bed bugs, but finally I had enough to move into my new house.

I decided that I would make a visit to Cornwall in August and see how things were. I could also look for a house in the Looe area with space for Alice and perhaps for me to open a small school. I would need to return north and collect Alice too. I hoped that by then, Yorkshire would be more peaceful. I could then return to London for the winter and move back to Looe permanently in the following spring.

The day of my house move arrived, and I was delighted to see that the sun was shining, as all my things were travelling in an open cart and I did not want my new feather bed to be marked by rain and mud splashes. It did not take long to pack everything up in the cart, despite Ranulf and Rolf arguing about the best way to secure the ropes.

We trundled off in the cart, waving goodbye to Lady Sedley, Isabel and the servants as if we were leaving for ever, even though I had an invitation to dinner for the following week. It was very exciting to arrive at the house and much faster to unload the cart than it had been to pack it. It was decided that Ranulf would share the largest of the secondary bedrooms with Rolf until such time as he and Joan were married. Joan would have her own room until then, which left one spare room for Alice.

We had just carried in the last pots when there was a knock at the door. Joan bustled over to answer it and seconds later, a white coifed woman of middle age entered.

'Good morning, mistress, I am Goodwife Mason and I have brought you some pottage for your dinner.' She was followed by a man, who was entirely bald, carrying a large cauldron wrapped in cloths. This is my husband, Martin, and we live next door.'

'Thank you very much, Goodwife Mason,' I said, curtseying politely. 'I am Mistress Allerthorpe, and this is my maid, Joan Glasson. The other men are my servants, Ranulf and Rolf.'

'Delighted to make your acquaintances,' she said. 'Mistress Allerthorpe, if you need any help, you need only ask.'

The cauldron of pottage was placed on the hearth and Joan escorted Goodwife Mason out. Ranulf lifted the lid. 'Mmm, smells good,' he said. 'Joan, go and fetch some bowls.'

After a large dinner supplemented by cold meats and bread donated by Lady Sedley's cook, we all felt tired. However, I encouraged everybody to finish putting away our possessions and to get the fire going.

That night, we were all unpacked and I had made a list of what needed doing tomorrow, starting with bread making. Fortunately, it was only a few years ago that I had been fully involved with the daily chores in Cornwall.

'Fancy, a countess making her own bread!' said Joan sleepily as we got undressed.

'An ex-countess, Joan. Whatever you do, please do not call me "my lady" in front of people here. I am plain Mistress Allerthorpe now.'

A week went by quickly, and soon it was the day of Lady

Sedley's dinner invitation. 'You shall all come with me,' I said. 'You can eat with the other servants. I am sure that the invitation included you.'

'It will be good to eat noble food again, even the leftovers,' said Rolf, rubbing his stomach.

'Are you implying that Joan and I cannot cook?' I said aiming a cloth at his head. 'You could always learn yourself. I hear that all the best households employ male chefs now!'

We set out at half past ten according to the bells and arrived in time for dinner at eleven. As we dismounted from our horses, I saw Edmund's horse being led to the stables. Perhaps he and Lady Isabel's betrothal would be announced today! I was shown into Lady Sedley's parlour and was greeted enthusiastically by her.

'You must tell me all about your new home, and perhaps I could visit you next week?'

'Yes, that would be lovely, your ladyship. You could come to dinner, but I must warn you that the food will be quite humble. Indeed, Rolf has been casting aspersions on my cooking skills!'

'You must employ a cook, Tamsin. A lady like you should not be doing her own cooking!'

'I enjoy it, Lady Sedley, and I am not sure that I can afford a cook. Fortunately, I remember recipes that were made in my mother's kitchens, and Joan is quite skilled as she was formerly a general servant.'

Edmund and Isabel were sitting next to each other and he certainly appeared to be flirting with her. Isabel was simpering and smiling coyly. Both were richly dressed. To my horror, I felt an emotion that I realised was jealousy. This really would not do!

We processed through to the table in the main hall. It seemed strange to be using silver finger bowls again. The courses progressed and I found that my appetite had been fully restored. I must go and see the cook and get some of these recipes, but of course, I would need to be careful about expensive ingredients.

After dinner, we returned to the parlour, where we were served hippocras and sweetmeats. Eventually, Lady Sedley asked Isabel to fetch her lute. She was back very quickly, and I suspected that she had already been asked to play after dinner. Isabel embarked on a soulful love song, all the time gazing at Edmund. This was too much for me and all that rich food was making me feel rather sick.

'Lady Sedley, please excuse me but I must go outside for some air,' I said as the final notes on Isabel's lute died away.

'Perhaps you have already become accustomed to simpler food now that your status has been reduced, and our diet no longer agrees with you,' said Isabel.

'Perhaps that is so,' I said calmly, rising from the table. Outside, I breathed in a lungful of air but breathed it out quickly when I caught the undertones of fumes from a midden. To my astonishment, Edmund appeared silently looming over me. 'Are you ill, Tamsin?'

'I am just suffering the effects of over-eating. You should be careful; I might vomit over your expensive shoes! You should return to Isabel. She is doubtless wondering where you are. Indeed, I am surprised she has not followed you! I presume we may expect an announcement of your betrothal very soon.'

Edmund ignored this and instead said, 'When may I call upon you in your new house? I thought it best to wait until you were settled and ready to offer hospitality.'

'As you heard at the table, Lady Sedley plans to visit next week, and I see no reason why you should not at some point.'

'I accept your most gracious invitation, Tamsin.'

I was just about to make a sarcastic remark that he would doubtless be too busy wooing his lady love, when Isabel appeared around the corner looking cross. I could not help but notice that when she saw Edmund, her face changed to a sickly smile.

'My lord, it was so kind of you to assist Mistress Allerthorpe. Are you feeling well now, Tamsin?'

'Yes, thank you, Isabel. I shall return to the parlour now, but I fear that I must leave soon because I have other commitments.'

'Yes, of course,' said Isabel, looking relieved. 'Doubtless you have many household chores awaiting you at home, Mistress.' She took Edmund's arm and led the way back into the house.

After making my farewells, I left. Joan was grumbling about being dragged away from the kitchen, where she had been having a good "chinwag" as she called it, but I placated her with talk of future visits.

The following week was happy. We had all settled into a routine and I looked forward to Lady Sedley's visit, due on Thursday. Much cleaning and dusting took place on Thursday morning and I decided that I would cook a simple meal for dinner. With Joan's help, I made pasties for the main course. Fortunately, the ingredients were easily obtainable from nearby market stalls, but I decided to use the local baker's oven to cook them rather than chance my fire.

Joan had only just returned with the bag of cooked pasties when Lady Sedley arrived dressed as ostentatiously as ever. She had brought two guards and a maid carrying a large bunch of flowers, but there was no sign of Lady Isabel, for which I was thankful. As I went out to greet her, I realised that our neighbours were staring in amazement at her from their doorways. I would have some questions to answer from Goodwife Mason!

'Welcome to my home, your ladyship,' I said, curtseying in

the street. 'Do come inside and refresh yourself.'

Ranulf darted forwards to help with the horses which were tied to a nearby post. I saw him tip an eager urchin to watch them.

'Tamsin, dear. You have made this house most comfortable looking,' said Lady Sedley as the maid silently handed me the flowers. 'What a delicious smell. I declare it makes me quite hungry!'

'Please sit down and have some wine, your ladyship. Thank you for the flowers, they are beautiful. Dinner will be served presently.'

We occupied ourselves with small talk until a clatter from the kitchen heralded dinner. Joan appeared carrying a dish of pasties, followed by Rolf carrying manchet bread and well-cooked cabbage. Ranulf walked behind carrying jugs of wine and ale. I had already decided that we would all eat together, as the kitchen was not large enough for the servants to eat in. I hoped that Lady Sedley's generally cheerful attitude would allow her to accept this. I placed her at the head of the table and myself next to her while the servants took seats at the end of the table.

'Now, this is most charming,' said Lady Sedley, who did not appear to have taken offence at the informal seating arrangements. 'Tell me, what are these pastries, Tamsin?'

'They are called pasties, your ladyship. They are a traditional Cornish dish. Inside, you have meat and vegetables which makes a portable meal that can be carried around with you. Our tin miners carry them to work, but the gentry find them very convenient too, especially on journeys.'

'They are delicious, Tamsin. You must give the recipes to my maid so that my cook can make them.'

Conversation flowed easily between the two of us while the servants seemed to be having their own quiet conversation at the other end of the table. After dinner, the servants retreated to the kitchen and Lady Sedley and I were left to talk.

'Are you still grieving for Richard, Tamsin?'

'Not as much now. I am so busy and when I remember him, I try to think of the happy times.'

'You are not heartbroken then?'

'No, your ladyship. Richard and I had a good marriage and I miss him, but it was not what you might call a passionate love affair.'

'No, of course not. Such marriages of our class rarely are.'

'I hope you will not mind if I speak frankly, your ladyship. In truth, at first I was angry about what Richard had done, and hurt that he had not shared his intentions with me.'

'It is good that he did not, or you would have been in great danger, Tamsin.'

'Yes, I realise that now.'

'In time, you will marry again.'

'I do not have any plans to marry again, your ladyship. Speaking of marriage, I presume Edmund and Isabel are shortly to announce their betrothal. They seem very taken with each other.'

'Yes, Isabel is certainly very taken with Edmund, but I do not know his intentions. He has not said anything to me about marriage. No doubt it would be a most suitable marriage. Isabel is from a noble family, she has a large dowry and Edmund has, of course, recently inherited his father's property and title. However, his large estate is expensive to run, and I imagine the dowry would be of great assistance to him.'

'Yes, of course,' I said smoothly. Was it my imagination or was Lady Sedley looking at me more sharply than usual?

CHAPTER 35

The afternoon seemed to pass quickly and when Lady Sedley left, I felt quite sorry to lose that good lady's company. That night, Ranulf and Rolf decided to visit the local tavern. Joan and I went upstairs to prepare for bed. I told Joan that she need not assist me because she looked so tired. I lay down on my bed and reflected on the day. It had surely gone well. The only difficult time had been when Joan had only just returned in time with the baked pasties. The solution must be to take them to the baker's shop earlier and then perhaps keep them warm by the fire. I dozed.

I woke up with a jolt, feeling that I had heard a noise. I listened for a while but heard nothing and I was just going back to sleep when I heard something fall downstairs.

Angrily, I jumped up. Fortunately, the candle stub had not yet gone out. It must be Ranulf and Rolf. I intended to berate them for alcohol induced clumsiness. To my horror, the man who was creeping up the stairs towards me was William Hayes, the soldier who had murdered my guard. I screamed at Joan to shout for help from her window. 'Stay there until somebody answers, Joan!'

'Well, what a pleasure to meet the Countess of Allerthorpe again. I see you are not so prosperous now. I have a score to settle with you, madam. You have told lies about me to Cromwell himself and now I find myself without employment. You are obliged to help me out of your charity!' Hayes was brandishing a large knife, he looked drunk and dangerous, and I needed to think quickly.

'I see that I must indeed help you,' I said. 'Let us go downstairs where my cash box is hidden. First, I will light another candle so we can see our way.'

'No, you bitch, tell me where it is, and I will take whatever you have.'

'It is locked, sir. Come now, my maid will summon the watchman soon. Let us both go downstairs, and I will find the key.' I could now smell the drink on him and hoped his wits were dulled. I saw he was struggling between the desire to knife me now and grab a locked box or wait for me to find the key.

Boldly, I walked past him, and he followed me across the landing. 'Get the box and stay where I can see you.' He punched me in the face and I nearly fell down the stairs.

'If you kill me, you will not have time to get the box before the watch arrives,' I said through a mouthful of blood. I walked to the pantry cupboard. 'It is in here, sir.' I took out the box and carried it to the table. 'I will fetch the key,' I said. I went to the storeroom, rattled some jars around to delay things and returned holding the key in front of me. Surely the watchmen should be here soon?

'Give it to me, quickly.'

I pretended to stumble and threw the key under the table. 'Oh, how careless of me! You should have let me light another candle!'

'Pick it up, you evil cow.'

'I cannot see where it has fallen,' I said, making sure that the hem of my dress covered it as I pretended to look. Hayes advanced on me as I heard sounds of running feet outside. He seemed to panic. 'Get out of my way.' As he leaned down to pick up the box, I tiptoed up behind him, snatched a heavy vase from the table which still held flowers from today's dinner, and brought it down on the back of his head with as much force as I could.

He slumped to the floor, groaning, but to my horror, he was starting to get up again while clutching at his head. 'I am going to kill you, bitch,' Hayes said as he groped for his knife which had fallen on the floor. He staggered towards me.

Sweating with fear, I took out my dagger and stabbed Hayes under his ribs. There was a horrible gurgling noise. He fell on his back – blood was pooling around him. 'My murdered guard is avenged,' I said quietly, I hoped Hayes could still hear me.

Suddenly, faint and spitting blood from the punch Hayes had given me, I became aware of a loud hammering noise. I staggered to the door. It was the night watchman and several neighbours in their nightclothes. Meanwhile, Joan appeared at the top of the stairs and screamed, 'Tamsin!'

'You are hurt, madam? A woman was yelling out of the upstairs window,' said the watchman.

'This man is a thief and he tried to kill me for my cash box. I was in fear of my life. I had to defend us,' I said, pointing to the man sprawled on my kitchen floor.

The watchman went over to the man who now lay on the ground motionless. 'He is dead, mistress.' The cashbox, the key and Hayes's knife all lay on the floor. The watchman hurried to the back door. 'Your kitchen door looks as if it has been kicked in, Mistress.'

'This man broke in and attempted to rob and murder the lady. The evidence is clear, and I will summon the coroner,' the watchman said pompously. 'You are all witnesses,' he said to Joan and the assorted neighbours. 'I will need your names as you may be called upon to testify at the inquest.'

When Ranulf and Rolf finally arrived home, they were shocked at the scene that confronted them. Both were very remorseful that they had not been there to protect us. They took me to Lady Sedley's house for the remainder of the night and then returned to oversee the removal of the corpse. Joan and Goodwife Mason remained to try to clear up the mess and blood.

Fortunately, the porter was the only person still up at Lady Sedley's house and when Ranulf explained what had happened, he allowed them to help me up the stairs to my old room. A servant brought me water to wash and some clothes from the communal chest. I would have to explain all to Lady Sedley in the morning.

The inquest was arranged for three days later in a local inn, but the verdict was, as the watchman had said, a foregone conclusion; I had only killed in self-defence. Veiled and dressed in black, I made my statement to the jury and their sympathy was obvious. I knew that God had given me the opportunity to avenge my guard as I had promised, and although I prayed for forgiveness, I could not feel any remorse.

It was hard to return to the scene of that death but as I told myself, it was my house. William Hayes had clearly watched and waited until he saw Joan and I were on our own. I remembered that feeling of being followed that I had experienced outside the house a few weeks previously. Hayes had set out to do me damage because he knew I had the measure of him and had reported him to Cromwell. Somehow, Cromwell must have found a way to ensure that the Duke of Norfolk dismissed the guard, but Hayes must have worked out that I was behind his dismissal. Perhaps Norfolk had told him.

A few days later, when life seemed to be returning to normal, there was a knock at the door. Joan answered it and escorted a dishevelled Edmund inside. 'I have been away, ladies, or I would have been here sooner. I have heard of the dreadful events that have occurred here.'

'Well, fortunately, Tamsin kept her head and defended us since our guards had gone to the taverns,' said Joan sharply for the benefit of Ranulf, who was behind her. He seemed to have started taking his duties extra seriously since that night. He disappeared shamefacedly into the kitchen.

'It was a happy outcome for all concerned,' said Edmund. 'Firstly, Tamsin finally had the chance to use the dagger she has carried around for so long. Secondly, she awarded him a quick death which would not have been the case if he had starved in the gutter or hanged, which looked likely.' He took a breath. 'Thirdly, she avenged her murdered guard and fulfilled her promise.'

I said, 'You have overlooked the fact that I saved Joan's life and my own!'

'True, he would certainly have murdered you both to leave no witnesses.'

'Thankfully, that is all in the past now. We must look to the future now,' I said. 'I intend to travel north and collect my daughter in a few weeks. We will then return to Cornwall to live near my mother, but I may keep my house here too. I also propose to open a school for young girls and boys. I expect you will be getting married soon, Edmund. Isabel must be very happy.'

'Aha, now you have picked a wife for me! Is there no end to your talents, Tamsin? Have you also decided where we shall live and names for our children?'

'Do not be silly, Edmund. It is obvious to everybody that you and she are to be betrothed.'

'That is terrifying news for me, to be sure. I wonder, Joan, if I could prevail upon you to fetch me some ale? I feel that I may need fortifying.'

As I watched Joan go to the kitchen, I looked around for Edmund. He seemed to have vanished.

'I am here, grovelling upon the floor,' he said.

I looked down and beheld Edmund on his knees. 'What in God's name are you doing? Get up, you fool!'

'Tamsin, you are correct that I intend to marry, but not to Lady Isabel. Would you do me the great honour of consenting to become my wife?'

I found that my knees seemed shaky, so I sat down quickly. 'You want to marry me, Edmund?'

'Through the years, from the day you first corrected my Latin translation up to our daring escape from the Duke of Norfolk, there has been no other woman for me but you, Tamsin,' he said from his knees. 'There is much you do not know, including that I was sent by Cromwell to try to persuade your husband to abandon his hopeless cause. I tried my best, even though it meant you would be lost to me if I had succeeded. Tamsin, why do you think that I never married?'

'Edmund, I do not know what to say. I cannot marry until I have been a widow for at least twelve months; it would not be seemly. I was not expecting this, and I will need to think. What about my plan to open a school?'

'Yes, of course, I will wait, and yes, you could still open your school. Tamsin, if you marry me, you would be a lady of rank again with a secure home for Alice in Cornwall. You would be close to your mother and all your family.'

Joan returned with the ale and looked at us curiously.

'Please let me know when you have had time to consider this matter, Tamsin. Pray, do not leave me waiting too long! Ah, thank you, Joan.' He drank a mug of ale quickly. 'I shall leave now,' he said with a bow.

'No, not so hasty, my lord. I have thought about the matter and my answer is yes, but we will need to wait a while!'

Edmund took my hand, bowed to Joan. 'Behold, Joan, your mistress has consented to become the new Lady Boskeyn!'

Joan smiled, but her response was unexpected. 'At last!' she said. 'It has been plain to me for years that you two were meant for each other. Tamsin was that jealous of that jammy mare, Isabel, for all she tried to hide it!'

The next day, I returned to inform Lady Sedley of my news. She seemed delighted. 'I am glad that you will make a match with Edmund. It is the best possible outcome for you after all your struggles and that tragedy, and I think you will both be very happy,' she said, embracing me.

'Thank you, Lady Sedley. I am so grateful for all the help you have given me over the years.' I almost felt as if I wanted to cry.

'I heard about the verdict of the coroner's court. You were not at fault when you defended yourself and Joan from that murderous robber, William Hayes. You can now put all that behind you and look to the future, Tamsin.' Lady Sedley paused and said, 'You could be married from my house again, but of course, as a widow, you may prefer a quieter wedding.'

'Lady Sedley, that is indeed a very kind offer, but I have a fancy to marry in my family's parish church in Looe, and Edmund has agreed. It is not far from his estate. We will need to wait until a respectable period of mourning for Richard has passed and I need to travel north again to collect Alice before the wedding.'

'Yes, that would be most suitable, Tamsin, and of course, you will return to London from time to time as you have your house and Edmund may still have some business here. Perhaps you will stay with me sometimes and we shall go to court again and enjoy ourselves!'

'That would be lovely, Lady Sedley, and we may find a good husband for Alice in time.'

'You can depend on my help with that situation. I shall start looking at suitable bridegrooms who are aged around five now and keep a list for you.'

'But Lady Sedley, Alice is not even two years old yet!' I said, laughing.

'Experience has shown me that it is always good to be prepared, Tamsin,' she said.

'I suppose so,' I said, suddenly realising how fond I had become of this outspoken woman.

'I must say I was not quite prepared for you, Tamsin, but I do hope you will always consider me a friend. When you arrived as my new waiting woman with your shabby clothes, I am sure you did not expect to have all these adventures.'

'No, I did not expect a quick marriage, arduous journeys, rebellions, being arrested and imprisoned, having my husband executed for treason,' I said soberly.

'Tamsin, do not forget your recent triumphs. You apprehended and killed a dangerous man intent on robbery and worse. Oh, and of course, you also collected another husband along the way, one who has apparently been devoted to you for many years without you even noticing!'

'It is true, Lady Sedley, I did not even expect to marry, but yes, I have had some exciting adventures.'

'I would be surprised if you did not have more in the future, but let us hope they do not involve rebellions, kidnaps and murder!' she said cheerfully.

'I intend to live in Cornwall for most of the year with Edmund and Alice, and perhaps I will be able to open a small school to teach local children to read and write. Perhaps too, I will be fortunate enough to have more children and a quiet and happy life.'

'Humph!' said Lady Sedley. 'I am not sure that all your future will be quiet, especially when you are married to Edmund!'

'Who knows what the future may bring?' I said cheerfully.